Sin

By *Shaun Allan*

ISBN- 978-0-615-53931-7

Fantasy Island Book Publishing

Credits:

Structural Editor: J. Darroll Hall

Senior Editor: Alison DeLuca

Cover Design: Lisa Daly

Contact us at: **www.fantasyislandbookpublishing.com**

Dedication

To my girls, for keeping me the right side of insane
To Mr. Staniforth for opening the door
To Tony, for giving me a good kick through

* * * * *

Acknowledgments

I have a lot of people to thank for Sin, not least Sin himself. He's almost a real person, he's so vocal, hence his blog and even his own Facebook page.

I would like to thank Mr. Staniforth, my old English teacher, for reading *To Kill a Mockingbird* to the class and showing me what a book could do to its readers – carry them away. Tony, me old matey-boy, for bugging for all these years to keep writing his exploits. My wonderful partner Hayley for taking me to Egypt and giving me the opportunity to write 15,000 words whilst there, and enjoying me being 'in the zone' – and for all my girls for keeping me just the right side of *tapped!*

Thanks Dean, for believing in Sin enough to introduce me to the wonderful Fantasy Island Book Publishing family. Thank you Allie for your excellent edit and for your 'standing ovation', and thank you Lisa for creating such a perfect cover. It completely captures what and who Sin is.

*****

To read more from Sin, visit his blog – his diary from within his asylum – at **http://singularityspoint.blogspot.com**

Prologue

CASE REPORT 16703: Sin Matthews, age 35, disappearance of.

CASE CONTENTS: Statement written by Matthews. Two pence coin.

<Dr. Connors' note: This statement was written by the patient during his various periods of supposed lucidity. It's as crazy as he is. And yes, that is my professional opinion.>

Statement:

Name's Sin.

I always wanted to do that, but never got the chance. You know, sort of enigmatic. A bit like 'Bond, James Bond'... except it's nothing like that, really, is it? I don't know. Hey, I know what I mean.

Anyway - Sin. That's my name, don't wear it out, as I used to say once upon a very long time ago. I wonder if kids still say that now. The old ones are the best, eh? Actually, the old ones are not necessarily the best. The fact is, the old 'uns are quite possibly the worst. But such is life. That's another of my old favourites. I've got a whole pile of them. I can just keep chucking them out. Probably will too, knowing me, as you obviously do not. Yeah, I know you *think* you do, but you don't. Trust me on that particular little one right there.

Sin. It isn't short for anything. It's not a neatly trimmed *Cin*cinnati or a *Sin*gle-Cell-Organism that forgot half its name. It's not anything like that or anything else. Simple and short and not entirely sweet. Sin.

I blame the parents (see, there's another one).

Well, I do. My dear ol' ma and pa. It was their idea of a joke, I suppose. They thought it equally hysterical to call my sister Joy, except she didn't get the crap I did when I was struggling to grow up. She didn't get the beatings or the name-calling. She didn't get pushed or kicked or made a fool of. Oh no, that little pleasure was all mine. I don't even think my parents had the excuse of being drunk, drugged or insane. That last one is also my very own little pleasure. Insanity.

Am I insane? You bet your sweet little old botty I am. Loony as the glorious, big blue Sister Moon shining her sweet face down on me. Or so they tell me (don't you?). Crazy as a rootin' tootin' coot, that's me, yes sirree. What's a coot? No idea. Ask me another, and you might get an answer, except you know you probably won't. I don't get any, so why should you? Hey, I just do what the voices tell me to.

No. I don't hear voices. Well, there's my own of course, whether it's in my head or in my ears, except it's still in my head if I speak, isn't it? Anywho-be-do. I don't hear other voices, is what I meant, as you very well know. I don't hear demons telling me to get out of bed in the deepest darkest night and do unspeakable things. I don't get *those* voices. No. The demons are all out there anyway, doing their own unspeakable things. They don't need my help.

Even if I gave it to them anyway.

I never meant to! I'll stand up in the court of all Humanity and hold my hand way up high to that! I didn't mean to! But the jury is still out, I guess. Even though I'm locked up here, in my cosy little cell with that nice soft padding on the walls, all thanks to 12 good men and true, the jury is still out. The real one. The one that counts. The one that sits in session up in my head (where you thought the voices were). It's still out, wondering if I *did* mean to. But I didn't. Promise. Cross my heart and hope to... Well, you know how it goes.

Sin. That's me. Thanks mum and dad, God rest your weary souls.

I used to have a surname, once upon a time. I lost it back along the way. Can't remember when or where. It's probably lying around at the back of the settee with my car keys and the remains of a beef sandwich on brown bread. It's not important. I know me, and that's enough. Yeah, my parents had a surname. Yes, so did Joy. It was Matthews. Trouble is, that name just doesn't sit right with me, you know? It's like when you see someone, and you think they look like a John, or a Wendy, and hey! That's just what they are! Not Matthews. That's more like when you think the guy's a John and he's a Harry or a Wayne, or even, let's not be shy, a Wendy!

Sin Matthews isn't my name, and I know it. But it's only a name. Sin will do. Sin by name, but *so* not by nature. I think. Sometimes it's hard to remember. That's thanks to the drugs they give me, those nice men in their crisp white coats and their happy, happy lives. If only they knew.

Sometimes it's very easy, and that's the big baloozer of the problem. Sometimes I *can* remember.

Of course that's easy to sort out. I kick up a fuss and they very kindly come into my room with a needle. That sorts out the memories. Most of them anyway. And the noise.

It's hard to believe that this six by six box of nothing was my choice. Why did I do that to myself? What sort of crazy loon stands up and says "Hey! Stick me in a room with no handle on the inside. Lock the door, it's ok, I don't mind. You want to pad the walls? Knock yersen out, just so long as I don't, eh? Straitjacket? If I don't have to wear a tie with it, that's just perfectly fine and hunky-double-dory with me." What sort of durbrain no-hoper inflicts that on himself? Tell me that one, because I don't know. Ask me another, but don't ask me that!

Well, I do know, actually. Me, that's who. But later. Later I'll get to that, if I'm still here. If I have time. Time... Well, indeed.

I've a surprise for you. I'm not crazy. I never have been. Oh, maybe I might have gone a little loopy-doo on occasion, but crazy? Nah. Never fancied it. It's never floated my boat. Surprised? I can never remember if, let's say, 'eccentrics' say they are mad or not. I read it once. If you're a few raisins short of the full banana, do you say you're sane or is it the other way round? So, does that mean I'm crazy for saying I'm not, or sane for saying I'm batting on the wrong side of rational?

I'll leave that one for you experts. You guessed it, ask me another.

Why? That's a good one to kick off with. Why? Well, that's one I *can* answer. It's that damn coin, is what it is. That damn, stupid coin.

See a penny, pick it up and all day long you'll have good luck. How many times have I said that, knowing it was a great big shiny pile of doggy doo-doo? Hey! Maybe I was crazy to do that? Maybe, every time I bent down to pick up that solitary penny, I was actually offering my backside to the world to come and give it a right good kick?

See a penny. What about *two* pence? See *two* pence and pick it up? How long does the good luck last then? I'll tell you. It doesn't. In fact, all the good luck from all the pennies you've ever picked up gets sucked right off you and flushed down Life's big toilet. So now who's the lunatic? Me for saying that or you for actually pausing before you pick up that shiny two pence piece lying on the pavement?

You get one guess. Right first time! Me, 'cos I picked up *that* two pence in the first bloody place!

It's a coin. So what? Two pence won't even buy you a penny chew nowadays. It just adds to the shrapnel jangling about in your pocket. You still pick it up though, don't you? You bet you do. So do I, or I did. But not no more. I learned my lesson. You can't give an old dog new ticks. You can lead a horse to water, but you can't make it swim. That's what they say, isn't it, them who know? Well, hit 'em with a great two by four and you can! That was how I learned! I got hit by a metaphorical two by four. I've still got the bruises to prove it, except they're not the bruises you can see. They're the bruises to my metaphysical psyche, Dr. Connors me ol' china. That's psyche with an 'E', not with an 'O', thank you very much.

You say 'Tom-*ay*-to'...

I found it, or it found me, or whatever, on a Friday afternoon. Ah yes, I remember it well. It'd be about 3:30-ish. I was just walking along, minding my own, as you do, when it sure leaped up at me! Yeah, yeah, it didn't. Coins don't have legs. I'm crazy but not stupid, OK? But it was *as if* it had. It was bright - brighter than a mucky old tuppence should have been. Hindsight is a bloody terrible thing to have. Some idiots talk about the 'beauty' of hindsight. Personally I think that's crap. Sly Mr. Hindsight only tells you what you should have done if you'd known better. What's the good in that? It's obviously too late by then, else it'd be *fore*sight, and I'm not psychic! Septic, maybe, but not psychic.

I was scoffing a McDonalds. Double cheeseburger, with just cheese. None of that salad crap thanks. Why ruin the taste of a perfectly good burger by splodging sauce all over it and sticking a *gherkin* of all things inside? And they call me mad! Anyway, such is life and all who sail in her. I was just finishing my burger, happily wandering along the street when I happened to look down. I think I was outside Woolworths, which isn't even there anymore. What's insane is when a shop that's been around *forever* and is part of the furniture of the town centre can suddenly go out of business and close down. That there is crazy. People were scooting past me and I was just standing there looking at that coin. I don't know why. Staring at a two pence piece isn't something I normally do to pass the time. Here, though, I couldn't help myself. It looked lonely. I forgot about my cheeseburger (which kind of shows I wasn't entirely myself) and picked it up.

It was warm. I remember that. I could even feel the warmth later, when it was in my pocket. Now, of course, I know why, sort of. Cheers Mr. Hindsight, sir. Thanks a great big bunch. I owe you one.

Some people, it's a habit. They have a coin in their hand so they toss it. They don't even check to see whether it lands on heads or tails. Flip, catch. Flip, catch. Flip, catch. Flip... You get the idea. Sometimes they don't even know they're doing it. They flip it up and catch it down without even looking at their hand - it's just there under the coin, ready to snatch it out of the air. I'm not like that. Never have been, and certainly never will be, now. I didn't have that measure of accuracy for a start. If I tossed a coin, I'd have to watch it every spin of its way through the air, not taking my baby blues off it until it was safely in my hand. That's why I rarely did it. If a coin was in my hand, it went either in my pocket or in the coffee machine at work. The most I might do would be to run it through my fingers like Steve Martin in Dead Men Don't Wear Plaid. Well, not quite like that - it was a lot slower and took a few goes, but I'd probably perfect it one of these centuries.

Oh, my baby blues are green, sometimes. Depends on the morning light streaming lazy-daisy through the curtains. Depends on the lyrical tilt of my head on the pillow. Hey, that's what I'm told, more or less. Sometimes my eyes are green, sometimes they're blue. Baby green's doesn't quite roll of the tongue though, does it? Baby hazels. Baby browns. Dady Bavids. My arse!

Anywho-be-doo. I digress. No really? That's a habit of mine, a bit like tossing coins is for some. I start off on a subject, then end up about a gazillion light years and straight on till morning from where I began, with no idea how I got there. Done it again!

Where was I? Yeah, the coin. Always back to the coin.

So. Why did I flip this particular coin? Ask me another. I did though.

I think about four died that time.

Died.

That's what I said.

The bus (the number 5 - goes from Freeman Street to Saint Marks and back again, like a hyperactive yo-yo) swerved to avoid something that was never there. Luckily, the Post Office counters are mainly at the back, so there were very few people near the front of the shop. It could have been worse. If there wasn't this custom to have the entire front of shops as a massive window, maybe... I didn't catch on then. In fact it took a while. A good few more needed to die before I got the *point!* The number 5 smashed into the Post Office window and the driver, a young woman buying stamps, a sales assistant and a man who'd always been a nobody and didn't get chance to be a somebody, never got to check their lottery numbers that night. Their numbers were up, so to speak.

Am I making light of it? Yes. Got to. You've gotta laugh! So *they* say.

Afterwards, after the statements and the press and the ambulances, I found it hard to sleep. I've never seen anything like that up close. On the TV, sure. In movies and the news and the papers, there's much worse. But it's removed. It's distant. It's not there, full in your face. You're not in the middle of it, with breaking glass and screeching tyres and screams. You don't hear the screams. Should that make a difference? I suppose not, but it does. But it was only the beginning, wasn't it? Yes, Mr. Hindsight, I know.

I know.

Four days. I'd almost forgotten about it in four days. That was all it took. Like a day a death. It was like a fuzz. A blur in my head, smudging out what I'd seen. What I'd caused, though I didn't know it. Did I? No. I don't think so, not then. On the fourth day, God made Hell. So to speak.

I'd gone to work; an oil refinery. I was in the control room, a concrete and steel bunker built to withstand the blast of the refinery going pop. And wadya know. It works.

I was waiting for a permit to go on site. It's a pain and it can often take longer to get the permit than to actually do the job, but such is the will and the way. Necessary evil, that's what it's called. I wasn't even thinking when I took the coin out of my pocket. I wasn't even aware it was in there. Thing is, it should have been mixed in with the rest of my change. What are the chances of me picking that specific coin out of a pocket full of them? I guess pretty good, considering that's exactly what I did. It was already in the air when I realised what I was doing. I also, quite suddenly, remembered the crash. Even the jolt from the unexpected flood of images wasn't enough to prevent my hand from appearing underneath the smooth arc of the two pence piece as it lazily curved through the air. It was, you know. Lazily curving. Could almost have been a slo-mo replay of Beckham knocking one into the back of the net. Lazy. Carefree. All the time in the world, thank you very much.

Then my fingers closed around it. There was a dull thud, and the alarm boards all over the control room were ablaze in flashes of red. Screeching alarms made the air a solid wall of noise that had to be fought through. It was like wading through treacle. People were scrambling desperately.

That was inside, where it was safe.

Outside...

The death toll was two hundred and fifty one. The 'one' was my best friend, Dave. At least another eighty were badly injured, and that was without the damage to the environment. The Community Alarm went off, warning the surrounding villages, but it wasn't really needed. They heard the blast. They *felt* the blast. They saw the smoke. Cars five miles away jumped, startled. Windows eight miles away shattered, the glass falling like the tears of the bereaved.

Sounds quite poetic that, dontcha fink?

I've seen photos of Tunguska, in Siberia, where the meteor (or UFO if you believe Mulder and Scully) hit. It was like that, in a way. A real blast. Party on down to Hell's kitchen folks. Today's special, anything you can still recognise. Hurry, it's going fast!

The coin was warm. I could feel it in my pocket, where I'd apparently put it, although I wouldn't swear to that. The warmth was, I suppose, comforting, even though I barely noticed it in the midst of the melee. At least it wasn't the whole refinery. At least it was only a 'little' bang.

I'd be surprised if you thought I should have had an idea then. I should, you might think, maybe have had an inkling about what was happening. Nope. I was only tossing a coin – even though it was something I hardly ever did. That I'd been in two tragedies in less than a week was... unfortunate. It was devastating for those involved, yes. I'm not heartless. I do see that. But this isn't about them.

Well, it is. But it's about stopping it. It's about THEM, the 'them' that includes you, my dear Dr. Connors, not the 'them' of those already dead. I was the Big Bad Wolf come to blow their lives apart. But I didn't know it, not until Mr. Hindsight came along and shook me by the hand, and that wasn't for a while yet.

I don't know how long it took me to forget that one. Oh, I couldn't entirely wipe it from my memory - I had to work there, eventually, when they had made it safe again. But to forget the horror, to forget the impact? It wasn't long. Soon enough I was wandering around as if nothing had happened. Simple as that. Easy as sweet caramel and apple pie with *lashings* of vanilla ice cream, just like me old ma never used to even think about making. But I'm not heartless. It was the coin. The coin seemed to be making me immune. It seemed to deaden something in me, some essence of actually caring. Of course, me hearties, I didn't know. I carried on regardless, just like good ol' Sid James.

I had three weeks then. Three weeks of uninterrupted mundane brain drain. Normality was the norm, just as it should be. There were no nagging thoughts eating away at the back of my mind, like locusts feasting on a vast field of corn. I didn't look at myself in the mirror and see evil shadows running across my face, dancing gleefully at the carnage I was creating. Nope. Nothing like that. Everything was hunky-doodle-dory. Nice and normal.

Flip.

Catch.

The trains collided just outside of town. All on board dead. I was waiting in my car, impatient that they always closed the barriers about ten minutes before the train's going to arrive and about two seconds before I turn up. How was the coin in my jeans? Ask me another. How did it get into my hand? Ditto.

All on board dead. And the Post Office. And the refinery. They all screamed out to me.

Dead.

Say it enough times and it becomes just a word. Dead. Dead. Dead. Four letters thrown together to mean something that was so much more and so much less. Dead. An absence of life. An absence of anything. For the few days that it took my mind to wash away the spectacle of the train crash, I said that word to myself over and over. I didn't feel responsible for the accidents, for that was surely what they were, but I didn't feel quite... right. But, like I say, eventually it becomes simply a word. Meaningless. Emotionless. Dead.

Flip.

Catch.

An earthquake. Turkey I think. Somewhere over that side of the world, anyway. Rivers flooded their banks. Landscapes changed their features, as if they had suddenly frowned, angry at the little humans skittering over them. They don't know how many died that time. I do though. I know. Four hundred and seventeen thousand eight hundred and ninety two. Seems a lot written out longhand like that. Seems more than 417,892. Numbers are just numbers. Written out, it's more real, more horrific, more sorrowful. More like a kick in the teeth, to be honest. They estimated about 350,000.

They were wrong.

How do I know? How do you know the sun will rise tomorrow? How do you know that Sunday will follow Saturday? You just do, dontcha? You just do. Same here.

I just do.

I think it was around then that I started to wonder. I think I began to suspect something. I'm not sure. I mean, it's only a bloody coin! How can I, or it, influence world disasters? Besides, *Turkey*? I've eaten it, but I've never been there! I threw the coin anyway. Dropped it into the River Freshney on the way home. Here little fishies! It's a bit tough, but tuck in. Keep you going for weeks that will!

Flip.

Catch.

I didn't notice. I have all sorts of coinage passing through my pockets during the week. Newspapers, coffee machines, petrol, Mars bars all play their part in the ebb and flow of the Royal Bank of Pocket. How one particular two pence piece could manage to remain in there was a mystery. Why it hadn't been passed to a shop assistant in return for a bottle of Coke (diet) or a packet of chewing gum, I couldn't guess. How it came to be back in my possession at all after taking a swim in the river...?

WHY does the sun always rise? HOW does Saturday always follow Sunday? You know they will, but *why*? I don't know either. I don't want to know. It just does.

It was four days. The earthquake still dominated the news both on screen and in print. In my head, though, it was already fading. It was going the same dulled way as the rest. The feelings of being responsible were dissolving too, like sugar in water, diluted until, no matter how hard you looked, there was just a foggy liquid that tasted just a little too sweet. I didn't notice the coin in my pocket. I don't remember taking it out. I don't remember flicking it up. I just remember the arc of it through the air and the warmth as my hand closed around it.

A child. Perhaps four years old. Typical TV advert stuff to slow your speed. The ball bounces into the street. The boy runs after it. Laughing, naturally laughing. He doesn't see the car. The car doesn't see him. The driver feels, rather than hears, the thud.

The child bounces into the street.

It happened in front of me again, not thousands of miles away. Mere metres from where I stood. Hah! The ball even rolled to my feet! How's that? I turned and walked away. I could hear the young woman waiting for half a dozen first class stamps. I could see the drivers of the trains. I could feel the heat from the flames on the refinery. I could taste the water from the flooded, surging river as it swept away all that stood in its path. I could hear the laughter of the boy.

I just walked away. I think I maybe even whistled a happy tune.

That time the memory didn't fade. The horror stayed with me during the dark nights and darker days. As time went by, my oh my, my mood darkened too. I knew. I *knew* it was me. I *knew* it was the coin. I *knew* I was responsible. I went to the pier at Cleethorpes. It stuck out like a literal sore thumb, reaching away from the beach into the lovely waters of the River Humber, or is it the North Sea? Either way, it's muddy and murky. I certainly wouldn't want to swim in it – paddling when I was a kid was bad enough. Well, the two pence coin was going to find out if it could sink or swim. I knew which one I was betting on.

I held it in my hand for a second, then simply let it drop. It spun away to splash into the water. There was a brief flash of reflected sunlight just before it hit and it was gone. Good riddance.

I noticed that, as it spun, it almost looked like it would had it been flipped. I shook my head. Nonsense. Get a grip. Get a life. Get an ice cream. Yeah, I really fancied an ice cream at that point. A whipped 99, a chocolate and vanilla mix with a flake, juice and hundreds'n'thousands. I checked the change – the *safe* change – left in my pocket. Wouldn't you know it, I was two pence short! Typical. Oh well, that's the way the double-choc-chip cookie crumbles.

Ooh, I just had a brief Homer moment: Ahhh, cookiessss.

I felt a few spots of rain. Good job I didn't get the ice cream, really. My car was only a short distance away. By the time I'd reached it, the heavens had opened and it was heaving it down. Cats and dogs? Elephants and rhinos more like! By the time I was half way home, thunder was grumbling towards me with sheets of lightning to brighten its merry way. Remember that, Dr. Connors, me fella-me-laddio? Remember that? Rained for a solid seven days. Solid non-stop. Solid as Niagara Falls on a sunny Sunday afternoon. Except we forgot what that nice smiling sunshine looked like for a while there, didn't we? Too busy wishing our cars were like James Bond's so we could flick a switch and the wheels would turn in and we'd skim along like a boat. Too busy wondering if the insurance would pay to replace the carpets and suite and TV. Too busy eating your tea with ducks swimming around your ankles. Too busy watching your kitchen table float away like a raft with legs. It was as if the whole island, good ol' Great Britain herself, had been submerged under two feet of water. Someone had pulled up a zipper from Land's End to John O'Groats and the sea had come together from either side. It didn't matter that there was no electricity – the constant lightning lit up everything like a giant camera flash.

Remember Dr. Connors? Because I certainly do.

I don't think anyone died then, amazingly. Maybe there were one or two casualties, but considering what happened, it was a lucky escape. Did someone get struck by lightning? Can't remember. Maybe. Still, considering... Of course so many thought that their lives had ended, or wished they had. Houses were flooded, belongings were ruined. Most of the country had waded to a standstill. It took a mighty effort to get moving again. It took a mightier effort to shake the drowning feeling I was overcome by when the cries of my other victims echoed in my ears.

Anyway. I don't know why I ask if you remember it, Doc. I know you do. Everyone does. I just wanted you to think about it for a moment. Just hold in your mind's tiny grasp (or should that be 'tiny mind's grasp'?) for a second or three. OK? And on we go.

When things got going again and life returned to its quirky little ways, I bought a bus ticket. My car, the same as just about everyone else's, was knackered. It didn't want to play. Well, who can blame it, eh? How would you feel if you'd spent the best part of a week and a bit with your arse end submerged in water? It probably wouldn't do your plumbing any good either, now would it? I bought the bus ticket to town. I used to take the number 5, at one time. Never no more, oh no. 3C or 3F, they're the ones for me. No other number will do, thank you very much. The 3F costs 20p more each way and goes all around the houses (which all buses do, I know, but this one goes ALL around them) to get to the same place, so the ride lasts a good fifteen minutes longer, but it's not the number 5. The 3C costs about the same and only takes about five to ten minutes more, but it's not the number 5. What is it, every half hour for the 3F and every twenty minutes for the 3C? Something like that. The number 5 was every ten minutes. Of course, it still goes on its happy travels, round and round the same route it goes, where it stops everyone knows – all the bus stops and the Post Office. No, it doesn't. That Post Office stop was a little one off special, just for sweet little ol' me. Ain't it nice. Why, thank you ma'am. Thank you oh, so very much, indeedy. Still. Anyhow and anyway, the number 5's not for me, no way!

My friend, my chum, my pain in the bum was back to say a great big fat "Hello." Right on top of the ten pence piece, to make sure I couldn't miss it, was the two pence piece. Howdy, pardner.

Flip.

Catch.

You know how it goes.

Across town, apparently, a seventeen-year-old kid was fed up. He was bored with his life and himself. His dad was in a shooting club. The gun was locked away in a secure box hidden in the attic, in line with all the police requests. The boy knew where his dad kept the key. He got the key, then the gun. His name was John, which makes it every bit worse. I know his name. He's not anonymous. I know his name, I know *him*. He left a copy of

Terminator in his DVD player to make it look like he was influenced by action films where every gun held a million bullets. He wanted them to think that, even though he knew it was crap. People, he thought, did what they did because they wanted to. A film was a film, that's what he thought. Sure, Arnie might waste a few bad guys, but that didn't make *him* want to do it. No, John did it because he wanted to. He was bored.

Besides. His dad's .22 pistol only made a little hole.

He would have taken the 9X bus to town, I guess. At least the number 5 doesn't go that way. The shopping centre was, naturally, packed. It was a Saturday, so it would be. John chose the Starbucks coffee bar to start his little performance. He didn't think it should cost nearly three quid for a coffee, even if it was a Mocca-Chocca-Locca-Shocka-Artery-Blocka. It was as good a place as any. It wasn't what he expected. There were the bangs. There were the screams. There were the crumpled bodies and the pools of blood, but it wasn't what he expected. He expected to *feel* and he didn't. He just didn't.

So he used his last bullet on himself. He yawned as he pulled the trigger.

How do I know so much about John and his thoughts? Ask me another.

I didn't feel so much from him, as he didn't feel much himself, but I felt the terror and pain of those around him. Oh, an old woman of seventy-three, with two children and five grandchildren, was trampled in the stampede as Starbucks and the shops around it emptied in seconds, the people scattering like birds off a telegraph pole. The window of Clintons Cards was shattered and the grandmother was showered in a rain of glass slivers. She didn't feel anything either. Her heart had given up the ghost, so to speak.

I was sitting third from the front on the 3C, on my way to the war zone. I was staring out of the window watching the world go by, wondering if the bus was staying still and the Earth was moving. I remember seeing a young boy jumping on the bonnet of a Mondeo. I smiled to myself, knowing if it was my kid or my car, I'd go mad. By the time the bus pulled into the station near the precinct, only a few minutes away from Starbucks, I was shivering. I wondered if perhaps I'd cried out, as a few passengers were looking at me strangely. Or did they know? I didn't want to go in anymore. I knew what I'd find. People were running about. Some were crying, others were standing there, dazed. One or two acted as if nothing had happened. Which one did I fall into? I don't know. I don't think I was crying. I didn't run. I couldn't stand still. I think I acted as if nothing had happened. I didn't want to go in, but that's what I did.

It was just as I'd thought. Just as I'd *felt*.

I walked past the bodies and pushed through the crowds. I bought some cookies from Millies – the assistant behind the counter looking at me as if I was crazy buying cookies at a time like this, but not willing to miss a sale. Maybe I was crazy, but I was also suddenly starving. All thoughts of why I'd actually gone to town in the first place were forgotten. I turned in the direction of Starbucks and said goodbye to my very good friend John, a young lad whom I'd never met. I dropped the half eaten white chocolate cookie into a waste bin and walked home.

I slept well that night. Like a log. I had a dream. At first I thought I was in the middle of the Never-ending Story, you know where Fantasia has been consumed by the Nothing? Well. The world had broken into thousands of pieces and each was floating about in space like lifeboats after the Titanic. I watched as families smiled and waved to me as their little pieces of Earth crashed into their neighbours' and they spun off into space. I awoke knowing, finally, that it was all me. I was responsible. Me and that damned coin.

Joy convinced me. That nice Mr. Postman only brought me one letter that morning. He was early for a change. It was a white envelope with my address elegantly printed in blue ink. Joy only ever used a blue pen. She thought black was rude. She didn't write to me very often. I can remember only a few times in our lives that I'd received so much as a postcard off my sister. My heart drilled its way through my chest like John Hurt's Alien as I sat at my kitchen table. Hey, it could have simply been a 'Hello'. I hadn't seen her in a month or three. She could have merely been dropping me a line saying she was fine, sunshine. But I knew she wasn't.

Joy was a joy to be around. Everyone liked her and she made everyone happy. As I held the letter in my trembling hands with my coffee going cold and my Weetabix going soggy, I thought about that. It had never occurred to me before, but Joy was joy, and I, Sin, was basically sin. Good and evil, light and dark. Two sides of everyone's favourite two pence coin. Oh, I needed to get a life! I was talking crap! Yeah, everyone liked my sister – she was a nice person! Why wouldn't they?

But, sitting there, forgetting to breathe, I knew I was right, at least almost. Maybe I was a little wide of the wotsit, but I was close. You know how I knew. That's right. I just did. I opened the envelope, pulled out the neatly folded sheets of paper and started to read. Joy's handwriting was smooth and flowed like water running across the page. Everything about my sister was… *silken*. Her skin, her walk, her voice. Perhaps that was why she was always so popular.

Ah.

Perhaps not.

I read the letter three times, then calmly laid it on the kitchen table. I stared out of the window. A sparrow was flitting about on the window ledge. Something busied the bushes at the bottom of the garden. It wasn't just me. I wasn't alone.

Joy, it seemed, had found a coin one day. It was years ago when we were children. A two pence coin. I'd never seen it, nor had I seen her toss it. She had, though. But whereas I ruined lives, Joy… Joy *made* lives. "I make people happy," she said. And it messed her up. She caused couples desperate to have children to become parents. She rendered poor people rich. She stopped accidents from happening and natural disasters from occurring. It was as if I was looking into the dead eyes of my mirror.

You see, Dr. Connors, Joy killed herself. I'm sure that's in my notes, or you've found it out, but rather than simply being words on paper (even as these are), I want it to mean something to you. Joy, my sister, committed suicide. She even told me exactly what she was going to do, something I won't go into, as I'm sure you already know. My first instinct was to ring her, to try to stop her before she'd had chance to jump but I knew there was no point. It was too late. Joy was dead. I wanted to feel sad, but I didn't. I wanted to cry, but I couldn't. I *still* want to feel something. I *still* want to cry. But I can't.

"I make people happy," she wrote, "and it's killing me."

I found my coin a mere few months ago. Joy had been found by hers years before that. She'd know almost straight away what was happening. I had only known, for certain, that morning – that morning when Mr. Postman kindly brought me the letter. At first it made her content. She was bringing happiness and good fortune to almost everyone around her. That was at first. Being contented I mean. Then it stopped being a pleasure and became a frustration. The frustration turned to hate. Joy was alone in her world. While everyone else was enjoying life, my sister was drowning in the responsibility of keeping it up. She felt stripped. One more good turn was one more piece of her torn away. Every smile was another knife twisting in her heart.

She had tried, early on, to rid herself of the coin. She couldn't. No, really? It kept coming back like the not-so-proverbial bad penny. That's almost funny, dontcha fink, Doctor? No, me neither. So she decided, if she couldn't get rid of the coin, she would get rid of herself.

Joy had noticed something. At first, she said, the incidents were erratic. Flip, catch. A man would not take the step into the road as the car burned around the corner. Flip, catch. The bully would see the error of his ways and would apologise to his victims. Flip, catch. The baby would smile at her father. Flip, catch. The mother of seven would win the lottery. Some were big, others were small. One would change the lives of a country, another would make a man feel good for a second.

It didn't stay that way though. The results of her coin levelled out, then began to increase in both momentum and... Joy left the word out. She couldn't find it. I knew what she meant. Each time, it would be *more*. She saw herself being eaten away. She saw herself living only for the world and not for herself. So she planned to leave. She planned to jump.

She had realised something. She didn't know if I would believe any of what she had written, but she had to tell me. She realised it wasn't the coin. The two pence piece was simply the catalyst. It was the trigger.

It was her. She was the cause. Joy *was* joy. She said that, when she understood, she could throw away the coin. When she understood, it was as if a floodgate inside her had been opened and a torrent of happiness was unleashed. That was how she put it. If she didn't end it, she would drown.

I took the coin out of my pocket, where I knew it would be, and placed it on top of the letter.

The coin was the trigger. It was her. It was Joy.

It was me.

I felt something inside me twitch at that point. It was as if I shook without shaking. For the first time, I noticed the radio was playing. I didn't realise I'd turned it on. I looked at the clock. It was almost half past ten. Time for the news.

Here's the headlines at ten thirty. Seven hundred die as freak tornado hits sleepy Essex village.

The coin was resting on Joy's letter. It regarded me lazily. It knew. Flip. Catch. I had flipped. I had caught. Not the coin, oh no. Me, myself and Ay-caramba!

It felt like someone was poking me in the chest from the inside. It would happen anywhere and at any time. Relaxing in the pub. Flip. Poke. Catch. A motorway pileup. Watching the TV. Flip. Poke. Catch. Etna erupts. Sitting on the crapper. Flipety-pokety-catch. Earthquake in Northern Scotland.

Doctor, doctor, doctor. You can check on each and every one, as I'm sure you already have. You want dates? Times even? I've got the lot. Even the earthquake in Scotland. Doesn't happen very often that, does it? Two in one week is just the gravy on the Yorkshire Pudding, dontcha fink? Yes, Doc. Check it out. Three days, four hours, twenty-two minutes after the first, a seismic hiccup way on down in Loch Ness was strong enough to capsize a survey boat on the surface. Now, Loch Ness is very deep and very wide. An educated man such as yersen, Doc, would know that it'd take a good ol' bounce to even ripple the surface. Course, the survey crew reckon it was dear Nessie herself, and they're going to be wasting a whole heap of money and time on searching her out. I reckon if Nessie was swimming about down there she'd have gone a-running with her kilt hiked right up to her hips.

So I had to make a decision. I had to choose. For Joy it was easy. Well, maybe not so easy, but she was always the one who *could*. Me? I guess I could have tossed a coin… John did it with a gun. I couldn't do that. No-Guts was my middle name, and I wanted to keep them exactly where they were. I couldn't jump off a bridge, although the Humber was just murky enough to be inviting. Driving my car into a wall was an option, but my right foot decided to have a mind of its own and not want to push that pedal-to-the-medal. A train mashing me to mush was another idea, but it would probably hurt.

In the end I did decide. I couldn't kill myself, but I figured I could take myself out of the loop. I could disappear. I could forget myself – become a John Doe-zee-do-your-pardners. Yee*hah!* That's when I came knocking at your door, Dr. Connors. That's when I rang your bell.

It wasn't difficult. Not that you're not good at your job, Doc. I don't mean to imply anything like that. I have enormous respect for your abilities. I bet that surprised you. Honestly, I do. Granted, you are so totally off base with my case that you're not even in the same time zone, but that's just me. I'm a special case, so to speak. A real vintage.

But it was fairly simple to get my own room-without-a-view. Act nuts. A little doolilly, a little doolally. A little 'I'm-a-little-teapot' thrown in for good measure. You practically welcomed me with open arms, didn't you? Thanks for that. Really. I mean it most sincerely folks. Yeah, there were no '12 good men and true,' were there? Just that nice, bespectacled, slightly balding (yes, Doctor, everyone knows) man in the suit creased so sharply it could cut butter.

Thank you. You took me in and doped me up. Helped me pack up all my troubles. What a guy.

Unfortunately…

Should have known, eh?

It's almost like aerobics. And, one and two and one and two and step and slide and flip and catch and one and two and on and on. That's why I throw a wobbler. It's why I go Lala every so often. Not because I'm a Teletubby, but because it's still with me, in here. I can't escape it. Even with the world a fading memory, I *know!* The brakes on Brenda Thomas's shiny new Audi failed as she was driving her daughter into school. Not a single one of the Humber Flying Club's parachute display team's chutes opened as they attempted, and failed, to build a pyramid three thousand feet up. Flight HB762, returning from Palma in Majorca, forgot to give its pilot control when they were landing back at Humberside. Or the pilot forgot how to land. Or it was the wrong type of snow on the tracks.

And step and slide. And flip and catch.

You see why I wanted the drugs? I think Jeremy (who really doesn't have to be so nice to your patients – half of them wouldn't even notice) knows that I'm not really crazy. When he comes to calm me down if I 'wobble', bringing his trusty syringe, I'm sure he sees it in my eyes. He's a clever one, Dr. Connors. You want to treat him right. He does the same for your patients, and most would prefer him to be the doctor and you to be the orderly. Hey, just saying it like it is.

But the drugs are not enough, not any more. Were they ever? I think at first, when they were new, I think maybe I fooled myself into believing that they were working. They kept me out of it enough so I didn't feel the flip, and I didn't see the catch. It was still happening though. So they are not enough. Joy knew. She understood that there was only one way.

I've figured something else out, Doc, and this one will lay you right out. You know how that damned coin always kept coming back? It was like a pet dog I'd been trying to get rid of. Kept nipping at my ankles, never realising I just wanted to kick it. I threw it away. I chucked it into the bloody sea! Yet it was always there, in my pocket, on top of the tens and the ones and the fifties. Always ready to wave and smile and say 'Hi!' I figured out that *that* was me too. I was bringing it back.

Yup-a-doozy.

Have you ever seen the film Phenomenon, with John Travolta? Very understated and quite excellent. I wonder if it's a bit like that, except my light from the sky was a two pence coin. I did, for a little while, hope that I'd have some brain tumour that was eating away at my central cortex wotsit and that was causing it all. No such luck. Fine and dandy and healthy as can be, that's me. So I couldn't hope for Him upstairs to help me out. Old Mr. Grim the Reaperman wasn't going to come a-calling either. I was on my own.

But the coin, yes indeedy. The coin was the trigger, but, bless its sweet little copper heart, it was also the key.

"What's he on about?" I don't hear you say. Teleportation, that's what. If you're a believer, let me hear ya say 'I BELIEVE!' A little louder, please. I can't hear you! Well, actually, it ain't that at all, I don't think. Don't you think? A question without an answer. Yes, I don't think. No, I don't think. You could go round in circles with that one. Anywho. Teleportation makes it sound like some cheap sideshow conjuring trick. Cups and balls-a-go-go. It doesn't feel like that, though. It doesn't feel like teleportation. I don't know, but the coin always ended up back in my pocket, safe and snug and warm. Maybe it's a flip without a catch? Ha. I just thought of that one. That sounds more like it. A flip with no smack-in-the-palm-of-your-hand catcheroony. By Georgy Porgy, I think he's got it!

So I'm going to try it myself. I'm going to flip, and I'm going to let the Universe catch-me-if-you-can. Sound metaphysical enough for you? I can't shoot myself, not that I could get a gun in here anyway (or maybe I could?). I can't jump. Hey, I wonder if I'd bounce or just splat? So I'm gonna flip.

Flipedy-doo-da, flipedy-hey, my, oh my what a helluva day!

I know just the place. I don't know why I didn't think of this before. I could have saved a lot of pain and death. If my mind had not been fogged by those won'erful drugs, would I have guessed? Who knows. Refineries are magnificent places, you know? Ever been to one Dr. Connors? I don't suppose you have. They've got all sorts of deadly chemicals and things that, if they went bump in the night, would certainly make sure half the county wouldn't wake up the next morning. Well, we've had a little preview of that already, haven't we? Furnaces. Loads of them. Temperatures exceeding a thousand degrees centigrade held captive in a little tin box. Oh, yes.

You look into them when they are going, and the flames, fifteen feet high and more, look ready to jump on you for their morning snack.

Well, I reckon I might just be lunch for one lucky flame. It'd be quick, for a start. He didn't feel a thing, Miss.

I'm trying to avoid asking myself any questions about what might happen then. I don't know if I believe in ghosts or heaven or hell. Does reincarnation exist? Would I come back as a frog perhaps? I reckon sitting by a pond catching flies all day would be a pretty relaxing way to spend one's life. I wonder if Joy is driving a cloud way up there with a sticker in the back saying 'The Afterlife's a beach!' But enough of that. I don't know, so there's no point in worrying about it. Well, there is one worry. What if it doesn't stop? What if I'm actually *stopping* the bad things happening, apart from the odd one getting through? What if I'm some sort of dam with a few chinks in the armour?

No. If only that were true. It's not. I'm certain it'll stop. Just like with Joy, it ends with me. Which, in a way, is a good thing. I suppose. I've got to go to the great meringue in the sky, 'cos life here's a lemon, but at least it'll stop. So, yeah, it's a good thing.

Well, this is it. This is where I take my leave of Life, the Universe, and fish fingers. I wonder if it's true that the last thing the captain of the Titanic ever said was to ask for ice in his drink? I wish I had something deep and meaningful to say. Some inspiring words of wisdom to pass on. I don't.

This is one small step for Sin, and one giant leap for the rest of you Muppets.

So long and thanks for all the rotten eggs.

Take your pick, Dr. Connors. Take your pick.

<End of statement>

Report by consulting psychiatrist, Dr. Henry Connors.

Sin Matthews was extremely paranoid and intensely delusional. His frequent bouts of erratic and often violent behaviour resulted in the need to keep Mr. Matthews sedated for much of the time. The claims made in his statement are obviously ludicrous, although it is clear he has researched these incidents thoroughly. Mr. Matthews's reasons for this are unclear. As he stated, Mr. Matthews voluntarily placed himself under this hospital's care. As yet, the investigation into his disappearance is inconclusive. That he 'flipped' out of his cell is naturally not being considered. It should be noted that, on the day of his disappearance, there was a fault in the CCTV system and it is my belief that Mr. Matthews took advantage of this to discharge himself. He has been reported to the police as a missing person. As he is no longer a resident of this hospital, my involvement with Mr. Matthews has come to an end.

Dr. Henry Connors *MRCPsych, DPM*

<End of report>

* * * *

It was Tuesday night. The rain beat down outside like the cast of Riverdance in a Sunday matinee. Jeremy "Jezzer" Jackson liked this shift. Some called it the graveyard shift, and in this hospital, that wasn't so far from the truth. A sea of zombies lay staring sightless into the darkness in the wards and cells. For Jeremy, however, it was calming. The outside world was a shade, a silent shadow beyond the large reinforced windows that lined the walls. Apart from the occasional call, a lone wolf's howl from the abyss, and soft sounds of snoring, everyone's favourite orderly could believe he was alone in the world.

He'd been thinking about Sin. Jeremy knew Sin wasn't entirely what he made out to be. He'd had an idea that the supposed insanity that he showed was enforced for some reason, as if he was running away, or trying to forget something that even the Foreign Legion couldn't help with. Jeremy liked Sin. They'd had long, intelligent conversations, something that the orderly missed. The doctors here treated him as if he was retarded somehow, not like the qualified nurse and ex-teacher that he was. He'd left both professions because he wanted something where he could make a difference. He knew nursing was rewarding, and he wouldn't disagree that teaching was indeed worthwhile, but this job was different. He made people who couldn't help themselves feel that bit better. He didn't really have to try either. Jeremy had a natural air of peace that could pacify the most tempestuous of patients.

But Sin was different. Sin had been a friend. Jeremy missed him. He knew that Dr. Connors wasn't really trying to find out what happened. Oh, the doctor was a decent man, but he felt he had enough patients at the hospital to worry about without having to chase one that couldn't sit still.

It was a quiet night. Hypnotic. Jeremy had been to Dr. Connors' office and had taken the Sin Matthews case file. He was sitting at his own desk, having finished reading both Sin's statement and Connors' brief report.

He picked up the coin. It looked brand new, shining fiercely in the glare of the strip lighting. He turned it over in his hands. It was hard to believe all that Sin had said. But what if...?

Jeremy blinked. The coin was turning a long smooth arc in the air. His hand was beneath it already, the fingers curled ready to close around the two pence piece.

Chapter One

Sin.

Yep. You heard me right. Sin. Sin-sin-sirree, there's no place for me. Or 'thee' as my dear old father, God rest his weary shade, used to say.

"You're a waste of space, boy!" he'd yell when he was feeling in a good mood. "Sin-sin-sirree, there's no place for thee!"

And he'd laugh. He'd laugh until he cried.

I just cried.

But that was then and this is now. So no matter, eh? Let's be cheery. Let's be happy. Let's be a-smilin' all the love-long day. Why not? Life's too short, so they say.

Weird that. "So they say" is also something 'They' say. So really, I should put it as "Life's too short, so they say, so they say..."

Or not.

Anywho-be-do. Name's Sin. That's me. And, I should coco, me and nobody else. If that's not the case, then my apologies to any other Sins out there. I hope you either changed your name or had big, hard fists. Really I do.

Sin. The kids at school loved me for that one. I wasn't fatter than a turkey three days before Christmas grace, or covered in raging acne as if Vesuvius had decided to dine out on my face, being a right pig in the process by having starter, main course and a big old yummy dessert. I didn't speak like I'd had a hearty meal of helium for breakfast, nor did I wear specs the size of full-fat-full-cream-full-cholesterol milk bottle bottoms. It was just the name.

Sin.

That's worth a punch or two, don't you think? Worth a kick between my legs once a day and twice on Fridays, no? No, but I'm biased. I'd rather be the kicker than the kickee. Well, to be honest, I'd rather be neither, but if it came right down to dancing on the edge of a knife, kicking or being kicked, punching or missing teeth, a choice isn't a choice. Not really.

So. That's me.

I tried to kill myself once. I thought I'd mention that just to keep the mood up. Just to keep us all smiling, you know?

It wasn't with pills, or razor blades, or leaping from tall buildings in a single bound. I used none of those mundane, ordinary, everyday techniques. My method of self-destruction was (drum roll please) *teleportation*.

Hah. Got you, that one, didn't it? You were expecting, perhaps, that I'd tied myself to a train track like in some old black and white film. Maybe you thought I'd tell you I'd stepped out in front of a truck down on the M180, in the rain, and at night. Better to make sure the truck didn't stop. Better to add a little dash of Craven-esque melodrama to the mix.

I could even have said that I'd had an all-day breakfast (served until 3:00 pm) at that little cafe down the end of Freeman Street. You know the one - next to the shop that sells unusual pets; geckos, tarantulas and the like. Is that shop still there? I can't remember. I've only ever been in there once, just to have a look. They had a komodo dragon in there the size of next door's cat. It was in a case not that much bigger than itself. One long stump of old tree branch for company. No wonder it did little more than sit and stare. Maybe it was eyeing me up for lunch - it obviously wouldn't have fancied the rat-burgers from next door. It's been a while since I was along that way, so maybe it's long gone now. But me and King Komodo agree on one thing - apart from the fact that I'm not on the lunch menu (not even the Chef's Special). The cafe was Alfonso's according to the sign, but Greasy Joe's to everyone else. Their breakfast was not a preferable method of suicide, even though it would no doubt be a successful one. I mean, if one of Joe's homemade hash browns didn't kill you...

Teleportation. There, I said it again. No, before you ask, if you were going to, I'm not crazy. The fact that the teleportation was actually out of a 'loony bin' - a bona fide mental institution - doesn't sign, seal and deliver my certificate of insanity. I just told them that so they'd keep me pumped full of those nice drugs that let me forget. Well, while they worked.

So anyway. I had a cunning plan. It didn't involve turnips or pushing pencils up my nose and saying "Wibble," or anything so loop-de-loo. I was going to teleport (that word again - if I say it enough times, do you think you might start to accept it?) straight out of my cell, padded nicely in a lovely glaringly serene white, right into the fiery heart of a dragon. Well, a reactor at least. Being licked by 20 foot flames flaring at a sliver below 1000°C wouldn't have been entirely pleasant, but at least, I figured, it'd be quick. And if it wasn't quick, well maybe I deserved that.

Unfortunately, I didn't get the chance to find out either way.

Self preservation. What a wonderful, sick, twisted, spit-in-your-eye, spiteful thing it is. They should have a society named after it.

I couldn't do it. I wanted to, oh, how I *wanted* to! But I, the I inside, wouldn't let me. It didn't even ask if I minded. There was no conversation, argument or heated debate over coffee. I wanted to commit suicide, kill myself, end it all, but *I* wouldn't let me. I don't know whether I was doing it deliberately, or if it was the grand old Universe having it's little bit of fun. Maybe the school bullies had been replaced by something far greater, and the Cosmos was taking its turn in hefting a great size 10 where the sun doesn't shine.

Cheers, pal. Yeah, thanks a bunch. Remind me to return the favour one of these millennia.

So I tried. I clicked my little red shoes together three times and said "There's no place like death. There's no place like death". Well, of course I didn't. I didn't have any red shoes for a start. I only wore these soft black soled things. We used to wear them at school. What were they called? No laces, just in case I wanted to do exactly what I wanted to do. What damage I could manage with a couple of thin bits of string with plastic ends, I don't really know. I'm not particularly inventive when it comes to doing myself in. If it's quick and relatively painless, then yay! Let me at it. If it's slow and the equivalent of a body wide paper cut? Thanks but you can keep it. No really, you have it. I'm fine with the death I've got.

Hey, paper cuts really hurt!

So what did I do? I didn't have my trusty little tuppenny sidekick geeing me on. Not that I think that's a bad thing. Mr Two Pence had caused me a whole load of trouble and heartache and had then piled on a good wadge more for the simple pleasure of it. Nice of him, eh? Listen to me. Heartache. Trouble. ME! I sound like a right selfish arse. Sod all happened to ME, apart from the ruination of my life, of course, and the everso slight inconvenience of being stuck in a padded cell. But at least I had a life! Thanks to me, all those people...

All those people.

Deeeeep breath. In through the nose, out through the mouth. Focus.

Plimsoles. Crappy little fall-apart-if-you-sneezed soft shoes for PE. God I hated PE. Physical Education? My physique was educated enough, thank you very much. Maybe it would have gotten an F in the mock exams - well, maybe a C if I was a wee bit vain - but running around a muddy field in the rain in shorts in September was not something I thought my body needed to learn. And cross country?

Can I ask why?

A group of kids running (and I use the term about as loosely as the Weightwatchers Slimmer of the Year's old knickers) around the streets, ducking into alleys for a crafty ciggy or nipping home for a packet of salt 'n' vinegar before running across the muddy field, in the rain... You know how it goes.

Back to the molecular transference of my physical atomic structure from one spatial co-ordinate to an alternative one. Or good old teleportation to you, me and the lampost.

I'd built myself up to a grand old height for the big day. The hour of doom was noon, when the sun would be high in the sky, birds would be singing, kids would be playing and the plague that a pair of nice, sweet, stupid parents had named Sin would be incinerated. Was Justice ever sweeter? I think not. I had no real ideas about what I was going to do - the methodology of my madness. Well, you've got to be mad to kill yourself, haven't you? Mad, but not necessarily crazy, thankee very much. I was wound tighter than Donald Duck's behind, snip snapping at anyone who happened by my cell that morning. Not that there were many. Room W17 didn't get that many visitors under normal circumstances. It wasn't the local branch of Woolworths, nor was it the local drugs den. It was just a simple padded cell, or rather cushioned accommodation, a third of the way along a blazingly white corridor of similar such rooms.

I used to like the lights, recessed into the high ceiling (so, I suppose, I couldn't jump up and bash my brains in if I was so inclined), fairly subdued to help keep me calm and equally subdued. It meant that when I ventured out of my cell, either by choice or by 'request', six inch nails of light were immediately hammered into the depths of my optic nerves, at least until I became accustomed to the 600 watt neon strips they'd decided to install in the corridor. Yes, they probably were only 60 watt bulbs, but combining white light with white ceilings, floors and walls, and dressing the staff in the same colour, enough to make them often look like disembodied heads floating along the hall, was something of a contrast to the relative duskiness of my room.

On this fine morning, however, no amount of twilight could ease my tension. It was the right thing to do. Of course it was. End it all, and it all ends.

Such are the plans of mice and men and me, that not all goes according to said plan. It wasn't my fault, and yet it was entirely my fault. Pretty much the same as all this low down stinking pile of doggy doo-doo we call life, in fact. I had no real control over events, but it didn't stop me being to blame. The finger of guilt was pointing, Pythonesque, directly at my bonce. I could feel it close enough to scratch my head with or to pick my nose. Granted, this finger bore a striking resemblance to the one on my own right hand - I was the only one who knew of my particular gift. Dr. Connors, bless him, knew as well of course, but he only believed the sun rose in the morning because, as a young boy of only five, he'd somehow climbed onto his parents roof at the crack of dawn to see for himself. He'd also wanted to hear if Dawn actually cracked, but he's yet to confirm that fact either way. It's a story he never ceases to enjoy telling, and it's one I and many others never tire of nodding and smiling and pretending to enjoy hearing. Consequentially, he didn't give a flying fudge about my claims, they couldn't be true, because then the sun might actually go to sleep at night, waking up all refreshed in the morning, ready to face the challenges of the day. Or the stars might be fairy dust in the night sky, sprinkled by some wayward Tinkerbell who's lost her way to Neverland.

Who knows? Maybe they are.

So. I didn't have any ruby slippers. Scotty wasn't orbiting in a geo-stationary orbit ready to beam me up. I didn't even have my lucky two pence piece. I had me. Just because I'd realised the truth about my relationship with that coin didn't automatically mean I knew what I had to do. As far as I'd been aware previously, it was all flip and catch. Flip the coin. Catch the coin. Kill a few hundred people. It had been that simple. That direct. Except the coin had nothing to do with any of it, other than being a catalyst. It had been the coin dropped into the jukebox of my mind, ready for me to press the right combination of buttons to play the records of destruction. It was a lot cheaper than the £1 for three songs that my local pub charged, that was for sure. Except it was also much, much more expensive. Devastatingly so.

Ruminations had been ruminating around my head all morning. They'd been chased by packs of rabid doubts which had in turn been pursued by... well, by fact. People had died. People had died because of me.

So in the end, it was as simple as dear Simon.

How, though? I thought I'd have to screw up my eyes. Clench my teeth and my fists. Hold my breath. Squeeze my whole body. But it didn't feel right. No great efforts had been taken previously, when all had been needed, it seemed, was an unconscious flick of the hand to send a small coin spinning through the air. What if that was the case now? But to do something so *big* had to take *something*, didn't it?

I didn't get the chance to find out. I didn't really even need the deep breath I'd taken. I was about to say some magic word or other, like "Go," or "Now." Maybe Houdini or Paul Daniels or even Sooty the Bear would have scorned those words for not being as theatrical as 'Abracadabra' or 'Izzy Wizzy Let's Get Bizzy'. This, however, wasn't conjuring. It wasn't even, to me at least, magic. It just was. So "Go" and "Now" weren't needed.

I went, then.

Just like that, as the wonderful Mr. Cooper would say.

I knew exactly where I wanted to go. I knew just where my crypt, or rather my pyre, would be. Right on top of a 1000°C, hot as hell, flame.

So imagine my surprise when I found myself on a beach, breakers breaking against my cold ankles, my strait jacket lying folded on the wet sand struggling to avoid being washed away by the tide.

Chapter Two

I was shocked to say the least.

The strait jacket had been a parting gift from the hospital. Because of my supposedly unwarranted tension that morning, they decided I needed some help in calming down. Being trussed up tighter than a turkey eagerly awaiting Christmas lunch isn't as attractive a proposition as it might at first sound. Saying that, I'm sure there are those who would, and do, pay very good money for such a 'pleasure'. I, for one, am not amongst them, I have to say. Naturally, Dr. Connors didn't realise I'd be vacating my cell that lunch time. I somehow neglected to inform his good self of my intentions. I doubted he would be too happy.

But then again.

If he had, then maybe he'd have plumped for something a little more fashionable. Straps and belts are something of a fashion necessity nowadays, but there is a little thing called overkill. I didn't think the flames that would be dining on me would mind though, so I didn't mention it. I was pleased the good doctor had decided against medication and had restricted his treatment to just the jacket. Being pleased about one of his decisions didn't sit particularly comfortably at my table, but I needed to be at the very least lucid. I worried that any amount of drugs, even though I'd often requested their administration in the past, would prevent me from doing the diddly-doo. So, yes, I was pleased, relieved and not at all peeved that I hadn't had a breakfast of needle on toast, washed down with a cold glass of Risperdal.

As far as I was concerned, I was interred at Insanity Central purely of my own accord. It was for the safety of everyone else, not for myself. The medication was there to numb me. It was meant to blot out that damned coin, erasing the possibility of me taking another bite out of population's pie. I didn't need it because I was psychotic. I wasn't. Nor was I half a dozen different people all squashed into this one body, each vying for control of the only mouth. I was normal, in a completely abnormal kind of way, of course. But Dr. Connors didn't know that. Even if he knew it on some level, he couldn't believe it. I was talking crazy dude! Rambling-a-ho worse than Bender Benny down in Room 101.

There wasn't actually a Room 101. That was just a cell a little smaller than the rest, with a little extra padding, where they put you if they wanted to forget you. 'In need of extra support' was how they'd put it, but it essentially meant the same thing. Bender Benny was crazy. He really was. Nuttier than Dr. Connors thought I was. Bender Benny's mind was bent so far round on itself, it could tickle his tonsils if it so wished. Don't ask me to tell you just what was wrong with him. Dr. Connors is the expert in matters of the mind.

Hah, I made a funny! Dr. Connors was an ex-spurt. That's about as far as I'd go. Trust me to voluntarily put myself in the care of someone who needed treatment more than his own patients! To be honest, I should have known, really. That kind of thing just seemed to happen to me. Fate's fickle finger always ended up picking me out of its nose and flicking me flat splat on the dirty pavement. When Life played Spin the Bottle, that old empty beer bottle always ended up settling on me.

Bender Benny was a danger to himself, apparently. He mumbled constantly in fractured sentences that only ever made a weird kind of sense when you half heard them. I'd never seen him become violent. He'd never so much as raised his voice or his fist. He simply sat there in the so-called common room, chained to the tubular steel chairs which were in turn bolted to the floor. After five minutes of his nonsensical mutterings he was returned to 101 before he made the other residents nervous. Every three or four hours, sometimes it was as much as six or seven, he'd appear again, head slumped, shoulders hunched, mouth twitching an ever constant stream of nothing. But he was a danger. Apparently.

As I was nice and sane and crispy, Risperdal, Valium, paracetomol and vitamin C were far more than I needed, but Dr. Connors, as he would, disagreed. Maybe he had shares in a pharmaceutical company. Perhaps he was on commission. A couple of quid for every pill popped and every tonic taken. Nice little earner. He certainly believed that preventing, or downright suffocating, a problem was better than a cure. So a daily dose was an essential part of everyone's diet. What doesn't kill you, it seemed, makes you number. Not a number, like 3487, just more numb. Something like that anyway.

For some reason, this time, he'd forgotten to top up my levels. Sometimes I felt the patients, residents, grunts, whatever we were, were like cars. You had to keep up our levels of oil and water and olanzapine to keep us running smoothly. Otherwise we'd break down and need towing back to the garage to be worked on. It was as unpleasant as it sounded. Perhaps this time he'd met his monthly quota and had earned a nice fat bonus into the bargain, because the strait jacket was all I seemed to warrant. Strange how I could be happy to be wrapped up and buckled down like some reject from escapology school.

Maybe I am crazy?

Or maybe Bender Benny was the only sane one amongst us, and we were the manifestation, or infestation, of his ramblings? What if we were all in his head and this was simply a story what he wrote, guv'nor.

And maybe the moon really is made of cheese and Wallace and Gromit's day out really was as grand as it seemed.

The first thing I thought of - the first question that came to me - was how my strait jacket had managed to not be securely fastened around my torso and was, instead, on the verge of floating away on a whim and a tide. And how come it was so neatly folded, straps tucked in, arms carefully creased across the top. OK, so that was two questions, but my first instinct was not to ask why I wasn't a cloud of ash floating about on the thermal updrafts of my favourite hydrogen-sulphide furnace. Nor was it "Where the hell am I?"

That would have been a good one for Houdini. How to escape a locked room whilst wearing the prerequisite strait jacket, in less than one second, removing yourself and the jacket with both arms tied behind your back, one eye closed and whilst singing God Save the Queen. Granted I was doing none of the latter, but it would still have been a good one for Houdini.

I stared at the jacket for a long moment. It bobbed on the waves, threatening to let itself be washed away if I didn't quickly rescue it. I thought about picking it up because it seemed part of me. It linked me to who I was. And that's why I left it. It linked me to who I was. I nudged it with my toe, helping it on its way. The breakers broke and the waves took it. I watched its colour darken as the fabric soaked up the water enough to weigh it down and drag it under. As it sank, the arms drifted off the top, either waving to me or beseeching me to save it. I waved back.

Bye.

I watched my cosy little strait jacket, arms flailing, disappear beneath the surface. It struck me that I could easily have used this watery grave for my own benefit. Rather than turning myself into the Sunday roast, I could quite happily have become shark bait - brunch for Moby Dick while he was waiting for Roy Scheider to stick a gas cylinder down his throat. The bottom of the deep blue sea was a definite alternative to a smelly old furnace. If the weight of tonnes of briny water slapped right on top of my head didn't kill me, the distinct lack of gills surely would have.

Hello Hindsight, and goodbye.

Finally my brain seemed to click into gear and I realised I was actually still alive. I hadn't drowned, nor had I been flame-grilled for that extra succulent taste. No sesame seed bun wrapped me up and Flipper wasn't likely to happen by and tell me Little Johnny had fallen down a cliff. I was still a one and only, walking, talking, living freak. I wasn't happy about that at all.

Turning, I looked around at the beach. The sea was one thing - I had always loved to listen to its whispering heartbeat as it danced its perpetual waltz with Sweet Sister Moon. The beach was quite another kettle of haddock, chips, scraps and lashings of salt and vinegar if you please. No, no mushy peas thanks. The thing was with sand, it was sandy. It got into all your nooks and crannies if you so much as sneezed at it in the wrong way. When I was younger - young enough to not question wonder and not to care about ordinary - I thought nothing of building sandcastles, kicking footballs, rolling around and mucking in. The sand would poor out of my trainers, my socks would shake and my jean's backside would brush clean. So simple. I reached a point, though, when I realised not all the sand left my trainers, and no matter how hard I shook my socks I'd still end up with sand between my toes. I'm not sure how old I was when that happened. I grew up, I think. How sad is that?

If you're ever contemplating growing up, don't. Take my word for it. *Boring!* That's my word. What difference does it make if your toes are sandy, or if you've a speck of muck under your fingernails? It really doesn't matter a flying fig. Not that I'm sure whether or not figs can fly. So don't do it. Stay a kid for as long as you possibly can. You hear about men hitting 45 years old and falling under the spell of the Wicked Witch of the Mid-Life Crisis. They buy flash sports cars and try and cop off with young pert-breasted blondes to recapture their youth. Personally I never owned a flash sports car, and I preferred redheads, so I didn't really have that youth to recapture. I always figured that a man's mid-life crisis was just an excuse. Not for anything in particular, just an excuse generally. A bit like PMT is an excuse for a woman to tear a man's balls off. As women don't have balls, a man doesn't have anything to aim at, so we're not that fussy. I'm still a long way off of 45, and don't have the money for a sports car, so I'll stick to trying to be a kid again. I'll continue to attempt to ignore sand, and to try to run between raindrops and see if I can jump in a puddle right up to my muddle.

But facing that beach right then, having realised I was still breathing, I was repulsed. I hated every single grain of sand and every tiny shell. It was personal. The beach was to blame. The water around my ankles had joined in for good measure. They'd clubbed together to abduct me, taking the piss and rubbing my nose in the fact that I could still feel the sun on my face. I could hear seagulls laughing somewhere off in the distance and I wanted to shoot them, one by one.

Let's see them laugh then!

I'm not normally the sort of person to get angry. I get down, maybe moody, pissed off and peeved, but not really angry. I don't fall into helpless rages, tearing through a room like a tornado, or a poltergeist who's had one too many coffees that day. That's not me. I'm fairly chilled, not tending to get worked up about things over which I have no control.

Perhaps that's hard to believe seeing as I committed myself to a lunatic asylum and then tried to toast my tootsies in a flame that Zippo or Clipper would have been proud of. The thing was, I didn't see it - the disasters, the death - as something out of my control. At first it was just a matter of ridding myself of that damned coin. Once I realised the coin was simply a focus and it wasn't going anywhere if it didn't want to, I'd hoped the heady mix of drugs, padded cell and strait jacket would do the job for me. I always thought there would be *some* way to stop it all. In the end, there could be only one, as the Kurgen once informed a young Highlander.

The Kurgen. Big, bad, mean-mother-hubbard. If ever there was a guy, immortal or not, who had a terminal case of PMT, Kurgeyboy was he. Anger was his middle name, or it would be if he'd had a last one.

So. My one chance to end it all - the pain and suffering and death - and I'd ballsed it up.

I was angry. Angry to be alive. Angry at the sea and the sand and the shells and the laughing seagulls. Angry at the fact that I could even be angry! One of the gulls landed a short distance away and peered at me gloating. "Ha! Got you!"

My anger switched up a notch. I realised my fists and my teeth were battling it out to see which could clench the tightest. The gull continued to mock me with its gaze, telling me what a sorry excuse for a suicide victim I was. A breeze picked up a few grains of sand and tossed them casually in my face. I could feel them scratching my eyes and working their way into my mouth. The sea seemed to surge around my ankles. I felt it wet my crotch and spray my fists as it joined in with the ridicule. The breeze became a wind that ruffled my hair the way a patronising uncle might his nephew.

I cried out then. Whether it was in anger, frustration or desperation I'm not sure. Probably it was all three mashed together like emotional bubble and squeak - except I had bubbled, but this was no squeak.

"AAAAAAAAHHHHHHHHHHHHHHHHHHHHHH!"

My throat was sore. My breath was gone. My anger had vanished. I felt empty. Lifeless. Dead.

That word again.

I shut my mouth and opened my eyes, not realising I'd closed them. The gull had gone, no doubt scared off by my shout. The sea had gone too, though obviously not frightened by me - I was no King Canute. I looked back to see the tide sweeping towards me, a stampede of angry looked white froth. If you don't think froth can look angry, maybe you'd like to kiss a pissed off Rottweiler. This froth was ticked off and it wanted a piece of me. Not wanting to become any wetter than I already was I ran backwards a few feet further onto the sand. The water crashed into a dip where I'd been standing, splashing me as if to say "I'll get you some way."

I wiped the salty water from my face wondering at the sudden tide. Had the waltz become a tango? Were the sea and the moon having a brief lover's spat?

I turned once more to face the land, stepping backwards slightly as I moved. I felt something crunch under my heel and looked down.

A wing, or rather the remains of one.

I crouched for a better look, not really wanting to but not being able to help myself. The crunch had been the small piece of bone still attached to the tattered and bloody section of feathers. Small pieces of gore were slimed across the wing, sand sticking to them like icing sugar sprinkled on a cake.

I vomited. Twice. The first was at the sight of the shredded wing. The second was either because of the smell of the first, or because the wing was now covered in my own puke, making the scene, somehow, more horrific.

Spitting a few times to clear my mouth, I stood again. Without looking back, I started to walk away. Without thinking about the what or the why, and certainly not the how, I walked away. I was sorry for the gull, but I didn't genuflect or say a prayer. I didn't look around for the remainder of the remains, if there were any. The thought of a burial, even one as simple as kicking sand over the wing, didn't enter my head.

I walked away and whistled a happy tune. Tra-la-la. No. I didn't. I just walked. I didn't look at my surroundings, sing a song, or even think. I just walked.

Chapter Three

Sometime after, I don't know how long or how far, I stopped and vomited again. As my breakfast that morning had been the usual two slices of toast, undercooked eggs and tepid coffee (they know how to look after you in that mental home), my previous efforts at throwing up had relieved me of the contents of my stomach. Dry retching was about all I could manage, but my body had a good attempt at more.

I'd left the beach behind a while ago, not noticing as the sand gave way to rough brush, which in turn transformed into grass. At some point the grass had met up with a road, maybe for a few drinks and a pizza, and I'd automatically turned along it, my feet taking me along their own path without actually letting the rest of me know. Perhaps they fancied pizza as well. Pepperoni, probably. Or maybe a meat feast. Just no tomato on the base please. I hate tomato.

I walked in a daze, feeling amazed, phased and, sadly, not erased. For a long time, I didn't actually think anything. I didn't notice flies on my face, though I perhaps brushed the odd one away. I didn't hear squirrels scooting along branches of trees or rabbits scurrying through the long grass. I never noticed any cars driving past, except for the one with the music blasting out. Music, nowadays, is a phrase that gets thrown on any pile of notes chucked together, however loosely. This particular harmonic car crash consisted of a bass beat I could feel in my bones, and someone swearing in rhyme, shouting to be heard above the relentless drums. The car was a pale metallic blue, small but with a rear spoiler so disproportionately large that, if the car hadn't have been doing 80 miles an hour, it would surely have tipped backwards. As it was, I expected it to achieve lift off at any moment, its escape velocity taking the vehicle into near orbit.

I didn't see the driver, but I assumed he wore a baseball cap, the peak curved down, frowning at the fact it covered the head of an idiot. He'd be on his mobile phone, shouting to be heard above the guy on the CD who was swearing at the top of his voice above the beat. He'd drive like this whether he was on the open road, or whether he was driving past a primary school. It was cool. He was invincible.

I vomited again at that point. Or tried to.

I hadn't seen the small dent on his bonnet. But I knew it was there.

I hadn't seen the single strand of strawberry blonde hair that was still, no matter how well he'd tried to clean the evidence away, trapped in the arm of his wiper blade. But I knew it was there.

He hadn't seen the girl. He was reading a text message on his phone from one of his drinking-smoking-drugging buddies. He hadn't felt his car hit her. The only thing he could feel was the beat driving its way into his soul. It wasn't until he'd pulled into his mother's drive and was walking away from the car that he saw the dent and he saw the hair and he saw the blood. I think he probably vomited then, but it was a club I didn't care to share membership of.

Up ahead the road curved to the right around a small copse. I saw the blue car with the enormous, phallic spoiler take the curve way too fast. The driver drove this way normally, so he could, most likely, have handled the skid. He would have laughed as he turned into it and accelerated away. Adrenalin, food of the yobs. Except he wasn't laughing. He didn't get chance. I'm quite sure the tree didn't leap into the middle of the road. I'm equally certain its branches didn't reach down, snatching the car off the road.

I didn't see the crash, but I heard it. I couldn't smell the smoke but I knew it was there. I couldn't see the strange angle his bloody head was hanging at, or the way his right arm didn't seem to be fully attached at the elbow anymore. But I knew. I knew.

I didn't run to the accident. I didn't believe it was entirely an accident. And when I rounded the curve in the road, I looked at the wreckage just as I would have roadkill, although for the squashed remains of a hedgehog or pheasant I would have felt something. Here, I felt nothing. No sympathy and no sorrow. I didn't feel numb, as I thought I might, I just felt nothing for the man, little more than a boy, who had driven too fast for too long and had mowed down a young girl on her way home from school without even noticing. I felt nothing for the person who could clean his car, polishing till his arms ached, to try and hide the fact. I felt nothing for the mangled corpse of someone who, the next day, could climb back into his car, turn up his music, talk on his phone, and forget it had even happened. The expanding pools of blood and oil, merging together like a ying-yang pictogram were just something to step over.

It would seem that, apart from our mutual queasiness, we also shared a lack of guilt.

I looked at the wreckage and continued to walk. I didn't stop to see if I could help - it was obvious I couldn't. I'd be hard pushed to say which was in a worse state - the car or the body.

It had been, apart from that spoiler, a nice car though.

Leaving the shattered remains of man and machine, car and corpse, fillet o' fish, behind me, I continued to let my feet take me where they wanted. I felt detached as if the only thing keeping me in contact with this world was the touch of my feet on the road. If I'd jumped, separating me from the tarmac, perhaps I would have winked out of existence faster than His Royal Deceasedness back there could take a corner. I didn't jump, to test my theory, just as I didn't feel bad that I could make light of what had just happened. I maybe felt bad about not feeling bad, but that was a bizarre spiral I didn't want to get tangled up in.

It dawned on me, like the sun rising refreshed after a good night's kip, that, as well as being still in the land of the living, I didn't actually know where I was. I hadn't recognised the beach I'd arrived on, washed up survivor of the shipwreck called my life, but that meant nothing. Apart from the glorious golden stretches of Majorca's Alcudia or mainland Spain's Costa Dorada, as the brochures insisted they were, I'd only really been to Cleethorpes. Golden, it wasn't, but it was all we'd had as I grew up. There were infrequent visits to the seasides of Skegness and Mablethorpe, and even less so to Scarborough or Bridlington, but none of the sandy stretches had any distinguishing marks to stick in my head. They all looked, like the grains of sand on their very own beaches, pretty much the same. They had pubs, they had souvenir shops and they had tourists. If it wasn't for the much hotter weather and the fact that the Mediterranean Sea is a tad cleaner than the River Humber, you could have been sunning yourself anywhere.

I'd been walking with no sense of direction and no sense of destination. Even if I'd had a destination, somewhere to rest my weary bones and, under the circumstances down a few neat vodkas, I wouldn't have known what to do once I got there. Except down a few neat vodkas, of course. That in itself raised a problem or two. I didn't have any money. The slacks they dressed us in were the poor relation of hospital scrubs, and were pocketless, not to mention styleless. With the asylum to bleed us dry of any finances we might have, residents, patients and grunts together were provided with their every need so personal money wasn't an issue, nor was it a temptation to anyone else. Providing us with our every need meant feeding us slop and doping us up, but that was just incidental. No need to be picky is there?

One thing Joy had done for me was make me comfortable. I don't know how she'd managed it, but she must have been a far keener financial wizard than I'd ever hoped to be. Because she'd taken her own life, her life assurance, to the sweet tune of £100,000, had not paid out, but her shares and various other monetary wotsits certainly had. I knew nothing about tax and accounts and bonds and such myself. I'd never had the money to warrant me finding the knowledge. As far as I was concerned, a bank account was somewhere to pay your wages into before everyone else leeched them out. My future-thinking financial security extended to a limited stakeholder pension, but that was about it. Everything else seemed as complicated as Sudoku, so I kept well away. Joy, it appeared, didn't have that problem. She'd invested extremely wisely, in such a way as to ensure her standard of living well into her twilight years. It was a pity her twilight had come so fast, like a candle snuffed out by an errant breeze.

More surprisingly, though, was the fact that I was named beneficiary of the whole shebang. Not because I wouldn't be, don't get me wrong. Joy and I were as close as any brother and sister might be. Granted she never, ever wrote me a letter, except one in particular, but we always shared a bond. I always thought that bond was one of simple sibling love. Naturally it wasn't. Joy was joy and I, Sin, was sin. I found out too late how closely we were connected. Too late to save her and, perhaps, myself. But whip-de-do. At least she made sure I could afford Dr. Connors' rates.

I think, sometimes, I sound callous and uncaring. I make light of the deepest, darkest subjects, as if I couldn't give a rat's banana. That's not the case, though. I might joke about my sister jumping off the Humber Bridge to take a little dip in Pollution

Central, but it doesn't mean I think it's funny. It doesn't mean it didn't tear me apart. It doesn't mean it doesn't still.

Perhaps it's because that's exactly what happened. It tore me apart, just as everything else I've caused has done. The bus smashing into the post office. The seagull ending up as if it had been supper for a pack of hunting dogs that had somehow mistaken it for a fox. The boy, a young *boy*, driving his car into a tree. Each time something happened, I was fed through the shredder, then stuck back together with a great, hefty staple gun and a few rusty nails. With some blu-tac and spit to make sure I didn't come apart at the seams. After so much of that you either deal with it or you end up insane.

No comments about my previous residence, please.

So that was my way of dealing with it all. That was how I bit the big cookie. I took the piss, just a little. It was either that or gouge my eyes out with a rusty fork. They didn't give us metal forks, rusty or otherwise, in the mental home, so I didn't really have that option. Humour, however inappropriate, was my only course of action, my only weapon and my only form of defence.

So, I wasn't rich, not by any stretch of the imagination, but I was comfortable. I couldn't buy a twenty seven bedroomed, eighteen bathroomed, ten kitchened, six garaged, one partridge in a pear treed mansion, not could I fork out for a Ferrari or two to run about town. I couldn't afford eight cruises a year. I couldn't afford one really. Well, maybe I could, but Dr. Connors' vampiric fees made sure I didn't take it. But that was OK. It was all well and fine and dandy. I'd voluntarily incarcerated myself into Hell's Kebab House and accepted the fact that they'd bleed me like a leech, all nicely bloated and disgustingly fat.

It was a good job their standards of care were right up there with the monkeys. I imagined Dr. Connors performing lobotomies with a steak knife and a knitting needle, giving the knife a quick wipe before he sat down for a nice bit of sirloin, chips and peas, hold the mushrooms. Was I being unkind? Perhaps. The good doctor might well use a clean knife for his dinner. Was it deserved? Yes. It was. Dr. Connors was like Stephen King's It. All smiles and happiness while he eviscerated you.

Apparently he liked Chianti too.

My problem was, although I had money in the bank - assuming that it hadn't been totally siphoned yet (and we know that assuming anything turns me and you into a right donkey's arse) - I didn't have access to a bank. I didn't even know if there were any banks around here, not knowing precisely where 'here' was. I could have been in my home town, or I could have been in Outer Mongolia. Both options were pretty much the arse end of Nowhere to me, but at least Grimsby had its fair share of banks, building societies and those cash-point machines that rip you off a couple of quid every time you make a withdrawal. I knew that Outer Mongolia had come a long, long way since the days of Genghis Khan, but I was sure trying to get hold of any cash, if indeed that's where I'd landed, would have presented me with one or two wee problems. All I could do, in my current situation, was keep walking and see where I ended up.

I just hoped I'd end up somewhere fairly soon. Dark clouds were looming ominously not too far away. I could see them planning their attack on me, making bets on which would manage to drench me the quickest. I wished I'd brought me brolly.

My thoughts, drifting like a strait jacket on the water, returned unbidden to the crash scene I'd left behind me. I'd trained myself to not dwell on the things that happened, that I caused. 'Trained' might be too structured a word. It wasn't really that conscious, or that regimented. It was more a case of I'd learned, through instinct or pain or sweet self-preservation, to not think too much about the deaths and the screams and the things I knew. The fact that I had wanted to turn myself into a strawberry Pop Tart might decry that admission, but, while I could want to rid the world of Me because of everything I'd done, I didn't concentrate on individual atrocities. The situation as a whole made me want to, let's be blunt, kill myself, not because of anything specific, but because I was a monster ass-ay-hole.

I think that makes sense. I could turn a blind eye to causing the death of a family, but not to the fact that I'd caused death.

I looked back, briefly. I couldn't see the remains of the car. The scene back there seemed as peaceful as if it was an autumn's day, just before the rain. The trees and hedgerows stood out in stark relief against the blackening clouds. The air felt charged as if the sky was winding up a dynamo ready for a lightning display. I certainly didn't want to be caught in any downpour but didn't see the point in quickening my pace. I could be 100 metres from sanctuary, just around the next gang of elms, or it could be 100 miles, over the hills and far away. Who knew? I, for one, didn't, so why bother breaking into a sweat when it might be pointless? If the heavens opened, as they surely were planning to, I'd take shelter under the branches of a tree and wait it out.

The car. The boy. The blood and the broken glass and the crushed metal.

I flashed back to him flying past me. He'd been a blur, but I saw more in retrospect than I had at the time. He was driving on the left hand side of the road. He was sitting on the right. The number plate was a UK one. FX56 something or other. A new car. Nice one. I wasn't in Outer Mongolia, nor was I in deepest, darkest Africa. Darkest England was a fairly safe bet.

I smiled. It had been a long time.

There was a body. There was a wreck. There was death. But hey, there was also the chance that I might be able to find a pub and have a few neat vodkas. "Yippee-ki-yay, you mothers," as Bruce Willis might say.

I blotted the crash out. What could I do, that I hadn't already done? Come on. I'd rid the world of an idiot driver, one that had gotten away with running down a young girl? Was the world a better place? Was it sweeter smelling and fresher? No. Not to my nose anyway. Not to my senses. Not to my heart. He was an idiot. His idiocy had resulted in the death of a girl. Who was I, though, to dictate that he should die? I didn't wear a great black hooded cloak and swing a scythe like Tiger Woods does a nine iron, or my old mate Tony tries to. I don't live on a cloud, have a long white beard and lightning shooting from my fingertips, having to be careful if I wanted to pick my nose. I was just me, Sin, a mortal more mere than most.

But anywho-be-doo. Hi-ho, it's off to wherever I go.

The light was fading and the distinct lack of any street lighting meant it was becoming much darker than I was used to. I hadn't thought enough time could have passed since I left the hospital for the day to be leaning towards night. I knew I'd been walking for a while, but I had nothing to track the hours by. Watches weren't allowed - yes, you could possibly hang yourself with the strap if your shoelace happened to snap, and I didn't have Tonto's skills in telling the time by the position of the sun or the song of a cricket. If I didn't have my Pulsar or my mobile phone, an hour could last five minutes or be about five days long. It meant the few years I'd spent in Dr. Connors care had lasted about six millennia. Even so, I would have guessed that only a couple or three hours had loped by since I'd blown apart that gull. Even in September it doesn't begin to get dark until around seven-ish. The clouds, my Reaper's cloak made real, were dragging across the sky, as if they were readying themselves to wipe us all out, although that was perhaps wishful thinking. The sun had disappeared, either behind the cloak or beneath the horizon I didn't know. Still, it didn't *feel* that late. It didn't *feel* like I'd been walking seven hours instead of two.

I wasn't hungry, nor was I tired. My legs weren't heavier than a mobster's hit, concrete shoes and all, and there were no stitches in time to save nine digging their wee ways into my side. So why was it getting darker than Dr. Connors' mood the time Bender Benny told him he (Dr. Connors) was the crazy one and everyone else was saner than a rattlesnake on ecstasy? I didn't quite get the rattlesnake analogy, but sometimes Bender Benny talked a lot of sense. Mr. Shrink-o-matic 2010 didn't appear to think so though, and had made sure Benny had realised the error of his ways.

We didn't see the Bender for a few days after that. It might have been about a week. He was quieter.

I figured that, if I could have been plonked on a beach somewhere when I'd intended on ending up in the belly of the dragon, I could, I supposed, equally have been plonked a few hours later. Maybe teleportation included a slight risk of time travel. Perhaps it was the equivalent of turbulence on an aeroplane flight. No oxygen masks were there to drop in the case of an emergency, and no air stewardesses were on hand to show you the wheres and whyfors of a life jacket. If you hit a cosmic air pocket on your teleporting way from one place to another, maybe you hiccupped a few hours into the future. Hey, if we're walking in the realm of Star Trek, why not add in a dash of Doctor Who for good measure?

I was new to this. Even I didn't entirely believe, deep inside, that I could teleport. Even I still thought I hadn't done exactly what I *had* done. It was all madness. Maybe I was in my padded cell, strapped up tighter than Scrooge and doped up to Alpha Centauri. Maybe none of this was real and I was a pigment of Bender Benny's emancipation.

But the death told me it was real enough. All the souls, torn from their bodies like giblets from a chicken, en-masse screamed at me that it was real enough.

Still. Time travel, on top of everything else, was just a step too far over the border into Crazytown, population 1. I'd just been wandering for longer than I'd thought. Time flies by when you're having fun, or causing youngsters to plough their cars into the trunk of a tree. Apparently time is relative. Who's relative, I don't know. Does time, his cousins, his mum and dad and the dog gather around the table for Christmas dinner, ready to tuck into too much turkey and pigs-in-blankets? Which one refuses to wear the paper crown from the cracker, that's what I wanted to know.

I did begin to feel tired then. The energy drained from my body like a light bulb being switched off. I was suddenly knackered and the thought of taking any more steps was so daunting, I'd have rather kissed a pissed off Rottweiler. I stopped and stood there, looking at nothing in particular, feeling... feeling floppy. I just couldn't be bothered. I didn't know how far I had to go, mainly because I had no idea where I was going. A house could chance across my path, but would I stop there? What if I did? What then? Would someone open the door, a big old farmer or a young, vulnerable farmer's wife?

"Hey there," I'd say. "I wonder if you could help me. You see, I've just escaped from a lunatic asylum..."

Would the resident reach for a gun to shoot me? Would it be a phone to call the police? Perhaps it would help if I mentioned how, precisely, I'd managed my escape.

"I teleported out," I'd tell them. "It's a simple trick of matter transference. You should try it; it'd save you a fortune in taxi fares."

Perhaps not.

It did occur to me, as it would have had to, that I could use my new found talents of space shifting (as opposed to shape shifting which, to my knowledge, was beyond my abilities) to get myself somewhere else. The problem was, of course, that I might well end up back in the mental home. Or on a beach in Outer Mongolia, if they have any beaches. Or even sitting in a furnace with a great walloping flame up my backside. Right now even my original plan of action had become a plan of inaction. Suddenly death, my own anyway, was something I didn't fancy trying out. Death was a bright spangly pair of purple trousers that I wouldn't be seen... dead... in. I didn't want anyone else to die because of me, but I wasn't keen anymore on biting the big apple myself.

Call me selfish if you like, I don't mind, but not shellfish. Well, maybe a bit crabby.

As such, with my possible destination being either the inside of a white dwarf star or sitting on Dr. Connors knee while he ate his supper, I decided to keep on walking, exhausted or not. Thunder rumbled, fairly closely. The clouds were chanting their song of attack and I was right in the firing line. Maybe walking would do in preference to getting wet.

Off to my left, to the side of a freshly ploughed field, was a small copse of trees. They were obviously an artificial planting, the trunks marching in even ranks across neatly trimmed grass. All were of the same make, model and serial number, but not being a botanist I wasn't sure which. Maybe willows or something. They weren't oaks or elms, I knew that much. They could have been baby redwoods, waiting to become fully grown so a car could drive through their bases, but I doubted it. It didn't matter anyway, though I did briefly think I should take better notice of the world I seemed hell bent on destroying. Whether willow, redwood or bonsai, they were enough to offer me shelter from the coming storm, and if they didn't want to offer, I'd certainly take. The sky had turned angry and I didn't want its temper taken out on little old me, thank you very much.

The first spatterings of rain were throwing themselves at me as I left the road and, by the time I had reached the cover of the first branches, the spatterings had become an onslaught as each drop did its very best to hit me. They weren't bothered which part of me they made a target, any would do, but I felt like John Cleese accidentally saying Jehovah in the Life of Brian. A good stoning had taken place, albeit with water instead of rock, and I was battered and served up with chips and mushy peas.

So much for not getting wet.

Wiping the rain from my face with my sleeve I looked around for a nice comfy tree to sit against. It looked like I was going to be here for a while, so I figured I may as well get myself settled. The branches and leaves above me served their purpose in protecting me from the rain well enough for me to remain soaked and not to progress to drenched, not passing go and not collecting £200 - which was a bit of a pain because I could have done with the money. Vodkas don't buy themselves. One tree looked to be not quite as knotty and knobbly as its neighbours so that's where I parked my behind. It wasn't exactly the most comfortable place I'd ever rested, but it would have to do. I contemplated removing my wet clothing, but without a radiator handy to dry them on I decided my own body heat was the nearest I'd get. Besides, I wasn't sure whether I'd be colder with them on or off, so I chose wet and clothed rather than cold and nude.

I looked at the forest around me. It was nice. Now nice is a word I don't like to use too much - thanks, pretty much, to my old English teacher. I remember he banned us from using it in essays once because it was so insipid and overused. This is nice, that's nice, they're nice, I'm nice, you're nice, mice are twice as nice. Using it in conjunction with other words was fine and double dandy, but on it's own, it wasn't nice at all. The forest, however, was nice. It was pleasant. Not insipid by any means, but restful. Even with the raindrops drumming along to their rock-steady-beat, peace seemed to reign beneath the blanket of leaves.

It was nice. Sorry Mr. Staniforth, but it was.

There weren't any birds whistling or whooping, but I did hear the odd scurry of a squirrel or rabbit hidden nearby. I didn't really know where they'd be hiding, as the ground between the trees was covered in a thick but neat carpet of grass, as if it had been a football pitch a couple of days ago and someone had accidentally dropped the trees here and hadn't got round to picking them up. But they scampered thither and to, keeping their distance from me and from the downpour beyond. I didn't mind them staying away from me. I wasn't in the mood for company, and trying to hold a conversation with a squirrel was something I was too tired to bother trying. They can be skittish creatures and tend to have a short attention span, so any chat is liable to dip and dive from subject to subject faster than I could make a banoffee pie disappear. Rabbits are different but just as hard to please. They simply look at you with blank faces, making it obvious that, no matter how riveting your conversation might be, they just wanted to know where you kept the carrots. I couldn't blame them. My stomach was starting to growl so a carrot or two, while not banoffee pie, would have been quite welcome.

I wondered if anything was happening anywhere else. By that I meant did the Grim Reaper owe me any thanks for chucking a few more shredded souls his way. I thought not. I'd know. I wondered if the boy in the car had been missed yet. Or had he been found. I wondered if I'd get some sleep. Then I slept.

Do you remember your dreams? I didn't. Not very often anyway. Sometimes, if I woke in the early hours then drifted back off to sleep again, I'd have snatches of a dream still clinging to me when I awoke properly. Occasionally those snatches would be full episodes and I'd recall them for a few hours or so before they would fade. Usually, though, I didn't. Sleep is a coma that only the insistent blaring of an alarm or the not too gentle shaking of a burly hospital orderly can rouse me from. And if I still retained glimpses from a dream, I rarely believed it to be my subconscious trying to communicate some hidden message to me. I'd like to, really. It would be good to have your brain ticking over problems while you're out for the count, supplying you with the answers in the form of little soap operas ready for when you wake up. I'd like the human brain to be capable of stuff like that. Perhaps it is, Who knows? In my case, though, it didn't happen, or if it did, my subconscious kept the solutions to itself. Maybe my dilemmas were too much for me to handle and I didn't realise it? Or maybe there aren't any actual solutions. My inner demons wouldn't stay inner enough for me to resolve them. They had a habit of escaping every so often and people died. I always wished I could dream more - or at least remember them. That would mean that things were getting better. That would mean the Reaper was doing his own dirty work.

"Hey, Sin," said Joy.

Chapter Four

I looked up. The trunk was obviously not as smooth as it had first appeared. Knots as big as fists were digging their knuckles into my back and no amount of squirming on my part could ease the discomfort. Even so, I didn't bother standing or moving away. I supposed I could have lain on the ground, but I knew I'd have felt exposed. With my back against the bark, as much as the bark tried to put me off, at least I felt I had some protection. Protection from what, I didn't know. I was fairly sure that, if I didn't know where I was then Dr. Connors and the rest of the 'sane' world wouldn't know either. That was unless they'd subcutaneously implanted a tracking chip somewhere on my body and satellites were currently spinning across the sky, homing in on my location so the hounds could come a-calling.

Oh my, wee doggy, what big teeth you have!

All the better to tear you limb from juicy limb!

"Always one for melodramatics, eh?" Joy commented. Her voice was like warm chocolate, velvety and smooth and, no doubt, high in calories.

"Oh," I said, smiling, "you know me. Why make a molehill out of a mountain?"

Joy was standing in front of me, looking much the same as the last time I'd seen her. Her hair was just past her shoulders, brown with blonde streaks that were not-so-fresh out of the bottle. Her eyes sparkled their usual green, smiling even when her mouth frowned. She seemed taller than I remembered, but then I was slouched against a tree that was doing its best to make sure I never stood straight again, and she was...

... She was dead.

"You're dead," I said, matter of factly.

"You're not looking so good yourself, mister," she said. "At least I can make a clean job of it, not like some I could mention."

I assumed, by that little comment, that she meant me. Joy had a habit of, where I'd make jokes, she'd make jibes. Usually it was all in good humour, just a different slice of the funny pie to the one I tended to munch, but I couldn't always tell if she was being serious or not. She looked fairly stern right at that moment.

"Hey," I defended, "I tried. It's not my fault I didn't end up where I wanted."

It sounded like I was sulking - a petulant child with my bottom lip dragging the floor. I knew Joy was only teasing, but I couldn't help it. Perhaps I was just pissed off with myself. Perhaps I was just pissed off with the world.

"Anyway," I said, picking my lip off the floor in case it got dirty. "You're dead. You don't have an opinion."

"Who are you to say what I can and can't have?" she huffed. "You're still, even after that mightily pathetic attempt to do otherwise, alive. You don't know the first thing about being dead, so I suggest you keep your *opinions* to yourself, thank you very much."

"Sorry," I said, dropping my lip again. I was angry enough at myself, not least because a seagull and boy were gone thanks to me. Having my own sister picking on me was a shiver past too much.

"Sin," she said, the melted chocolate back in her voice, "Get a sense of humour."

I looked up at her again. She winked and I realised what I should have known anyway - she was teasing.

"So," I said. "Death hasn't dulled your edge then?"

"Not a bit," she replied. She stepped to my side and sank down to the ground beside me. Her movements were as fluid as if she'd poured herself. I imagined the whole cast of the Royal Ballet performing Swan Lake, or some other famous ballet dancing show thing (I wasn't up on my classical dance) pirouetting through her body. Grace would have been an appropriate name for her, but then so would Sarcky Cow.

"Death," she continued, "isn't really as bad as it's made out to be. Granted I can't enjoy a Big Mac anymore, but at least I don't have to buy tampons either."

"What a lovely thought," I said. I would have assumed that being deceased would have more going for it, or against it, than the simple pleasures of fast food and periods. Not that I'd have thought a woman's monthlies was exactly a pleasure, but you get the point. Not that Big Macs and large fries are necessarily a pleasure either, for that matter.

"Indeed," said Joy. "Now do you want to get that lazy arse moving or are you going to stay moping here for the rest of your miserable life?" She poked me in the shoulder, quite sharply actually.

"Ouch," I complained.

"Sin, when did you become such a wuss? Has having that nice Dr. Connors looking after you all this time turned you into a big baby?"

I wouldn't have called Dr. Connors care 'looking after me', nor would I have called it 'care', but I didn't think I had to point that out to my sister. I'm sure I wasn't still the handsome hunk that had checked himself into the institute. Granted, I'm sure I wasn't a handsome hunk at all, but if I looked rough back then, I'd certainly be on the dark side of shabby now. Joy, on the other hand, was glowing. I don't mean in that aural angel kind of way, but rather in that healthy holiday in the sun three times a year, gym three times a week and cleanse three times a day kind of way. More radiant than... I don't know... a radiator. A white one. With a light shining on it. Or something.

"Death's been good for you," I commented, changing the subject. A weird thing to say, perhaps, but I was talking to my dead sister, so I figured it was ok.

"I wouldn't say that," she said. "I've a devil of a time trying to get my roots done."

So there I was. Unsuccessful at suicide, hiding in a forest, talking to the ghost of my suicide-successful sister. It had been a busy day. I'd escaped a mental home, killed a bird and a boy and I still had time to watch Eastenders and maybe grab a bite to eat. Chit-chat with Joy was pleasant and totally irrelevant. I was confused.

"This is a strange dream."

Joy smiled. The dimples in her cheeks made her look, as ever, like a mix of cute and sultry, carrying her smile up to her eyes.

"Who says you're dreaming?" she asked.

How did I know she was going to say that? I felt like I was in the middle of a horror movie, where I knew I shouldn't go down into the cellar - especially with the light not working - but I was going to go anyway.

"So, I'm awake and you are really my dead sister's ghost, come to haunt me?"

"What makes you think I'm a ghost? What makes you think I'm haunting you at all? Just because I'm dead doesn't make me a cliché, you know."

Fair point, I thought.

"Well, if you're a zombie," I pointed out, "you're not baying for blood and you haven't got half of your head missing. I know you don't like horror films, but remember when we watched Dawn of the Dead together?"

"That was Shaun of the Dead, and if you'd prefer I look the part just to convince you, then I suppose I could play along."

As she spoke, I noticed movement in the corner of her eye. At first I thought it was a tear forming and was going to ask her why she was crying, but when I saw it wriggle and plop out onto her lap, my mouth dried up. There on her tan coloured trousers, creamy and bulbous, was a maggot. I stared at it for a moment, my usually smart mouth staying dumb. When it was joined by a second, equally bulbous cousin, I looked back at my sister's face.

Or what was left of it.

OK, so her roots needed touching up before, but now they were a mass of movement as maggots swarmed across her skull making her look like an adolescent Medusa. Sections of hair, along with the skin it they were attached to, slid down across her face leaving streaks of red and brown. Carried by the added weight of the larvae, they dragged over her still sparkling eyes until they reached her jaw and fell onto her lap. She smiled again and a cockroach worked its way out of her mouth, all spindly legs and antenna at first, then seemingly all body, hard, black and glistening. The cockroach joined the scraps of head and crawled over the writhing maggots until it fell onto the ground and scurried away, thankfully in the opposite direction to me.

One shining eye bulged outwards at me until I thought it would explode, spraying me with gloop and cornea. Instead it popped out and hung by its optic nerve, swinging lazily on her cheek. It still sparkled, even though it was now bloodshot and yellowing.

She raised one hand. The hand was missing its flesh. Skeletal, with withered tendons struggling to stay attached, it pointed at the remains of her face.

"Is this better?" she asked. Her voice oozed from between decayed lips, no longer velvet but slime, still smooth but bubbling slightly and on the edge of coagulating in her throat.

I regarded her for a long time as the maggots feasted on her flesh and wriggled into her ears and nostrils.

"Nothing a bit of foundation wouldn't fix," I said.

She laughed, spraying blood and teeth on the ground between us. A molar landed on my foot and I picked it up and handed it back to her.

"You dropped this," I said. Whether Joy was a ghost or not, this was a dream, so there was no point in being disgusted or frightened. None of it was real.

"That's the Sin I know and love. Thank you Doctor for injecting some humour back into the old misery!"

This was how I remembered our relationship. We always seemed to bounce of each other, sometimes like Sumo wrestlers but more often than not like two balls in a Newton's Cradle - tick-tack-tick-tacking, trading funny little comments with smiles on our faces - what was left of them in some cases. I relaxed and Joy's face returned to its normal pretty self. She picked up the sections of scalp off the grass and laid them back on her skull, pushing her eye back into its open socket. I'm sure this was more for theatrics than necessity as, when she opened her mouth all her teeth were back in their original places, lined up on parade for inspection, Sergeant. The maggots were gone, though I didn't notice them disappear and the bloody streaks across her face faded to nothing.

"Ugh," I said, pulling a face. "You can take off the Halloween mask, it's not for a couple of months!"

"Oh, funny boy," she smirked. "You should be on stage."

"Thanks."

"Sweeping it."

I laughed anyway, even though it was an old joke and not particularly funny. Sometimes, without being able to help myself, I'd be on the precipice of laughing at a funeral, looking down the pit of complete embarrassment. You know when it's so wrong you can't help it? Like Death By Chocolate cake smothered in double cream? You know you shouldn't but you grab the biggest spoon in the drawer anyway? It was like that, almost. I knew I was in a bit of a state. I was an escaped mental patient, had no money, no real clothes, no idea where in the world I was and I was chewing the banana with my dear old sister, R.I.P.. You've got to laugh.

No, really. You have to.

"Come on. Buck up bucko!" She jabbed me in the arm with her perfectly re-fleshed finger. It hurt. Well, at least it meant she wasn't a ghost and this had to be a dream. And at least I wasn't naked or running around school in my pyjamas.

"I'm ok." I almost meant it. "Just been a bad day, you know?"

"Oh, I know. You've the world on your shoulders, and you're no Charles Atlas!" Her voice had returned to its previous silkiness and no longer sounded like she was going to choke on her words and her own blood. "Been there, done that, bought the t-shirt, taped over the video, bit the Big One. Trust me, when I bit the Big One, I think my eyes were too big for my belly. It's a pity you can't take a bite, and then if you don't like it, spit it out."

"You mean like Marmite?" I asked.

"Marmite?"

"Yes. I tasted it once. Bloody disgusting. I spat it out and it took about an hour to get rid of the taste."

"Yes, then," she said, a little sadly, "like Marmite. I took a great chomp at a Marmite sandwich and now I'm not living to regret it."

"So," I said, wanting to bring the conversation back to something resembling normality, even though the subject matter was far from normal. For someone who could kill people thousands of miles away and who could teleport his body in the blink of a wink with no strings or mirrors required, what really counted as normal any more, anyway? "What can I do for you?"

Joy frowned playfully. "Can't a sister visit her brother nowadays?"

I nodded. "Of course she can," I said. "But since you're dead and I'm supposed to be, I figured you were here for something else. Are you in my head, conjured up just to keep me company? Or am I actually dead and this is hell?"

"So you think I'd have ended up down there, do you? Thanks a bunch bro'!"

"Well, I don't know. Did you?"

"Do I have horns and a sexy little tail? Not as far as I can tell. So no, I didn't end up 'down there', but thanks for thinking I might."

I shrugged. How was I to know what went on after death? I'd tried to take a peek but the door had been slammed firmly in my face. There might be Heaven, there might be Hell, there might be a great white light or there might be endless repeats of Crossroads with nothing to eat but cheesy Wotsits or prawn cocktail Monster Munch. I didn't want to piss Joy off whether she was real, ghost, dream or cannibalistic zombie eyeing up my liver for lunch, but I hadn't had the best day. Give a guy a break, eh?

Still. She was my sister. I hadn't seen her since before she'd killed herself, naturally, so perhaps I should be nicer. Depending on your religion, by committing suicide you could either be a blessed martyr or damned for all eternity, doomed to walk the earth in new shoes with no plasters. Did your religion dictate your afterlife - if there was one? Just because I was having a wee tête-à-tête with her didn't mean life after death was a reality. Maybe it was a surreality? I was dreaming and she was a conjuration of my mind, a sleight of hand illusion performed by the snoozing synapses of my brain. But it made me think. Did your own personal beliefs create your Heavens, Hells and Asguards? Was reincarnation real for those that believed in it, but if you didn't you had no chance of coming back, whether as a dolphin, a butterfly or a fresh pile of steaming doggy-doo-doo? And what if you believed in nothing? Was death the snuffing of your not so eternal flame?

Who knew? Ask me another.

Either way, I was pleased to be reunited with Joy, even if it was all in my not completely stable head. I'm not saying I was as crazy as Dr. Connors liked to insist I was, but there had to be something a little whoo, a little whee up there, didn't there? I hadn't lost the plot entirely, but I'd possibly skimmed a few pages. Otherwise I'd still be sitting in my cell waiting for the needles to come and pay a visit. Saying that, if all was jolly double-dandy, I wouldn't be at the hospital at all. I'd be in a comfortable job, earning a comfortable wage, maybe even with a comfortable girlfriend. I'd have a dog called Frank and be trying to stop next door's cat from leaving little presents between my lobelias.

Hmmm. I'm not sure which is the better deal now.

Hey ho, away we go.

"I don't think that," I said. "Of course I don't. I don't even know if there is a 'down there' for you to end up in." And besides, this was Joy. She'd made so many people happy it had sent her over the edge and she'd felt forced to take her own life. It was better than taking other lives like I had a penchant for doing. How could someone like that end up 'down there'?

Not that I'm implying Australia is all that bad.

"Well, alrighty then," said Joy in her best Ace Ventura voice. It was, basically, crap. My sister was always one to get up and sing at a Karaoke or dance on a table or see if she could down a pint of lager in three seconds without it coming out of her nose. She knew magic tricks which, though recent events and discoveries dulled their shine, Siegfried & Roy might not exactly be impressed by, but they'd certainly appreciate the effort. When it came to voices and such, though, Joy was pants. Her Welsh accent sounded Pakistani and her Sean Connery was akin to Father Ted after he'd had a few. As for Ace Ventura, I didn't think Jim Carrey had anything to worry about. She sounded like Joy doing an impression of Joy, but badly.

I smiled anyway, deciding to leave the deep and meaningful behind. Thoughts of life and death and cheesy Wotsits could wait for another day. Enjoy the dream because when I awoke I'd be back in the nightmare.

I belched loudly. It was one to be proud of and Joy slapped my arm in mock disgust. She could lay a good one out when she wanted to, so she was probably only jealous.

"You horrible, stinking, filthy pig!" she said as she smacked me again. "You really disgust me, you know that?"

And everything was ok. I was sitting in the woods having a laugh with my sister. The fact that she was dead was irrelevant. The fact that, but a short time before, I'd caused a young lad to make his car more intimate with a tree than he'd have probably wanted to was also, for now, irrelevant. Old times and daisy-chains were the tea on the table tonight, with a healthy helping of nostalgia for dessert.

"You couldn't help that boy, you know."

Well that was a custard pie in the face of memories.

Chapter Five

"Pardon?"

I was shocked at the abrupt change of mood. A second ago we were laughing and now laughter had fled screaming into the night. The forest had darkened and the trees had closed in making me feel suddenly claustrophobic. I almost waited for feral eyes to open like slashes in the darkness. None did, so thankfully my dream hadn't travelled that far on the express train into Nightmare Station.

Joy seemed unaware of the sudden suffocation. She wasn't looking at me, instead picking some invisible piece of cotton or dirt from her trouser leg. Whatever was there was stuck fast and she stayed intent on it as she spoke.

"The boy. He crashed and there's a better than good chance that he wouldn't have if you hadn't been there, but you couldn't help him. He was lost anyway."

My heart was suddenly squeezed by an invisible hand that had reached inside my chest and taken a hold, long, cracked and yellowing nails digging in. I couldn't speak.

"He killed that poor girl. He would have done it again. He would. More than once. It wouldn't have stopped him and it wouldn't have slowed him down. He would have begun to look for it. The rush. The danger. The badness of it. He would have become addicted. He was rotting from the inside out and you did him a favour. You did those little girls he isn't going to mow down a favour. Hey, you did the world a favour."

Joy's voice wavered, a ripple in the velvet. I could only stare at her, the hand around my heart squeezing rhythmically. What was she doing? Justifying murder? That's what it was! Manslaughter at the very least because I couldn't help it. But what if I could? What if there was some sick core inside me, rotting like she said the boy was? What if I meant for him to die?

What if I wanted it to happen? I knew. I knew what he had done. Eight years old. That's all she was. But I didn't feel anger or pity for him. I felt nothing. So what if that nothing was concealing my pleasure, or my desire? If I'd reached out to his car with whatever twisted thought or idea crawled beneath the nothing and made it swerve, and made it crash...?

What then?

Maybe this was hell and I had ended up in that furnace and I had been char-broiled and I was dead. And Joy. Maybe she believed in Heaven and Hell. And maybe, because of that, we were part of each other's damnation. She was doomed to try and make me feel better - something that, on a grander scale had bled her to a husk - and I was doomed to listen. Her Purgatory was a much more focused and personal version of the life that had led her, or pushed her, here. Mine was to relive my own, the tales retold in my sister's vain attempts to justify and reconcile and appease.

And I hadn't even brought a picnic.

I mentally gripped the metaphorical hand around my heart, wresting its grip and flinging it away. What if, what if, what if. What if Willy Wonka had made flour instead of every kind of chocolate? Charlie Bucket would never have been the hero he was and Violet Sludgemonkey, or whatever her name was, would probably be a redcoat at Butlins by now. What if Man really had landed on the moon, or men in black really did protect us from illegal Aliens and the scum of the universe? What if, in space, someone *can* hear you scream? What if curry night at the Trawl pub, Toothill, was on a Wednesday instead of a Thursday? Would the world come crashing down around our ears like a Paris Hilton CD?

No. I doubted it. So why worry about it. Or, at least, why dwell on it. Blank it out. Smother it in Nothing. No pain, no brain. Or something like that.

Of course that wasn't how it worked. It didn't work much at all, really, but...

Hey ho, daddyo, away we go.

It didn't matter if Joy was right or not. If I'd saved half a dozen or more children from being hit-and-run victims at the cost of one stupid, stupid boy's life, it didn't matter. It *did* matter, but it didn't. Not really. It was what it was. Life and death. Heaven and Hell. Black and white.

Heads and tails.

Flip and catch.

"So?" I said.

Joy frowned, puzzled. I could see why. My reaction, or lack of one, would puzzle me too, if I wasn't me. In fact, it did to a certain extent. Why wasn't I breaking apart, little bits of me drifting off into the Nothing that waited in the shadows to engulf me? Why was I just hey-diddly-dee-a-normal-life-for-me?

"So?" she asked. "What does '*so*' mean? Is that all you can say? 'So'?"

"Yes," I answered. "So. So what if I am responsible. So what if I'm not. It's done."

I realised, suddenly, what was wrong. I knew why I was numb. The same sweet self-preservation that stopped me knock, knock, knocking on a furnace door. It was too much. All of it, and if I let myself feel that, I'd be dragged down Life's little plug hole into the sewers below.

"I can't take it," I said. "I don't know what to do. I don't know what to say. I just... I just can't do it."

Joy put her arms around me. She smelled of Jasmine. Her cheek was warm and soft against my own. Were my dreams torturing me now? All these memories of my dead sister pummelling me, taunting me. It wasn't FAIR! I felt like a yo-yo, spinning between laughter and sorrow, smiles and frowns, mental clarity and mind-numbing despair, my string wrapped around the finger of some demonic child who was having simply marvellous fun at my expense.

I pushed Joy away and stood up. This was a lovely dream, what with the ghost, maggots and rotting flesh, but it was only serving to make me feel worse about myself than I already did. Joy's reassurances did more to wind me up than calm me down. I knew she wasn't being patronising, she wasn't like that. Well, my sister wasn't like that when she was alive. This deceased version was an invention of my own psyche, so I supposed it could be as patronising as my mind felt it wanted to be.

I was going round in circles. I should have stayed, happy as a hamster with my very own wheel, in the mental home. Dr.

Connors would look after my bank account and me, and everything would have been hunky-dory, Jackanory. Yes. Of course it would.

I feebly tried to push Joy away again as she moved towards me, arms wide. She batted my attempts away and wrapped me in her Jasmine blanket. I let my breathing settle and slumped against her. She held my weight easily, obviously empowered by my subconscious - she could never have carried me in reality.

Her voice smothered me in velvet calm, easing my anguish. "Sshhhh," she whispered, though I hadn't said anything.

I took a deep breath, my face buried in her shoulder. A second one succeeded in steadying me enough to support myself. She let her arms drop and looked at me, her face full of concern.

I smiled weakly, then took a third deep breath and smiled again, stronger this time.

"Fartypants," I said.

"That's better," she said, the concern fading. A hint of it lingered still, but she looked more her usual perky self. I hoped I appeared the same. I hoped that, if I looked happier then I would be. If I seemed more confident, that confidence might worm its wicked way inside. "Plonk it, rancid pits," she ordered, indicating the base of the tree I'd been sitting at.

"Yes, Miss."

I eased myself back down onto the grass and leant against the trunk. My back protested as the lumps and bumps of the bark found more places to dig into but I ignored it. I wasn't into self-mutilation or any of those whipping rituals religious types indulged in, but I did feel that a taste of pain myself was somewhat deserved.

"So," I said, hoping again to bring the conversation back on track. I left the word hanging, not really knowing where to take it. This was my dream, but I figured Joy could lead the way for a wee bit. She left the word where it was for a long time, head low, face expressionless, except for the eyes a-sparkling. Then she picked it up and had a play.

"So indeed," she said, lifting her eyes to me. The corners of her full lips raised slightly: "What are we going to do with you, brother of mine?"

I didn't answer. I wanted the question to be rhetorical so she'd provide her own response. Perhaps then I might have some idea myself. If not, this would be a short chat and, as good as it was to be reunited with Joy, I may as well wake up. If my mind, in the form of my sister, wasn't going to give me any answers whatsoever, then I'd have to fumble my own way - and that thought scared me way down the road to Shitless and half way into Witless.

"If only I could tell you the things you need to know," she said. "It would be so much easier. You'd be so much happier." She paused and chewed her bottom lip, a habit I'd grown tired of trying to slap out of her. "Maybe you wouldn't be happier actually, but at least you'd *know*."

"Know what?" I asked. Things I needed to know? I wasn't appearing on Who Wants to be a Millionaire. I didn't need to phone a friend or ask the audience. Good job really because the only audience I currently had was maybe the odd owl or squirrel. Anyway, what did I need to know that I didn't already? This dream was going the way of a Twin Peaks episode. It was following some twisted path I couldn't see, swinging back on itself and then taking a completely different route. I felt like Kyle MacLachlan was conspiring with David Lynch to hijack my brain and turn it on its end. All we needed was some cherry pie, a damn fine cup of coffee, and we could all sit down, have a picnic and figure out which outcome would be the weirdest and as such the one we'd use. At least Kyle was investigating a murder whereas I was committing them.

I wondered if, in a court of law, murder in absentia was a punishable crime. If I had an alibi tighter than Jacob Marley's business partner, even though I admitted to having done the crime - and thanks to Mental Homes R Us, done the time - would I still be sent down, joining the chain gang on a one way trip along the Green Mile? Maybe I could get Tom Hanks or Michael Clarke Duncan to sign autographs.

I doubted a defence of "I wasn't there m'lud" would be sufficient to get me off. But death by proxy. What would be the maximum sentence for that? Six months? Life? Would there be a frying tonight, with old Sparky, the electric chair?

Ask me another.

Death by proxy. That's a phrase and a half, ain't it? *Murder* by proxy, perhaps - get some other schmucky-duck to do the deed. But *death* by proxy? How did that work? If it's my time that's up, is DBP (as we affectionately don't call it) giving my extinction ticket to the next customer, like at the deli counter in Asda?

"I'll have half a pound of bullet to the brain and three slices of cardiac arrest please. Oh, hold on, you go first, pal."

"Cheers mate! Make mine a quarter of honey roasted dismemberment please. No, wait. Make it six ounces."

"Certainly sir. We've got a special three-for-two offer on aneurisms this week. Can I tempt you?"

"No thanks, I'm good with the dismemberment."

Death by proxy - giving your place in the queue for Snuffit & Keelover to the next bloke, nice guy that you are.

My sense of dread and guilt, which had been rebounding around the forest like a squash ball shot from a cannon, slammed back into me once more. What if that was exactly the case? What if I was missing my appointment with the Other Side by passing it on to other people?

If I was meant to die the day the number 5 bus drove into the Post Office instead of into me?

If I was meant to die today, the next victim of a teenage idiot more intent on his mobile phone than on the road?

I jumped when I felt Joy's hand on my shoulder.

"Sin?"

"Sorry," I said, shuddering. I suddenly felt cold even though the temperature hadn't dropped noticeably. The closeness of the trees, the canopy of leaves and the blanket of clouds all did their bit to keep the afternoon's warmth from escaping.

And me.

"What is it?" she asked.

I shook my head. What was the point? She'd only tell me I was being stupid. Maybe she was right. Maybe my head was running after David Lynch, hoping to be sucked down the convoluted drain of his imagination.

But still. As ever. What IF?

I *so* needed to get a grip! What if the world really was flat, with only the 150 foot wall of the Southern Ice between us and an eternal drop into Oblivion? What if the Bermuda Triangle was an extra-terrestrial King's Cross, with trains (or ships and planes) leaving every fifteen minutes or so, stopping at Peterborough, Newark, Doncaster and Alpha Centauri?

What if anyone actually gave a toss?

I took another one of those deep breaths people recommend to steady your nerves. Was there some magic medicine in air? I suppose there was. Oxygen. Daft question really.

"Nothing," I said, managing a half hearted smile. The other half had a go, but couldn't quite manage it. Oh well, a smile is always half full rather than half empty.

I needed to get this dream going, if, indeed, it was going anywhere. For all I knew it could be tomorrow or next week by now. It had been so long since I'd had a sleep that wasn't drug induced, I figured my body could be making up for lost time. Perhaps Joy was here to keep me occupied while my body recuperated. Dreams being what they were though, I could have just dozed off for five minutes. Either way, if there was a point, I wished Joy would get us to it.

"Are you sure?" she asked. How could anything be wrong with that voice caressing me? How could any problem be a problem while those eyes sparkled?

"I'm sure," I said. "I'm fine." I sat a little straighter, my slump becoming more of a slouch. It wasn't much, but it was an improvement. "You were saying?"

"Was I?"

"Yes. You said you wished you could tell me something. Something I should know."

"Oh, that." She shook her head. "Don't worry about it."

What? She couldn't do that!

"You can't do that! You can't lay something like that down, and then take it away again."

Joy looked nervous, as if she'd let a secret out and had only just realised.

"No, really. Forget it. It's nothing."

I wasn't about to let it go. Joy could be in this dream to carry me through to next year for all I cared. Or she could be here for a reason, the voice of my subconscious working its way up to granting me an epiphany of some kind. Or, of course, she could be a zombie deciding whether to start on my nose or a nice bit of rump.

"Joy," I said, gripping her hand. It was warm. I would have thought zombies would be cold to the touch, so that was comforting. Maybe she wasn't wondering if she should have mustard or plain old ketchup. "Just tell me."

She snatched her hand away as if she thought I was trying to steal it. *"I can't!"*

"I don't understand," I said. "You can't tell me? What? What's so big a secret you'll implode if you share it? It can't be that bad, can it?"

"It's not that. Nothing like that. I just can't tell you."

"Why?" I insisted. There had been times in our lives when, although we normally hid nothing from each other, we'd had to keep certain things to ourselves. I don't believe anyone is totally open about every tiny little thing with anyone else - siblings, partners, no one. Whether it's down to guilt, embarrassment or sheer spite, some things are simply meant to kept to one's self, hidden away, held close to your chest lest they get snatched away and held up to scorn, ridicule or horror. Usually it's something small and petty and not worth worrying about, but not always.

Joy and I didn't share our biggest secret with each other. The fact that we could manipulate others' lives, destroying them in my case and making them so much better in hers, was something we'd not told anyone until it was too late. Joy let me know by posthumous letter. I'd told Dr. Connors in the comfort of an asylum; padded cells, padded seats, padded wallets.

This wasn't the time for my sister to be reticent. And anyway, it was *my* dream. If I wanted her to talk, shouldn't she concede? Was I, in effect, arguing with myself? Did I have not-so-hidden schizophrenic tendencies? At least I wouldn't be lonely.

Joy looked at me, her eyes doleful. She seemed to be struggling with something and I wished she would just let it go and tell me.

"You don't understand," she said sadly. "I want to tell you, but at the same time, I don't." She was right. I didn't understand. "Part of me wants to, but when I open my mouth to, the urge goes. It's like the words are stolen away."

"Who by?"

"I can't say."

"Come on," I said. "Is it the Big Man Upstairs? Is that it?"

"I can't say, Sin. I really can't."

"So, God, in all His infinite wisdom, chucked you back down here, to invade my dream and to tell me a whole lot of nothing. That was nice of Him."

"I'm not saying that, I'm..."

"You're not saying a thing," I interrupted. "You 'can't say' anything!"

"Stop it," she said fiercely.

I stopped. Joy was many things, but very rarely was she fierce. Pissed, peeved and, currently, paranormal, but not fierce. I let her continue, running my fingers across my mouth as if I was closing a trouser zip.

She smirked a sarcastic quiver of the mouth. "I'm not saying there's a Big Man Upstairs. I'm not saying there isn't. And don't ask me about lights, tunnels or bloody escalators! I just can't say! I won't tell you there's a Heaven or a Hell or a great bloody evangelical shopping centre with shops selling halos and Hail Mary's. You're not going to find out if the Jews were right, the Christians, the

Muslims or the Jehovah's bloody Witnesses! I cannot say! Nothing and nobody has a hand clamped over my mouth, the words just don't want to come out, OK?"

"OK," I whispered.

"There's things I want to tell you, to help you, but I can't. I'm sorry."

"Help me with what?" I dared to ask. Silly me.

"I CAN'T SAY!" she shouted. I winced. Her velvet voice had developed some sharp edges. I wanted to file them away as soon as possible in case they cut me.

"You can't say," I repeated quietly. "Sorry."

"No," she said, reaching out to hold my hand. "I'm sorry. More than I can say."

"Or can't say."

Her smile was real this time.

"Yeah, or can't. Just... Just be careful." She squeezed my hand. "Be careful."

I wanted to ask why, but there didn't seem to be much point. She wouldn't have been able to tell me, it seemed. But I trusted her, so I supposed I'd be careful.

"I will," I said.

Joy looked out towards the edge of the forest. It was dark beyond the trees. The rain could be heard but not seen, like children supposedly should be. Or was that the other way around? Occasionally a flash of lightning was chased quickly by a throaty rumble of thunder. I followed her line of sight and was startled to see, as the lightning burst across the landscape, the after image of a figure on the edge of the tree line, silhouetted in my eyes. Another flash showed there was no one there, but I was suddenly uneasy.

Why was hard to say. I'd voluntarily walked in to the mental home. I'd given myself to the doctor and his drugs. Why couldn't I walk freely from it when I decided I'd outstayed my welcome? You'd better ask the doctor about that. Once he'd had his hands on me, he didn't seem to want to let go. At first, he'd talked me around, his words trying to be as smooth as my sister's but tainted with a saccharin aftertaste. I didn't see him in his true colours, the monster beneath the sheep's overcoat until later. At first he could manipulate me under the guise of guidance. Once I'd realised the dark inner soul he festered, I found it was too late. My requests or demands to be discharged were met with denials and heightened dosages.

Once, I'd tried to just walk out. I'd walked in, so why not? Jeremy had stopped me then. He was the most human and humane of the orderlies at the institute, the majority of whom were pissed off Rottweilers who would be as happy restraining a patient as they would be tearing a young animal limb from limb. And they put as much fervour into their duties as said canine would.

Jeremy was different. He was a nice guy, and as such was completely out of place in the home. He cared about the residents and treated most as if they were members of his own family. If I hadn't been a resident myself, I could have come close to calling him a friend. Unfortunately, my address was 18 Looney Bin Hill, so the invisible but tangible line between psycho and social created a barrier to any such relationship being nurtured. Jeremy was pleasant and caring, but he was there to help, not to be your best pal.

So around tea time one day - a Tuesday I think - just before the soaps were piped in to keep the crazy hoards appeased, I had decided that I'd had enough. I didn't want to be there anymore. I knew what could happen if I left - that people could die - but I couldn't stand being trapped in that antiseptic, bleached environment any longer. I hadn't figured out the whole matter transference thing back then, so I had to rely on my two little legs. They managed, bless 'em, to get me to reception before Big Jeremy's big hand was on my shoulder.

"Come on, Sin," he said, his voice softer than his size implied. "You're going to miss Eastenders."

I thought about running. I thought about fighting. I thought about a swift kick in his prize begonias. And I thought better of it. His hand was firm and insistent. It told me that yes, Sin, you could run, fight or kick, but I ain't about to let go, so it's probably not a good idea. I agreed.

"Cheers Jezzer," I said. "Can't miss that."

Why was I uneasy about being discovered? Even though I'd caused the boy to crash, there'd be no evidence to point at me. To my knowledge there was no forensic test for a psychic push. A mental fingerprint wouldn't be detected with a bit of talcum powder and a brush.

Psychic push... Psychic... Was I? It hadn't really occurred to me before. A fortune teller? Medium? What?

No. I didn't have time to think about that. Whether I was cousin to Uri Gellar or ready to set up a tent at a local fair, professing to be able to read palms, tea leaves and the bumps on your head didn't matter. Not right now. I'd deal with thoughts of psychobabble later.

The fact remained that, contrary to the wishes of my beloved shrink, I'd escaped the institute. I had to assume Dr. Connors wouldn't be happy about it. That I was there voluntarily obviously meant nothing to his lordship. I'd given myself over to being his property, so I was certain he'd try to reclaim it. I could see pictures of myself plastered all over the morning papers and the six o'clock news:

"Mental patient escapes! Assumed to be dangerous! Do not approach!"

Of course, no one needed to approach me to put themselves in danger, but it wasn't something I could help, or control. It just was.

Dr. Connors would be looking serious but calm as he was interviewed and photographed. He'd be saying that I would be a danger to others and myself. Call the police. Call him. Call anyone, but get me back in the home. It was for my own good. I had problems and couldn't be trusted.

Then he'd smile, the caring, professional hero that he was. The mask would never slip. The wolf behind would never be seen.

I wonder if he bayed at the moon.

Joy letting go of my hand brought me back from my thoughts. I blinked.

Standing again, she looked at me, her face serious. She gestured towards the edge of the woods.

"You see that storm out there?"

"Yes," I said, nodding slowly.

"Take it as a warning, Sin."

"A warning?"

"Yes, a warning. There's another one coming, only this one won't have rain and lightning. You could still drown though. And you could still get burned."

I opened my mouth to question her, but she held her up hand.

"Don't," she said. "I can't. I'm trying to tell you things without telling you anything. Just listen."

I listened.

"The storm. Wrap up warm. Watch yourself."

"I will," I said. I assumed my sister wasn't telling me wasn't telling me that El Nino was planning on dropping by for a visit. Or maybe she was, after a fashion.

"Good," she said. She rested her hand on my brow briefly, then let it drop to her side. "Bye."

I nodded and she turned and began walking away, heading out to the rain.

"Thanks for the weather report," I called after her.

"No worries," she called back without turning around. "Maybe I could get a job on morning television!"

"Nah," I shouted. "You haven't got a ghost of a chance!"

She did turn then, almost at the edge of the forest. Her faint laughter drifted across to me, fading in and out with the sound of the downpour as if some mad DJ were playing with his panel, sliding the controls up and down to mix the next chart smash. She stood there and I watched, waiting for something to happen. Would she walk off, or disappear, or fade away with her laughter? Nothing happened. Joy simply stood looking back at me.

"Well, blink then!" she shouted.

Blink? Even as I told myself I wouldn't, my eyes flicked shut for a fraction of a second. She was gone. There wasn't even the pleasure of an afterimage.

I watched the spot where she'd been, this time not blinking for a long while. Lightning speared the sky, tearing the darkness. The rain, invisible against the black backdrop, beat down incessantly like a thousand tiny Duracell bunnies banging their drums, racing to find out whose battery would last the longest. My sister wasn't there, if she ever had been.

I wanted to wake up. The dream was draining and I was already tired, but wakefulness would have had to have been preferable to being visited by the dead. Why couldn't I had just slept normally, maybe dreaming of being in my pyjamas at school or knocking off my next door neighbour's sister? What was wrong with just a smidgeon of normality for once? I wondered if a load of miniature rabbits were running around in the woken world with AA's stuck up their behind. Was it dark? Was I still leaning against a tree with knots the size of Ayers Rock determined to dig their way into my spine? I wondered if, in a dream, I should be wondering about the world outside anyway. Wasn't a dream, whilst you were immersed, your reality? I was sure you weren't supposed to know you were dreaming. No outside world was supposed to exist because your subconscious was your universe. Wasn't that right?

So if I knew I was dreaming, and I knew there was an existence beyond this fake reality, didn't that suggest that I wasn't actually dreaming? Was it like a crazy man knowing he was crazy, hence making him sane? Oh if only it was so easy - I could put Dr. Connors out of business.

But now I was confused. Was I awake or asleep? Was it live or was it Memorex?

I pinched my arm, hoping it would prove to be the latter. If I wasn't knocking out the zeds, that would mean I really had been visited by the spirit of my dead sister. It didn't work, but I realised that nothing was proven. If I could pinch myself whilst awake, there was nothing to stop myself doing so whilst snoozing. All I could do was wait. Whether I was in the land of the living, or in the Land of Nod, I'd either wake up or not. I stared into the wet night, listening to the drumming. At first chaotic, the sound seemed to slowly settle into a haphazard kind of rhythm. Almost hypnotic.

Almost...

Chapter Six

I woke with a start. Was it possible to do that with a stop? Or with a finish? Why is it always a start? Not too long before I'd have been happy to wake up with an END. As my body jerked awake, the knotted tree trunk gave me a good kick in my back to remind me where I was. I could have told it that I hadn't forgotten, but trees are notoriously bad conversationalists, especially in the mornings. Well, without a hot Cappo and some toast, who isn't?

But... was it morning? Dewy webs dotted the ground like a warped game of Twister where all the spots were white or silver. Now that would be confusing – you wouldn't know where to put your foot or hand. I stretched, wincing as my back breathed a sigh of relief at finally being released from the bark's surface. I wondered at who spun the wheel and who did the twisting. Spiders could cheat and squirrels only had short legs. It wouldn't really be a fair game. I'm glad I'd only played with my sister and friends.

The light had a hazy feel to it, as if it was on a dimmer that hadn't quite been turned all the way up. I could see a vague fog drifting across the fields beyond the forest, aimless and lost. I knew how it felt. The mist failed to reach into the confines of the trees, perhaps lying in wait for me when I emerged. No matter, I thought. I could handle a bit of fog. It was hardly a case of Mr. T versus Rocky Balboa, was it? Of course John Carpenter or James Herbert might disagree, but I'd have to take that chance. If the mist thought it was hard enough to try it on with me, let it have a go.

Big words from an escaped lunatic, don't you think?

It certainly felt like morning time. How early I couldn't tell, but the air had a definite crispness to it, like it was just out of the wrapping and hadn't been used yet. I felt guilty taking a breath, as if by exhaling I could possibly taint the atmosphere - but hey, I felt guilty taking the last jaffa cake from the box. It didn't stop me. The freshness of the air was sharp in my throat and nostrils, cleaning them out as it passed on through. I felt like someone had stuck a Dyson down my throat and sucked out all the grimy remnants of modern day's pollution. It was as if every breath I'd ever taken had traces of muck and sludge mingled in it, and this clear morning air had scoured me out better than a hydrochloric enema. I could have been breathing for the very first time, instead of the twenty millionth or so.

How often do you breathe in a life time? I think I read somewhere that it was around twenty thousand times a day. It sounds like a lot, but it's only about fourteen times a minute, give or take the odd yawn or hiccup to spoil the flow. So that makes it about... erm... put the 1 on the doorstep... about seven hundred million or so in a century? Of course, if you're still breathing at a century then you're doing something right - breathing for one.

Anyway, today's felt like Numero Uno for me. My lungs had been plucked from my torso, chucked in a washer on 40° and hung on the line to dry, thereafter being shoved back in my body to start all over again. Refreshed, revived, replenished and renewed. I guess I'd been RE'ed in every which way but loose, Clyde. It was great. I was Samson before he'd nipped to the hairdressers for a quick wash, cut and blow dry. Whether it was Androcles or Saint Jerome who pulled the thorn from the lion's paw, I could do it with my teeth whilst blindfolded and with both hands tied behind my back. Unusually invigorated by the morning, I pushed myself to my feet, ignoring my protesting joints, and decided I was going to get my shiny metal behind into gear. If the men in white coats came a-hunting-we-will-go, then they'd have to catch me. If Dr. Connors was on the prowl, he'd have to find me. And if my dead sister wanted to stop by for a chat again, a-haunting-we-will-go, then she'd just have to call first so I could check my diary. Either that or she'd have to bring some Viennese Whirls. I hadn't had any for ages, and I just fancied one.

Of my sister, there was no sign. Maggots weren't wriggling towards the morning sun like turtles to the sea and the grass wasn't flattened where she'd stepped. No cockroaches crunched underfoot and I failed to see any globby bits of flesh, with hair still sprouting, hiding between the roots of the trees. My dream had been a dream and no more. Of course it had. Why did I feel the need to convince myself? Yes, it had *seemed* real, apart from her eye popping out and the like, but she was dead. It hadn't *been* real. Just a dream veering precariously close to the edge of nightmare without quite careening over.

Not that I'm saying my sister was a nightmare. She could sometimes be, though, a bit wee, a bit woo, a bit wah, if you know what I mean. Often even a bit WOAH! I didn't know whether to blame that on hormones or just general femininity. Who understood a woman? Not even women was my guess. And isn't any sibling a nightmare at times? Isn't it always a case of 'I can call you but if anyone else does I'll rip their head off?' Such it was with Joy and me. She did my head in, big style, sometimes, but she was still my sister. So why dream of her with a face melting faster than hot wax?

Go on, ask me another. Dare ya.

My shiny metal behind was loitering, I realised. It was looking for a reason to stay put and to not enter the big, wide, scary world. It didn't have to look too far, of course. Being the right hand scythe of the Big D was reason enough to cower, head between the knees, mooning the world, but I was having none of it. What could I do? Sit here, waiting to see if Joy would call again, or how long it would take me to starve or freeze to death? Sure, that sounded like a plan. Do nothing and nothing could happen. I liked it. But it didn't work like that. People died if I was simply walking through town. Hell, people died if I was sat on the toilet! Sitting tight and waiting for the end to see how bitter it would be wouldn't stop people joining the queue for the one last dance with the Reaper. No. I couldn't do anything so I had to do something.

A light breeze stroked my face and I smelled Jasmine.

Joy.

No again. It was probably the endless sea of rapeseed or maybe a farmer had fed his cows some new additive so their doo-doo wouldn't smell quite so much like doo-don't. My mind was playing tricks and fooling me into thinking I was smelling my sister when I couldn't have been. Dreams didn't leave odours. Go on mind - play your tricks. Have a laugh on me, I've got plenty to spare. God knows I didn't need them myself.

Get going!

I walked to the edge of the trees. For some reason I was nervous about stepping out. The tree line felt as if it was the edge of a cliff, the outside world an abyss daring me to leap. Naturally, that was nonsense. OK, so maybe there were snipers hidden in the bushes along the roadside, waiting for me to make the wrong move so they could take me out with a single shot? I checked my body to make sure there were no red dots giving me the targeting equivalent of measles - a fatal dose. There were none. Obviously. I was being silly. If 'they' were looking for me - the men in white coats, the police, the nameless, faceless, *They* - I didn't see how they could possibly have found me yet. If I didn't know where I was, how could anyone else? Short of hiring one of the Charmed Ones to swing a pendulum over a map, what could they do?

A tracker. Perhaps not all those injections were the happy drugs being pumped into me. Maybe one little prick (ooer missus) really was a microscopic, subcutaneous computer chip and right now satellites were spinning high overhead shouting down to the Big Bad Wolf that *"HEY! HE'S OVER HERE!"*

And the Big Bad Wolf, or Wolfey as he likes to be called, will huff, and he'll puff, and he'll bloooooow me away.

Well. Here's one small step for Man and a dirty great jump for little ol' me.

I stepped forward. I didn't feel a bullet tear through my chest and bury itself all nice and snugly in my heart. Half a dozen SWAT teams didn't fall from the sky as helicopters zoomed over. And the men in the nice white coats didn't rush me and bundle me into the back of an unmarked van ready to return me to my very own padded cell. I was still alive, untouched and currently unnoticed. I had to admit to a little disappointment. Not at the absence of a bullet through my brain - the suicidal tendencies had realised I was a bad bet, so they'd left me in favour of some other troubled soul. The disappointment stemmed from the fact that I hadn't thought beyond that one step. Because no one had pounced on me like a cat on a rat, it meant they also hadn't taken my choices. I still had them laid out before me like a car boot sale, some going for 50 pence and some for the grand price of a couple of quid. And I was the boy in the sweet shop unable to decide between the gob-stopper and the jelly worms.

Staying where I was would cost about £1.50. It had its merits but was overpriced to be honest. Besides, I'd taken that step now. I was out in the world and as comforting as the leafy canopy behind me might be, it was really a slow grave to China. I'd come from the right, so all that lay for me in that direction was a burnt out car and the corpses of a boy and a gull. My strait jacket could be in the belly of a whale for all I knew. So right was wrong. Left was best. Straight on would take me across fields and ditches and, in the distance, a small lake. It meant effort and no visible destination. Turning left and continuing along the road also had no visible, and possibly viable, end but it was more likely that a house or village would be that way. Roads generally went somewhere. They could take their time arriving, meandering about, taking in the sights along the way, but they usually got there, somewhere, by the time they were finished.

So the road it was. Its surface was smooth as if it had been newly lain only last week. The central lines, a white seam stitched into the black, were as sharp and as crisp as the day they'd been painted. Either the road was a brand spanker, which would wind up all those guys with their fancy sat-navs, or it was hardly used - a back passage to the arse end of nowhere. Whichever it was, it still had to have a purpose. A to B or Y to Z. It couldn't be just A to ?, because what would be the point? Would the road be bothered, in that case, by its aimlessness? It could be that the road was sentient. Perhaps it wandered the world, settling where it wanted, and was just having a rest here in the countryside. And I was an itch on its back, an irritation disturbing its slumber.

I walked to the sleeping asphalt serpent, unsteady across the freshly flooded furrows of the field. More than once I stumbled, and my feet were becoming weighed down with the mud they were collecting. I'd easily gained a couple of inches in height by the time I exited the field, a much cheaper option, I thought, than a pair of heels. I could market this to those who were vertically challenged or catwalk models. I could just see Naomi Campbell flashing a pair of sludge-covered plimmies the next time she was showing off Versace's latest collection. My shoes were slurping each time they were pulled from the mud, and my legs began to ache with the effort. I reached the road with relief and stood for a long moment, enjoying the feeling of increased height while the ache seeped from my legs. Top of the world, Ma!

It only took a few steps along the road for me to realise I'd have to clean my shoes. Apart from the telltale footprints I was leaving as a trail for any possible pursuers, every step was awkward and a struggle. I stopped and knelt at the roadside, peeling my plimsoles off gingerly between my thumb and forefinger. The edge of the road merged with the stumpy hedgerow that ran along the side of the fields as if the workmen who'd put it down had thought to nicely tuck it under. It meant that there was no kerb to scrape the muck from my soles so I tried to use them heel to heel, toe to toe, one shoe being the spatula to clean the other. I suppose partial success can still be classed as success, if you're a half-full kind of guy (which I like to think I hopefully am), so I should have been pleased that the mud didn't want to leave its new home having finally escaped the field. As much as I scraped, it simply served to swap the mud from one shoe to the other. Finally I dropped one shoe, the left, to the floor and used my fingers, the middle and index serving as a mini plough driving through the muck and flicking it off back towards the field from whence it came. I was half way through the second shoe when I heard the squeal of dirty brakes and looked up to see the back end of a van pulling towards me, reversing lights lit, as lights have a habit of doing.

Chapter Seven

Do you think lights sleep when they're switched off? Taking the chance to snooze a while before being called, once more, into action, capes flaring in the wind and capital L emblazoned on their chest? Or do they just sit there, bored, twiddling their filaments, hoping someone would wander by and give their switch a little flick? Do they burst into brightness and savour every moment of life until they are condemned to go back into the darkness again by a second casual flick? Maybe, baby, they prefer the darkness. Could it be that the sixty-watt bulb hanging leisurely from your living room ceiling dragged itself into powering up.

"Oh, no. Here we go again! Can't a bulb just be left in piece?"

Who knew? "Not I," said the fly, chomping away on a big meat pie. "Ask me another."

OK. Flies buzz. They don't talk. And they don't chomp either. They vomit and suck. So sue me.

The van was white, or at least it had been in a former life. Hysterical comments such as "Clean Me" and "I wish my wife was this dirty" were finger written into the grey grime that coated its surface. There was a covering of dirt so even it could almost have been sprayed on, a sexy new alternative to the usual metallic blue or red of lesser vehicles. The originality of the graffiti raised a smile on my weary lips. They were the sort of slogans that were very funny and at the same time were decidedly not so. A bit like "Computer users do it with lots of RAM."   I mean, come on people! Nevertheless, I smiled, just before I thought...

..."Shit!"

Panic overtook humour in the outside lane as I saw a white van coming towards me. They'd found me. They'd found me and they were about to run me down! At that moment I knew what a deer or rabbit felt like. Ambling across a road, minding their own business, when suddenly they're blinded by the glaring high-beam headlights of a car or truck bearing fatally down on them. Feet became fused with tarmac as if roots had somehow grown and eyes stared unblinking into the bright, smiling face of Death. Reversing lights - headlights. Same thing. Either way, a few tonnes of metal was heading my way and it meant business.

But I couldn't move. I knelt, frozen, one filthy shoe hanging from my limp filthy fingers. I couldn't breathe, let alone flee. How had they found me? I glanced up at the sky half expecting to see the tracking satellite hovering overhead, waving to me.

"Gotcha!"

Brake lights replaced the white reversing and the van slowed to a stop a few feet away. I dropped my shoe and reached down to retrieve both it and its partner. It was an automatic move as my eyes were fixed firmly on the bringer of my doom. I heard the crick of the hand brake being yanked on, the cogs clicking in derision of my fate. The red lights, feral eyes watching me, winked off. A click. The driver's side door opened slowly, as if whoever might be there was intent on dragging out my terror. Time became the tortoise to my heartbeat's hare, anticipation the razor blade of my nerves' wrists.

A booted foot, the wellington once green, now brown and streaked settled onto the road, the extending leg clothed in worn, equally dirty jeans. I could see the hand that gripped the door handle. Big. The type that could grip my throat and happily squeeze. A beaten red checked shirt sleeve covered the arm.

Then the man himself. Bigger than he could possibly be to fit inside the van's cab. The shirt strained across his huge barrel chest. It was tight enough across the biceps to look sprayed on. A few days growth of brown-on-the-cusp-of-red bushed across his chin. Cold blue eyes, startlingly clear against the muddy exterior of the figure - not muddy in the same way as my shoes, more so in his complexion and general state. As if he'd worked for a hundred years in the open air, shovelling and digging and building. He was muddy. Almost craggy. He smiled, his teeth as startling as his eyes.

"Ey up, mate," he said, his voice rising up from his boots. "You after a lift?"

I opened my mouth, but couldn't think of what to say. A lift? He wasn't going to drag me up and throw me into the back of his paddy wagon? He could have easily, probably with his little finger. Well, maybe with both. A lift?

I blinked and woke up, a baseball bat whacking me into reality.

The van. It wasn't any sort of paddy wagon. The institute, the police, the CIA, NSA, FBI, OAP, VIP, QED, KFC wouldn't have vehicles as dirty as this one. They'd either be a crisper white than untrodden snow or a darker black than midnight's shadow. They'd have a Transit as a minimum, not this. What was it? An Escort van? Astramax? Small, nippy and suitable for shifting a few bags of fertiliser. Or, maybe, the odd body. They'd be high-tech, this was low spec.

And the man. He didn't wear black, have shades and talk into his cuff. He didn't have a long white coat and I was fairly sure he wasn't as dextrous with a hypodermic as he was with his milking hands. I wondered if his surname was Giles. He looked so much like a typical - stereotypical, in fact - farmer he'd probably left his flat cap on the passenger seat.

"Erm," I said. It could, under the circumstances, have been "Blah, blah, bleeh, blah," but I'm sure it was "Erm."

Farmer Giles stood looking at me with eyes cut from topaz. I stared back with my mouth hanging open and my hands still limp. I could have been Bender Benny's buddy Micky for all the life I must have seemed to have in me.

Micky, as was the norm in the home - Home Away From Harm was the humorous twist on the classic phrase that Dr. Connors liked to employ - had a nickname. Mucous Micky. Unless the cold floor was the only option, you just didn't sit anywhere Mucous Micky had previously been. The guy could snot for England. A hook had been fastened to his colostomy trolley specifically for a roll of tissue to help keep the streaming snotties at bay. He couldn't help it. I think that every wayward flu bug that wandered through our illustrious halls fancied a bite of Micky's bum. The fact that he was permanently drugged up to Heaven on High didn't help. It meant he forgot how to sniff. He forgot how to tear off a square or two of Kleenex and wipe. He forgot how to use the innate talents of a three year old and use his sleeve. So you didn't sit in the same seat as Mucous Micky - not unless you actually wanted a sticky yellow or green patch on your derriere.

Mucous Micky was Bender Benny's buddy. He was about the only one who couldn't easily get away from the Bender's ramblings. A captive audience, I think it's called. Micky may not even have known the Bender was sitting next to him most of every day, but it didn't stop Benny from claiming Mucous as his own.

Nicknames were our - the residents' - way (or one of them) of bringing a hint of normality into the home of Abnormal. We were almost human if we could call each other something other than Patient XYZ. There was One Eye Joe, an old Scouser who's penis had a life of its own and steadfastly refused to stay 'indoors'. Jazzy Jazz Jaroo, the loony formerly known as Jarrod, had an incontinence problem surpassed only by the ferocity of his night terrors. Others in the Pseudonym Posse, as no one called us because it's only alliteration if it's written down, included Big 'Un, a quiet man called Ian who was not much more than five feet and a fag paper tall. Penny Drop was Penelope, a woman of around fifty who, once upon another life, lived in a house with five bedrooms, three cars and a Chihuahua. She'd lost her son in a car accident whilst driving over the limit and had never recovered - mentally at least.

No, that one wasn't down to me.

Eddie the Eagle wasn't called Edward, but he did have a nose so long and sharp he could have skiied along it. I didn't know the reasons for his particular internment, as he apparently hadn't spoken a word in the seven years he'd been at the institute. There were others - Windows with her obsession for all things glass; Muse and his epiphanies - such as when you turned the handle of a tap, water actually came out; Billabong who told everyone he was a kangaroo, even when he was quacking like a duck; and Car Crash Kenny, a sad man who could only talk in short mumbled sentences thanks to the fact that his head still had the dent from the accident that gave him his nickname. They all had their own story. They each had a tale to tell and some even made sense occasionally.

Like Polly, the dolly lolly. She was beautiful. Slim with hair the colour of sunshine and a smile even brighter. That was when she wasn't crying through the night, mourning a daughter she'd never had or punching the face of any man stupid enough to come within a few feet of her. When she was... normal... she was wonderful. Sweet. Silly. Sharp and shining. Unfortunately, the normal fought a losing battle with the madness and her lucid episodes were fewer and further between as each week passed. As with my name, I blamed the parents. Her father at least. She still bore the scars on her stomach from when he couldn't or wouldn't accept she could be pregnant.

Then there was me. The Vicar. Reverend Sin. Stitching good and evil, holy and un into one neat little moniker was a stroke of warped genius and I can't remember who wove the weave. It didn't matter whether I liked the name or not. Once given it stuck like Mucous Micky's mucous.

As "Erm" didn't particularly convey my preference either way when it came to the proffered lift, Farmer Giles, or whatever his name might be, waited patiently for a few moments for me to answer properly. I couldn't really improve on my initial reaction - I was so sure that I'd been found the discovery that I hadn't been discovered was taking its time sinking in. While it did so the rest of me was waiting along with the big man before me. I blinked again. In so many films and stories, blinking is magical. It breaks a spell or gives ghosties, imaginary or otherwise, the chance to appear, disappear or sink an axe into your forehead. In my case it snapped me out of whatever zone I'd been visiting and brought me back to life, back to reality, back to the here and now with a high and mighty splat.

"Erm," I repeated. I know - not very original. "Sure. Thanks."

Well, it was an improvement.

Mr. Giles smiled. His teeth showed, even and white, and I had the sudden impression of a bear. I wouldn't have been surprised if his next comment had been a growl. I don't know if bears have white teeth, not having been close enough to one to find out, but I've never seen Sir David Attenborough squeezing a bleb of Colgate onto a big toothbrush for one of his ursine friends. As such, they may or may not have a lovely set of pearly whites. The farmer type bloke smiled, I saw his teeth, and I thought BEAR.

He nodded his head, a shock of mussy hair falling over one eye.

"Come on then. I want to get back in time for breakfast."

The magic word. It didn't matter whether breakfast was a full English, with bacon, sausage and fried bread hiding out beneath a runny-yolked egg or a dry round of toast with not even a hint of butter. I could happily have scoffed dog biscuits at that moment. Just as blinking had broken a spell, the word 'breakfast' had opened the floodgates of my hunger. My stomach grumbled in protest at being denied sustenance and I had to agree with it. Just a nibble would have been wonderful. My meagre last meal had ended up being splattered over the ragged remains of a gull's wing so my body hadn't had the chance to digest it fully. As such my belly felt like someone had taken a big shovel and dug all the way to China. I stood, forgetting I had my shoes in my hands rather than on my feet. I was sure I heard my back pop, still recovering from a night snuggled up to the craggy bark of a tree.

Gilesey-boy saw my mud sprayed sandshoes and shook his head.

"Don't worry about those." He pointed. I saw dirt hiding beneath the ends of his fingernails. I don't know why it bothered me - the man was a farmer so muck was part of his daily life. It did though. Maybe it was because I'd spent so long in the confines of Sterility Central. I shook off the feeling of... not unease, just... not easy. "The truck needs a good clean anyway. I'll get round to it one of these days."

I thanked him and slipped the shoes back on my feet. I'd scraped enough mud off them to no longer feel a foot or two taller and went over the passenger side of the van, holding my breath as I pulled the door open. I expected, given the state of the vehicle's exterior, that the inside would smell. Maybe not stink, but have the fusty aroma of dry dirt and stale manure. The seats would be stained and torn, the stuffing poking up like a meerkat sentry watching out for hyenas. Empty food wrappers would give me a rustling foot bath while we drove and an ancient Magic tree would be spinning from the rear view mirror, probably still hanging from the day the van was driven out of the showroom when Smiler Giler had promised himself he'd clean it every week. I paused as I moved to get in, shocked that the interior was so clean. The seat covers looked almost spotless. The dashboard gleamed as if it had only been polished that morning. There were muddy marks on the mat in the footwell of the driver's side, but that was all. The mat on my side could have been bought new not five minutes before.

"Jump in. Don't worry about a bit of dirt."

I followed the big man's instruction. I wasn't too sure that, if our positions had been reversed, I'd have appreciated a stranger dragging his filthy arse in my nice clean cab but I wasn't going to argue. He hadn't mentioned feeding me, but his mention of breakfast had temporarily overridden my fears about him being an Agent of Doom for Dr. Connors. I smiled and, whilst I didn't exactly jump in, I was quick enough in gaining my seat and strapping myself in.

He nodded and turned the ignition key, spurring the van into life. A moment later, after he'd checked his mirrors, we were away, the radio informing us that the station was playing the best of the eighties, nineties and the noughties, which was probably spelled naughties. A song I didn't recognise sung by a group I didn't know filled the cab with music and I settled back into the seat, staring out of the window and feeling relaxed.

After a while my new farmer friend turned the music down and smiled at me.

"You okay Doc?" he asked.

Doc?

"You must've been in a rush to not change out of your scrubs," he said, gesturing at my clothes.

Damn.

Gotcha, I thought. I tried to think quickly, to come up with a spontaneous response. Unfortunately, the faster I tried to think, the less spontaneous any response became. I suddenly felt like a crash test dummy flying full pelt towards a brick wall. Hmmm, hmmm, hmmm, *kaPOW!* My mind was whirling and I tried to grab it with both hands to steady its dervish. Doc, Doc, Dockety-Doc. Go with it, like a leaf on a river flowing to the sea. Let's just hope I didn't follow my strait jacket down to a dinner with Davy Jones.

"Sorry," I said, managing a somewhat lopsided grin. "Long shift."

"No worries. I don't know how you guys manage it sometimes. My job's long hours, sure enough, but at least it's only a day at a time, not two or three like your lot."

"Yeah," I said. "I think I started my shift around March-time."

Mr. Giles laughed, a deep boom that threatened to blow the windscreen out.

"I don't doubt it," he said as his laughter turned into a fit of coughing. I waited for his cough to settle, wanting to let him lead the conversation rather than me volunteer a lie. "Got to give up the fags!" he grinned. "But I don't have to tell you that, Doc!"

Slipping into the persona of Doctor Sin was easier than I'd expected. Smoother than a leather glove and twice as snug. For some reason, I could see my whole life as the good doctor and was ready to fill in any blanks I might have to. Or at least I hoped so.

"Hey," I said. "You don't have to tell me. I'm trying to cut down myself."

I'd never smoked a cigarette in my life apart from trying one in the school playground when I was around 12. He didn't need to know that though. I figured that even an imaginary bond like nicotine addiction was better than none at all. It would help ease things along and make this stranger less prone to being suspicious of a supposed doctor wandering around in his scrubs in the middle of nowhere.

"You and me both," he said.

I saw his eyes flick to his rear view mirror and the paranoid little imp sitting by my left ear whispered to me that he might be checking for company. My heart started to flutter as I glanced in the wing mirror to check for myself. The road was deserted. Stop it, I told myself. Checking your mirrors is a normal part of driving. He probably didn't even realise he'd looked. Chill. And, whispered the imp, they'll probably be waiting for you wherever he's taking you anyway.

Well, that could quite easily be true. The farmer's disguise had taking me in immediately, but he was big enough to swat me like a fly if I tried to buzz off. Not that the idea of jumping from a moving vehicle appealed to me.

No. Stop it. If he was, he was. If not, then fine and diddly-dandy. I'd just have to play the game and wait until the fat lady sang. Hopefully she'd do a better job than the noise that was spewing forth from the radio.

Could music change so much in so little time? It wasn't like we'd taken a leap from the Sixties to the Eighties. It hadn't been decades, yet the racket that was happily dancing a jig on my ear drums was a far cry from the stuff I used to listen to before my days of piped Musak. Thinking about it, though, I had to admit that the stuff I enjoyed was more from the Eighties than the Naughties. Rock anthem more than pop-pap. The odd song would catch my attention and set my fingers tapping but in the main, it probably was a good deal more than a mere couple of years since I'd properly taken an interest in who was reigning supreme at the top of the pops.

"Not enjoying the music?" he asked.

I didn't realise I'd been that obvious. "Not my sort of thing, really," I admitted. "But if you like it..."

"I can't stand this racket myself. I just like a bit of noise when I'm driving. It helps numb the brain!" He laughed again, this time managing to avoid the coughing fit.

If he needed something to help numb his brain, I could point him in the direction of a man who'd be more than pleased to help.

"I know what you mean. I just prefer something a little less... noisy I suppose."

"No problem," he said pressing the button on the car stereo to find something easier on the ear. He settled on some Bon Jovi, one with a good ol' geetaaar solo and big chorus. At least it had a tune. "That better?"

"Spot on," I said. I found myself tapping my fingers on my leg as both the music and my driver's attitude helped me relax.

There was a long period of silence during which neither of us spoke. I didn't mind as it let me breathe and think. I had no idea where I was or where we were going. That wasn't particularly a good thing. I could easily be being driven into a den of lions and, however innocuous my ride, I didn't fancy being prey. Of course they'd be nice : "Come in. Here's a made-to-measure jacket for you. Honestly, you'll look fabulous. Trust us." It would only be a small prick, missus, and all the pain would go away - for a while at least.

On the other hand, and this was a scenario I daren't hope too much for, Farmer Giles here could be genuine and simply be helping a guy he'd passed by on the road. He could be driving home for his breakfast before ploughing a field or mucking out the pigs.

Well. You never know.

"You're a long way from the hospital, then."

I jumped. Here we go. Doctor Sin ahoy. Be still my thumping heart.

"I broke down." I didn't say that too quickly, did I? I felt like my palms were suddenly sweating but resisted the urge to wipe them on my trousers. What was I guilty of? All I had done was escape from an institute I'd voluntarily walked into. Was that a crime? Why was I panicking?

What was I guilty of. Yeah, right. I know a few corpses who could answer that one.

"Oh?" The big man frowned. "I didn't see your car. It wasn't that smashed up one, was it?"

Smashed up? The boy.

"Smashed up?" I deliberately looked surprised. "No, just a break down. I didn't have an accident."

"I didn't think so," he said, not seeming in the slightest suspicious. Was he just a very good actor? "You probably wouldn't be walking if it was you! Besides, there's an ambulance there. They seemed to be pulling someone out."

"I didn't see any smash. Where was it?"

"Further back from where I picked you up. Where did you break down?"

"No idea," I said. I once broke down driving along the M180, and my car wouldn't start in a Mablethorpe car park one summer, but I doubted he meant that. "I hung about for a bit to try and flag someone down, but didn't see anyone so started to walk. I hoped I'd find a house or something."

"It's a quiet road, this," he said. "Barely half a dozen cars a day come along here. You would have been waiting a long time. Where's your car then?"

In my driveway back home. Unless it's been nicked in the time I've been in the mental home.

"It's a few miles back," I said. "I saw the rain threatening, so I took cover under those trees back there. I only just made it before it started pissing it down."

"Didn't it?" he said, nodding vigorously. "I half expected to see Noah sailing by on his ark! That's why I've spent the morning in my back fields. The rain buggered up one of my walls. Rebuilding a stone wall buried in a ton of sloppy mud isn't my idea of a fun-filled morning."

"Mine neither," I agreed. Despite myself and despite knowing much better, I was warming to him. I wanted to stay suspicious, and it was becoming more of a struggle. The odd pangs of panic jabbed at my insides, but he was doing a good job of dulling their edges. I had to keep them sharp though. I had to keep them keen. Just in case. I thought it sad that he was accomplishing this simply by being nice to me. Apart from Jeremy back at the institute, I'd almost forgotten people had that capacity. Firm hands and sharp needles had become the norm and I couldn't help but be taken off guard by someone being actually pleasant.

If I could have slapped myself without him thinking I was more of a weirdo than he probably already did, I think I would have done. I was pretty sure I wouldn't have picked up a guy in the middle of nowhere, looking somewhat past his sell by date and wearing a fashion victim's version of hospital scrubs.

I don't pick up hitchhikers though, not after my one and only attempt at that particular good deed. I was driving through Healing, a smallish village on the way from Grimsby to Scunthorpe. Yes, I know, classy towns. Anyway. There's a sharp corner just after the school. Right on the corner of the corner was a man. His thumb was out. I didn't think or give myself the chance to keep on running, I simply pulled over.

"Where you going?" I asked, pleased that I was doing my bit for the common good, although I wasn't sure good was all that common.

"Brigg, mate."

He was tall and he was gangly. He wore what looked to be Status Quo cast-offs (including the long hair) and I remember thinking that if I have my X-ray specs on, like those you could buy from the back of comics when you were twelve, I'd be able to see the tattoos of big breasted beauties or dragons (big breasted or otherwise) adorning his forearms. Maybe a heart with an arrow through it and a banner sprawled across with Mum inked in fading blue would beat its tune with every flex of his bicep. All he needed was a warm can of Carling lager to be the icing on the stereotypical cake.

I didn't say yes, I didn't say no, all I had said was "Where'd you want to go." The next thing I knew, he was sitting beside me and I hadn't even seen the door open. I almost threw my curds and whey in his face and ran off, leaving my tuffet far behind. But I didn't. It was a warm and sunny day. My window was down and the fresh air was blowing my cares and my good sense away. I told myself to not be so quick to judge and pulled away. Brigg was on my way, more or less, so it was no bother to drop the guy where he wanted.

Chit-chat-rat-a-tat. Nice weather, blah-de-blah. Are you from around here, blah-de-blah. No, just been released from a spot in the cells, blah-de-er... huh?

Apparently my new denim coated friend was on his way home from spending the night in a police cell. It was nice of those policemen to let him have a rest and sleep off his alcohol-induced rage. Even more so when he was suspected of grievous bodily harm. He was angry they'd kept his knife. I supposed I would be too.

I suddenly entered one of those dark corridors on horror films where they inexplicably extend until the far end is lost in blackness. I was driving along expecting my passenger to introduce himself as Johnny and start discussing Redrum, but not in an equine sense. His name, apparently, was Kev, but he could have been using an alias to escape the mighty sword of justice. Police response units could have been mobilising right at that moment, hut-hut-hutting into the back of a discreetly large black van, armed to the nose-hairs, waiting for the nod to spring into action if your friendly neighbourhood murdering son-of-a-gun so much as picked his teeth.

Strangely, after my initial shock had subsided and we'd moved on from the subject of beating someone to a pulp because they pinched your girlfriend's arse, Psycho Kev turned out to be a fairly pleasant, and almost eloquent, companion. Who'd have thought serial killers could be so personable.

OK, so Psycho Kev, the Denim Demon probably wasn't a serial killer. He may well have simply had a moment of drunken stupidity and his confiscated blade could easily have been ritualistic rather than murderous - defensive rather than despicable. Still, I breathed a heavy sigh of relief when Brigg appeared out of the darkness of that tunnel and my new mate, pal, old bone china said his farewell.

It was his farewell too, rather than his farewells. Singular as opposed to plural. Considering I'd taken my life, limb and testicles into my hands and thrown them out of the window, I at least expected something along the lines of "Thanks a lot. I really appreciate it." Instead I was treated to a barely heard "Ta," as he climbed out of the car and disappeared around a corner. I think there may have been a newsagent along that road that he wanted to relieve of some cigarettes. He might actually have been planning on paying for them too. What a guy.

"We'll get you cleaned up, then I can bring you back to your car."

I jumped. This zoning out was getting to be a habit, and one I couldn't afford to fall into. I thought it strange that, after the past few hours, I was thinking about picking up strangers of all things, but I knew I needed to focus. I needed to be aware and be awake.

"Soz," I said, stretching to pretend a tiredness I wasn't really feeling, at least not too much. I felt wired. I felt as if I'd had a gallon or two of coffee washed down with a few cans of Red Bull. "I think I was drifting off a bit there."

I faked a yawned and he picked it up and ran with it, taking my yawn and raising it. At least my faux fatigue was real enough to be infectious.

"That's OK," he said. "After a night in a forest, I think I'd be flaked out myself."

I smiled and nodded, then realised what he'd said. He'd take me back to my non-existent car.

"I'll just call the AA," I said, hoping I didn't sound too panicked. "I'll let them pick it up and I'll make my own way home, thanks."

Of course I didn't know where I was, or even if I dared return to the house I used to call 'home' before taking up residence in a padded cell, but I had to play it by ear, even if I was a little tone deaf.

"You sure?"

I nodded. "That's what I pay my membership for."

"OK," he said. "It's up to you." He paused then reached out to me. I flinched before realising he just wanted to shake my hand. "Martin Collins," he said.

I took his hand, trying to be firm and manly, and wondered if I should give him my real name. How many questions would it prompt? Could I be bothered to tell him that yes, I did get bullied at school because of it and yes I did hate my parents, but for entirely different reasons. How far would I go? Would I tell him that the Universe had decided to let my life mirror my name literally? That my Sin-o-meter had filled all the way up to ding-a-ling?

Well, hate is a strong word. Perhaps pity is more fitting.

I took his hand. "Sin Matthews," I said before I'd given myself the chance to think of anything else. I decided I had to pepper my lies with some form of truth to help avoid being sucked in too far. I'd avoid the facts about the life of Sin-sin-sireee, of course. He might want to get me locked up in a mental home.

"Sin?"

"Sin."

He pressed his lips together, obviously wanting to ask the same tired old questions I'd answered so many times before. He apparently realised I was long done with the name game.

"Bacon butty do you?"

Magic words.

"Oh yes," I smiled.

Bacon butties. Food of the gods, no less. None of that Ambrosia nonsense. Rumoured to have been how Delilah really made Samson fall head over ponytail for her, and what Nero was actually doing whilst Rome became a dusty pile of ash, possibly even cooking it over the embers of the Coliseum. Crispy, salty and hot enough to melt the butter. Yummy, scrummy in my fat tummy. Delish, in fact. Giles had used his whiles to make me smile. Or Martin Collins as I should now call him.

The road was long and, yes, many a winding turn meandered it's way to who knew, or cared, where. For the most part, fields stretched each side, some furrowed and muddy, some smoothly tilled, as if an enormous rake had been dragged across the surface. Patches of wooded areas, second cousins twice removed to the semi-forest I'd spent the night in, dotted the landscape, lonely and forlorn with so much distance between them and their relatives, with not even a telephone to keep in touch. Long hedges snaked along the edge of the fields, dividing the landscape into a huge chessboard, perhaps for the pleasure of the giant Mister Rake Man.

I hadn't seen a sign or a distinctive road marking since passing a National Speed Limit indicator a few miles back, and there had been nothing before that. I could have been in the middle of nowhere or the middle of Lincolnshire. Trees were trees and fields were squares of mud. I hadn't seen a Yellow Bellied oak or a Scouse hedgerow to show which county of Paradise I'd landed in and didn't want to advertise my ignorance to all and farmer.

Did trees have accents? Apart from the fact that you didn't often see a giant redwood or palm sprouting on your way through town, did they have regional idiosyncrasies? Did a wee northern birch spread its branches wider than its southern brethren? Was the midland elm a touch more nobbled in the trunk area than those in, say, the Shetland Isles, or Deepest Dorset?

Ask me another.

We'd passed the odd turn off now and again, little roads that lead into the back, front and side of beyond, but none had anything to show what might be at the far end. I didn't know if there were towns, villages or simply the Flat Earthers' Abyss. Yesterday I'd have been happy to go along one of those small asides, just in case the fabled Abyss did exist for me to throw myself from, but I'd slept since then and my failed attempt at suicide had cleared the cobwebs of my miserable whinging arse away. The future was bright. The future might not have been orange, but it was definitely not so black. Maybe a murky grey perhaps.

Well, sitting in the cab with Farmer Collins on my way to a mighty bacon butty, it certainly seemed to be on the right side of wrong, the bright side of billabong. Shadows were still stalking the edge of my vision, flitting away if I turned to see, but they seemed not brave enough to venture closer. Don't go near the light, chappies.

I wondered if the road to hell wasn't actually Chris Rea's M25, but was in fact this black streak across the countryside. I'd read, once, a story about a man in a department store who'd taken the down escalator. He'd zoned out, a little like me, while it was descending and hadn't noticed, as he moved to the next and the next, that no one else was aboard, cap'ain. Then he noticed that he wasn't in Kansas anymore, and he was on an ever-descending escalator to nowhere. I can't remember what happened to the poor guy, but I think a combination of my night in the woods and the looming prospect of crispy paradise had dragged the end of this particular road on towards the horizon. I felt sure that Martin's farm should only have been around the corner, but some unseen hand had grabbed that corner and wrenched it off into the distance, purely to spite me and my screaming stomach.

But brighty-bright, lighty-light.

I was just about to ask how far away we were, and if it could be measured in light years, when a gate appeared in the hedgerow with a small hand painted sign attached. The sign was somewhat mud splattered, and the writing was blurred in the muck, but I could just about make out what it said.

"Shadow Hill Farm."

"Shadow Hill?" I asked.

Martin smiled. "Don't ask me," he said. "It was already called that when my grandfather bought the place. I seem to remember a big hill out back when I was a kid, but it's gone now. I don't recall it being flattened or anything but I suppose it must have been."

"Didn't you fancy changing the name? Cherry Tree or Pig Swill Farm perhaps?"

Martin laughed. The sound came from his boots and I could almost feel the bass through the seat, as if he'd had a subwoofer in his backside.

"Pig Swill, I like that. Maybe I will. I don't like cherries though. Besides - Shadow Hill. Sounds a bit mysterious."

I nodded my agreement. I would have preferred Shadow Hill to Cherry Tree myself. Pig Swill had a certain ring to it though.

Chapter Eight

The house we pulled up to didn't suit itself to the scruffy mud-slopped sign that greeted us at the gate. If there had been a traditional old farmhouse on this site, with knackered sash windows and drafty wooden doors, it had long since been knocked down. In its place was what I suppose looked like a mini-mansion. Windows were everywhere, and across the two floors looked to be a multitude of rooms. I didn't have time to count, but it certainly wasn't a mere two-up two-down. A gorgeous garden, filled with any number of colourful blooms - hey, I know what a rose is and that's about it, remember? - spread from the front door, almost as if it had been spilled. The door itself was a great uPVC affair, half glazed with rose leading, that still looked dwarfed against the rest of the structure. I wondered if the wicked witch of the west was buried under there somewhere, the house looked so out of place.

"Come on in," said Martin.

He stepped from the cab and walked to the entrance, pulled off his boots. I did the same, noticing the mud on my shoes was dried now and flaking. He pushed open the front door and stepped in. Instantly I was assaulted by the smell of cooking bacon. Assaulted - that has got to be the wrong word. Caressed? Washed? My belly growled, a wolf waiting to dine on the carcass of a dead animal. Martin looked and me and grinned.

"That's what I like to hear," he said. "Appreciation of the meal before the first bite."

I laughed and followed him in through the hallway that was all washed laminate and pictures to the massive kitchen. Was it a prerequisite of farmhouses that they had big kitchens? Was more cooking done down on t' farm than in the suburbs? I didn't know, but this particular kitchen was enormous. Stainless steel appliances were everywhere, from the triple hobbed cooker to the four-slice toaster. A large island sat in the middle of the room covered in the same black granite worktop that adorned the rest of the surfaces. Hanging over it were pots and pans and spatulas, all keeping with the same steel theme. It could have been the main showroom of a Kitchens-R-Us catalogue, front page spread and centre page special pull-out.

Bent over the oven, pulling out a grill pan covered in the best looking, crispiest bacon I'd ever seen, except maybe since the last time I'd had bacon (a long time ago), was a slim, small vision. She had short brown hair, large brown eyes with high arched brows. Slender fingers that deftly moved the bacon to the ready buttered buns, somehow without the hint of a burn. Small breasts that didn't look undersized on her equally small frame. Legs that seemed long. Behind that looked so right in her figure hugging jeans, Michelangelo couldn't have done better.

I couldn't decide, for a second, which I wanted more, the bacon or the girl. Then I realised where I was and tore my eyes away from both. Some of the nurses in the hospital had been pretty, one or two even beautiful, but their simple white uniforms stripped away any semblance of sexuality. This was my first 'proper' female in a hell of a long time. She could have looked like a bag of spanners and it probably wouldn't have mattered. The fact that she looked elfen only added to her glory. But I needed to stop being the ignorant sexist I knew I wasn't and get back in the groove.

"Hey babe," said Martin.

The woman nodded and smiled. "Morning Marty." Her voice was soft, warm and just on the upside of a whisper. How else could it have been? "Timed to perfection, as usual." She indicated the bread buns steaming at the sides. "You didn't mention any guests though or I'd have made more."

I felt my cheeks redden as she mentioned me. I took a deep breath to steady myself. Spinning a yarn longer than a spider's web was hard enough with one person. Adding another into the mix complicated matters.

"Sorry about that," Martin replied. "I picked up a stray along the way. Couldn't you just chuck another slice or two on the grill? My man here could just about kill a pig himself I think."

I didn't know about that, but I could feel a black hole forming where my stomach had been, threatening to suck the rest of me in along with it. The point of singularity was just about where my belly button had once been.

"I don't want to be a pain," I said. "Don't worry about me."

"I'm not," she said. "But I can still manage another sandwich. Have mine and I'll do another."

Martin, the Mighty Marty, indicated a seat at the large terracotta topped table he was sitting at. "Plonk it."

I did as instructed and within what seemed like seconds, had devoured the buns on my plate. Somehow a coffee had appeared before me, hot, strong and black ("Just like my men," Joy used to say) and I'd downed half the cup in one gulp before realising I was being stared at.

"Hungry?" said Martin's wife/partner/sister/mistress. She was filling her own bun with bacon hot enough to make the butter sizzle. I bet myself she could make plenty of things sizzle.

Stop it.

I stifled a belch, not entirely successfully, and nodded.

"Sorry," I said. "I was just a bit peckish."

"A bit? You want me to fry up the whole pig?"

She was smiling. It was like a beacon in the darkness. The sun on a spring morning. A punch in the face from her fella if I didn't snap out of it and sort my head out. Where was my focus? Where was the idea of not bringing more attention to myself than an escaped lunatic could bring? I wasn't completely stupid - some of the parts were missing. If I didn't get it together, I'd be back in pokey gnawing the bark off twigs for lunch while they had fun flicking the switches to the electrodes they'd stuck on my head. While the electrified Medusa image was something of a fashion statement, I didn't really see it catching on at the next Clothes Show catwalk.

"I'm fine thanks," I said. I turned my attention to Martin, partly to avoid showing too much where I shouldn't, and partly to move this little interlude on. I needed to find out where I was and get out of here.

Would I have been better staying where I was? Would doing my Johnny Blaze impression in the furnace have been preferable to going on the run and panicking at the hint of a wrong look or phrase or phone call?

The telephone rang. The sudden noise scared the Beetlejuice out of me, making my heart jump high enough into my throat it made my ears ring a karaoke duet along with the phone. Neither of my hosts made a move to answer the call and after a few seconds it clicked off, an answer machine kicking in to, no doubt, invite the caller to leave a message after the beep.

How original were answering machine messages? And how many people suddenly found themselves at a loss for words when confronted by the expectant silence of the waiting tape? Why did it feel strangely like you were standing naked in front of a thousand faceless shadows, each of which was expecting you to spout forth insight and genius, instead of the "Erm..." you managed?

Or was that just me?

The telephone was a folding design I'd never seen before. It seemed a curious mix of mobile phone and standard cordless handset, but was struggling to decide which. Martin caught me looking.

"We never answer it at meal times," he said. "If it's that important they'll leave a message or ring back."

Great sentiment, I thought, but I wasn't aware it was humanly possible to not answer a ringing phone. Just like you're going to say "Ouch" when someone kicks you in the gazoingas, you're going to pick up a phone when it rings.

Or, I say again, was that just me?

Sometimes, I'm like a human cucumber. No, I don't mean a bit green or a bit bent, although I'm not actually denying either. I mean I sometimes repeat myself.

I decided to do my gadget-geek bit and ask about the telephone. Partly this was to avoid any possible questions about myself but also because I really was interested. If it took batteries (and didn't have the words 'rabbit' or 'rampant' in the name) or plugged in, I was automatically interested. Hey, even if it was based on a decidedly bunny design. I was energised by energy and electrified by electricity. Or something like that anyway.

"Good, isn't it," said Martin. "It's great for if someone calls while I'm out in the back barn or mending a wall or something."

"Oh?"

"Yes," he said. "It's a landline phone in the house and a mobile outside. It's even an internet phone if I want it to be."

"Cool," I said, meaning it. Sad, I know. And?

"Except he never takes it with him," said Mrs. Martin. The big man rolled his eyes and she playfully slapped him. "What's the point in having a gadget if you don't use it properly?"

"Oh don't nag, Sarah," he said.

So her name was Sarah.

She flicked his nose and then kissed it. I pulled the spear from my heart.

Martin stood up, taking his arm from around Sarah's waist, then smacked her bum. Like I needed an excuse to look in that direction. He walked over to the telephone.

"May as well listen to the message now, seeing as we're talking about it."

He pressed a small button on the top and a young man's voice said: "Hey boss. Not going to make it in today. Feel like shit. Off to doctor's later 'n' I'll let you know what he says then. Soz. Hope to be in tomorrow." There was a cough and then a long beep, silenced by Martin pressing another button.

"Great," he said. "That's Dean off sick. Just what I need."

Great, I thought. That's one less person to lose in a lie.

"He might be back tomorrow," said Sarah hopefully.

"Oh, he might be," said Martin looking doubtful. "He's not sick often, but when he is he makes sure he milks it more than he does the cows!" He looked at me with a wry smile. "You any good with animals, Sin?"

I'd once trained my dog to sit when commanded. If a cat sat on my lap, I'd be happy enough to scratch it between its ears. I didn't think he meant that.

"Not really," I answered.

Even if I could turn a foal in utero or spin a tractor around on a penny, including trailer, my answer would still have been in the negative. I wasn't entirely sure why, but I saw myself as a fugitive on the run, Harrison Ford fleeing Hannibal Lecter. Well, Dr. Connors was certainly no Tommy Lee Jones. Saying that, Lecter might have liked to dine on your doodads, but even he was something of a refined gentleman, with morals and standards - however warped they might be. Connors was three steps down from base. But continuing the line of thought, was I so very different? It's fine and dandy likening myself to a wronged man running because he could do nothing else. I was escaping a prison I'd incarcerated myself in, and from deaths - or murders - I'd committed myself.

I couldn't help seeing myself as a good guy, though. I wasn't bad, I was just drawn that way. Death, destruction and misery weren't my friends - they were my shadows, my stalkers. Was the fact that they picked me up Pinocchio-like and strummed my strings like a harp my fault?

But I killed people. Like it or not, I killed people. Innocents. Sure, the kid in the car had knocked down a girl. He didn't mean to do it - it was his own ignorance and arrogance that caused it. If I can excuse my own horrors why couldn't I excuse his? Why was he in the wrong, but I was still goody two-shoes? Ask me another. I could say that it was because the boy was reckless and stupid. He was an accident waiting to happen. I would rather have killed myself than another person. I wanted to control this demon writhing in my gut and exorcise it. That kid was the demon and was out of control. I really wasn't bad, I was just drawn that way. He was his own artist.

But who was I to judge? Who was I to sign-seal-destroy?

How could such a monster as myself be a 'good guy'?

But I felt that I was. If you looked past the body count, and you'd have to stand on your tippy-toes to do so, I was pretty much Mr. Ordinary Joe. Unassuming, apart from the power to rip seagulls apart. Almost shy, if you ignored the ability to throw a bus through the window of a Post Office.

Of course, I might simply have had a 'dark half'. Hiding under the double divan of my conscious mind, a sinister shade could have been waiting for me to be looking the other way so it could slip out and wreak a little wreckage. No uncontrollable power, no terrible curse - just the darkness stalking the edges of where I could see or think or imagine. Subdued by the dark side was I. Flip and catch. Heads - Obi Wan, tails - Darth Vader. Except with better dress sense. And without the asthma.

It was me. Of course it was. But I refused to believe it was some monstrous part of my psyche that acted on urges I pretended I didn't have. It was my power, or my ability, or my curse, but it wasn't *me* that wielded it. It was me, but not *me*.

"So how about it?" Martin said.

"Huh?"

"If you don't fancy it, fair enough. After the night you've had, you'll want to just get home and get your head down, but you'd be doing me a real favour."

"Huh?"

"Maybe the bacon was too much for him," said Sarah, her voice sparkling with humour.

"Or maybe you are," answered Martin.

Oh. He'd noticed my interest. Ah.

Martin stepped towards me and I resisted the urge to flinch.

"I asked if you minded taking a look at Dean for me. I could really do with him here today, or at the very least tomorrow. If you could check him out, cos I know he'll not get round to visiting the quack today, I'd appreciate it. You could call it payment for the ride and the butty."

Damn. He wanted the Doc to play doctor. I knew that you fed a fever and starved a cold - or was that the other way around? I knew that dock leaves were good for nettle stings, though I didn't know what a dock leaf looked like. I knew that paracetomol got rid of a headache and ibuprofen eased back ache, and I knew that it's good to let a cut breathe. I really couldn't do this.

"Sure," someone who sounded like me said.

"Excellent! Ready to go now?"

Blimey, I thought. On the case, ready to race! Come on man - give me a chance to wangle my way out of this.

"Sure, why not," that person who sounded so much like me said.

I stood and made to walk to the door then stopped.

"I feel a bit..." like I've slept in a forest with only my decomposing sister to keep me company... "dirty. Any chance I could... " run away and don't stop until my feet are stumps or I fall off the edge of the world... "get cleaned up?"

Martin looked at his watch. He wanted to get the doctor making his house call so he could get the hired help doing their work.

"Well...," he said, implying that me getting cleaned up was a great idea but time's a-wasting matey, so let's get this show on the road and worry about sprucing ourselves up later.

Sarah smiled. "Of course you can." She put a hand on Martin's arm to silence his obvious protest. I didn't think he was against me using his shower, but he seemed to be a time-is-money kind of guy and while I wasn't working, this Dean person was shirking.

Martin shrugged and smiled. Argue with a woman? Not me mister.

"Of course you can," he said. "Bathroom's top of the stairs, first door on the left. I'll grab some clothes for you. They might be a bit big but they'll do you for now."

"Are you sure?" I asked, thankful for the chance to avoid playing doctors. I was no George Clooney, and I doubted my ability to successfully pull off a Dr. Ross act. With my history it'd be more Crippen or Frankenstein than Dr. Jack Shepherd, though I was definitely lost. More Hyde than Jekyll. More Donald than Duck.

Well, maybe not that last one.

Martin nodded and I thanked him, heading towards the stairs. As I walked I looked for any hint of an address or a location of some sort. Mail or photo or anything that would give me a clue.

Perhaps I should have just asked "Where are we?" but I felt like I was crazy now I was *out* of the mental institute. I didn't want to help confirm the diagnosis.

There was nothing. No stray letter lying on the hall table. No big map with a neon blue arrow proclaiming 'YOU ARE HERE!'. I was up crap creek without a shovel, and I couldn't find my way back.

Hey-ho, daddy-o.

With my mind wandering, my feet did the same and, instead of turning left at the top of the stairs, I turned right, finding myself in a spacious, minimally decorated bedroom. The master suite, it seemed. All chromes and chocolates, the bed looked almost as inviting as Sarah's smile, but I turned quickly and left the room, closing the door quietly behind me. As I moved across the short landing towards the first door on the left and straight on till morning, I heard Sarah's twinkling tones from below.

"He's not a doctor."

Chapter Nine

"What do you mean?" Martin said quietly. The rumble of his voice carried through the bones of the house. The words made my own rattle. They must have heard me close their bedroom door and mistaken it for the bathroom.

"Those clothes. They're not hospital scrubs. He's not a doctor. He's a patient."

"A patient? How do you know? He said... He didn't deny it."

"I know because I wore the same clothes when I was... you know."

"Oh."

Oh.

"Are you sure?"

"I'm sure." Sarah's voice had lost its shine. Cracks had appeared in the velvet, rents that ripped their way into me. "He made everyone wear them. Part of the process, he said."

He.

Dr. Connors. It had to be.

Oh.

"You never said."

"You know I don't like to talk about it. I'm better now, no thanks to him. It's the past. You're the future."

I heard Martin's footsteps. I could feel him moving towards her. Putting his arms around her.

"Still. We should call them. If he's wearing those clothes, he might have escaped. He might be dangerous."

"I know," she said. "I thought I was done with that place."

"One call, and then you will be."

A cold tingling started in my calves and worked its way up my legs. Goosebumps prickled my arms, Braille for 'What the hell do I do now?'

Then I knew. It was one of those, I just knew moments we all love so much. I could almost feel it creeping up on me that time though, much like a putty tat. Instead of the knowledge simply being there, I could sense it appearing. Like night becoming day, gradual enough for you to not quite notice until the change was done. A bit faster, of course, because that would have taken hours, but still steadily blossoming in my head. I knew.

I knew why she was in the hospital. Why she didn't want to go back.

I knew more than she did.

I knew about the rape one night after the club. The baby that was a result. The stillbirth of the child she'd come to want and to love. Her breakdown. Her committal. Her abuse at the hands of the orderly. How Jeremy, good ol' Jezzer himself, had discovered and stopped it. Her recovery. I knew that and she knew that.

But more. I knew more.

Martin. Farmer Giles. Loving husband. Carer. Friend and lover. Rapist. Father of her stillborn child.

I didn't realise I was standing on the top step until I almost fell down. I was dizzy and sick. A deep, slow breath steadied me and I took a step back. I heard pages turning from the kitchen. They were looking up the number.

"Hello?"

Pause.

"Yes, hello. Can I speak to Dr. Connors please."

The line went dead. I knew that too. I could almost hear the silence as the receptionist on the other end - probably Claire, all chubbiness, smiles and red hair - was cut off. I knew because it was me. I wanted it to happen. I made it happen. Yes, I crashed the bus and the car and did all those other horrible, awful things. But this time, somehow, I *made* it happen.

And the Braille on my arms had gone. In its place was the uncertainty of what the hell I was going to do now.

Martin was trying to get through to the hospital still. He would be unsuccessful. I returned to their bedroom and opened one of the built in wardrobes. It was his. I took a pair of jeans and a t-shirt from hangers. The top was a light brown with cream horizontal stripes. Not my colour really, but I was going to pass on the Catwalk of Chaos for now. I changed quickly, the clothes too big but more than suitable under the circumstances, and went back to the landing leaving the wardrobe door open. It wasn't going to matter in a few minutes. I walked down the stairs, my panic gone. I was calm. I was... I was smooth. A windless lake. A breath held.

There were no sounds from the kitchen. There wouldn't be. Sarah was sitting in her chair, holding her coffee. She wasn't noticing the heat was burning her hand. Martin was holding the useless phone in his hand. He was staring out of the kitchen window, possibly at the spot where the famous hill had once been.

I picked up his keys from the hall table where he'd left them and walked out of the front door. I didn't hear the flames start to lick the wall behind the cooker, but I knew they were. I didn't smell the smoke curling along the hallway but yes, I knew it was.

Perhaps it was following me. Perhaps it was saying goodbye. Perhaps the smoke was reaching out to coax me back, so I could enjoy the same fate that I'd handed to poor Sarah and her wonderful rapist husband.

He'd engineered their relationship. Bumping into her so she'd spill her drink on him only days after her discharge. The old ways were the best. He knew her history. He could be sympathetic. Was he a monster for doing so? Needing to be so much in control raping her wasn't enough - he had to dominate her entire life?

No. That wasn't it. Yes, for the rape he was a beast. But the rest? It was his reparation. His repentance. To care and to provide for the woman who he'd torn apart. To help mend the wounds, even though she didn't know he was the one who wounded her. It was his purgatory to be reminded each moment of each day of the vile act he'd inflicted upon her.

Did that forgive him? Did that make amends for his actions? Did that make him a good guy? A saviour? Beast become Beauty? Was I defending him in an attempt to defend myself? *Was* there a defence, or did one's actions taint one's soul for the rest of one's sorry life?

Ask me another. Anyway it wasn't Martin's past conduct that had damned him, it was his current. I wasn't going to let him hand me over. I wasn't going to let the good doctor get his greasy hands on me again. The drugs don't work, the Verve once said. Dr. Connors didn't give a flying flip about that. How Sarah had managed to escape his clutches I don't know. Perhaps that was down to Martin too. History, and my inner voices, didn't relate. All hail the laydee.

I had to stop them. I had to. But by killing them? Could I not have talked to them? Reasoned maybe? Look guys. I'm not that bad. I'm not crazy. True, I can teleport and kill people with my mind, but I'm not insane. Honest!

What would I have said? Hardly the truth. They would have been on the phone quicker than a rabbit out of a fox hole, with Connors as the fox and me as the gory remains of the cute little bunny.

I have a tattoo of a fox on my upper right arm. It's a symbol, to me, of freedom. But the doctor is the dark side of the fox. Vulpine instincts drive him. Why kill the chicken for lunch when you can slaughter the whole coup?

I'd taken three steps towards the dirt-washed van when I heard it. I might have missed the sound at any other time. Would have in fact. But around me all had become suddenly hushed. Mr. Bluebird on my shoulder, or at least the crows in the fields and the light buzz of insects had been muted as if by a great remote control. In space only Sigourney Weaver can hear you scream. Her Majesty the alien queen could have been standing behind me and I wouldn't have heard her. The sound had been sucked from the world like lemonade through a straw till not a drop remained. Were the fauna in the flora biting their collective tongues in protest at what I'd done?

Did it resent me causing the fire that would soon consume this house and all who sailed in her? Perhaps. The silence echoed around me, non-existent whispers crawling up my spine. Not a whistle or a rustle or a caw. Not even the crackle of a flame.

Except...

A baby.

Crying.

From inside the house.

The spell was broken - the hex halted. The sound rushed back into the air like the seal on a vacuum suddenly fractured. Crows yelled from the trees at me. A bee had given up on bumbling and was spinning around my head in a crazed dervish. A buzzing had erupted from around me as if the ground itself was vibrating.

Everything was screaming at me.

THE BABY.

I could tell myself - fool myself if that's what you want to call it - that Martin and the boy deserved their fates. In fact I may well have been Fate's own personal gopher, doing the job's he, or she, hated. Why would Fate get his hands dirty when I had a perfectly good pair to sully?

Actually, I always thought of Fate as a woman. Definite female tendencies there, don't you think?

The baby.

I turned and I ran. The front door had been drifting shut, a feeble attempt to bar my way. I crashed it open and took the stairs three at a time. I didn't need to think about which door to open; my hand took the handle, turned and pushed.

The nursery was decorated in yellow and Pooh was dancing across the walls with Piglet and Eeyore. And in a wooden cot (all the better to go up in flames, my dear) just inside the door was the baby. She had her mother's eyes and had stopped crying as soon as I entered. I took her up in my arms and was back out the front door before I'd taken another breath.

I stood trembling for the longest time, still not breathing. I didn't deserve a breath. The girl, doe eyed and pink romper-suited, looked up at me and...

Cooed. Then smiled.

Her name was Morgan. Morgan Alexandra to be precise. And she had just forgiven me.

A silver Mercedes was parked to one side. A car seat was in position behind the driver's. The car unlocked automatically as I approached and I gently fastened Morgan into her chair.

I walked as calmly as I could back to Martin's van and climbed in. As I drove away the couple in the kitchen slowly stood and left the house, collecting the keys to the Mercedes on the way. The flames in the kitchen died as they smiled at Morgan Alexandra and started the engine. I turned left out of the gate, knowing they'd turn right, and knowing that they were just going into town to buy a few essentials. Disposable nappies. Toilet roll. Baby wipes. You know the sort of thing.

It would be three days before they noticed the van missing. Probably a week or two before they decided to redecorate the kitchen. It was looking tired. Needed a face lift.

"A bit like me," Sarah would joke.

They wouldn't see the scorch marks or the smoke damage. And they wouldn't remember me.

Two miles? Three? No more than that. No more than three miles before I had to stop, open the door and vomit my bacon breakfast onto the side of the road.

Shame, that. I'd enjoyed it.

My shaking stopped after a few more minutes and I could get my breath and think again. I'd still not passed any signs or indication of where I might be. I needed to stop and get my bearings.

The van had almost a full tank of petrol, which I was sure would get me to some semblance of civilisation. Guessing that Martin's farm wasn't just a single dot of life in a vast expanse of nothing, I'd have to find a town or village eventually. Wouldn't I? I could drive until I did, of course, but I preferred to have some sort of warning as to what I might encounter. The glove compartment was suddenly very inviting.

A couple of CDs, old when I was still in the land of the living - before my incarceration. A small unopened packet of tissues. A cigarette packet with four fags left. A pen. Blue. Leaked. That was it.

I slumped back in the seat and flipped the glove box shut. The latch didn't catch and it fell open again, one of the discs slipping out and falling into the footwell. Sighing I leaned down to pick it up, and saw a corner of white stuck under the passenger seat. An envelope. Maybe Fate was lending me a helping hand. Perhaps the glove box was supposed to fall open and let a disc drop out. That would be the only way I'd find my salvation - if salvation was what it was.

The envelope was dirty and water stained and had the look of something that had been kicked out of the way, forgotten about for a long time.

"A bit like me," I joked to the magpie that was watching me from a few feet away. It stared at me then dropped its gaze to the puddle of sick on the road. Was it hoping for a free lunch, or was it calling me a disgusting slob? Maybe a bit of both - I was a disgusting slob who'd just provided lunch.

The envelope had been opened. Inside was what appeared to be a bank statement. Hadn't this guy heard of identity theft? Wasn't leaving something like this just lying around, an invitation to be robbed blind? I felt sure that even the most casual thief would have a credit card, flat screen television and designer wardrobe by the end of the week based on a find such as this. Luckily, at least for Sarah and Martin - my latest victims - I wasn't a casual thief. Nor was I an experienced one. Their statement would serve only to give me an idea of where I was and that was all. I wasn't interested in fleecing what was essentially an innocent couple.

Yes. Innocent. Martin had been a monster, but he was trying to repair the damage. I didn't believe he was still the same man. Perhaps it was a case of Jekyll and Hyde, that old horrific double act whose sense of humour was surpassed only by the Two

Ronnies or Morcambe and Wise. Would it be a case that, if Miss Temptation walked in front of him, wiggling her sexy little behind, Martin's dark side might re-surface, the monster reborn?

I didn't think so. Just like my father's abuse of me was another life, the farmer's abuse was dead and buried, complete with a marble headstone reading: "Here's lies the black heart of Martin Collins, beloved husband, father and rapist. R.I.P."

There was I, again, defending what some people would call the indefensible. Martin had torn young Sarah's life apart. String him up, slit his throat and leave him to rot. I couldn't say those people were wrong. But I... I knew him. Or I knew that part of him. I'd felt it. Another aspect of that darkness permeated my own soul. Was I, again, trying to forgive myself?

Who cares! Whether I was innocent or guilty of mass murder was irrelevant. I'd gone and done it, guv'nor. Fair cop. String *me* up, why don't you?

But I was just trying to live my life. I was trying to escape from the death and the devastation. I didn't want it to happen. So go easy on me, ok?

Anyway. The envelope.

The statement was in Martin's name. A quick glance, out of curiosity rather than possible profiteering, told me that his account was in exceptional order. He could keep his wife and child in a very healthy lifestyle for a long time to come. But that didn't interest me, not really. It was his address.

Martin Collins

Shadow Hill Farm

Grainthorpe

Lincolnshire

LN...

My eyes barely registered the postcode. They'd noticed the town and they'd noticed the county. Home Sweet Home - give or take a few miles or so.

I knew the name Grainthorpe. From somewhere it swam about in my head, hinting at its location. I'd been there, or at least I'd been through there. A few houses, a main road. Perhaps a small shop. I could just about grasp fragmented images. But even if I hadn't known the town - although I knew it was only a village that might have aspired to township - Lincolnshire, in all its green and pleasant glory, I knew well. The town I'd grown up in, Grimsby, was slap bang in the middle. OK, it was slap bang to the side. On the edge of falling into the North Sea and swimming away to sunnier climes. But let's not be pedantic. Euphoric yes, but not pedantic, if you please.

Lincolnshire, or more generally Lincs if you happened to be an envelope or a postcard, was split into more then one county. North, North East and simple Plain Jane Lincolnshire. I didn't know where the Southern part had disappeared to - perhaps it was on holiday in those aforementioned sunnier climes. Parts had lost their way for a while and called themselves South Humberside, but they'd recovered and reverted to their proper name eventually. Grimsby, named after the Dane who'd settled there to protect the heir to the Danish throne, wasn't as Grim as the name might suggest.

Ok, so the fishing industry had floated away, but it was still prospering. Or so I thought anyway. I'd lived in nearby Scunthorpe, a town held hostage to its steel industry, for a good few years and Grimsby might have faltered along its path while I was away, but I'd grown up there and both Joy and my parents had remained there. I'd moved back after Joy had died, taking up residence in her house. Maybe I did that to bring myself closer to my sister and maybe it was because I needed the cocooning blanket of somewhere that wasn't mine. Joy's house, which would still hold a connection to her, could offer some illusional protection against my demons.

Or not.

So.

Grainthorpe, Grainthorpe, Grainthorpe.

I wiped a small dribble of vomit off my chin and flicked it towards the magpie. It regarded me with watchful eyes, much like HG Wells' Martians. Was it drawing its plan against me? One for Sin, two for Joy, wasn't it? Sorrow, Sin - it was all the same. Why did

I know Grainthorpe? Lincolnshire had a million small villages scattered about, some no more than a house and a post box, some lacking even the post box. So many of them were less than dots on a map to me, so why did I remember this one. Then I remembered why I remembered.

Ice cream.

I scream, you scream, we all scream for Armageddon. Or Robbie Williams. Or vanilla with cinder toffee and a flake. On the road (A18? A16?) out from Grimsby to somewhere else was Applebys Ices. Applebys was one of those old family run businesses that was soon to be celebrating or recently had celebrated its centenary. Ice cream made the way it used to be before Walls and Nestle muscled in. A hundred different flavours, ranging from mint choc chip to Magic Mandarin and beyond. I couldn't remember exactly which post box it was near, but I was sure you had to pass through Grainthorpe to get there. That meant, if I followed this road, with all its bends and wiggles, I'd either be scoffing a 99 or hitting my old home town.

I could have, should have, appeared in the middle of a furnace. I could have popped up in a nowhere town in a country I hadn't heard of. The potential was there, I supposed, for me to resurface on the event horizon of a black hole. That would have been some event - me, my very own *Sin*gularity point. But I didn't. I'd hop-skipped-and-teleported to just down the road from an ice cream parlour. And a good one at that.

Who'd have thought it?

With a smile, the first really real one of the morning, I gave the eye-spy-my-little-magpie the one finger salute and pulled the van door shut. The engine growled into action and I started along the road. One bend was basically the same as another, each too close to get much past about 35 miles an hour, but that was fine by me. I had the window open, the crisp morning-after-the-storm smell of the air singing in my nostrils and I knew where I was - give or take. Dennis Hopper could be riding nice and easy along sweet old Route 66 and it wouldn't feel this good.

"Hi ho, Sliver," said Joy from the passenger seat.

I looked over but she wasn't there. The smell of jasmine drifted past me and out of the window and I smiled again.

Hi ho indeedy-o. Where we'll stop nobody knows. Well, if I was driving towards Grimsby, I knew exactly where I was going to stop.

Chapter Ten

The road curved and swung more times than a ride at Alton Towers, but without the queues. The odd long stretch let you build up some speed (as much as the van could give a pretence of speed), lulling you into a false sense of security before a bend leapt out to slow you down again. I went through a couple of villages - houses crowding around the road like spectators at a race track - but didn't catch their names. Not that I would have readily recognised them anyway. But then, in an open field to the right of the road, was a tree. I recognised it immediately. It was dead, that much was obvious. One lone branch stuck out and up, and just above where the branch jutted out, the tree stopped, looking like its head had been lopped off. Was it waving to passers by, just being a friendly headless tree, saying "Hi, how's it going?" Was it a warning? Signalling people to STOP! DON'T GO ANY FURTHER! THE MAD TREE-HEAD-CHOPPER-OFFER IS LURKING HEREABOUTS AND HE'S HUNGRY FOR MORE TROPHIES! Or had it been pointing up at something in the sky - a UFO that, upon being spotted, had zapped it with its green death ray, petrifying the tree where it stood so it couldn't tell anyone else its secrets?

Ask me another.

Either way, I knew it and I knew that onward bound was home sweet pseudo-home.

A bend and the magical sign for Horseshoe Point. Magical, I hear you say? No such thing. It's easy-ish to believe in teleportation and murder-by-mind, but magic? Nah. But this sign, that'd have you convinced, I'm sure. Sometimes, driving along this road to Appleby's and beyond, you'd reach the turning for Horseshoe Point, a small sandy bay with a couple of grass patched dunes for company, in the blink of an eye. You'd be there before you knew it. But go again, and it would seem to have moved - taking an age and a half to find. So yes, it was magical.

I saw a sign for Tetney and knew sanctuary was close. Tetney was a strange little place, a little more than a village but a little less than a town. It had pubs and some small shops and even more than one post box. What made it strange was the curious practice of, once a year, making scarecrows. Yep, scarecrows. Like a summer fair but held in each resident's garden, scarecrows would be made and put up in all manner of curious guises such as Mary Poppins, burglars and Spiderman. Dressed not to scare any black feathered birds, but to scar and invade the minds of the young. Well, actually it was a quaint custom which brought more smiles than scares, but what happened at night with those straw stuffed characters, eh? Did they party hard, or creep into bedrooms wielding knives? Just a thought, you know.

It wasn't Scarecrow Weekend, thankfully - I had enough nightmares whilst awake without anyone holding my hand as I wandered through the Land of Nod.

Through Tetney's double bend and onto the Grimsby straight, and, finally, into Grimsby itself. I was breathing hard, as if I'd run all the way here from the Collins' farm. Perhaps it was the impending relief of being able to rest properly. Maybe get a shower. A bite to eat. Or perhaps it was because it had been too long without anything happening. No deaths due to me. No sign of pursuers. It was too quiet for too long.

Sod it. Enjoy the peace, however short-lived.

It wasn't too far from the mini-roundabout that told me I was in Grimsby to my destination. I hoped it wasn't my Final Destination and Death wasn't hot on my heels, clawed hand reaching out for the scruff of my neck. If I was forced to have these special gifts, or curses, it would have been nice for Fate, God or whomever to chuck in a sprinkling of Spidey sense for me so I could tell if I was going to be discovered or attacked or torn limb from juicy limb. But there were none so I had to put my trust in a whole heap of nothing, and not for the first time.

So just keep on trucking, matey. I couldn't help, hinder or do diddley-squit. I had no choice but to keep on a-trucking.

It was good, wonderful in fact, to see people. Normal people who, in the most part at least, weren't high on drugs or babbling nonsense. Ha! Was life so different from a mental institute? Anywho. *Normal* people. *Sane* people. Ones who wore colours other than white. Ones who were allowed spectacles and watches and laces and, gosh almighty, a belt! Couples hand in hand or arm in arm. Smiles. Vacant expressions that weren't drug induced but were simply normal people getting on with their normal lives in their normal way.

LIFE.

What an absolutely joyous thing it was. I felt like an evangelist bursting to spread the Word (and rake in the donations), but I wasn't the Messiah - I was a very naughty boy. I felt like winding the window down and shouting, with my head sticking out, wind in my hair like a spaniel: "Hey you lot! Do you know how lucky you are???"

Of course, they wouldn't know how lucky they were. They just got on with living the same way they got on with breathing. It was free and they did it without thinking. There were no direct debits being drawn from their bank accounts every month to make sure they received their quota of breaths and heartbeats. They didn't have to swipe their credit cards or remember a pin number to make sure they woke up each morning after falling asleep the night before. It was just there. The way electricity is when you flick a switch or water is when you turn on a tap. No thought, no messing, just good old Existence. Do with it what you will.

Naturally a shed load of stuff went on to get electricity to the socket or fresh water to the tap, just as plenty happened to get life shoe-horned into the tiny body that popped out of your mum's bottom bits. But once it was done and you flicked that switch or turned that tap or cried that first slapped-arse cry, who thought there'd be a time when it wasn't there? Unless someone didn't pay the bills and you were cut off...

In the matter of Life, your Honour, that'd be me.

The traffic lights in front of me were at red. I stopped, pulling behind the yellow Toyota in front of me, and had a flashback to a game I used to play. Yellow cars were rarely seen at one time, with blues, reds, silvers etc. being the norm. Yellow was too bright - too in yer face. So when you saw a yellow car, you'd shout out "Yellow car!" and smack the arm or leg of the person you were with. Crazy little bit of fun, I know, but the thought of it still made me smile.

Raised voices dragged me back from the brink of a happy memory. An argument between a young couple. I didn't hear what she'd said to him but I heard him shout back at her that 'it didn't mean anything.' Well, wasn't that a statement that needed no explanation? Even if it had, however, I'd still know, in that wonderfully twisted way I had.

The man, about 22 or so, partially raised his hand, then clenched his fist and lowered it again. I could tell the intent. It was a habit of his. A nasty habit because he wouldn't always lower it, but he would often clench the fist. The bruises on the girl's face had faded but I knew there were some still lingering on her upper arm and on her abdomen. He saw me looking and made a what-are-you-looking-at-face before spinning away from his girlfriend and storming off. She stood there for a moment, trembling, and then ran after him, the word 'sorry' forming on her lips.

He was right. It hadn't meant anything. None of the other women had. Nor did she, not to him. She was a trophy to him. An accessory. Someone to prove his manhood because she was so pretty and he could treat her mean and she'd still stay keen.

I felt the creeping sensation I'd had earlier. I saw the dog wander from nowhere into the road. I saw the Mondeo coming up behind me start to swerve to avoid it and bear down on the boyfriend. I could feel how his bones would break and could hear the noise his head would make when it hit the pavement.

Then the lights changed to green. The yellow Toyota pulled away (smackety smack) and I drove after it, frantically pulling myself in, clenching my body tightly, screaming inside myself to suck it in, suck it in.

And the Mondeo stopped inches from the boy. And the dog sniffed at a dropped crisp packet in the road and trotted away along the street. And the girl caught up to her man, because he was such a man, and they both threw evil looks at the Mondeo driver, who was sitting there not quite comprehending what had happened. And they walked off arm in arm, her kissing his cheek, him strutting because he wasn't just a man, he was *the* man.

And me? I drove down a few streets, across a couple of sets of traffic lights (both at green) and around one or three corners. I parked up at my parents' house. And then I cried for a little while.

A woman, old, wrinkled and looking like a sofa that had been left out in the back garden over winter was walking her dog. The dog, a Pug, glanced at me as they passed the van. I half expected it to shy away or start growling at me as if I was the spawn of the devil (and wasn't I, effectively?), but it didn't. It paid me less attention than it might a lampost it had just peed up. The woman, her long scruffy brown coat hanging around her four sizes too big, seemed to want to say something. Probably ask if this dishevelled man, wearing clothes that were too big, crying alone in his van was ok. The terrier pulled at its lead, eager to claim a small gatepost as its territory, and the woman forgot all about me and hurried along, as much as her shamble would allow, after her pet.

I wiped my eyes and then remembered the tissues in the glove box. Helping myself to one - Martin wasn't going to miss them - I blew my nose. I should move the van. Park it somewhere else. My parents' house had been standing empty for the couple of two years and more. A stolen van outside a supposedly empty house? Not the best idea in the bargain basement of Ideas Inc., purveyors of the finest thoughts, anecdotes and concepts money can buy. I moved it. Not far away was a supermarket, one of those that stayed open 24 hours a day, except on Sundays, just in case you needed a loaf of bread or a tube of toothpaste at two in the morning. Cars were parked there at all hours of the day and night, so one more wouldn't hurt, I assumed. And if, three days from now, it was noticed that this particular mucky white van had been there for a while, then Mr. or Mrs. Collins would come and collect it, with no idea how they could possibly have forgotten to take their car when they'd stopped off to buy a newspaper and some tea bags, or a tube of toothpaste.

Oops, eh?

The walk back to the house was difficult. I kept not wanting to notice anyone or anything. I stared down at the pavement trying to block out any tempting morsels of nastiness my inner beast might feast upon. Luckily there were no arguments between arrogant bastard boyfriends and their submissive other halves. I didn't cross paths or swords with any robbers or muggers or rapists. But still, try clenching your entire body from teeth to toes and mouth to mind. Then hold it for an extended period whilst trying to walk and avoid coming into contact with that anyone or anything I mentioned.

Didn't think so.

The street the house was on was quiet. It always had been. The type of street that didn't exist in too many places any more. There had never been, in all the time my parents had live there (which was from around when I was twelve or so), any muggings or rowdy neighbours to complain to the council about. I didn't recall any burnt out cars and could only pick out one or two burglaries from behind the mist of my memory. It was sleepy. A little boring in fact. But right then I was pleased and welcoming to Sleepy, Boring and all the other Seven Dwarves. They could cosy on up with me any time. Room and board, bed and breakfast, milk and cookies.

The house backed onto a playing field. Cricket used to be played on a Sunday afternoon, the lazy ones with light aircraft buzzing across the sky and the smell of fresh cut grass sitting at your window. Five-a-side football was Tuesday nights and the rest of the week was taken up by kids on bicycles and dogs off leads. A high wooden slatted fence separated field and garden - high enough for the spectatorship of any matches to be only possible from either the bathroom or my childhood bedroom - but I'd long had the knack of scaling it thanks to an old post, a tree and a lot of bruised knees. A hollowed out stone with a concealed compartment held, as ever, a key to the back door and I let myself in, locking the door behind me.

Chapter Eleven

The kitchen, which the back door opened into, was cold. Icy fingers reached into my lungs, dripping icicles as they passed. The house had been empty for a long time, and it felt like it. Barren. Lifeless. Soulless. I was an intruder, undesired and undesirable. Even my breath seemed to echo and I was half surprised that I couldn't see the cloud as I exhaled. I stood still for a long moment as I waited for the house to recognise me and welcome me into its bosom, a long lost child come home from the wars.

Except the wars were still being waged, and I'd wager I was the one doing the waging.

After a while the house seemed to relax a little, allowing me in but still not dropping its guard entirely. That was fine. I couldn't expect any more. I doubted I'd welcome myself back if I'd known what I'd done. The temperature rose slightly to a more acceptable level and the icy fingers melted in my throat enough to let me breathe easier.

I stepped forward and suddenly I was home. I was the little kid bouncing down the stairs on my bum. I was older, being told off for dragging mud in from playing football on the school fields. Older yet, my head down the toilet as I 'celebrated' my first attempt at being drunk, swearing I'd never touch alcohol again - until the next time. Bringing home my first girlfriend and being told that the only pair of tits that were going up those stairs were my mother's. Storming out after yet another argument over something that just wasn't fair. The last day of my last school. The first day of my first job. Memories filled me up and spilled out, bursting from my eyes in the form of tears. Not tears of regret or of pain, but of relief. Of release.

Home. It hadn't always been sweet - it had, in fact, mostly been sour - but it had always been home. Regardless of whether I'd been in exile in Scunthorpe or living with friends or girlfriends, this house, with its high back fence and its crappy mobile phone reception and its ever-flaking banister running up the stairs, was still home with a capital aitch. How crap was that then? Wherever I may wander? Oh yes. There was no place like it. A father who seemed to think I was an irritation rather than a blessing. A mother who seemed to let him. And a name that made sure the kids at school rubbed my parents' contempt of me right in my face.

The name's Sin. Spit in your eye, wish I could die.

But hey, what doesn't kill us can only make us stronger, right? So I'm the sum total, carry the one, of my father's distaste and my mother's disinterest? It's a wonder I turned out normal, don't you think?

The tears dried and the house became less of a mystical being, guardian of my childhood, and more of a simple building. It was, finally, exactly what it should have been - a refuge. Joy and I had kept the house on after our parents' death, her not needing to sell it and me not wanting to. It had become our escape from the pains of the world; somewhere we could go and just be. No phone calls (the phone had been disconnected when dear dad spent the bill money on a nag in the 4:30 and had never been reconnected) and no visitors. In the street that time forgot, we were able to kick back and chill. Dad had never won on the horses, but Mum had once won on the only lottery ticket she'd ever bought. Not a single penny of the hundred thousand or so she'd received came the way of either myself or my sister, but there was enough left after their death to keep paying the bills for their house. As such, we didn't touch their money but came and went as we pleased and the house stayed in the family.

Maybe it was a reminder of our childhood. Weren't they supposed to be the best days of your life? Perhaps we kept the house to make sure the thorn of memory stayed stuck in our side.

It might seem strange that, when others had their own home and a villa in Spain, we kept one in the same town for our sanctuary, but a change was as good as... well, a change. 'Different' was sometimes all that was needed to recharge our Evereadies and spring that spark back up our behinds. Maybe a villa, complete with pool, palms trees and piñatas, tucked away on a Mediterranean beach would have been better. Then we could *really* get away from the grinding and grouching. But our parents' was, obviously, much closer and you didn't have to book flights to get there. And everyone spoke English (although they might be as difficult to understand), and you could be sure not to miss an episode of Coronation Street or some other wonderfully exciting television program. It was only odd days, or the occasional weekend here and there, but it still felt like we were getting away - packing up our troubles in our old tote bag and trying to find that smile, smile, smile again. In more cases than not, it was successful.

The house wasn't entirely as it had been when we'd taken over ownership. We hadn't quite stamped our own brand of melancholy on the rooms, but we'd modified them enough to dilute some of the memories and exorcise most of the Ghosts of Childhoods Past. Simple things like changing a carpet here, painting the walls there, emptying a room and sealing it off completely... That was the main bedroom. Ma and Pa's Love Pad, as he used to call it. Calling it that was one thing. Advertising it as such at any time of the day or night, was quite another. Didn't he know doors were meant to be closed? Once the door was plasterboarded over, both Joy and I could walk past it without having to suppress a shudder. We tried hanging a picture - the Grand Canyon at sunset - over the area to distract us from what was behind it, but the picture never wanted to stay up and would often try to leap off as we walked past. We put it down to the weight of our footsteps on the landing, or maybe an earthquake in Central China - or anything close to normal. Of course we didn't know then what we, or rather what I know now. Now I'd be more inclined to think the house was shuddering along with me. Or that my own shudders were not confined to my body, and were reaching out, holding the wall for support.

I looked around the kitchen. The toaster was in the same place as the last time I was here. The kettle too. The clock on the oven was lit and the little colon in the middle of the time was blinking, so the electricity was still on. It felt as if there should have been a layer of dust across everything and that I would be brushing aside cobwebs as I moved. It had lain empty, dormant, for such a long time that, if this had been a Hammer film, the house would have given itself over to spiders and rats and bears, oh my! Well, maybe not the bears, eh? Not in Grimsby - except for after kick out time at the Tavern on a Saturday night.

Ah. Olivia.

Joy, bless her little rotting eye socket, had the foresight, long ago, to employ a lovely old Philipino woman from three doors down as a cleaner. Apparently (I'd only met her a couple of times), she was known to be both meticulous and thorough, and her mouth would stay zipped into the bargain. Discretion was all part of the job description Joy told me once, a fact that was confirmed when it emerged that the doctor whose surgery she kept spick and span and shipety shape was using his after hours appointments for certain liaisons he might want to keep to himself. Olivia had discovered him whilst looking for a socket for her hoover. The physical examination he'd been performing had much less to do with medicine than it had to do with, well, let's say biology. This discovery only came to light three months later when Angela Simpson, the 'patient', went about as public as she could to a packed waiting room, because Dr. Hurst wouldn't keep his promise to leave his wife of thirty years.

So Olivia, it became known, was one woman whom you could trust, and this prompted an influx of requests for her services. Whether that was due to her cleaning abilities or her silence, I was never entirely sure, but you had to hand it to her. She knew how to whip a duster across a coffee table as well as she knew how to keep incidents such as the good doctor's dilly-dally to herself. And she could vacuum in all the nooks and crannies too, much the same as Dr. Hurst seemed to be attempting to do, by all accounts. The kitchen surfaces were testament to one side of her talents, and I hoped, if she came whilst I was still here, that me remaining undiscovered would be testament to the other.

Because Joy and I were not at the house too often, and we were house trained, Olivia was only asked to visit once a month for a spruce up here and there. That could have been four weeks ago or that morning, I didn't know, but the lack of dust on the worktop implied that I had at least a week or two before I'd have to think of explaining my surprise return from my travels across South America. Well, Brazil and Mexico sounds so much more exotic than a mental institution, doesn't it? It also meant that she'd kept up her job, and there was still money being paid into her account. Aren't direct debits a wonderful thing?

So. Ghoulies and ghosties and all manner of ferocious beasties were not, one would hope, lurking in the crevices and behind the furniture to gobble me up for lunch. Yay. Christopher Lee wasn't ready to jump out, gagging for a pint of my very own ruby red. Hammer was humdrum and Craven was calm and a zombie wasn't poised to rip off my arm. Yay, again.

I still felt as though the house was watching me, remaining a touch wary, waiting for... something. Well, let it. I wasn't an intruder, I was just maybe the prodigal son returning. If the house didn't like that, tough. It wasn't as if I had a lot of options, was it? I daren't go to my own home, just in case there'd be an unwelcoming committee. This was our safe haven so it would just have to get a grip and be safe, and a haven.

I briefly thought about checking the fridge and cupboards to see if there was any food, but then decided that, after a couple of years, I'd rather hope there wasn't. I didn't want to be accosted by a rogue ciabatta or raving pot noodle. I decided the toilet was my best bet. Let my bladder relax a bit before it burst its banks. The bathroom was upstairs, but there was a small room with a toilet and wash basin at the bottom of the stairs. The 'little toilet' as we'd always called it. Not little as in a five year old could sit on it comfortably, but little as in big brother, little brother, red lorry, yellow lolly. Thinking about it had suddenly added about a gallon to the confines of my bladder, so I figured Little Bro was my best bet. I left the kitchen and walked along the hall. The walls and the pictures and the light bulbs all kept their beady eyes on me as I went and I almost asked for a little privacy please!

But that would have meant I was talking to a house. Haven't I mentioned I wasn't quite insane?

Anyway. I gave my bladder the relief it deserved, washed and dried my hands, then stood in back in the hall. I didn't know what to do. Sit and watch television? Sleep? Shower? After so long with my daily routine being firmly regimented, I was somewhat lost at the prospect of having to make a decision myself. My escape and the events since had more or less played themselves out, with me simply being a participant swept along with the current. Now I'd washed up on the shore of my own free will, and I didn't have a clue which direction to take. I'd only planned, after changing from suicide to flight, to find out where I was and end up somewhere. I was Somewhere.

So what now?

I looked down at myself and realised the clothes that I'd taken from Martin's bedroom were more than a little too big. They hung off me as if I was an extra in the next Rick Moranis film, Honey

I Shrunk the Neighbour's Postman or something. It didn't matter now. Within these walls I no longer had to be the escaped lunatic, nor did I need to pretend to be the dedicated doctor. I was just me, Sin, a lost boy. If only Peter Pan or Kiefer Sutherland were here to help me. Well, maybe not Kiefer, he'd be a pain in the neck. But young Pan. A quick trip to Neverland, and straight on till morning, would be mighty fine. No passport required. Did Neverland have duty free? Could you buy alcohol and cigarettes cheap? Did Captain Hook have a black market in Bells or Benson & Hedges? Customs would have a job trying to impound that little lot.

A shower. That would be good. Wash away the grime both inside and out. Maybe even a shave, if the battery on my razor that I kept in the bathroom cabinet still had a residue of charge left in it. My own clothes. It would help me feel sane. Normal. Even if I wasn't, entirely.

An hour later I was looking at myself in the mirror in my bedroom. It was a three bedroomed house, and Joy and I had taken one of the smaller two each for when we visited, the main one - the Lurve Pad - being wiped from the memory of the house like chalk off a blackboard. The rooms were almost identical to each other. We'd refrained from applying any of our personal touches here. We didn't want this place to be a surrogate home, merely a refuge. So there were no photos or knick-knacks or stuffed toys dotted around. A wardrobe, double bed, bedside cabinet and mirror. That was it. Functional rather than fancy. Downstairs, I'd upgraded the TV and the sound system, and Joy had brought one of her reclining armchairs, but nothing else. It stayed as it had when our parents had lived here. The same tired wallpaper and worn carpets. The same faded curtains and the same settee you sank into so far your bum was almost touching the floor. Neither of us had the inclination to improve something that meant so little to us.

And it wasn't home. It wasn't, however I'd felt when I walked back in. It was a house I'd lived in for a while when I was younger. Did I have a Home? No. I wasn't a nomad, but I hadn't settled in any one place long enough for me to become attached. To grow roots. Did I protesteth too much? Methinks, possibly, verily.

Oh well.

My reflection regarded me solemnly. What had I become? What was I reduced to? An outcast. A fugitive. But hold on a God-damned minuet! I'd walked into that place. Surely, now I was out, they had no claim on me? I hadn't been committed. I hadn't been dragged there by those men in their white coats. It was *my* decision to jump on the groovy train to Nutsville. So it should be *my* decision to get off at the next station. The thing was, I didn't think Dr. Connors would see it that way. He wouldn't appreciate one of his pets escaping. Once you were in his 'care', your own decisions were a thing of the past and became something he made on your behalf, for your benefit, of course. Such a nice man.

I regarded my reflection regarding me, reflecting. This felt like it could be the first day of the rest of my life. It could also be the last for a lot of other people. I was teetering on the edge. I wasn't sure if this precipice was an abyss, hungrily waiting to swallow me whole, or a whizzy-wee slide I could zoom down into the great big ball pool of everlasting contentment. I leaned towards the former, although leaning towards anything this close to the brink was a more than a little dangerous.

As I dressed, with jeans that fitted and a t-shirt that was much more my style, I pondered. Have you ever pondered? Streams of consciousness ping-ponging around in your head like some old arcade game, turning into snakes of thought that twisted and coiled? My mind was like Spiderman swinging through New York, slinging webs and swerving this way and that, his direction entirely dependant on which skyscraper his web attached itself to. I tried to focus, concentrate on one building in particular, aim for the Empire State of my mind, but the Green Goblin kept throwing exploding obstacles in my way, scattering my thoughts and sending me spinning to the ground far below.

Something was different.

Something had changed.

I could... I couldn't control it, but I could... feel it. I could rein it in. It started on its own, creeping out like smoky fingers, grasping at their victims, but I knew the fire had been lit, and I could extinguish it. I could STOP it.

The boyfriend who was a bastard and a bully. The former rapist and his wife and their fire, willing to hand me over because of the possible danger to them and their baby. I made it happen, but I made it stop.

Something was different. It had changed.

Was it me? Was the battle between good and evil, or at least grey and slightly darker grey, inside me finally being won? Was Anakin resisting the pull of the Dark Side? What? And possibly more importantly, how?

Could I hone it? Possibly gain enough control to stop it altogether? It might be, though, that it, whatever it was, had to be released occasionally - a safety vent to stop me exploding. If that was the case, then maybe I could direct it. Channel the force or the will or the power into something harmless or something that wouldn't be missed. A fence post. A round of toast. A politician. If I kept it inside, if I could keep it inside, and I did go pop, I didn't know what I might take with me. There could just be a puff of smoke with only my shoes left behind, or I could take the entire street along for the ride into death. Maybe not just the street. How about the town, or more.

I just didn't know. But something *had* changed. And I could only think that it was for the better. I could only hope it was for the better.

In a folder in a box on a shelf in a cupboard under the stairs was an envelope. In the envelope in the box blah-de-blah was my life. Credit card, bank card, passport, the lot. My life, such as it had been, could be stored in an A5 sized brown envelope. The sum of me, carry the one. Beneath my envelope was another belonging to Joy. It contained only her passport and her driving license, the credit and bank cards long since being defunct and cut up. These two items, though, I couldn't dispose of as easily as I could her credit card. Was it because they had her photograph on? Was it because, by virtue of being her ID, they'd somehow become part of her? That, I think, was closer to the truth. I'd lost her, but keeping these items, especially in such close proximity to my own, somehow meant we were still together on some plane.

I opened her passport and smiled. She'd always hated the photo. False smile to match the fake eyelashes. She was looking forward to renewing the passport and, along with it, her photo. It still had almost a year to go when she killed herself. I supposed, going by my dream the other night, she could pretty much go anywhere she wanted now, so a passport was somewhat redundant. Useful thing, death, then.

I slipped what remained of my sister back into her envelope and put it away. Taking my own little packet of Me, I went back upstairs to my room. The living room would maybe have been a better place to kick back and think, but I knew what I was like. I'd turn the TV on and watch inane programmes try to sort out the lives of inane people, from those that couldn't find a new home on their own to those that couldn't find themselves. Reality television in its many forms would latch on to me like a leech and suck the will to do anything from me until it was full and bloated and dropped off. By then the stars would have turned and the Doctor's friends would have come knocking, no doubt.

So back to my room. Maybe a short nap. Then lights, camera, *action*, with no need for a stunt double.

It was dark when I awoke. Well, night-time anyway. A street lamp stood guard outside, lighting the room with an anaemic glow that I would normally have blocked out with a blackout blind. So much for a short nap. Sleep had fooled me, hiding behind the curtain of my hyped up energy, sneaking out when my back was turned and my eyes were closed to steal the day from me.

Joy was sitting at the end of my bed.

Chapter Twelve

"Hey there, sleepy head," she said.

I smiled, yawned and stretched. "Hey sis."

Clearly I was still asleep. Maybe it wasn't actually night-time and the street light wasn't swathing the room in a sickly yellow. At least Joy's face was in one piece - for now anyway. I could do without having to hand her sections of skin while she spoke or flicking maggots that crawled my way, even if it was only a dream. She looked good. Better than the other night. Her smile was back to full power and her eyes flared with a fire that even the chill of a house left unheated for years couldn't defeat. I pushed myself up and looked around.

It was a little disappointing. My dream world bedroom was exactly the same as my waking world one. I didn't have a four-poster bed. There were no sumptuous carpets or fitted wardrobes and a huge plasma screen TV wasn't hanging on the wall opposite. It was the same impersonal (deliberately so, I know) room I'd gone to bed in. You'd think my subconscious would embellish things just a little wouldn't you? Just for fun?

Well, I suppose you could count my dead sister as an embellishment.

"Cheers," she said. "I'm just the best you could do next to a four-poster bed, am I? A decoration? An adornment? Thanks a bunch, boy."

I hated it when she called me boy. Always had. She knew it, which was why she did it.

"Think of it as an enhancement," I told her. "An improvement. You're giving the room some spirit!"

"You know," said Joy, "you should be on stage. Sweeping it."

"I know, you said that," said I. "I do have my moments."

"Unfortunately, that's all they are - moments."

Touché, said the turtle.

"Anyway," she said. "Enough of this frivolity. You'd sleep the world away, you know."

Would if I could. But uh-oh. I knew that tone.

"You've got your business head on."

Joy shook her head, her long locks putting Pantene to shame. The Grim Reaper should open a beauty salon. Death seemed to do Joy justice. She put her hands to her ears.

"This isn't my business head," she said, suddenly performing a perfect Worzel Gummidge impression by pulling up and separating her head from her body. While I stared wide eyed, she laid it down on the bed next to another that had somehow materialised. She picked up the new one, which was identical to the first, and put it on the newly vacant space atop her torso. "THIS is my business head."

I looked back on the bed but there was nothing there. A pair of small dips, though, were proof that something had been.

"Embellish *that*, boy," she said.

Well, that wasn't going to be easy. It would be hard for me to top a trick such as self-decapitation. Even I, the Mighty Me, couldn't outperform the dream of a ghost of a sister.

"You win."

"Yes," she said. "I do. And stop thinking of me as a dream, please! It's not good for one's ego, you know?"

"Well you please stop reading my thoughts, then."

"Hey," she prodded my arm. "You're the one who's convinced I'm actually *in* your head, so I'm bound to know what you're thinking if you're the one thinking of me!"

Erm... Hold one. Let me figure that out.

Right. Got it.

Hey, that proved me right, didn't it?

"Not necessarily," she said with a grin. "Being dead might just make me telepathic. I may be able to really read your thoughts. I could be a psychic spirit."

Septic, more like, I thought, my mind flashing back to her dripping facial features back in the forest.

"Yes, very funny. Let me get you that broom."

"So come on then," I said. "Convince me. Show me I'm really awake and you're not just a figment of my warped imagination. Prove to me you're the ghost of my sister and not just a recurring dream I'm having because I'm feeling alone now and need someone and you're all my mangled mind can manage."

"God," Joy said, rolling her eyes (but not literally out of her head this time). "The boy wants a soapbox now! Maybe he should see a psychiatrist to sort out his abandonment issues!"

"Stop..."

"...Calling you boy. I know, I know. OK. It's just habit to tease you."

Well, that was true.

"Listen," she said, resting her hand on mine. It was warm like before. Not chilled or clammy. Not ghostly or zombie-fied. "Believe what you want to believe. It's up to you. I don't have time, *you* don't have time for me to prat about proving myself to you. If I'm real then listen to me, if I'm not then still listen to me, because then you'd be listening to yourself!"

OK, I get the point.

"OK," I said. "I'll listen."

Joy smiled and I thought back to when we were kids. She could always make me feel better. Whenever I'd been the brunt of a particularly savage stream of abuse from our father, Joy just had to look at me, hold my hand and smile. Dad could shove it then as far as I was concerned. I realised, later of course, just how and why she could make me feel that way. Joy was joy and I was sin. Her curse had led her to her eventual death, but it had been my salvation at the time.

She suddenly hugged me, hard. When she pulled away she had tears in her eyes.

"Joy?"

"I'm OK," she said. "Just... thanks for that, that's all."

"For what?"

"For making me feel that I did something good. For making me feel like I wasn't a waste."

"A waste? Of course you weren't! You helped so many people!"

"Yes, but you're my baby bro. They don't matter. You do. And you had it harder when we were kids than I did. So thanks."

I felt that I should have been thanking her, not the other way around, but I didn't say so. She would, it seemed, know what I was thinking anyway, so I didn't have to.

"Let's walk," she said.

"Walk? Where?" I didn't like the idea of leaving the house. I was like Quasimodo but without the bell... or his hump. This was my Sanctuary. Joy was a sibling version of Esmeralda. Going outside held me open to attack and capture and all manner of unpleasantness.

"It'll be fine. Come on."

"Where are we going?"

"Seven Hills," she said.

The Seven Hills. Were there seven? I didn't know. It was the name, locally at least - it wouldn't appear on any map as that - for an area of waste ground near our parents' house. Perhaps waste was a little too harsh. Undeveloped was closer to the truth. They just hadn't managed to get round to building on it, a fact that constantly surprised me. They, the council, the developers or whoever, hadn't yet crammed three hundred or so town houses into the little plot of land. It wasn't so little but nor was it a vast expanse of unkempt and untamed wilderness. It was an opportunity untapped for some enterprising company, and that tap would be turned on full before too long, I shouldn't wonder. Near to my house in Scunthorpe there'd been a small area on the tight corner of a junction. You'd have thought a couple of houses with smallish gardens would have happily fitted on there. Nope. Forget the gardens. A communal parking area surrounded by a claustrophobic collection of almost a dozen dwellings that you'd be lucky enough to be able to swing a cat in, if you were lucky enough to be able to fit yourself and a cat in. On the Seven Hills you could probably slot a small town. Maybe a Tetney sized village.

The Seven Hills. Reputed to be inhabited by rats the size of small dogs that wouldn't so much as nip at your ankles as take your leg off at the knee. Maybe that's why it was left alone. Perhaps the Beast of Bodmin or the Hound of the Baskervilles wandered loose and people were too afraid to set foot in there. Or the dog-sized rats were a new, protected species, and scientists wanted their natural habitat to remain untouched so they could be studied. Nessie herself might be holidaying there, taking a break from her Loch and from the unending stream of tourists and investigators. Or maybe it was just that it would be such a colossal project to level off the wildly uneven and wildly wild ground that no one had been bothered. I mean, who'd want a house so off kilter the water wouldn't stay in the bath or you'd open the front door to go to work in the morning and fall out? It wasn't really a selling point, was it?

So the Hills, all Seven of them remained. Not quite Rome, but good for roaming. I just hoped I didn't become the Nero of this particular town. I couldn't play the fiddle so maybe that was a plus for me.

Joy and I walked in almost silence. I couldn't think what to say, because I knew I wouldn't be able to stop myself asking questions she wouldn't be able to answer. She might not believe it, but I did listen sometimes. She couldn't say, that's what she'd told me the last time we met. The words just didn't want to come out, like petulant children when they were refused an ice cream. So questions such as "What's it like to be dead?" or "Do you get cable TV?" were redundant. It would be like talking to a brick wall, except the brick wall wouldn't whinge at me for asking. Or if it did I wouldn't be able to understand it, not being fluent in Brick. A smattering of conversation stopped it becoming complete silence, but it was mainly silly comments about nothing. Talking crap to avoid talking sense. Still, it could have been uncomfortable, but it wasn't. We'd spoken enough crap to each other over the years for this episode to be less awkward than it might otherwise have been. I was sure all would be revealed when we were finally in the domain of the giant rat.

The air echoed in the darkness - if this was a dream, it added a touch of the macabre to my mental invention. I had to accept, though, that this wasn't sleepytime. I was wide awake. Night had fallen and the streets were drifting amongst the twilight, waiting for their chance to get a little kip themselves. I saw the odd moth battling with a street lamp – dusty winged Don Quixotes and their windmills. I saw my breath clouding in the light chill, hopefully not my soul escaping before the trouble to come that Joy had promised. I hadn't checked the time, my watch was still in the safe back at the institution, but it felt as if it was around 8 o'clock or so. I'd slept the day away. I was refreshed, but I wasn't sure I could afford to lose those hours. Dr. Connors might have simply thought "Oh well, that's one less loony to worry about," but I doubted it. Once you had handed yourself over to him, you were his property. Until he said otherwise.

As we walked we, naturally, passed other pedestrians. At first I didn't notice that anything was out of the ordinary. Or rather, I didn't notice that anything was *not* out of the ordinary. We could have been simply a brother and sister out walking - going to the shop or the pub or the cinema. Ordinary. No one would know one of us was serial killer and the other was dead. And that was the point. How could we be seen as a couple? Whether Joy was a spirit or just the product of my own tortured mind, she would be invisible, wouldn't she? I'd look like a loon, chatting to myself - or at best someone talking through a bluetooth headset which, on closer inspection didn't exist. But Joy wasn't there, not in corporeal, physical, real terms.

You'd think.

So why did the guy in the torn jeans, tinny music spilling out from his tiny earphones, make eye contact with her? And the girl who was only just managing to keep atop the heels she was wearing walk - after a fashion - around her? Why were people acting as if she was there when she couldn't, shouldn't, *wasn't*?

Ask me another. Unlike my sister who most probably knew the answer but wasn't allowed to say, I really didn't have a clue.

I wanted to ask. Did she know that? Had she read my thoughts - or even been my thoughts if she was part of my mind -

but was waiting for me to voice my question? To admit what it must mean?

OK. So be it.

I saw dead people and, it seemed, so the hell did everyone else. Unless I was somehow projecting my own brand of Krayzeee onto each and every person who happened by, Joy was a walking corpse, or ghost, or hallucination. Take your pick. What's your fancy? Reanimated cadaver anyone? Ghost of sister passed?

I said it.

"You're real."

"Well whup-de-do."

"I suppose I can't escape it."

"Nope."

"So what are you then? Are you a ghost? Or a zombie? Or one of my delusions made real?"

"Yep."

"Yes what?"

"I am a ghost, or I'm a zombie, or I'm a little pinch of Sin's Delirium."

She could be as aggravating as me sometimes.

"Sin's Delirium," I said. "Sounds like something you'd put in a curry."

Joy laughed and the world clicked back into its groove for a little while longer. At least until I derailed it again.

The Seven Hills were surrounded by four long roads. Littlecoates Road was home to Western School, which was my own seat of learning as a kid, a golf course, a hotel and a residential home for the elderly. Yarborough Road was a sweeping curve where, at its apex, had once been a video rental store owned by a friend of mine's family. They'd had an Alsatian dog that had suffered from a growth hormone imbalance. By the time it was fully grown you could have slung a saddle over its back and ridden off into the sunset crying "Yeehaaaah." On Chelmsford Avenue resided the water company's water tower (between the road and the Hills) and another school. Once it, the school, had been 'affectionately' referred to as Pram Land, a reference to the abnormally high pregnancy rate amongst its pupils. About ten years ago it had been turned into a sixth form college, quite a successful one by all accounts, and the prams had been traded in for a crèche. Along the fourth side was Cambridge Road and this held the main entrance into the Hills. For a hundred metres or so a low metal fence, less than knee high, served as the barrier between residential and run-amok. How anyone thought such a barrier would hold back a pack of raving rabid rats, I didn't know, but it did. There were never, to my knowledge, any reported cases of individuals being mauled or eviscerated as they walked by, nor were there tales of folk going missing in the Hills' vicinity, possibly being dragged under the barrier and off to the rats' lair for the main course of a Sunday roast, without it being roasted.

We were turning onto Cambridge Road when a high pitched voice clawed my ears from somewhere off to the side.

"Sin!"

Poo. I suppose it had to happen sooner or later, but why couldn't it have been so much later? And why did it have to be while I was with whatever remained of my dead sister, who refused to not be seen?

I recognised the voice immediately. Wendy Carpenter. Long time friend and co-conspirator of my mother. Putting the world to rights by tearing apart the reputations of their friends and neighbours. She had the dress sense of a hippo, bathed probably once every full moon, and was the proud owner of a voice that could strip wallpaper at twenty paces. I remember wondering, when I was much younger and she'd visited mum for one of their regular Saturday afternoon shredding sessions, if I held an orange near her while she was ranting, would its skin peel off by itself, helped along by her fingernails-on-blackboard voice.

I never tried it though, fruit being something only yearned for on a semi-permanent diet of chips and fried anything. I use the term 'diet' very loosely.

I stopped and turned, a smile trying desperately to not become a grimace.

"Wendy," I said. A hint of enthusiasm struggled to make itself heard and was very nearly successful.

"Sin! How are you! It's been so long, I almost didn't recognise you there."

Not long enough.

"Hello, Wendy. I'm doing OK. Same old, you know."

Her breath smelled of old onions. Her coat was the same one she'd worn so many years ago - grassy green with a faux-fur collar and cuffs. It seemed cleaner than I remembered. She was wearing her slippers, dark brown moccasin style ones with worn toes. I don't think she had ever had a normal pair of shoes on her feet. I could only ever recall slippers or those flip flops that slap-scrape-slapped as she walked.

"Cyril died, you know."

Cyril was her husband. I would say long suffering, as anyone married to Wendy Carpenter must be, but he spent so much time in the Oak Tree pub, drinking pints of bitter with his nicotine-stained fingers and his little coven of drinking buddies, enveloped in their impenetrable cloak of cigarette smoke, I don't think he really noticed anyway.

"That's a shame," I said.

"Yes," she said. "It was. He was a good man."

I didn't know why she was springing this little snippet of information on me. I hadn't seen her in something like two decades. Saying 'Hi' then jumping in with news of her deceased husband seemed a little random to me. Maybe it was because I was the only person along this street whom she hadn't told. Or because she'd spent so long in my company when I was a child, she felt a weird motherly connection and just wanted to share. Either way, I feigned interest, just hoping this encounter would be over with quickly so I could escape with my equally deceased sister to wherever she wanted to take me.

"Was he ill?" I asked. Yes, I know. Why lead the conversation on when I wanted it over and done. I couldn't help it.

My dislike for the woman was not as strong as I seemed to want to think. I did try to say that I wasn't all bad.

"No," she said. "It was a quick death. He slipped on a patch of piss in the Oak Tree toilets, and hit his head on one of the urinals. They said he wouldn't have known a thing."

If I'd been eating something at that point, I think I would have choked on it. If I'd been drinking, then there was a good chance that Wendy would have been wearing it.

"Really?"

"Yes. The Oak Tree were brilliant after. They didn't charge me for the broken urinal, and they let me hold the wake there after his funeral. They even paid for the first drink for everyone."

Such generosity, I thought. I couldn't help but feel for this poor woman. She seemed just a step up from pathetic. Lonely. No one to share gossip with and no one to complain to. Still wrapped up in a life that had left her behind, cocooned in its memory to avoid facing her empty house. She'd sit in Cyril's favourite chair, with its worn arms and dirty patch on the seat where he'd drop his ash from his cigarette, rubbing it in rather than brushing it off. She'd have the television on, but not be watching it. She'd stare out of the window but not be seeing, her eyes as vacant as her life.

"Are you ok?" Joy asked.

Wendy jumped slightly. Her eyes blinked and she looked at Joy as if only just seeing her.

"Sorry love," she said. "I hardly even noticed you. I must need these glasses checking."

I felt like telling her that it wasn't her glasses at fault, nor was it her eyes. It was her ability to see ghosts that, perhaps, wasn't quite as good as it might be. And no optician had a lens for that. I didn't though.

"That's OK," Joy said, smiling her smile.

You could almost have seen the candle that had remained extinguished in the depths of Wendy's gut for all these years suddenly ignite, a flame dancing into life and banishing the darkness. The change to her stance and her features was immediately obvious. She straightened, the slouch that had dragged her forward and down - in more ways than one - vanishing. Her eyes defogged and had the beginnings of a sparkle.

"Well," she said, her voice having lost the quiver that hadn't been noticeable until it wasn't there. "I have to be going. Things to do, you know."

"People to see?" asked Joy.

"Who knows," Wendy said. "I haven't seen my grandson in months. He should know his nanna."

"That he should," I said. "How old is he?"

"He's four. He's a bundle of energy with a mouth to match." Wendy laughed and I ignored the way her stale onion breath misted the air and seemed to float, semi-solid towards me. I suppressed the urge to swat it away like an annoying wasp.

"Sounds wonderful," said Joy. I could almost see her voice wrapping its velvet cloak around Wendy's shoulders.

"Yes, doesn't it," said Wendy. Her own voice had dropped an octave and no longer felt like splintered glass in my ears. "Take care, the pair of you."

"We will," Joy and I said.

I reached out and held her hand and she gripped mine back. I would never have suspected that Wendy Carpenter might have a human, or humane side, or that I would voluntarily touch her hand. I could only ever have envisaged her with a knife in her hand, spying out who's back she was going to bury it in. That she might have feelings or be worthy of sympathy - not that sympathy necessarily required someone to be 'worthy' - was something I would have bet I'd never consider. It was a warm moment, made all the better because it was unexpected.

"Come on," said Joy. "Let's go."

We turned and crossed the road.

"You did a good thing there," I said.

"Thanks." She sounded sad or wistful.

"See," I said, "it's not all bad."

"No," she replied, looking at me pointedly. "It's not."

I was sure more meaning was hidden in that statement that I could immediately see. She was telling me something without telling me. I wasn't going to work it out though. It was, I thought, something that would come to me in due time, dragging us with it.

"You can still do it then?"

"It seems so, doesn't it?"

"It doesn't stop when you..." I couldn't make myself say it.

"Die? Kill yourself?" I nodded. "No. As long as you're here, it's there."

"So..." I began, but she stopped me, her hand on my arm.

"So I didn't need to do myself in. It didn't stop." She dropped her hand and turned away. "It's different now. I don't feel such a need. I'm not suffocated by their problems. And anyway, I'm not here all the time. I'm only here now for you."

"For me?"

Joy nodded but didn't say anything. She pointed ahead of us and I knew the subject was closed, at least for now.

"Come on then," I said. Either all would become clear, or it wouldn't. If the hood stayed over my head, tied tightly at my neck, blocking everything out, then there was nothing I could do to untie the knot or cut the cord. I'd simply have to wait to see if Joy, or somebody else, would remove it for me. My life, their hands. I just hoped 'They' didn't drop it.

The low metal fence glowed in the streetlight and flashed in the beam of the cars that passed. Beyond it was a blackness that felt all consuming, as if it had eaten the land and the air and was waiting for us to cross so it could devour us too.

"Get a grip!" said Joy, shaking her head. "Life is allowed to be more mellow than drama, you know."

"Will you stop doing that! It's rude!"

"Well, stop thinking such crap then."

"If you stopped reading my thoughts, you wouldn't have any crap to complain about!"

"Nernerner," she said in a whine that a two year old would have been proud of. I didn't have an answer to that, but at least it managed to break the beginnings of tension. Joy's suicide might have been a complete waste, but perhaps it wasn't. If it was better for her then did that make it OK? Were we given these lives to do with as we wished? And if that wish included ending them, disposing of them, was that still fine because free will dictated it was up to us?

Of course that was if we were given these lives. If some Higher Power was running an assembly line of souls to populate the Earth and maybe the Universe (who knew?). Or Life could well have been an accident and we were just here. Living. No purpose or direction, just *being*. In which case, I don't think anything mattered, did it?

But hey-ho daddy-o, it's off to hell we go. Free will - or was it Free Will, Will being William, or Bill to his friends, a man locked up in prison for the past ten years for a crime he didn't commit? Anyway, free will was looking to be pretty scarce at the moment. My will certainly hadn't been free whilst in the mental home (maybe it had been locked up with Bill) and it had been hijacked by my sister since then. I felt as if I was just along for the ride and wished I'd had the foresight to strap myself in.

Still, whether I was being dramatic or not, I had to take a deep breath and steel myself before stepping over. I'd been in there more times than I could remember when I was young. The Hills were an adventure and a dare for a kid, and I'd had plenty of both. My courage, or innocence, had faded with the passing years, however. I could tell myself that it was only a sense of the danger in walking on such uneven ground in the darkness that was making me wary. I could tell myself that, but I didn't necessarily believe it.

Something else waited for me and I was letting the ghost of my dead sister lead me to it. I was walking into a cellar, with a light that didn't work, and I was ignoring the streaks of blood on the walls and the sinister scratching sounds from below.

Chapter Thirteen

History doesn't relate whether Jonah, Gepetto and Pinocchio sat around a table eating pizza, sharing stories of prophecy and puppetry while in the belly of the whale, but I thought that I could relate to being swallowed whole. It wasn't quite in the realm of my hand disappearing as I pushed it into the visceral blackness, reappearing again when I pulled it out. I could still see my body and I could still see my sister. When I turned around I could still watch cars drive by and the dog sniffing at the lampost. But I wasn't sure whether they could see me. It felt like I was looking at them through glass, as if they were exhibits in a museum. Or perhaps I was the exhibit. No. I was Alice stepped through into Wonderland - a dark, eerie, hollow Wonderland inhabited by all manner of ghosties and ghoulies and horrible beasties.

As long as Joy wasn't the crazy Queen of Hearts.

"OK?"

Joy was looking at me questioningly. Had she read my thoughts just then? Did she see the glimmer of distrust? I couldn't help it. The situation... I was being led blindly. I was accepting of so much. Ignoring the things I could do and had done, this was my sister! She was *dead*! I'd attended her funeral, scattered her ashes. Yet here she was, large as life and twice as wonderful. Cryptic conversations and unknown destinations. I doubt I would have trusted the Pope or a second hand car salesman if they'd have been here instead of Joy. But what could I do? Walk away? To what? No. I had to follow through like a wet fart. See what came of it and clean up the mess afterwards.

This was my sister. If I had to place my trust, however blind it might be, in someone it could only be her. In the absence of that second hand car salesman anyway.

"I'm OK," I said. "Just a bit nervous."

I'd presented Joy with the perfect opportunity for her to put my mind at rest. Ease my fear. Calm my nerves.

"I know," she said.

No "It'll be fine" or "Don't worry."

Great.

"This way."

She started off towards the centre of the Seven Hills and I, as quickly as my slowly adjusting to a distinct lack of light eyes would allow, followed.

The Hills of the Seven were all around the outer boundary. A ring of guardians protecting an inner treasure, or maybe a circle of judges presiding over a central court. In some cases the slope down to the middle was gradual, the odd pothole or dip the only blemish on the smoothish surface. In others, a sharp incline, broken by gashes and crevices, led a perilous path that only a mountaineer or a twelve year old could confidently descend. Far over to the right, towards the end of Chelmsford and its intersection with the middle of Yarborough a group of trees huddled, afraid to venture forth into the Hills themselves. The Copse. Or the Corpse as some called it. The rest of the area was, in some places sparsely, in others more densely, covered in patchy grass and low bushes. Certainly the odd tree sprouted here and there, but they were lonely figures and struggled to keep their footing in this naturally hostile domain.

I could see none of this. A greyish, off-white glow surrounded us as we walked - or Joy walked and I stumbled. At first I thought it was nothing more than my eyes becoming accustomed to the dark, but it seemed off. It seemed artificial. And I noticed it flickering at the edges.

"Are you making this light?" I asked in a hushed voice. I wasn't necessarily afraid of being heard, but the setting and circumstance seemed to command a level of respect.

"Yes," Joy whispered. She felt it too, then. "I wouldn't want you to break your leg or kill yourself."

I assumed that was a private joke amongst suicide committers. What did you call someone who killed themselves? A suicider? Suicidalist? Did they have their own private Comedy Store in the hereafter? Comedians standing up on a stage telling death jokes?

"I'm half the man I used to be," says Eddie, who threw himself under a train.

"Guess which instrument I am," says Denise, who dined on a three-course meal of paracetomol, washed down by a bottle of the finest triple distilled vodka. "Maracas!" She shakes herself so you can hear the rattle.

Barry, who led a piece of hose from the exhaust pipe of his car into his window while he left the engine running and listened to Barry Manilow, goes one better. "And they say smoking will kill you!"

Hilarious.

"But we'll be seen," I said. The isolation felt so complete, we could have been alone in the world, the last survivors of the Human Race wandering the Earth in search of scraps of food, some shelter, or a tanning studio. Priorities, people. But we weren't. During the day, the Seven Hills were creepy. At night, especially this night, with this companion, they were Creepy. We were so completely *not* alone, I almost felt crowded, hemmed in by persons or creatures unknown, always dancing just outside the circle of light that Joy was creating.

"No, we won't," she said. She stopped and turned to me. "We're not in Kansas anymore, Sin," she said.

"Not in...?" I frowned. "Pardon?"

"Don't worry about it," she said. Well that was easy, wasn't it? OK, I won't worry. Just like that. "Nobody will see us."

It wasn't some*body* I was worried about. It was some*thing*. But not in Kansas? I assumed she meant Grimsby. So where?

"Where are we?"

"Just somewhere else," she said. "I don't know how... It's difficult to explain."

"And this light? Have you swallowed a 40 watt?"

"Oh," she said gesturing. "This is nothing. Practically a parlour trick. You'd be surprised Sin. So surprised."

"At what?"

"At what a person can really do."

"A person? Anyone? So it's not just the two of us? And it's not just because you're dead?"

"Well, maybe not then."

"Not what? Dead or us."

"Both." She took a step towards me and I barely stopped myself taking a step back. "I don't know if it's just us. It might be. We could be an accident or we could be a design. I don't know."

"And you couldn't tell me if you did, I suppose."

"Probably not. But I don't. But this light, yes. It's because I'm dead. It's like... ectoplasm or something."

I laughed and my voice sounded empty, as if someone had turned my bass right down, and still had their hand over the dial marked Treble.

"Ectoplasm? This isn't Ghostbusters, you know!"

Joy laughed then and she didn't sound flat. She sounded her usual vibrant self.

"No, I know, but I don't know what else to call it. It's like I'm the light. It's part of me, and I'm just... spreading it out."

"Well that makes sense," I said. Of course it didn't, except in a weird way, it did.

"Does it?"

"No. Not really."

Joy laughed again. The laugh was full of body and vigour, like a fine wine, but the magic she'd always had was missing. I wasn't suddenly uplifted. I didn't shine inside at the sound of it, as if I'd swallowed a box of Christmas decorations and someone had switched them on. She was right.

We weren't in Kansas anymore.

I shivered.

Joy had set off again. She was heading, as far as I could tell, towards the centre. Of course she was. Where else? The big nasty Thingy in films or books was always there. An altar had to be in a clearing in the middle of the forest. Clearings naturally didn't exist anywhere else. A pentagram to summon your friendly neighbourhood Djinn would be in the centre of the attic room. Not in a corner. Not etched in the floor of the downstairs toilet. Granted it could be painted (in blood, most likely) on the floor of a cellar, but if you didn't have one (and I didn't think many - if any - houses in Grimsby did) then the attic, loft or whatever you wanted to call it, would do. But the middle of the floor or no more. Why? Why not in front of the TV? You could catch Top Gear or Doctor Who whilst dripping blood from your self-sliced palm into a chalice to call your favourite hellish minion to do your bidding. Nope. It probably had something to do with the heart. The core. The centre of the Universe. The centre of the soul. Or even the centre of a ring doughnut, where all knowledge is alleged to exist, at least so says the Gospel According to Homer J. Simpson.

So down and in, down and in. I didn't remember the climb down being so steep or treacherous. I didn't remember gashes the size of a small car being rent out of the ground. Were they clawed by whatever beastie lay in wait below? Had it tried to escape once and the ground I now scrambled across had suffered the consequences?

Happy thoughts. Happy thoughts. Flowers and fairies and pixie dust. Hey ho, it's off to certain death I go. If the Great Green Oogly-Boogly wanted a piece of me, then it looked as if I was serving myself up for dinner. Don't you just hate it when you haven't got any condiments to hand. A little salt. Maybe a sprinkle of paprika. I didn't want to taste too bitter. Didn't want Oggle-Boogle-Schmoogle to be any greener than he already was.

The light Joy was creating, ectoplasm manifest, moved with us as I hurriedly tried to catch up. It flowed over the rocks and dirt like lava down a mountainside, solid become liquid, lifeless become living. It felt as if we were in some sort of dome of luminosity, protection from the darkness haunting the area beyond its reach. Did it hurt? Was it like an energy she was releasing, the discharge draining her of strength? Or was it more like wind? One long, satisfying fart that just keeps on going and earns a round of applause once it's finished rooting and a-tooting?

Ectoplasm. Where were Bill Murray when you needed him? And was Slimer, all hunger and... well, slime... going to burst from the night and Tango us?

Down and in. Down and in.

Could they, the monsters that dwelled hereabouts, not have installed an escalator? A lift maybe? At the very worst, some steps to aid our decent? I'd prefer to go to my doom in comfort. And my knees, backside and knuckles were becoming scuffed and bruised from the number of times each of them had helped prevent me falling.

Joy stopped suddenly and it was a second before I realised we were on level ground. The Hollow. The hole in the great doughnut. Unfortunately, I feared it was going to be me that was eaten. D'oh! She put a long manicured finger on her lips. Did the dead have nail bars?

Sssshhh.

Suits me, I thought. I hadn't intended on announcing my presence with a hearty proclamation of "Grub Up!"

She walked forwards, slowly, a few steps then motioned for me to follow. I did so and stepped to her side. Her close proximity seemed to bolster my flailing courage (although that implies that courage had existed in the first place), but only to the extent that I didn't run away screaming. She held my hand and squeezed tight, and the light around us went out.

Did I scream? Squeal? Like a kicked piglet? Or was it only in my head?

All I could feel was Joy's hand in mine. The world had been snuffed out, a candle on a birthday cake blown out by the birthday girl.

Make a wish.

I couldn't feel the air - no breeze nor breath brushed my face. I couldn't actually feel my face. The ground beneath my feel had vanished and I felt as if I was standing, but not floating, on nothing. Terra Firma had become Terror Firmless. Was this sense depravation at its most extreme? People paid money to float in tanks of water, lying in an insulated cocoon to become one with their innermost being. Or some such nonsense. Maybe it works, or maybe you just go crazy from the complete lack of stimuli. Was I going crazy? Or was I still one stop away, clinging onto my ticket, but wondering if I should get off at this station rather than at the end of the line. Because it could quite literally be the end of the line.

A spark. A prick in the black. Was it real or were my eyes tricking me, creating light where there was none? Ha, got you that time. Nothing here but us Nothings. No. There was definitely something there. Maybe it was a cluster of Nothings, gathered together, and that many in one place created a *Something*. But a group of Nothings? What would that be called? And why would my mind insist on thinking of the term for a collection of crows - a Murder.

The Murder of Nothings was getting bigger. Not brighter, but it was certainly growing. It was a ball now, or at least not just a dot. No. Not a ball. A box. A spinning cube that was either becoming much larger, much faster, or was far away and was flying towards us, a speeding train with us on the tracks. I tried to let go of Joy's hand, intent on turning and running. I had no idea if I could actually run anywhere, suspended as I was in the night. But either way, Joy held on fast. She wouldn't let go and was somehow far stronger than I'd ever remembered her. My hand was in hers, and it was staying that way. The box continued to spin and grow or race wildly towards us. At first I'd thought it was featureless, the sides plain, but soon I could see detail. Blurring patches of greys and almost blacks.

Then there was a whoosh as the void we were in was suddenly filled with substance. My heart had been racing faster than the cube had been approaching, yet between one heartbeat and the next, the Nothing had disappeared and the Something had taken its place.

And I knew that place. I knew it better than the fluff in my own navel. I didn't need to read the sign on the door that had materialised in front of me to know what lay beyond it. I could feel it in the air tonight, oh Lord. The smell. The sense. The blinding white that should have meant purity but instead signified Purgatory.

Home sweet home.

I looked at Joy. Stared at her. The question must have been written all over my face in black permanent marker, perhaps by the same birthday girl who'd so successfully blown out the candle of the world. Why had she brought me to the office of Dr. Connors?

Chapter Fourteen

"There's something I want you to see," she said. She smiled, a sorry effort that, if it had been in a grinning competition would have come right near the bottom. The edges of her mouth twitched in a vaguely upwards direction as if they knew there was nothing to get excited about, and any attempt would be meaningless and futile.

We no longer needed to be quiet, obviously. She hadn't whispered so any semblance of sneaking sneakily had snuck away. Did I feel betrayed? By my own sister? Was this a knife so deep in my heart the blade was playing hopscotch with my aorta? You might say that. Part of me said 'I told you so,' and another part of me wanted to slap the first part. Yet another piece of the jigsaw that had a picture of me and the name Sin on the box told the other two to shut up and get a grip.

The others shut up and got a grip.

"What's going on?" I asked.

"You need to see something," Joy said. "You need to be prepared."

I had never been a boy scout, and I doubted Baden-Powell had this situation in mind when he founded the movement. I was certain there wasn't an arm badge for letting your dead sister deliver you into the waiting arms of your former psychiatrist. What would such a badge look like? It would probably, I think, be similar to the No Smoking sign, except the thick red line would be cutting across my face. Would it be the same picture that was on the jigsaw box?

Ask me another.

So. I prepared myself. I'd entered this room on more occasions than I could count, at least not without taking my socks off. The door handle needed an extra wiggle - sort of a twist-lift-push kind of thing - to get the door open. The bottom hinge creaked, and half a can of WD40 had failed to cure it. A keypad lock had to be tap danced with to pass through. So many certificates and qualifications lined the wall in gold coloured frames, you could have been entering the Louvre, except the Mona Lisa would have been dragged off and drugged up. A desk, massive and leather topped for extra executive effect was the first thing you saw when you walked in. A little OCD tempered the good Doctor's habits, enough to make sure the pens were all blue and they were lined up parallel with each other and the pencils on the desk. A notebook and diary, each leather bound the same colour as the desk top (a blur of maroon into crimson) would be squarely placed in front of the large swivel recliner that enthroned the big man when he was holding court. A large grey flat screen monitor and a cordless mouse were the only other occupants of the desk top, perhaps to ensure nothing diverted your attention from the Doctor.

There were no pictures, unless you counted the proclamations of Connors' vast intellect. No indications of any family. No handshakes with politicians. No faded photo of a wannabe psychiatrist's graduation. The office was clean and sharp and pure Connors. It was as focused as a laser and the man behind the desk could do as much damage. More perhaps.

My preparations took a matter of seconds. I'd long since discovered that nothing could prepare you for entering this office. He was the spider and you were the big juicy fly caught on his web, accepting the invitation into his parlour. And you didn't need to worry - Dr. Connors would supply his own condiments. They came in needles and pills. So effectively, there was no preparation. It was a simple matter, if you were able to and were not under the influence (so to speak), of tapping, twisting, lifting and pushing.

So Joy gripped the handle, then... tap-tap, twist, lift... breathe... push.

I've read that there are police dogs that can smell death. They know if a body has been in the boot of a car, or crumpled at the bottom of the stairs. They can tell if you've touched one, and it can, supposedly, be weeks after the contact. That's amazing, isn't it? They're called Cadaver Dogs. Pretty name. The same goes for fear. Dogs, and other animals, can smell fear. They can taste it. I think it's something to do with, at least in the case of fear, endorphins or something. Maybe sweat. I'm no dog. The only canine in my body is in my teeth and just as my molars don't enable me to dig dark tunnels in the ground, I don't have the olfactory abilities of your local Fido.

But this room. It wasn't a smell. It wasn't even a sense, not in the way of the five senses.

Now that sounded like the something Grasshopper would say to David Carradine. The Way Of The Five Senses is fraught with danger. To overcome them, you must overcome yourself. The way of the psycho is the way of the butterfly. He who laughs last, didn't get the joke. A wise man knows that if you throw up on a roller coaster, you might just be wearing it on the next loop-de-loop.

Did we have a sixth sense? Were people psychic? Could they contact the dead and move objects with their hands? Could they know who was going to call even before the telephone rang? I didn't think so. Which is strange, of course, seeing as I was currently standing, with a ghost, in a room in the middle of a mental institute I'd recently vacated.

Or had I? Was I still strapped to the low bed in my room, flying high on the wings of drugs?

I wondered how I could still think clairvoyance was a whole load of tish-tosh on quick-wash yet accept my present company and the fact that I'd mentally torn a sea gull apart. Men, eh? And if you press the button on the remote control *really* hard and *really* fast, it would miraculously work even though the batteries were deader than... my sister.

Whatever the reason, whatever the explanation, you knew this room bred fear in anyone who was called here. Prickling sensations crawled up your arms. Your spider sense started to tingle. Your stomach knotted. Even your breath was afraid to show itself, choosing instead to stay hidden in your lungs until you forced it out in ragged pants. And behind the desk, basking in the effect he was having on you, like a leech sucking blood, would be Dr. Connors. His smile, plenty of shine but oh, so malign, could chill the balls off an Inuit. He knew it and he loved it. Almost as much as he loved himself.

Tap, twist, lift, push. Creak.

"Close the door."

What little breath I had froze in my chest as I looked at him and he looked, in turn, at me. I automatically went to close the door when I heard a voice that was not my own but came from my body say: "Yes, Doctor."

I felt a pull and the door closed, my hand sliding through it as if it was nothing more than smoke. Another pull, harder this time, and a bulky man in the white coat of an orderly stepped into view. I was confused for a moment as to where he'd come from, and then I realised. He'd come from me! Like Patrick Swayze in Ghost, I'd just been walked through. Was I now dead? Had I passed over into Brian's Bright Side of Life only to find it darker than midnight in a coalmine in December? Then I felt Joy's hand in mine again. Something was still solid. Unless, because she was a ghost and I now was, we were solid to each other...

My head spun and I felt faint. When had I died? Had I slipped while stumbling across the Seven Hills? Did I lay, a twisted broken mess in a hollow, food for the monster rats and other creatures that dwelled there? Was it in my sleep back at the house? Would Olivia discover me lying in a pool of my own bodily fluids, three weeks from now? Or... no, it couldn't be... Had my suicide attempt worked? Was I a cloud of ash and cinders floating on the thermal updrafts of a furnace's radiant section? Had my escape, the crasheddeadmangled boy, the rapist farmer and his abused wife and everything else been some sort of mirage as I walked in the Valley of Death? Has it been an illusion of life to protect, or to fool, me?

Did a ghost vomit? I felt as if I was about to find out, but Joy put her arm around me and turned my face to hers. I could see she'd read my thoughts.

"Don't worry," she said. "You're not dead. I wouldn't do that to you. I'd tell you."

She would, that's true. Joy hated lies. She found it difficult to even handle fibs that were just a darker shade of pale. And an omission of the scale of this would probably have made her as physically sick as I was feeling. She would have told me.

So I wasn't dead. I didn't feel particularly comforted, but I was back in the office of my former tormentor. Or should that be saviour? I forget. I could be forgiven for being somewhat dazed and confused, and so not amused. Someone had just walked through my body as if I was a shadow of a shade of a shiver.

"Trust me," Joy said. What else could I do?

The burly body that had used me as a door it didn't need to open belonged, I saw, to Jeremy. I automatically smiled and took a step forward to say hello to the only person in such a long time that I called a friend. Even though I'd been a patient and he was the guy who stuck the needles in, we'd become, I hoped, friends. Joy held me back, though.

"He can't see you," she said. "Neither of them can. Or hear you. Just watch."

The perfect opportunity presented itself for me to tell the doctor just what I thought of him and his practices. I wondered if I slapped or punched him, would he feel it. I had opened the door, but to Jeremy I'd been as nothing. So the chance, I guessed, was a chance missed. Such a shame.

"So what are we doing here? Why here? I left here. I don't want to be back."

"You left here to kill yourself. You don't want that anymore, but if I don't bring you here now, you might just get it."

What?

"What?"

"Just watch and listen, Sin. And don't ask questions I can't answer. Just do as I ask, please."

Ok, ok. I'll be a good little puppy dog. I'll sit at your heel and wait for any tasty treats you might have to offer, and I'll watch the show.

"Fine," I said. It wasn't fine. Of course it wasn't. 'Fine' was like 'nice', meaningful and meaningless at the same time, but without 'Fine' I wasn't going to get anywhere. Of course I wanted to know what we were doing here. If it was a grown up version of show and tell, or if this was some sort of virtual reality television where you could sit in the Rovers Return whilst Jack and Vera argued next to you, then great. Excellent. Maybe Eastenders would be on afterwards. But I didn't think I'd be able to change channels and walk along any cobbled streets. Strange things were afoot and, even though I didn't think feet were all that strange, I needed to find out what they were. So I said: "Fine," once more, with feeling.

"Sit down, Jeremy," said Connors. He was smiling his smile, straight out of the freezer. Did the temperature in the room drop a few degrees?

"Thank you, sir." Jeremy settled his bulk into the only other chair in the room. It was a simple seat with legs. A back lent some support, and I'm sure it was designed by the man himself in a, very successful, attempt to make you feel even more insecure and insignificant than he thought you already were. As his chair was the throne, this could almost have been the stocks. It groaned in protest at the weight of the orderly, but Connors had long since stopped listening to such complaints. The chair had objected for a number of years and still stood, albeit sorrowfully, in front of the desk, a naughty pupil before the vengeful headmaster.

Did Jeremy notice? Not the chair - he'd been here long enough to not notice its grumblings either. No. Did he notice Connors' manner? The way he spoke. The smile that could melt a relative's resolve yet reduce a patient to a babbling mess. No one who worked in this hospital, or resided here either, was addressed by their first name. Not by the Doctor at any rate. To do so would place them on an even footing with him. It would make them his equals. And although he'd insist that all were equal within these walls, he was plainly more equal than anyone. Or so he thought.

Connors had called him 'Jeremy.' I think that would have been my cue to run-baby-run right there. I'd be watching my back to make sure no blades were sticking out at odd angles making me look like a drug crazed knife block or a not so glamorous assistant for a failed circus act. Dr. Connors being nice was like a vulture at a funeral - it might be wearing a dark suit and shedding a tear, but you knew there was an ulterior motive there somewhere. You knew that, once everyone had retired to the wake to eat, drink and tell their stories, it was going to be there, spade in wing, digging up its supper.

I shuddered but Jeremy seemed oblivious. He had the prerequisite timidity, giving the impression that he was kneeling before his lord. I think he could have been called 'Monkey Breath' and it would have been acceptable. The fact that he could easily have crushed the man he faced seemed to emphasise the smaller one's power.

Dr. Connors was Napoleon before his generals, or at least one of his foot soldiers. Small in stature but huge in ego. He wasn't really a short man - his height was a fag paper shy of average, as if one last mighty stretch would settle him nicely into the realms of medium - but his overall appearance was... minimising. He was balding, and had once, up until very recently, favoured a toupee that hadn't particularly favoured him. He wore rimless spectacles that seemed to pinch his head between their arms and squeeze his eyes into a permanent squint. Perhaps he thought the look gave him an air of Clint Eastwood, his eyes tight to focus his gaze. Did you feel lucky, punk? No, not really. If you passed him in the street, you wouldn't look twice, but he commanded a room with a sort of compressed regality. He believed in himself so much and kept himself so tightly bound, you became convinced he was about to explode with a wondrous cacophony. He was his own spin-doctor and his conviction was so convincing you couldn't help but be dragged onto the merry go round as well. And if you felt dizzy afterwards? Well, he had just the right medicine for that.

Jeremy, orderly of the month for the past two years running (if such an accolade existed, which is didn't, but if it did, it would be his) sat patiently. He knew better than to say anything unless he was spoken at, or on rare occasions to. Connors made the pretence of being busy on his computer, the delay a long mastered way of serving up the other person another mighty slice of discomfort pie. It felt as if it had been weeks since I'd seen my friend, since he'd last strapped me up in my snug little strait jacket. I couldn't believe it had been only so very recently.

My last day in the mental home was a lifetime ago, and I felt as if I'd aged thirty years. The world had turned in that time and I felt as if I'd been cast off, landing on a celestial rollercoaster that had been through loops and twists and was just about to enter a very long, very dark and very steep tunnel.

Click, click, clickety-click.

It seemed that Connors was actually doing something other than simply dragging Jeremy's nerves over a line of razor blades, each stood like dominos so that, once they'd flayed his nerves they could topple over to maybe slice a wrist or two. The mouse movements and clicks weren't random jabs in the eyes. Probably, he was upping the dosage of Car Crash Kenny or ordering a little extra electro-convulsive therapy for dear Dolly Polly. As far as ECT was concerned, more than enough was about half as much as was really required in the Doctor's eyes. I could imagine that, if he ever fancied a change of scenery, a job on Death Row would suit him. He'd be like Percy Wetmore from Stephen King's wonderful Green Mile, taking sadistic pleasure in the dip of the lights and the screams and the smell of cooked flesh (you want fries with that?) as he flicked the switch to spark up the electric chair. I wondered if he pulled the legs off spiders. Probably not. They only had little mouths so you couldn't hear their screams. He'd hate it in space then, because, so we're told, in space no one can hear you order a Big Mac.

Finally Connors was finished. He pushed the mouse forward, leaving it perfectly perpendicular to the monitor, and leaned back in his chair. Turning to face Jeremy he was silent for a long time. He stared at the big man, his face expressionless except for the occasional dark shadow that flitted behind his eyes. Now you see me, now you don't. What was he thinking? Had Jeremy done something wrong? Connors leaned forward, resting his elbows on the desk. It was a familiar pose. He adopted it when he wanted to appear concerned but was instead planning his attack. He smiled again. Jeremy, the poor naive soul, smiled back. The doctor's was warm and fake, the orderly's hesitant and doing its best to be real, and the mismatched smiles met each other across the leather desk top and dissolved.

"You seem nervous," said Connors. "Why would you be nervous?"

Jeremy looked shocked. He hadn't expected that. Dr. Connors believed pleasantries were verbal banalities for people who had nothing better to say. They were grass cuttings - snippets of waste cast aside to die. Of course, if you thought about it, once they died they provided fertiliser for the conversations to follow, but he didn't see that. Dead and gone, and superfluous when alive. Small talk was no talk. While others might see speech as corn that, when the heat was applied, popped and overflowed its container, spreading in all directions, to him it was a straight line. You could get in your car and drive from A to B and the indicator light would never blink once. A surgical incision from which any words that might leak out were quickly mopped up and tossed in a yellow sacked bin for disposal in an incinerator. He was more to the point than Robin Hood, and his aim was twice as deadly. But no one would challenge him. Nobody slapped him for an abruptness that was often on the wrong side of rude. He didn't believe that he was wrong and so others tended to follow the same train of thought, even as it drove them off a cliff and onto the rocks far below.

No one would expect him to ask how their day was going or how the kids were. Would he even remember you had children? Perhaps. Knowledge was power and even knowing the details of a person's family made you stronger because it could be used to take them off guard. If they knew Connors would not ask, if he did they would be disarmed. And a disarmed individual was practically sprinkling the paprika on themselves. I said, do you want fries with that?

Still. The fact that Dr. Connors avoided the niceties of conversation as if they were an angry wasp to be swatted away (an act that sometimes made them more insistent on being noticed), didn't forgo the chance that he might ease into a dialogue rather than ploughing in all guns a-blazing. Rambo, he was not. I doubted he could sew a suture Stallone style, sans pain relief, but he'd gladly do that to you.

This. It was... sly. Unexpected. Direct, but off topic. Not that Jeremy seemed to know what the topic was, but the look on his face implied that he was expecting to be torn off a strip or two. It was an almost considerate question, and that made it all the more disconcerting. And clever. Disarm and beguile, then decide whether you want rump, fillet or sirloin as they roll over for you.

"I..." Jeremy floundered. Was the doctor being nice? Or was he trying to trap him? What to say? "I'm fine, sir."

That's right. Deny everything. It came off in my hand. It was like that when I got here. She told me she was 18. I couldn't see Jezzer ever saying that last one. Sure, it's always the quiet ones, but he had honest eyes. Intelligent eyes. If there was a type, he wasn't it. He was... He was nice.

Connors smiled again. If I gave him a warm beer, I was sure I'd see condensation forming on the glass.

"Good, Jeremy. That's good." His name again. Leave, friend, leave. The false sincerity - surely you can see through it?

Jeremy looked blank. He didn't know how to respond. *Leave!* That's how you respond! He nodded. It was the best he could do.

"Now Jeremy," said Connors. He leaned back, his elbows on the arms of his chair and his fingertips together. He was the picture of pleasant, the epitome of ease. How could you doubt him? How could you wonder? "We seem to have a small problem, don't we."

Not a question, a statement. Lay it out, bait it and wait.

"I don't know, sir." Jeremy straightened in his chair. The seat creaked, possibly in fear. It had been in this office for a long time. It had, no doubt, seen many things. Perhaps it knew what was to come and wanted to escape. I could sympathise. I tried to will my friend to hear me. If my sister could read my thoughts then maybe he could read mine too. If I could only project them to him. If I could shout enough in my head then maybe he'd hear me.

"It won't work, Sin." Joy shook her head. "We're here but we're not, not really. Nothing you could do would make a difference. If you picked up one of his pencils, you could stab it in his hand, but he wouldn't feel it. He wouldn't see it."

"I could?"

My spirits lifted suddenly. The chance to hurt him and for him to not know it was me. I couldn't pass on that. He was looking at the orderly without saying anything. He was waiting. Watching. He saw the sweat bead on Jeremy's forehead. He saw it run into the corner of his eyes. He saw Jeremy try to blink it away, not wanting to move to wipe it in case the doctor took it as some sort of admission of guilt. For what, I assumed my friend didn't know. But guilty until proven innocent, your honour. I walked over to the desk and picked up a pencil. There were three, all as sharp as the other. I imagined he honed each to perfect points after every use. No matter. All the better to maim you with, my dear.

His hands were still up in front of him, but I didn't want them. He was watching my friend like a buzzard watches a dying cowboy in the desert, waiting for its last breath to expire so it can peck out the eyes. That suited me. I didn't even pull back for extra force. I just raised my hand and plunged the perfectly pointy tip of the pencil into Dr. Connors' right eye. The eye popped, optic fluids squirting onto my hand. Blood and cerebrospinal fluid - brain juice - seeped down onto his chin and along the pencil, dripping slowly onto the desk. That'll stain. He didn't move. He didn't blink, although a length of wood encased graphite poking out of his eye might have prevented that. There was no reaction whatsoever. I twisted the pencil savagely. Nothing.

This wasn't me. I wasn't savage. I wasn't even particularly fierce. I was confused for a moment. Back when I counted the institute as a home away from hell, I'd always had a grudging respect for my doctor. Up until the point of discovering he wanted me to stay awhile, regardless of my own intentions, I'd thought he was good at his job. Where did all this anger come from? How did I have this newfound knowledge of his inner demons? At first I thought it was one of those 'I just knew' things. Maybe finally getting away from this place had opened my eyes. The absence of the drug infused regimen had cleared the fog of the last couple of years and I could see what he was truly like. But I didn't think so. There was no feeling of knowing. I'd begun to recognise the signs, or the symptoms, of my curse, and none were present here. I did just know, but I didn't 'Just Know.'

But the pencil. The stabbing. I was sick at myself. I pulled the pencil out. It made a sucking noise - the last dregs of water down a plug hole - and a pop (goes the weasel). I threw it onto the desk, partially in disgust at myself and partially in disgust at the fact that it was a wasted effort. Connors was still sitting there and he was still watching my friend, albeit with only one eye. I walked over to Joy, my head hung.

"See," she said with barely a hint of 'I told you so.'

She pointed to the desk and I turned back to look. The pencil wasn't where it had rolled after I'd cast it aside. There was no mix of blood and fluid, like a half fried egg, pooling on the leather surface. Connors' eye wasn't a punctured wreck, dribbling down his cheek. All was normal. All was right. All was very wrong.

"What?"

"We're not really here, Sin. Well, we are, but we're not. It's hard to explain. You could throw things, smash things, trash the place if you want, but it won't make any difference. It won't be real."

"So where are we then? How come I could pick up that pencil?"

"Because we are here, sort of. It's like we're looking through a mirror, but we're in the reflection."

So. We'd climbed through Alice's looking glass. Maybe Joy really was the Queen of Hearts then.

I shook my head. I didn't understand and I couldn't be bothered to try. Joy kept seeming to be making sense, but the real meaning was always evasive. I'd grab for it and it would jump back, staying just out of reach. Catch me if you can! Besides, Dr. Connors seemed to have grown tired of making Jeremy squirm. He'd placed his hands on the arms of his chair and, with a sigh, he stood up.

"Yes, Jeremy. A problem. I would like, if you don't mind, a little help in solving this particular problem. Please."

The 'please' was separated from the rest of the sentence. Not an afterthought, more an emphasis. Go on mate. Give us a hand. Please? Be a pal. Or else.

"Of... of course, sir. Anything I can do to help."

"I'm pleased to hear that. Very pleased indeed." Connors was walking around his desk smiling his smile, crocodile, circling the room and Jeremy, like a hyena waiting for the poor animal to get on with it and die. Jeremy stayed facing forwards, his head down. His eyes flitted from side to side nervously. I wanted to tell him that it was ok. Tell him that I'd sort out Dr. Connors in my own inimitable way. But I couldn't. Jeremy wouldn't hear me and turning Connors innards into outards wasn't something I'd be able to do, as much as I might want to and actually be able to. It appeared the devil on my shoulder was a monster, but he had morals after all. I was sure the angel on my other was smirking a conceited twist of the lips.

"Do you know which problem I'm referring to?" Connors was behind the chair now, looking down on the back of Jeremy's head. He reached into his pocket and, unseen by the orderly, pulled something from his pocket. Still speaking, he pulled a sheath off the needle and pushed the plunger of the syringe up slightly.

What the...?

I shouted out, ineffectually. My warning went unheard as Connors took a step forward.

"We seem to have lost a resident, Jeremy. One Sin Matthews has been... Let's say misplaced."

Displaced was more like it. Me. This was all about me. Why bring him into it? What did Jeremy have to do with anything? He didn't help me escape. In fact, he was the one who trussed me like a Christmas turkey in my strait jacket. He left it tighter than Michelle Pfeiffer's Catwoman suit and only stopped short of handing me a ladle to baste myself with - and I almost laughed, considering where I'd planned to end up.

"Yes, sir. Sorry sir." He could almost have been saying 'Sire.'

"Sorry, Jeremy?" He took a step forward. The syringe was a sword poised for a beheading. Considering I'd been pumped full of drugs for the past two years or so, I had no idea of the colours or viscosities of what they'd injected me with. The yellowish fluid could have been happy juice or a massive dose of morphine. I doubted Dr. Connors wanted to plant a big cheesy grin on his minion's mush. "Why would you be sorry?"

I wished he would hurry up. Get to the point or give Jeremy the point. I was standing useless, knowing I couldn't stop whatever might happen and this cat and mouse game was driving spikes beneath my fingernails.

Jeremy shook his head. "I don't know sir. I don't know what to say."

"Well, would you care to enlighten me as to how he managed to leave? You were overly close to him. Did you help him? I am correct, am I not, in assuming that you were tasked with jacketing him? Did you not fasten the straps tight enough? Perhaps you wanted to give him a little room to breathe. I can understand that. They are constrictive, aren't they?"

"Yes, sir."

Another step forward. Still the smile. He knew that how something is said carries into the tone of your voice. Scowl and it can be heard. Smile and you could be ordering the drowning of a litter of kittens and it would still sound light and uplifting. Well, more or less.

"Yes what, Mr. Jackson? Yes, you helped him? Yes, you didn't do your job properly and now we have a deeply disturbed and psychotic escapee?"

"No, sir! No! I was agreeing with you, sir. The jackets. They... They're tight, sir. But I didn't. I wouldn't help someone escape sir. Never."

"Well, Mr. Jackson. That's good. I had complete faith in you. You're an excellent employee. I do have one other question though, Mr. Jackson."

Mr. Jackson. No longer Jeremy, friend, pal. Connors had grown tired of his Mr. Sunshine charade. It no longer served a purpose and had been tossed aside like a pencil that refused to impale an eye.

"Yes sir?" Jeremy looked as if he was shaking. I could have happily launched a size nine between Dr. Connors' legs hard enough to send his testicles up into his eye sockets to replace the ones I wanted to gouge out.

"The report. Matthews' case file. It's been moved, Mr. Jackson. I wonder, have you been through my files?"

My case file? I bet that made entertaining reading. I'd written a statement a short while ago telling the good doctor why I was there. He didn't believe a word of it, but he'd said that admission was part of the process of relinquishment. Spill the beans to rid the dreams, or something similar. So I played along. I told my story openly and honestly. It hadn't helped me, but then my demons had their claws so deep into my soul that a few words on a couple of sheets of A4 wasn't going to dislodge them. Unfortunately. And I could see that he'd know it had been moved. I was sure that each file was placed so precisely in its hanger that a micrometer couldn't measure a difference. But why would Jeremy take it out?

"Me, sir? I wouldn't. That's not my place." His shakes were more noticeable. I didn't think he was telling the truth. Bad move, especially when a viper with a potentially poisonous fang was coiled behind you more than ready and willing to strike.

"Are you sure? You didn't sneak a peak? A little late night reading for your so-called Graveyard Shift?" He lowered his hands and put them behind his back, hiding the needle. He sidestepped slowly, circling his prey once more. "Are you sure, Jeremy?"

Jeremy looked up. His brow was furrowed, his eyes wide. Sweat rolled down his forehead like boulders chasing Indiana Jones. If he didn't tell the truth, and Connors obviously knew what that truth was, he'd be liable to be crushed under their weight. Just tell him. Don't lie because he'll know. Just tell him. He went to shake his head, but seemed to think better of it. Good. Better. Don't be a fool.

"I..."

"Yes?"

"Yes, Dr. Connors. I did read the file."

Connors straightened up and smiled. The mouse had just taken the cheese and the trap had caught his leg as he scurried off, the bar slamming down to crush the tiny bones.

"Would you like to explain yourself, Mr. Jackson? I'm sure you have an explanation. I'm sure you don't make a habit of rifling through patients' private records, do you?"

"No, sir! I don't." He was fidgeting more than a Jack Russell told to sit and stay. Calm it man! So you read a report. A slap on the wrist or a dose of Diamorphine in the neck, which would you prefer? You decide. "I just... He was my friend, sir. I just... I was interested. I'm sorry sir. I don't make a habit of it. Honestly. It was just..."

Connors held up his hand - the one not holding the syringe. That stayed firmly behind his back. Jeremy knew when to shut up. I couldn't help the smile when he said we were friends. I had a distinct lack of them recently, but now wasn't the time for warm fuzziness to butt in with its hot cup of cocoa and big bar of Dairy Milk.

"Just, just, just. I know." He was smiling that razor sharp, frost bitten smile again. Relax, it said. I'm just going to slice your throat. It's only be a little cut, honest. It won't hurt for long. "I do understand. I fancy that I'd do exactly the same if I were in your position. Don't worry."

Don't worry, said the spider to the fly, the fox to the chicken, the iceberg to the Titanic. It'll be reet.

"Thank you Dr. Connors." He looked as the iceberg might after getting off with a charge of GBH. He could melt with relief.

"You don't need to thank me, honestly. It's nothing." He paused and his hand returned to his back. Both hands were holding the syringe now, brothers in arms, partners in crime.

I looked at Joy and saw she was entranced by the unfolding scene. She could have been at the cinema watching the latest Bond movie or George Clooney flick. All that was missing was the popcorn, the overpriced Pepsi and the idiot at the back who wouldn't shut up. Perhaps that was unfair - about Joy, not about the idiot at the back. She'd brought me here to show me this, though I couldn't see why or what good it would do. But she knew that we couldn't stop or change any of it so she - we - could merely watch and wait. Feeling impotent, that's what I did.

I found it odd that Jeremy was so docile in the presence of the doctor. He was a trained nurse and I was sure he'd once told me he'd been a teacher, so I would have thought he'd have had experience of dealing with the more difficult or overbearing among us. So why was he such a lapdog, scurrying around desperate to be petted? Was Connors so charismatic that he could charm or hammer anyone to his bidding? I had a vision of the institute becoming a cult under his pervasive aura. I wondered if a mass suicide was on the cards. And was I the first follower to go? I had, after all, tried to take my own life. The fact that I'd failed possibly showed that he wasn't as all powerful as he seemed to think. I didn't believe that, though. I don't mean about him being omnipotent. Rather, I was not under the influence of a crazed psychiatrist. Currently I was being led by the ghost (or whatever she was) of my dead sister. It was semi-voluntary, like being told I had to steal the crown jewels or I'd lose my little finger. I could say no and wave goodbye to my pinky, or I could go ahead and ram-raid the Tower of London and have all ten fingers on the hands that they'd clap the handcuffs on.

My choice. I could have refused to follow Joy and in doing so missed this little show whilst waiting for either Them to find me or Never Mind The Buzzcocks to start on BBC 2. If I'd known for sure that Bill Bailey and Phil Jupitus would have been on hand to make me chuckle rather than the costume department of Loonies UK PLC, then Joy might have lost out. I still didn't see the point of my spectatorship here but hoped all would become clear. Or at least less opaque.

I doubted that Connors really thought this invasion of his inner sanctum that would no doubt have tainted the very air he breathed was nothing. It was something, hence the needle that was so lovingly being stroked behind his back. His fingers were running along the metal needle, back and forth as if masturbating it, the forthcoming ejaculation of serum the closest a person like Dr. Connors might ever get to real orgasm. Maybe that was his problem. Maybe he just needed a good shag and he'd drop the demigod persona.

"So, Mr Jackson. What did you think to our friend's little story? Entertaining, no?"

I was pleased that he thought the tale of my terror was so enjoyable. I do aim to please, when I'm not, as I wished I was at that moment, aiming to tear his face off and ram it up his backside. If I can buy someone a birthday or Christmas present that will really make them smile, instead of the fake 'oh that's nice, hope you kept the receipt' kind of grin, then I'm happy. If I can help a little old lady across the road, make a cuppa with just the right amount of milk or pee straight then hunky-dory-do-dah-day. I may not be in the same league as my sister, but I do my bit. So if my file provided some small measure of amusement, jolly dee.

Jeremy frowned. Entertaining, it seemed, wasn't exactly the word he'd use.

"I don't know, sir." His head was bowed as he spoke, either because he was trying think what to say, or because he was trying to think what he *should* say. "It was unexpected."

Unexpected. I can imagine.

"Unexpected. Yes." Connors scratched his nose leaving a small smear of blood from where the needle had pricked his finger. Small boys shouldn't play with matches, and big ones shouldn't play with needles. You're gonna get burned. Well, I could hope that he'd somehow accidentally inject himself, freeing my friend from his ordeal and the patients from theirs. And me from this. Obviously he didn't. It's rare that the pyromaniac is caught up in his own inferno, the torch bearer becoming the torch. The doctor had wandered back behind Jeremy's chair. He made it appear as if he was simply ambling about, meandering while he mused, instead of stalking a prey that was presenting its throat for a quick slaughter.

"But believable?" A step closer to the orderly. A step closer to the kill.

"Believable sir?" Jeremy looked up but without turning in his seat, he couldn't see Connors. And turning in his seat wasn't something he dared do. Sit down, face forward, soldier. Chest out, back straight. Drop and give me twenty.

"Believable, Mr. Jackson. The wildly delusional claims your friend made. Did you believe them?"

Jeremy shook his head as, behind him, the doctor licked his lips. Dinner's ready kids. All you can devour. Tuck in.

"No, Dr. Connors. How could you believe any of that?"

"How indeed, Mr. Jackson. But he's your friend. Didn't you at least think there might be a chance some of it was the truth? Just a hint?"

"No sir. Killing people with your mind? Teleporting? There's no such thing."

"Are you sure about that?" Connors was fishing. He was making sure Jeremy was saying what he felt and not simply trying to escape the slowly tightening noose.

"Of course, sir. He was my friend, but he wasn't one of the X-Men. He was just... ill."

Bless him. If only he knew. Part of me was offended. Slighted by the fact that he, to some degree, *should* have known. But hey, teleportation? Come on. I could do it and I didn't entirely believe. I wasn't, as had been pointed out, an X-Man.

"X-Men?" Connors questioned. Of course he wouldn't know. His world didn't include comic books and movies, fun and escapism. Reality and realism were his world. I wasn't a superhero in a tight lycra/spandex suit. I couldn't fly or bring lightning down with a snap of my fingers. I was a mortal, more mere than most, and I was crazy as a loon.

Isn't that right, Sister Moon?

Wibble-me-ree.

"It's a film, sir. It's based on a comic."

"A comic? Like Spiderman?"

I was impressed. I didn't think he'd know comics existed as, from conception, he'd had his head inside the pages of Megalomania for Dummies. But I supposed he would know Spidey. After all, Connors was adept in capturing people in his web.

"Yes, sir. Like Spiderman. They're a group of super..."

"Mr. Jackson, we're not here to discuss popcorn pap cinema or the futile methods the masses employ to escape their dreary lives. I don't care what an X-Man may or may not be. I don't care if my postman can read my thoughts as if he's prised open the envelope of my mind. What I do care about is do you believe the deranged ramblings of a psychotic man."

He was good. He was, wasn't he? The envelope of my mind? I might use that one myself some day. I think he knew exactly what the X-Men were, and had secretly wished he had an adamantine skeleton like Wolverine or dated a beauty such as Storm. I bet he'd had a box under his bed crammed with Marvel and DC comics and had hidden under his quilt with a torch whilst reading how Lex Luthor had smuggled kryptonite into Superman's cornflakes. Or something.

In fact, it might still be a guilty pleasure of his. Something he did late at night whilst other men were surfing porn or pleasuring their women in the good old Viking way along Testosterone Terrace. He'd never admit it, of course. Oh no. An intellect and ego as inflated as his? It was his own private form of fornication. Anyone who discovered it would have to be disembowelled whilst writing out one hundred times on a blackboard "Dr. Connors does NOT read comics. Dr. Connors does NOT enjoy himself." Life was for the common man and the good doctor would definitely not class himself as common.

Jeremy shook his head. The rest of him was shaking too and for a moment I thought he'd shake himself apart. Well, it was one way to get out of this.

"No. I don't believe it, sir. Sin was, unfortunately, ill."

He sounded so sincere I felt my stomach fall away inside me, leaving a hole the size of... I don't know. What's big? Besides Connors' ego. The Empire State? The doughnut of Homer's dreams? J-Lo's bum (in a nice way, of course)? He really didn't believe me. He really did think I was lying or delusional. At least he was referring to me as ill and not insane or doolally or a sandwich short of a picnic, meat short of the two veg. I'd take those small mercies wherever they were served.

I saw Connors relax. His shoulders, normally so fixed in place they could have been stand-ins for the Dallas wardrobe department, dropped a fraction and the syringe was returned to his pocket. From the corner of my eye I saw Joy relax too and felt a sense of relief wash through me like the falls of Niagara.

Nice one Jezzer. A bit touch and go there, walking the tightrope of terror up in the heights of the big top, blindfolded and sans safety net, but you got to the other side with barely a slip. Take a bow.

A "Thank you, Jeremy" from the poised cobra allowed my friend to join the ranks of the relaxed and he visibly slumped in his chair, his tension spilling out onto the floor to lap at my ankles, mixing with the waters of my own release. Finally the doctor believed him. As did I. He thought I was first mate on the slow boat to Crayzee. Cheers bud.

I couldn't blame him, could I? I hadn't sprung from the prolific pen of Stan Lee or been bitten by a radioactive cheesy wotsit. I didn't rescue cats from trees, swipe children from the path of oncoming buses or make the Earth spin backwards to save the woman I loved. No. I split the cat apart along with the tree. I threw the bus through the window of a post office, taking the child along with it. And as for making the world spin in reverse to change the course of time, I'd probably cause its axis to shift and plunge us all into the next ice age. The Day After Tomorrow would be today. But Jeremy wouldn't, and couldn't, believe this. I was ill. I was delusional. I was raving and rabid and unreasonable.

And I wanted to leave. I'd had enough of this. Connors had played his games. Maybe he did know how to have fun, and reducing grown men to quivering wrecks was his idea of a good time. His equivalent to ten pints and a kebab. Either way, the show was over and I wanted my taxi home. What use was this? I'd learned that I was on my own. My only friend of the past months thought I was demented. My only support was a ghost. I wanted to leave. I wanted to turn my back and hey, maybe keep that appointment with the furnace.

Nah. Maybe not, but I'd seen and heard as much as I wanted, and more. I'd been a captive audience to a ritual humiliation and Dignity had left the building. I felt Joy take my hand and let her. My body hung there as if it was the remains of the practice dummy on a rugby pitch. No, this is how you take an opponent down! Run, smack, crack. Again. Run smack, thud. Again. Run, smack... Back to the house and stare at a spot on the wall for a few hours until I decided what I was going to do, or Judgement Day arrived, whichever came first. If that happened, I figured I'd be at the back of the queue. Sorry, Sin, we're full up. I believe there's room for one more down below.

Connors had stepped forward. He was now standing behind Jeremy, his hand on my friend's (yes, a sense of betrayal hadn't changed that) shoulder.

"Thanks you," he repeated. "I'm so glad we agree."

It happened so fast I didn't realise what was going on until it was already underway. Until Connors' hand had left his pocket, holding the hungry needle, desperate for its vampiric bite. Until it had pierced the neck. Until the thumb had pushed the plunger. Until Jeremy had gasped, stiffened and slumped.

Where was slow motion when you needed it? If John Woo had written this scene, I might have had time to intervene before the syringe had completed its fatal fall. If Spielberg was bankrolling the action, I could have leapt to his rescue, Matrix-like, taking the doctor's arm and twisting it, the needle puncturing the throat of the attacker instead of the attacked.

But this was reality. Or it was reality's closest relative. Brother. Cousin. Whatever.

I stared. Joy stared. Dr. Connors smiled.

"I believe you, Mr. Jackson," he was saying. "I really do. But for me to be safe, you must be sorry. I'm sure you understand."

He pulled the needle from Jeremy's neck. He tossed it onto his desk as if it was nothing more than an eye gouging pencil. Jeremy didn't move. He didn't breath. Of course, being dead, he couldn't.

Connors returned to his own chair. He was humming. Almost whistling a happy tune.

I looked at Connors and Jeremy, first one then the other as if I was watching a macabre tennis match. A rotting heart was being volleyed back and forth, my attention captured like a dolphin in a tuna net, unable to take my eyes off the decomposing flesh as it was batted to and fro. Except the only rotting heart was deep inside the doctor's chest. And I so much wanted to rip it out. Finally, deuce. Match point. Game. I turned to Joy and I saw the tears in her eyes. She hadn't known my friend. I don't know if I'd ever spoken about him. Said his name. Hinted that he existed. But the tears were there. I had none. I had nothing. Rage had wiped remorse out like the nuclear blast of a Terminator film.

I wanted... I needed to hurt Connors. A pencil in the eye wasn't enough. Decapitation. Slow. Not enough. I wished, briefly, that I'd lived on a farm when I was younger instead of a flat on a council estate, where the nearest greenery was the square of grass that I'd played football on, using the 'No Ball Games' sign as a goal post. I wished I'd learned how to skin a rabbit or pluck a pheasant. He would have been plucked and skinned. Boiled perhaps. Alive, obviously.

But my visits to farms were restricted to the play farm at Rand with its pigpens and lamb feeding days. And its trampolines and witches' hat rides. Taking the foil off a chocolate Easter Bunny was the closest I came to skinning a rabbit.

Joy breathed in deeply, exhaling slowly. It was a version of my own method of focussing. Breathe in, and on the exhale move your index finger away with the breath. Banish the bananas, you might say. Well, you might not, but hey ho daddyo. My impotence at being able to only stand and watch was threatening to screw me up into a tight little ball and play ping pong with me. What was the point? What was the reason?

"Come on," I said. "Let's go."

Let's go. Simple as that. Leave Doctor Death and his victim and just walk away. No calling the police - not that I'd be able to use the phone - and no goodbye to my friend. I'd had enough.

"Wait," said Joy, her hand gripping mine.

"No more," I said. I didn't see how there'd be anything left to show me. Anything that I'd care about, anyway. Anything that mattered. No more. Done. Enough.

"Sin," she said, her voice hushed, which seemed strange since we couldn't be heard anyway. "Wait."

Chapter Fifteen

Well. Joy had her ways. With a look you'd be walking on clouds, almost paddling in the break waters of the sky. But she also had a way of, when she meant something, you knew it. It was more than a woman's wiles. More than one of those stares you get that say, just because I haven't told you how I feel, doesn't mean you shouldn't *know* how I feel! Was it an inflection in her voice? An underlying tone that grabbed you by the shorts and made them curly if you didn't stop, look, listen and not bother thinking because she was going to do it for you? Was it a shadow in the glitter of her eyes? A slumbering demon that you really didn't want to be stirred? I don't know. I don't think it was any of them. When Connors spoke, people listened. He pretty much commanded it - or demanded it. When Joy spoke, if she spoke in a certain way, people also listened. But she didn't command it, she deserved it. Or requested it. Or maybe it was just that you could feel everything she'd done, and you knew without knowing that she'd earned it. I wouldn't say that to her face though. She'd dig me in the ribs and tell me to get a grip.

But Joy had spoken. So I listened. When it came down to it, what else could I do? I wasn't, as had been pointed out, in Kansas anymore. I'd neglected to pick up an A to Z to help me find my way back to the land of the living, if Grimsby could be called that. For all I knew, if I stepped back through that door, I could end up like Alec Baldwin and Geena Davis in Beetlejuice. Open the door and try to escape, and I'd find myself in a vast desolate land of sand with huge razor-toothed snake like creatures hungry for a piece of Sin Steak Pie, just like mamma used to make. Yum.

Sod that. And besides. I think any fight or life left inside of me disappeared with Jeremy's final breath. Strange how that could change in a second. Only a moment had passed since I wanted to feed Connors to a pack of the giant rats that wandered the Seven Hills. Now I was suddenly deflated. Fine. We'll wait. We've paid the entry fee. Got the popcorn and drink. A small tub of Ben & Jerry's Cookie Dough ice cream. The main feature had been on, or at least I hoped it had, and now perhaps they were going to show some trailers. Maybe a cartoon.

Click, click, clickety click.

Connors' finger tapped his mouse button in quick, successive strikes. He didn't look over in the direction of the body on the chair, which seemed now to be someone other than the orderly who'd been nice to me on so many occasions. Jeremy had done his best Elvis impression and had left the building. What remained now was a husk, the cast off skin of a snake in human form. No, not a snake. The doctor was the snake. The doctor had waited, played his game, got his answers and struck anyway. Why? Why kill him? He'd admitted he thought I was crazy. He hadn't used those words, of course. 'Ill' was a much nicer way of putting it and I did appreciate the effort, even though I had plastered over the disappointment with a trowel the size of the QE2. But he didn't believe me. So why? What did it matter? Why kill him?

Click, click... pause... Connors leaned into the screen, his icicle inducing smile playing across his lips. Something had captured his attention.

Click. Drag. Click.

Voices.

Something was playing on the computer monitor. I heard Connors' voice as it said...

"Do it, Sin. Do it for me. Do it. Do it. *Do it!*"

Did I run? Ask me another. I only know that one moment I was standing next to my sister and the next I was behind the doctor's chair, staring at his screen, not entirely sure what I was looking at, but at the same time very sure.

CCTV. The miracle of the modern age. They say in the UK there's one camera for every 14 people. You get snapped something like 3,000 times a year. Say cheese! Sizzling Sausages! Monkey's knickers! Of course none of this would mean anything to the viper sitting so close I could wrap my hands around his throat and squeeze. I could imagine the uses he would put hidden cameras to, all under the umbrella of care and healing of course.

The camera angle was awkward. The room was being viewed in isometric, from a high corner and the lens seemed to have a curve that was distorting the picture - not quite like looking through a fish bowl but having at least a hint of the aquatic. Two people were in the picture. One was the doctor, white coat and tight spectacles. The other was me.

Or it looked like me.

I was once on television. I used to, years ago, run an online magazine for stories and poems. Nothing major certainly, but people liked to see their work published, even on a small web site that not too many people had visited. Still, for all of its lack of size, and size isn't everything so we're told, the magazine managed somehow to gain the interest of a computing program on Sky's now defunct .tv technology channel. They wanted to do a piece on the pros and cons of web based publishing as opposed to its more usual paper form. Nervous? Me? Damn right I was. But they wouldn't take no for an answer. Maybe I didn't fight it too hard though.

Anywho. Off I jolly well trotted on the choo-choo down to London. It was an experience, that's for sure. This was long before the days of coins and flips and catches and death. I felt normal. Special, in fact, that I was going to be on the tele! Me! I didn't expect that I, a nobody who just put a few stories and poems on the web for people, would be faced off against the chief buyer for a major publishing agent. Hmmm. David? Goliath? Where's my sling?

I almost hesitate to use the word 'fun' but it was, really. At least it got me on the box. Except when I saw it, and I waited and waited and scored the TV guide to make sure I didn't miss my 15 minutes of Warholean fame, it wasn't me. Was that what I looked like? Did I really sound like that? It was a surprise. Not necessarily unpleasant, but unexpected. Was that the way others saw and heard me?

The 'me' on the monitor was yet another person, or persona. It seemed a shadow, as if part of me was missing or had forgotten to turn up for the session. My 'I' inside was still in my room, slumbering in a drug induced daze and had missed the call for a one-on-one with the head Shrink-o-matic.

Examination Room One. Connors lair. Well, Lair Mark Two, as we were currently in Mark One, the seat of his highness's personal madness. Not a nice room. It'd had more names than Prince or Puff Doodad across the years: The Hole. The Closet. The

Inner Sanctum. They were the nicer ones. Sometimes, when you thought no one was listening, it might be referred to as The Screamer, or simply The Room.

Nothing wrong with calling something The Room. It's what it is, anyway. A room. Four walls. A door. A recessed, naturally, light. The camera in the corner that I'd never even noticed was there. A basic screwed to the floor table. A couple of chairs, one of which was screwed to the floor and another that Connors used, and placed wherever it might make you the most uncomfortable. But when those words were used they were always dripping with dread. They oozed fear like butter melting on a hot plate. Seeping. Bubbling. And crap on toast.

The Room. I was in the chair that was screwed to the floor. There were badly filled holes by the legs where someone, I don't know who as it was before my internment, had managed to rip it from it fastenings and launch themselves at the doctor. It was purely the fact that his chair wasn't fixed in place that a lucky squeal and fall backwards saved him from having his nose bitten off.

The Room. Always colder than the rest of the hospital. Your breath could often be seen escaping your body - if you couldn't then something may as well - on the warmest August day.

The Room. If rooms or buildings have souls, then this one's was noticeable by its absence.

Dr. Connors was sitting in front of me. His face was so close to mine I'd have been able to smell what brand of coffee he'd had with his breakfast. I was sure I remembered all or most of our sessions together, but I really couldn't place this one. He was saying over and over, almost as a chant:

"Do it. Do it."

Do what?

Ah.

The image on screen seemed to blink or to blip. There was an almost imperceptible flicker. Then Connors was standing up and turning towards me. Except I was no longer strapped to the chair screwed to the floor. The strait jacket I'd been so comfortably cocooned in was no longer strapped tightly around me. Where the table had been clear, there was now the aforementioned garment, neatly folded, arms tucked in and straps tidy.

I was in the far corner, crouching. My arms were around my knees, my head down. A foetal huddle.

Connors crouched in front of me. I couldn't see his face but his voice implied a chilled smile.

"Well done, Sin. Good boy."

He reached over and patted my arm. I touched myself where his hand had rested and shivered.

The screen went black, the video file ended. Connors nodded.

"Yes, Sin. Good boy." He clicked an 'X' in the top right corner of the screen and the window closed leaving a smattering of neatly arranged icons against a pale blue background. "Except now you've been very bad, running away like that. I'm afraid that I might have to punish you."

The doctor chuckled, a high sound like a lunatic on helium. Oddly appropriate on one such as he.

I jumped as I felt a hand on my arm where I'd been rubbing a moment earlier and Connors had been patting who knew when. It was Joy.

"Now we go," she said quietly.

Now we go.

I'd been wrong. Jeremy's death was the prelude to the main feature. He was the trailer and the adverts for hot dogs and dream cars. His part in the performance had lasted for much longer than the (literal) movie, but it paled beside this last revelation. I was shocked at how the death, the murder, of someone could possibly seem secondary, but it did. He knew.

Connors knew.

Joy had been right when she'd visited me in the forest the previous night. There was a storm coming, and I didn't have a coat thick enough to protect me from its force.

"Sin. Come on."

Fair enough.

I turned and we went to the door. I didn't look back. I didn't need to be reminded of how Jeremy looked, mild surprise on his face, his hand hanging limp, a trace of drool on the corner of his mouth. I didn't need that memory burned onto my mind any more than it already was. I pulled the door open and stepped out, automatically holding it for my sister. I did turn back then, for one last look at the man I was going to make suffer and at the friend I'd lost.

But they weren't there. The office was gone. The door had gone. I could still feel the handle in my hand, but when I looked, my hand was empty. Darkness was around us and I felt so small.

But Joy was light and lo, there was light. Well, the ghostly ectoplasmic variety anyway.

My mind was racing, a scalextric set where the car was predesigned to fly off at the corner just as they all did. I turned my mental back on the track. Let my thoughts race where they wanted, I didn't have the time to be a spectator to their inevitable collision. If a wreck was going to happen, I was going to be caught in the mangled remains anyway, so why look out for it? My brain would let me know.

"Hey Sin."

"Yes?"

"This is your subconscious. How goes it?"

"Not bad. Fair to crap, you know?"

"Well that's an improvement then."

"Sure is, what can I do for you?"

"Oh yeah. Thought I'd let you know that the race is over."

"Cool. Who won?"

"Well, it wasn't us, I'm afraid. It wasn't pretty. You know what those bends are like."

"Sure do. Tighter than..."

"A barnacle on the bum of the Titanic. Indeed. Anyway. Thought you should know you're now officially insane. Mind is in shreds and there's guts and thoughts everywhere."

"I'd hate to have to clean that up. Thanks for the nod."

"Welcome. See ya. Wouldn't want to be ya."

"Yeah. Unfortunately, you already are."

"Oh yes. Oh well. Shit happens."

Yes it does. It was whether or not we carried a pooper scooper around with us that mattered, or at the very least a carrier bag. I had neither. Bummer.

Chapter Sixteen

"What now," I asked Joy.

She'd brought me here. I'd let her lead me like a bull to a china shop or a lamb to the kebab house. It wasn't like I'd really had much of a choice, was it? Joy said 'Jump' and I asked off which cliff. I'd at first thought I was simply, and it had been simple at the time, on the run from the mental institute. An escapee who should have been able to walk out, seeing as I'd been the one to voluntarily walk in. Now, though, the wolves were baying for blood, and my jugular had been well and truly sliced open, spraying great crimson swaths that would most probably lead them to me like the breadcrumb trail of Hansel and Gretel. Maybe I should save the witch a job and stick myself in the oven, gas mark 7 for the rest of my life.

Dr. Connors would like that, I'm sure. Wine and dine like Lecter on happy pills.

Joy didn't speak for a moment. She was staring at the ground, her face sad. I followed her eyes, for a second wondering if I'd see Jeremy looking back at me, smiling. "Only joking!" But he wasn't. There was just mud, sick and pallid in the light oozing from my sister. She looked up at me, her eyes watery.

Ghosts could cry. Go figure.

"Come on," she said, starting to walk off. I almost automatically took a step to follow, but then stopped.

No. Not this time. I needed to know.

"No," I said. "Not this time. What was all that about. Where are we going?"

Joy stared at me without speaking. The moisture cleared from her eyes as a grim determination crept in, turning them grey. I didn't like that look. I never had. Steely and soulless, as if her eyes had been replaced by those of the Terminator. All that was missing was the red light signifying life.

But then, my sister was actually dead.

"Come on," she repeated, her voice as cold as her stare. I'd forgotten my warm, loving sister could be like this. Happiness normally drifted from her like pheromones, as much a part of her as the colour of her hair or the scar that crossed from her middle right knuckle to her thumb, a keepsake from falling off her bike when she was twelve. And I still say I didn't push her, even though my backside was singing that same song for two days afterwards (thanks dad). It was as if she'd tossed a coin, possibly a two pence piece, and it had fallen face down in shit.

I could have said no again. I really could have. I'd learned long ago, though, that you didn't argue with my sister when she was like this. Puckering up to that not-so-friendly Rottweiler was like kissing a new born baby when compared with standing up to Joy. I opened my mouth, not entirely sure if acquiescence or opposition would leap out into the maw of the lion, but it seemed Joy took my slight pause to mean the latter.

The light from her went out and the clammy touch of darkness stroked my cheek.

There was a brief growl to my right. A dog? A demon? A rabid rat? My stomach clenched. My legs went cold. My heart missed a beat, then another, before picking up the pace to start racing.

Then Joy's voice. "Open your eyes, Sin."

I didn't realise I'd closed them.

Name's Dorothy.

Yep. You heard me right. Dorothy. I was only missing the blue chequered dress and pigtails to complete the picture. Scampering along beside me could even have been Tonto. Oh, hold on, that's the Lone Ranger. Toto then. I hear those drums echo in the night, guys 'n' gals, and they're beating for me.

I didn't even have to click the heels of my ruby slippers together. Not that I had any, of course. Red is so not my colour.

What planet is this guy on, I hear you ask. Well I don't of course. You're not the voices in my head. Are you? Nah. The voices in my head sound more like Joe Pasquale on helium or James Earl Jones in his best Darth Vader incarnation.

"Sin. Come over to the Dark Side."

Jimmy-boy, I'm already there.

Dorothy, that's me. And Joy was either the Good Witch of the North (or whichever direction she came from) or the Wicked Witch of the West, except she wasn't wearing stripy tights and curly shoes. Oh, and a house hadn't fallen on her. But, either way, we were no longer wandering the yellow brick road of the Seven Hills. Nope, we were back in Kansas. Or Grimsby to be more precise. If we'd even left. Joy was sitting in her recliner, feet up, looking at me. Her face was expressionless, neither smiling nor frowning, angry nor happy. A blank canvas perhaps waiting for me to be the artist of her mood.

I was standing in the middle of the room, my back to the television and the bay window. I felt exposed. The light from the streetlamp outside seemed to stop just inside the window frame as if fearful of venturing further. I could feel its fear prickling my back. Well, maybe I just had an itch, but right at that moment the light was scared of stepping too far over the boundary into this room, whether because of the occupants - myself and my sister - or because of something more sinister. Saying that, what could be more sinister than two siblings who could, with neither thought nor whisper of a breath, alter the course of someone's life. Sure, in Joy's case it was for the better. In my case though, altering the course of someone's life meant diverting them over the Niagara Falls into a fire pit below.

I didn't blame the light. I wasn't too fussed about being there either.

"Don't doubt me again, Sin." Joy's face was grave. There could almost have been a tombstone about her head. Her voice was a monotone that held not a single inflection, yet carried such a mighty weight of meaning, an ant would have struggled.

"Pardon?"

I was, to say the least, miffed. I hadn't broken out of a mental home just to become the lap dog to my deceased sister! I was so used to following her when we were kids, it came naturally now. And she seemed to have a touch more of a clue about what was happening than I did - which wasn't surprising seeing as I had no clue whatsoever. Even Sherlock Holmes, had he gone for a wander around the recesses of my mind, would have found it far from elementary to find clues of any sort in there.

"I said..."

Sod this. I wasn't going to take it. So she was my sister. So she was dead and seemed to be party to knowledge that she couldn't, or maybe even wouldn't, share. So what? I'd just gone for a stroll in the Twilight Zone and had seen someone I'd considered a friend killed. And the killer knew all about me and my funny little ways. So excuse me if I have to wonder what I'm doing. Excuse me if I don't automatically fall into step behind the Squadron Leader. Excuse me if I happen to want to know what the hell is going on!

I interrupted her with the only thing I could think of at the time. A classic line. One to be proud of.

"Whatever."

I stormed off upstairs to my room, a petulant little boy who'd been reprimanded and didn't really understand why.

I sat on my bed, hands clasped, thumbs rubbing against each other. I was slumped forward, my shoulders hunched and neck at such an angle that I'd be sure to suffer later if I didn't move. Well tough titties. Let me suffer. Let me be in pain. Would it be so much worse than the way I was feeling? I doubted it.

"Sit up, Sin. You know that does your back in."

Joy was standing at the door. Had she walked upstairs? Drifted through the floor like Casper? Disappeared from her chair only to reappear at my door like... well, like me I suppose.

She was right. I'd be a walking grimace if I didn't sit up straighter. I was a martyr to the red hot poker that every so often was shoved between my shoulder blades. Straightening up, the grimace playing on my lips for a moment like a pond skimmer racing across the surface tension of the water, I looked at her. I tried to return her stony stare but managed little more than a slightly muddy look. I felt drained. Not really sorry for myself, but somehow lost. Perhaps it was because I had expected to have been found by now. Not found by the men in the white coats with their happy needles, but found by myself - not lost inside of me anymore. Instead I was still wandering aimlessly, being led rather than leading, a horse being taken to water, and if I didn't drink I'd be chucked in and drowned. Should I give in? Succumb to whatever wanted next to take a bite out of the Sin pie? Wallow in pity with a capital *SELF?*

It would be so easy. Drift beneath the waters of dismay like a strait-jacket on the sea, waving goodbye to any who might notice. Who needed breath? Who needed life? Wasn't it better than all the pain, fear and strife? Well, to be honest, for seconds that felt like a week and a half, I thought it was. Time had stood still and was waiting patiently for me to decide what I was going to do. In that pause between one heartbeat and the next my mind was made up. Give up or give 'em the one finger salute.

Aye, aye, cap'n.

I smiled. It was pretty much, from the middle to the ends, genuine. Maybe a little dip to the left of centre, but only a little.

"Go on then, you frippet," I said. "What now?"

Joy smiled then. Like chocolate sauce drizzled over profiteroles, all was well once more.

"What now?" she said, walking over to the bed. She sat down beside me (a spider to my Miss Muffet?) and took my hand. "Now I apologise."

Apologise? I was surprised.

"Apologise?" I asked, surprised.

"Yes. I shouldn't have spoken to you like that."

Should I tell her that no, she shouldn't have. I wasn't a football to be kicked about when she was bored and stuck under the bed when she wasn't. I was the one going through this crap. She could vanish off to whichever cloud she liked to plonk herself on and play harps all the live long day. I had to hang around here and face whatever music wanted to batter my eardrums. I'd tried the cloud approach, but it hadn't quite worked out as planned. Should I tell her that? Probably. In fact, absolutely.

"Don't worry about it, chick. You've got your reasons."

See, I knew how to stand up to her.

"Perhaps." She squeezed my hand. "But still. You don't know what those reasons are, so I have to make allowances for that."

My sister, apologising. Wow. It had to happen sooner or later, like me bedding a nymphomaniac fetish model. It had to happen; I just didn't expect to be drawing my breath if it did! Don't get me wrong, Joy didn't automatically assume she was always right. I think it was more a case of everyone else assuming that. And if she actually was wrong, I'm sure she would admit it, just as she was now, but I could never recall witnessing such a monumental moment. Just as I've never bedded a nympho fetish model resplendent in PVC and strategically placed clamps.

I smiled again. What was the point in arguing or griping or holding a grudge? For all I knew I could still be locked away in my padded cell, drugged up to heaven upon high, and this could all be a hallucination. But while I had my sister back, I'd accept that and anything she had to throw at me. I'd just maybe get better at ducking.

"It's fine. Don't worry." An edge of me felt that it wasn't fine, not really, but Joy had a habit of dulling the sharpest edge, so it was fairly easy to run my finger along it without drawing blood.

"Sure?"

"Sure."

And I was sure. There were bigger fish to fry, and they weren't all haddock in batter. One or two sharks had swum into the net too - a net that, I figured, would be closing in on me fairly rapidly. I was a dolphin caught up with the tuna and I didn't know if I'd be able to free myself or whether I'd end up in a can on a shelf in Asda. Sin in brine. Delicious with mayonnaise.

"Good."

She kissed my cheek, then stood up and started pacing. My room isn't as palatial as I might have liked. Even though its furnishings were sparse, a cat could be swung with just about enough room not to take its head off on the wall as you spun. Around the bed there was floorspace for some jeans and duds to be thrown without tripping over them the next morning, but that was about it. It mean that Joy's pacing would, if it went on long enough, wear a rut in my carpet. I assumed a ghost's or zombie's footfalls would have some effect similar to my own anyway.

Besides. She'd just used the word 'good.' Pacing, to me, didn't appear to be good at all. Pacing appeared to be, in fact, bad. The distant frown on her face did nothing to change my opinion of the complete absence of 'good,' convincing me instead that I was in the company of awful, appalling and dire, the three blind mice of my mood. Well bugger how they run, and bugger chopping off their tails with a chainsaw. Whack 'em over the head with a hammer instead. Say it like you mean it.

"Joy."

She stopped her striding and turned to me. She tried to look at me but for some reason couldn't quite make eye contact.

"Come on," I said.

We had to get this, whatever it was, over with. I understood she was unable to tell me whatever it was she knew. I didn't quite understand how she could have that restriction and yet still take me to Connors' office to witness a murder, but I was sure there was a completely irrational explanation. Whatever her reasoning, it was all irrelevant. We had a situation here, folks, and my fretting or her carpet thinning would have only a detrimental effect on the outcome. Not that trailing a rut in the rough pile of the polyester-wool mix could really influence the life and times of a raving loony and his deceased sibling, but you never know. Maybe it was taking Chaos Theory a step beyond the beat of a butterfly wing, but maybe that step was right on the line proving that no, officer, I hadn't been drinking or smoking something I shouldn't have been, and I was perfectly capable of driving this here automobile of my life right into the nearest tree. Thank you and good night. Wish I had an airbag.

To be honest, and I'm nothing if not honest...

Hold on. Does that mean my honesty is the only thing I've got going for me? Does that mean I'm a hollow shell of a man if I'm not a fine, upstanding, paid up member of Honesty International? If my family motto isn't 'Tell a lie, gotta die, stick a penguin in your eye' then I'm a mere shadow, a shade of substance with neither hope nor honour?

Nah. Don't be daft.

So. To be honest, and I'm lots of things if not honest, Chaos Theory may well play its subtle, sinister part in all of this, but it was like an extra in a Lord of the Rings battle sequence. There were thousands of others in the fray and unless it was wearing a pink hat, feather boa and a frilly little sequined tutu, it wasn't really going to be seen amongst the polystyrene armour and fake blood. No, this time it was... erm... Time. Something we were in as short supply of as we were salt and vinegar Pringles. It was a Mother Hubbard day today and the cupboard, both of Pringles and Time, was bare. With every tick of the clock, Connors and his hounds were closing in and once they popped, I doubted that they'd stop.

Tick, tock, tick, tock. What time is it Mister Wolf? Time to bite off your head from the twinkle toes up.

My 'what now' question hadn't been answered, but I hoped Joy would have some idea. I figured she'd have a plan that she'd love to come together. I also hoped that either one of us, but preferably both, would drag themselves up out of the Drums of Dol and get this showboat steaming along the Mississippi. The hesitant smile that played hopscotch across my sister's mouth indicated that she might just be the one to pull the whistle and yell out 'All aboaarrdddd!' And I would help by weighing anchor.

I was going to make a joke there about the anchor weighing 18 stone 4 pound, but I won't. Especially as it would be more like around 30 tons or more. And 'weigh anchor' doesn't mean that anyway. But that's the point of the joke. But I didn't make the joke.

Erm... Anyway...

Anyway... I was beginning to feel like I'd swallowed some chewing gum and my shit was twanging back. The mood in this house was bouncing up and down faster than Zebedee on ecstasy. Or in ecstasy. It was a coin, yes, two pence probably, that was being constantly tossed. Flip and catch. Happy and sad.

"Come on, indeed," said Joy.

'Eileen?' Oh, sorry, 'indeed.'

"We need to get out of here." She reached out for my hand and I automatically held out my own. Before I stood, though, I asked:

"Where are we going?"

"Somewhere."

"Somewhere? Where's that?"

I'd have to look at a map, or Google at least, one day and see if there actually was a town called Somewhere. It'd make a change from living in a town called Malice. Oooh, yeah.

"I don't know," she said. "We'll find out when you take us there."

When I...?

"When I take us there?"

"Yes. We can't stay here. He'll find us. He doesn't know this house yet, but it probably won't take him long. His pet has escaped and he wants it back in its cage."

"His pet? I'm his pet? What do you mean?"

"Sin, you saw what the video. He knows. He knows! He's not going to let a prize like that get away, not while there's a chance he can use it - control it."

A pet? A prize? I was neither of those. I was a person. I was me! I wasn't sure who that murdering, teleporting me really was, but it was still me! As for controlling me!?

I realised I was shaking my head and stopped myself, but Joy responded to it.

"Yes, Sin. As much as you might not like it, he knows. And he's known for a while. That was a fairly recent video, but there's others. So many others. Don't you remember?"

"Remember what?" I remembered, or thought I did, pretty much all of my time in the hospital. I couldn't recall any gaps. There were no slices of my memory's steak and ale pie being munched on by the Spirit of Forgetfulness, with a few chunky chips and some garden peas covered in lashings of gravy.

Saying that, I didn't remember, not even with a whisper of recall, the episode in The Room that Connors had been watching. What else was missing? What else had he made me do? I felt my face drop, the muscles sagging suddenly as if they'd been tensed up for days and the weight of all that skin had become too much for them and they'd had to let go, breathing a hefty sigh of relief as they released their grip.

He did know. That much was obvious. But how much did he know? Moreover, how much was there to know?

"He's had you as his little lab rat for months now." She sat on the bed beside me, her hand on mine. It felt cold. I felt cold. My blood had gone the way of my face - south for the winter - and I was shivering. Even her arm around me failed to give me any warmth.

See? Shit twanging day, all right.

A lab rat. That was what I'd been reduced to. I wondered if I'd even been an actual bona fide patient. But then, were any of the patients really patients, or where they merely a hobby to the Doctor, passing away the days whilst giving him something to vent his megalomaniacal tendencies upon. I know which I leaned towards, and it didn't involve a modicum of care or a Hippocratic oath. Hypocritical, perhaps, but Hippocratic? I think not. When had I been promoted from mere loon to Teacher's Pet? When had I scampered up the ladder of Life, Love and the Lunatic's Way to become Connors' personal plaything? And what had I had to do to get there?

These questions and more were unlikely to be answered in the next thrilling episode of Sin: A Life Unfolding. Or should that be Unfeeling? Or perhaps even Unravelling. If only this had really been a Hollywood blockbuster, or even an old Ealing comedy. At least I'd have had a script and could potentially have looked ahead to see what was going to happen to my character. Was I going to go out in a blaze of gunfire, leaving behind the beautiful accomplice, her bosom heaving as she sobbed for her loss? Would I ride off into the sunset on my trusty steed, with only a trail of settling dust to show I'd ever passed this way? Would I wake up in the shower to find this had all been a horrible dream and that I was actually married to Victoria Principal?

Hmmmm...

No.

The doo-doo was twanging with yo-yo like precision and all we could do was duck to avoid getting whacked in the eye.

So, (deep breath) I was a lab rat. Well, this rat was going to bite back. This rat was badder than its Seven Hills cousins and was going to crap in the lunch of the good doctor. This rat was going to give Connors a nice unhealthy dose of rabies before the day was out. Granted that was a metaphorical dose of rabies and a probably metaphysical bite. The crap in the lunch was too tempting an offer though... Either way, some arses need to be kicked and I had a size 9 ready and waiting.

I just had to figure out how. Well, I had a lot more than that to figure out. How? Why, Where and When, and their little brother What all wanted to join the club, become fully paid up members and sport the flash little badge and cap. Sign up here, guys. Thirty days free subscription and you get a nice shiny pen to boot!

This was making me crazy. It felt like I had a steering wheel down my pants that was driving me nuts. Yeah, yeah, so up until very recently, I was supposedly officially crazy anyway. Is that going to be held against me forever? Does shit stick like bugs to a windscreen? Give a guy a break and let bygones be gone by. I'm not, your honour, and never have been crazy. Teleportation, mental mayhem and seagull slaughtering might test that denial, but hey, you never believe the Wet Paint sign unless you're wiping it off your hands because you just can't resist checking. If you want me to prove to you that, with a thought, I can turn those innards into outards, then just say the word.

Hmmm. Didn't think so.

But obviously I jest. Even though I probably could, I didn't know how. It was all subconscious. All that death was dealt by the shiver that lived in the hell of my heart. He and I, Shiver and Sin, weren't on speaking terms. We didn't share a morning coffee while chatting about the weather and whether anyone had been ripped apart recently. So you're safe.

Not that I would anyway, of course. I might be a little strange, in fact I hope I am (besides the obvious talents), but I am not crazy.

Promise.

So. Labus Raticus was I? Fine. Pet project? Double fine. Snivelling little victim on the run and in hiding? I think not.

I didn't remember any videos. I didn't remember that session with Connors, nor any others where my particular brand of barbarism exhibited itself. I didn't remember being pushed into performing, like Marcel the monkey, missing only a tiny fez hat and a cup to collect money in. To my knowledge there were no blanks in my memory, no jagged edges where pages had been ripped out, screwed up and thrown into the bin, but that didn't mean they didn't exist. I wasn't sure if I ferreted enough I might be able to unearth them but I supposed it didn't really matter. If those memories were windows into the past, their glass shattered by the Doc swinging a nice big hammer, then there was nothing I could do. If, on the other hand, I could call in a glazier to do a quick repair job, then all the better. I'd flick through the yellow pages of my mind later. Right now there was a fan that was in dire need of some shit hitting it.

And I had a fistful ready to throw.

Joy leaned away from me at that point, a quizzical look on her face.

"You okay?" she asked.

Was I okay? We didn't need to take a stroll along the prom-prom-prom of my tattered life to see the myriad reasons why I wouldn't be okey-dokey-pig-in-a-pokey, but strangely, I was. A light bulb had been flicked on inside of me and all the darkness has fled for the hills. Well, most of it at least. A few shadows still lurked there in the nether regions, but I was sure I could handle them. So yes, I figured I was okay.

"I am," I said.

Joy was still looking at me as if I had grown another nose or something, maybe sprouted horns and a yukka out of my ear.

"Promise?"

To Joy and I, a promise was never made lightly. A promise was just that, a promise. If you said it, you meant it. It stemmed, I think, from an upbringing where not every word that came out of our parents' mouths could be trusted. You always had to take what you were told with a pinch of Lot's wife. Even if that magic 'P' word was used, we made sure to count to ten, then again, then not believe it anyway. Far safer that way. If you set yourself up to be let down, you were never disappointed when it actually happened. And if you weren't let down - if by some crazy fluke what you were told actually happened, then bonus. Small things or big things, it didn't matter. Disappointment was disappointment to a child. Whether it was asking for a Six Million Dollar Man toy and a Thunderbird 6 (was that the blue one where the middle came out and the dinky submersible appeared?) for Christmas and getting nothing, or finding out that cheques were written drawing money out of your account, but you weren't the one who'd signed them, it boiled down to the same thing. If the kid expected it, it didn't hurt him as much.

Or at least he could pretend it didn't.

So. We made sure that, if we couldn't trust our parents completely, we should be able to trust each other. Perhaps that's a fairly grown up attitude for an 8 year old, or however many solar revolutions I'd seen. Perhaps not. But we seemed to realise that we needed someone who we knew, if they said something, they meant it. Someone who wasn't going to 'borrow' our paper round money and never pay it back. That kind of thing. Sibling rivalry was one thing, and we had our fair share of bickering and battling, but when it came down to it, as I've said, a promise was a promise.

"Promise."

"You're a strange one, Sin."

"I take that as a compliment, sis. Especially from a walking corpse."

She smiled and I returned the grin. The pair of us had joined in the game of doo-doo-twanging and, even though we were up to our elbows in it, for a moment it actually smelled sweet. For a moment.

"So where are you taking us?"

She had to go and spoil it, didn't she. A second or two of actual semi-normality shattered by a simple question. If this had been another life, another pair, another world, that question may well have simply meant 'Pub or restaurant?' or 'Park or beach?' Unfortunately, this was this life, this pair and this world. It meant one thing.

Flip and catch.

My problem was that I didn't know how to do either. Dr. Connors had obviously been pushing me to discover exactly that, but it was under the influence of drugs. It was chained to a chair. It certainly wasn't sitting on my bed at my parents' house. True, I'd managed to flip out of my cell hoping a nice passing furnace would catch me, but that hadn't quite worked as I'd planned. I'd figured out how to do that, after a fashion, but I'd ended up on a beach that was only by chance not in another country. What if, this time, we did end up in Outer Mongolia. What if we landed right smack in the cooking pot of a lost Amazonian tribe of cannibals? What if, indeed, we ended up in the fires of hell itself? I couldn't control it. The fact that I'd managed to get myself out of the hospital at all was something I wasn't sure I could repeat. The possibility of what could easily go wrong, basically, scared me.

I was still okay. I was still positive. The non-existent plan of action was still, essentially, a plan. But to take my sister's hand and jump to who knew where wasn't something I felt I could risk, and I told her so.

"Sin," she said quietly.

"Yes?"

"It's up to you, brother. We could simply wait here and face whatever consequences are dumped on our heads. Or we can do something and get out of here."

"But you could get hurt," I insisted.

Joy laughed then. A sparkle of real humour. I didn't see the joke.

"I'm *dead!*" she said. "How am I going to get more hurt than *dead?*"

She had a point. But she could, it seemed, come and go as she pleased. She could, it also seemed, take us into a crazy Twilight Zone version of the Seven Hills in which psychopathic psychiatrists murdered friendly orderlies. Why couldn't she get us out of here?

I asked her. If you don't ask, you don't find anything out.

"Because I can't," she said simply.

Well that told me.

So, it was down to me. Teleport (even the word made me cringe) or wait. Hold on...

"Why can't we just walk out of here? Get a taxi or something and go somewhere?"

"We could," she admitted. A flash of relief sparked inside of me at the prospect. "But there'd be witnesses. There'd be a record at the taxi office. We could bump into someone we knew, like Wendy. If you take us, then even we don't know where we'll end up.

My point exactly! But the brief spark was extinguished. I took a deep breath and...

A knock at the door.

Chapter Seventeen

Joy and I stared at each other for a breathless moment. I wasn't sure if she was actually breathing anyway, being deceased, but it was a breathless one for me. My whole body went still. I think even my heart stopped beating for a second.

Yes, I know. Joy's wouldn't have been beating anyway.

A knock at the door again. The doorbell.

Joy stood and moved slowly to the window. Even though I hated them, a simple net curtain draped across the glass. I'd always meant to take it down, perhaps replace it with a blind, roman or venetian maybe. Or a tab-bottom, I sort of liked them. I just hadn't got round to it. I was thankful now. It hid my sister from sight as she peered down to the front door. I could see by the look on her face that the visitor wasn't just the milkman wanting his money. It may have been a Jehovah's Witness, but her look was blacker than the night sky with your eyes closed. Santa Claus hadn't passed by and not been able to get up to the chimney. It wasn't the tooth fairy on the hunt for a molar or two, bag full of coins strapped to her waist for the exchange.

It had to be him.

"It's Connors," she whispered.

I didn't think. I didn't hesitate. I don't recall even standing up, but I suppose I must have. Somehow, though, Joy's hand was in mine and we were no longer in my room, sitting on the bed. We were... somewhere.

It was dark. It was black. It was as if it was night. It was as if all the light had got scared and took flight. Well, it was night, that much I already knew. But the sound and the air had joined in with the light and skedaddled. There was an absence of anything other than the feel of my sister's hand in my own. Was this what a flotation tank felt like? Sensory depravation? The situation was pretty depraved so we were on to a winner there. But where had everything gone? Or rather, where had we gone...?

Suddenly I could feel the blood pumping in my right ear. A rushing sound with a rhythmic beat that made me feel as if I were walking in my own heartbeat. The sensation lasted for no more than a few seconds, little more than a short stroll, before the rushing sound increased and the world flooded back around us. There was still silence and darkness, but now there was also substance. I could feel the air. I could feel the breath entering and exiting my body. I could hear faint sounds of life.

Yes, I know I said there was silence. I didn't mean there was a complete lack of sound, a void where sound had lived until it had been evicted by a jobsworth council for not paying council tax. I didn't mean sound had vanished as if a flying saucer had plopped down out of the sky and zapped it away to poke and prod and analy probe. I meant it was quiet. Very quiet. Not the silence from before my ear decided to run a river through itself, but the silence of a late night, when only stray cats and restless dogs wandered the streets, and fallen leaves drifted across roads travelled, normally, by the metal behemoths that could crush them in a second; cars. The silence that was only that because it was such a contrast to the cacophony of the day.

After sound had crept back from whence it had fled, light followed warily after. Or wearily. A smattering of stars sprinkled themselves across the sky, a light icing on the Victoria sponge of the night. Vague shapes formed around us. They began as shadows that feinted about, threatening to join together but deciding not to, rather preferring to fool us into believing they were something they weren't, before finally giving in and coalescing to become something indistinct but almost recognisable. My eyes adjusted slowly, seemingly taking their time, enjoying the fact that I had no idea where we were and wanting to drag the suspense out for as long as possible. Well jeepers, peepers, let's wait for those creepers, eh?

Did Joy's eyes needed time to adjust? Did being dead give her the ability to see better than someone who still had the beat of a heart to chase the blood around their veins. Did the jeeping peepers of a corpse dilate or were they lacklustre and lifeless. Well, I actually knew that already, at least in the case of my sister. The sparkle of a thousand stars still shone in her eyes and even the unfortunate fact of being an inhabitant of the afterlife hadn't dimmed its shine. That led to another thought. I'd kind of had the idea that this was Joy, as I knew her. This was physically her. I'd touched her. I smelled her. This was my sister, in body, mind and what was left of her spirit after the Grim Reaper had done whatever it was that Reapers did. Sure, she'd let herself melt back in the forest, flaps of maggot riddled skin sliding off like butter on hot toast, but other than that, this was Joy. Once she'd plopped her eye back in and the cockroaches had finished crawling out of her mouth, my sis was back, as good as new.

But was she? This couldn't be her actual body, even though it looked, smelled and felt like her. It couldn't be. I doubt even Mr Grim was good enough at jigsaw puzzles to put all those tiny bits of ash back together. He might have been World Champion at the 500 piece landscape or the 1000 piece Where's Wally Super Edition. Perhaps he could even put all the Corn Flakes back together to make them look like the cockerel on the box, but a human body, with thoughts and feelings and attitude was something else entirely. I didn't think even the mighty Death himself could manage that particular feat. Maybe that was just me, though. I was rubbish at jigsaws. I never had the patience for them to be honest. Even a 500 piecer would bore me after about twenty-five or so. So maybe Death could rebuild her. Maybe he did have the technology, and a staple gun, super glue, and double-sided sticky tape, to get the job done. I didn't know. The chances weren't good though. So this wasn't Joy, but it was. It wasn't her body reformed. She wasn't a phoenix risen from the ashes of her own cremation. But it was still her.

Was it an illusion? Was it all in my mind? No, because that would mean that it was all in the mind of Wendy as well. Or Wendy was in my mind. Or I in her's. Or this was the Matrix and we were all in the mind of a machine, sleeping like batteries... erm... babies. I supposed that would make the cell I'd been incarcerated in fairly appropriate. Dry cell as opposed to padded cell.

So what then? Was she a ghost? Like Casper or Swayze? Were we Matthews and Matthews (Deceased)? Or did George A. Romero have dibs on her life story?

It didn't matter. My head had spun this little web already and I was likely to get stuck fast if I didn't pull free and focus. Joy wasn't going to tell me and I didn't know how to find out myself. I didn't know if she was a spirit or a sprout. A ghost or a gherkin. It didn't matter. There were bigger fish to fry in the chip shop of our little drama and if we didn't sort our heads out - if I didn't sort mine out at least - we were likely to get drowned in a great dollop of mushy peas at best or curry sauce at worst. And we'd be battered in the process.

The shadows had stopped pratting about and had taken on more distinct shapes and my eyes had decided they'd had enough of winding me up and were prepared to do what they did best and let me see, albeit it still vague and grainy in the low lighting.

We were inside a vast room, so large it almost felt like were outside rather than in. The ceiling was completely clear and apart from a very few support struts it appeared to be made totally of glass. The smattering of stardust across the sky could easily, I suppose, have been a splattering of bird droppings, but either way, it had the same effect. Even being inside, I felt exposed. I felt vulnerable. And I still felt at risk, even though no one else could know where I was, since I didn't know myself. I was an insect on a slide, and not the kind found in a playground amongst the swings, Witches' Hats and bruised knees. The glass roof was the microscope lens that was peering down at me, an ant struggling to survive.

Shake it off, shake it off. Twang the shit back into the butt-cheeks of Life.

I grabbed my composure off the hook and wrapped it around my shoulders, slowly feeling its warmth settling through me like a log fire in an Alpen lodge. Not that I'd ever been in front of a log fire, nor had I visited any lodges, Alpen or otherwise, but I imagined that's how it felt. Calming. Dousing the chill flames of fear like frostbitten fingers returning to life. Trying my best to keep the cloak of composure tight around me, not quite as effective as Harry Potter's cloak of invisibility but close, I looked around. Joy was in a semi crouch and I realised I was too.

"Where are we?" she whispered.

I could have laughed, but I didn't. A giggle threatened to well up inside of me, maybe morphing into a snicker or possibly even a guffaw on the way out, but I held it in check. I might laugh at a funeral, but I didn't want that funeral to be my own.

My own funeral. I wondered if I would laugh then. If I were there in body and in spirit, though not actually in body-and-spirit - if I had moved on, passed over, stepped on a crack to never look back, would I laugh? Old Uncle Alfred and his ridiculous tie?

A rack of people I didn't really know wondering why the song I wanted playing was Simple Minds' 'Alive & Kicking'? A eulogy by someone who had never even met me waffling on about how wonderful I was? Which, naturally, was the truth... Would there have been something to amuse? Amidst the tears, some real and some more crocodile than Captain Hook's arch nemesis, was a little entertainment to be gleaned?

Well, hopefully, it would be a while before I had to find out. In the meantime...

'Where are we?' Wasn't the whole point of me being the one to take us from the house that we wouldn't know where we were? It wasn't as if I had a built in satnav - a SinNav perhaps - and could pinpoint our exact GPS position down to a whisker off a metre. Unless that tracking chip really was in my arm, of course. I was just pleased we hadn't popped up inside the furnace I'd picked for my original jump, all toastie-roastie together, if Joy could actually be toasted or roasted when she wasn't really alive. We didn't appear to be in Outer Mongolia either, which was good because it would have been a hell of a long walk back. We were where we wanted to be. We were Somewhere.

Jump. Was that what we'd done? Jumped? Was that the correct word to use? It still grated to say we'd teleported. This wasn't science fiction. Scotty wasn't upstairs not wanting to give her any more because she'd blow and we weren't Jeff Goldblum in disguise. So was it a jump? Or was it... was it a flip and a catch? Were we living (and I use the term loosely with respect to my partner in grime) two pence coins? Had we flipped and let the world catch us as it spun on its wobbly little axis?

'Where are we?'

Who knew? Should we jump again? Then again and thrice again? Let the trail criss-cross who knew where, so much so that we were dizzy with the flipping and the catching and the spinning and the...

But I did know.

I realised suddenly, with the impact of a short length of two by four across the back of my head. With the force of a bus through a post office window, I knew exactly where we were. Was it chance, happenstance or seat of the pants? Was it the Universe have a little giggle, or Fate's fickle finger once again? Or was it me? Some warped, deranged, completely bing-bang-boggley insane part of my mind that had a sick sense of humour and thought it would be hilariously funny to drop me slap-bang-bill-a-bong right into the lion's den?

My breath caught in my throat, frozen as if the temperature had just dropped to a couple of degrees above Kelvin and it was no longer today, but time had travelled and taken us with it, maybe in hand luggage, to the day after tomorrow.

Educational. That was what it was called. Stimulating. Enjoyable, even. It was, supposedly all of these things, and was, actually, none of them. To the suits and the auditors and the mighty They, this horticultural paradise was an essential part of the treatment for those fruit and nutters that could go a whole ten minutes without the drool having to be wiped from their faces or their backsides. Under Connors' loving care and attention, that reduced the possible number of those who might be educated or stimulated down to about four and a simple one-two-buckle-my-shoe-three-four-give-'em-some-more kept even those a smidgeon short of comatose.

We were at the hospital. The mental home. The lunatic had returned to the asylum. He hadn't taken it over yet, but hey, the night was still young.

Who sang that song...? Hmmm...

To please those that required pleasing, and to garner funding from those that had fat wallets and fatter bellies, Dr. Connors had built a nursery. It wasn't the kind of nursery where babies were taken to be looked after, although this version wasn't so far removed from that. It was the floral variety where adults requiring the care of babies were taken to be supposedly looked after. Of course, once the money was banked and the curiosities were satiated, I'd have been surprised to see even one patient pass through the vaulted doors that led to the hospital proper. No. It was far cheaper to hire the services of a gardener to tend the plants once a week than it was to let loose a bunch of shambling wastes of space and have half the workforce tied up watching them. No. Educate? Hah! Stimulate? Why? To Connors, I'd come to realise, the patients were a means to an end and nothing more. He could be mean and there'd be no end.

But it looked good on paper and it looked good to any who happened to look. So a purpose was served and no dolphins were harmed. Oh, sorry, that's porpoise. My mistake.

For a few seconds, I didn't know whether to be happy or sad. Happy because I knew where we were and it wasn't just somewhere, it was Somewhere. Happy because we were not crispy chicken. Happy because the world had turned and we hadn't burned. And sad? Sad because we'd returned to my own personal hell. Well, my personal purgatory was the reason I'd come here in the first place, but it had been the physical hell to my emotional one. Sad because we were sitting on the tongue of the mighty beast, waiting its mouth to close and swallow us whole.

Sad because all of my running; the gull, the boy in the car, the farmer, his wife and their child, and watching Jeremy die - it was all for nothing. I may as well have stayed put and kept my mouth shut. Or perhaps I should have tried harder when I clicked my ruby slippers together to leave here in the first place.

Was it a blessing for Joy to not have to breathe? On a cold December morning, when frost lay like icing across the pathways and parks and one small slip for Man could be one giant fall on your backside, did it please her to not breathe in and have her lungs turn to ice? After a hundred meter sprint did she have to worry about the breath being torn from her lungs by a rusty garden rake as she stood bent, hands on knees, panting and wheezing? Probably not. I hadn't noticed if my sister breathed at all. Maybe she did and possibly she didn't. It could be that she breathed normally. Or out of habit. Or her chest moved as if air was being sucked in whilst carbon dioxide was being expelled, even though it wasn't. Or it could be that none of these were true. Either way, I didn't have that option. I needed to breathe. My lungs were still intact and had a basic oxygen requirement to keep on working. Hey, it might be boring being lungs just expanding and contracting over and over in an incessant monotonous rhythm, but someone had to do it. A job was a job, however tedious, and they should be pleased they weren't rectums. Not that I could tell if they were complaining or not. They were doing what they were designed to do. Or at least they were when I remembered to breathe again.

My breath, once it kick started again, came in short rasping jolts, as if it wanted to stay away and not be seen to be associated with me. I think not, I thought, and did my best to steady myself. I wasn't suddenly centre stage on Britain's Got Talent, my voice all nervous crackles as anxiety strangled the words before I could squeeze them out. I also wasn't a deer, casually crossing a road to see my friends in the forest on the other side, a night of beer and Wii playing planned, caught in the headlights of a gas-guzzling gargantuan that was bearing down on me, wiping all thoughts of alcohol induced wiimote twirling from my mind in a blaze of headlamp and radiator grill. I was simply a normal guy, with his dead sister, suddenly teleported back into the mental institute from which I'd escaped.

Simple.

I settled somewhere in the no-man's land between a smile and a frown. I gave myself a mental botox boost that fixed my face, and my mood, in a grim but fairly relaxed mask of emotionless resignation. Not that I was emotionless - I'd yo-yoed so much I could practically do a cat's cradle or walk the dog with neither a canine nor feline to hand. Nor was I resigned - the fact that I'd just popped up to say hello and couldn't go back down below, much like a rollicking burp after a nice cold glass of coke, wasn't here nor there. The situation was the situation. Deal with it or don't. Do or die, tuck into a big steak pie.

Yes indeedy.

I broke the glorious news of our current location to my sister. She took it rather well I thought.

"Are you *insane??*" she bellowed. I was sure I felt a sprinkle of spit and the heat of her breath as she brought her face close enough to mine for me to see her nasal hairs. She'd always kept herself preened to perfection, any stray hair or zit banished post haste, so I declined to mention the odd nostril sprout. I thought that best.

Perhaps I should have returned the bellow, standing up for myself and pointing out that location, location, location was a Channel 4 television programme. If she'd have wanted to go somewhere specific she should have gone with my original idea of calling a taxi. But then I figured it wasn't necessarily a point of going somewhere specific as it was of *not* going somewhere specific. Either way, though, I didn't tap in an address into a control pad in my stomach and then follow the directions. It wasn't an exact science, if indeed any science was involved. We just went. Put your lips together and blow. Much like a hot air balloon or a leaf on the wind, I couldn't say let's go left or right or up or down. Before about two minutes previous, I didn't actually realise I could properly go anywhere.

Yes, I know I deliberately evacuated my cell at this very institute. Yes, I know I had figured out that I could teleport. And stop, please, sniggering at that word. It is what it says on the tin, with no preservatives or E numbers added. That was me then and this was me now. It had all seemed so simple - jump into a furnace and die. What was so difficult about that? Quite a fair bit, it appeared. Now I was on the run. Now I had my dead sister accompanying me. Now I'd seen that the doctor who'd 'looked after' me was, in reality, a cold-blooded killer who knew all about my particular gifts and had even tried to train me to use them. Albeit under the influence of drugs. Now I'd witnessed a murder, killed a boy and a bird, and almost killed a family and more. Now, I had to admit, the days of being locked in a padded cell whilst a needle was jabbed into my arm and sweet oblivion washed over me seemed to be the greener side of the grassy knoll.

But anywho. The knowledge was gone. Someone had closed that particular book, without noting down the page number or, at the very least, turning down the page corner. Not that it was knowledge exactly. It was more of a feeling, and I'd lost that feeling, loving or loathing. I was walking a blind line between me and who I needed to be. My arms were outstretched and my eyes were closed. I was feeling my way, stumbling and crashing into things that I couldn't see, hoping I wouldn't trip and fall on my arse. Whilst in my cell, I had some confidence in my 'ability'. I wanted to go and I went. But now the hunt was on and I'd left that confidence behind in my hasty departure. I could still hear it in the distance, calling out to me - reaching out beseechingly. Come back! But this blind mouse was running away with his tail between his legs while it was still attached.

That Connors had forced me to practise the teleportation (the phrase 'stop sniggering' includes the implication not to smirk) was not lost on me. From the brief video clip we saw in his office, it seemed I should have this down pat by now. I was sure that that hadn't been the only session he'd had with me, not by a long way. I'd have been surprised if I hadn't had daily 'treatments'. I mean, if the shoe was on the other foot, plimsole or clod-hopping welly, I'd quite possibly have done the same myself. Would you be able to stop yourself? It'd be like a boy in a toyshop after closing - it would be possible to play with all the things you always wanted for Christmas but knew you'd never get, because buying you a present tapped into your parents' alcohol budget. Besides, Christmas was all about commercialisation now, and it had lost its original meaning. So toys and other gifts were simply different ways to line the pockets of the retail giants. Not being bought them made a statement to... someone or other... and was character building into the bargain.

A little like being given the first name Sin.

Apparently.

So my father used to tell me anyway.

The thing was, I didn't fancy pumping myself full of drugs, as Connors had, just to rediscover my lost talents. Only a short time ago I was welcoming of them - the drugs that is. They helped me forget. They helped me believe it had all stopped and I was normal - as normal as a man locked up in a padded room floating on a nice fluffy cushion of Risperdal could be. Even if I did want to get my daily dose, I didn't expect to be buying them over the counter at Boots, at least not without one or two questionable eyebrows being raised. I felt under the spotlight enough without elevated bodily hair adding to the interrogation. Low 'brow' joke about things getting 'hairy' tried to skim through my mind, but I resisted their push, knowing that my sometimes inane sense of humour was out of place in situations like this. Joy was glaring at me with the heat of a solar flare and I needed to appease her before I got radiation burns.

I realised that I was being a hypocrite, or something like. I'd lost myself to drugs to smother and suffocate this beast that coiled inside my belly, and then I'd used that same beast to try to end my life. And just now I'd let it out of its cell again, like a prisoner on his hour in the exercise yard, to escape from the clutches of another monster. I wasn't sure just how many times I could do that without it taking its chance and breaking free for good. It was on a fairly tight leash, but I didn't know just how strong that leash was, or even what it looked like. It could be a solid thick chain that could hold the hounds of hell, or it could be as tissue, only 2-ply at that, not even strong enough to wipe your arse with.

In Farmer Giles' van, I'd had an idea that I could control it. I felt something different - something change. I could quite easily, whether I liked it or not, have torn that bully apart, and quite possibly everyone else in the street. I didn't though. I reined it in. I pulled it back. But how much of it was a breath held? And how much would it take for something to punch me in the stomach, and the breath be expelled and the demon within me to dance, or dine, or dilly-dally on till Doomsday? If that happened, Doomsday would be here a little early, much like the Number Five bus that had passed a couple of stops without having to pick up any passengers, right before ploughing through...

"Sorry," I said quietly.

I thought that appearing meek might sooth her savagery. And the meekness wasn't merely an appearance anyway. Coming to the nursery wasn't the cleverest matchstick in the box, but if the blue touch paper was lit, it'd certainly go up with a bang. I knew that. Of course I did. But choosing where to go was akin to throwing sand in the wind and deciding to surf on one particular grain. *That* one just there. It couldn't be done. The breeze scattered them all too far too fast, and your foot was too big anyway. Now that analogy might seem to be one of my shadier ones, with the meaning only vaguely clinging on to relevance - praying no one would stamp on its fingers and have it plunge to the depths below, but on some level in my head it made perfect sense. But then I've been told I'm a touch... touched. But then, again, I have just escaped a mental home.

My not so fake submissiveness didn't work. Why did I think it would?

"Sorry?" Joy shouted. "Sorry?!"

I tried not to concentrate on the light dusting of hairs up her nose. It wouldn't help my case.

I once had a cat. His name was Magic and he was part Persian and part tabby. He used to sit on my shoulder while I was at my laptop or watching TV. Not when I was on my Playstation, though. That was his cue to fight with my thumb as I battled with aliens or uncovered lost treasures. But anywho. He'd be perched there, on my shoulder, and I'd feel like Long John Silver with his pirate's parrot. With two legs, of course. And both eyes. I never managed to get him to say, repeatedly, "Pieces of eight," or "Pretty Polly," though. Not that I tried as I didn't think that feline vocal cords would stretch much further than meowing to be fed or stroked.

He was much cuter than my sister was as she began repeating, parrot fashion, "Sorry! He's sorry! Sorry! He's sorry!" to anyone that might be listening.

Given our location, I hoped that 'anyone' was limited to just me. I also hoped that her ranting wasn't going to draw any unwanted attention. We shouldn't be there, we didn't want to be there, and we would be in a humungous pile of poo if we were found to be there, but there we were nonetheless. Deal or don't, do or die, stick a pinecone where the sun don't shine. I needed to calm her down and decide what the next part of our little adventure might be. Well maybe she needed to decide, as I'd been led by the hand like a four year old to the ice cream van up to now. But there'd be no chocolate flake, strawberry sauce or hundreds & thousands as a treat for me.

I could slap her, shocking her into silence. She was, mostly at least, substantial. Whatever post-death version of flesh and bone comprised her body, I figured it'd react fairly normally to the palm of my hand coming sharply into contact with it. I could out-rant her. Talk louder and more insistently than her babbling. That, of course, was defeating the object. Silencing her by being Mr. Mouth Almighty myself would probably be the equivalent of picking up the PA microphone and announcing the Return of the Mighty Sin to the grateful listeners of Radio Nutsville FM. Our adoring fans, in the shape of Dr. Connors and his merry men would pour in through the burst open doors in seconds, and they wouldn't be holding out autograph books or left boobies for signatures. And, I'd assume, the sharp objects in their hands would more likely be needles than blue Bic pens. Knowing Joy, though, she'd slap me back - with her fist. We'd had a few scuffles, as siblings do, during our childhood and teens, so I knew that she was a little whirlwind when she was riled. I didn't want to find out what a touch of the supernatural might do for - or to - her. Angry ghosts became poltergeists and that normally meant things being thrown about and smashed up.

I didn't want 'things' to be me.

Then I heard something. Or felt like I'd heard something... or something. It was like feeling a breath of sound across my ear. A tickle of tone. You hear it but you don't. You feel it but you're not sure if it's in your head or in your ear. And then there was silence. Real silence. The kind that exists after a storm, when thunder and lightning have been very, very frightning. The hush after the horror. The peace after the party.

The silence after the sister.

Joy had shut up. I'd turned away from her ranting, almost in shame. I'd brought us here and I was being reprimanded for being a silly little child. How could I do something so foolish? How could I be so thoughtless? How could I lose his comb? I'd have to pay for being stupid. I'd have to pay for being useless. I'd have to...

Joy was gone. I looked towards the absence of noise to see a great big bundle of nothing where my dead sister had been. Now abandonment was something I'd been used to. Even whilst still living with my parents, I may as well have been dumped in a gutter outside a half way house, or given a one way ticket to nowhere. At various points I'd also felt as if the world had turned its back on me, like an ostrich burying its head in the sand. Can't see me so I don't exist. At various times during those various times, I'd wished I didn't.

Hence, I suppose, the attraction of toasting my tootsies.

But those feelings of being sole-shit had faded. Some of it had followed my parents into their respective graves (or urn in the case of my mother - they could never agree on anything) and some had just got lost along the way, probably along with my surname. We'd all hung around for a while years back, chewing the fat - a disgusting sounding phrase that I doubt really has anything to do with dining on blubber - until we'd become bored with each others' company and drifted apart like old school friends or the post-Pangean continents. I didn't realise it until Joy had returned but she had, eraser-like, rubbed out the final remnants of my life-long wallowing whimsy. I was ok with myself. Mostly. Apart from the obvious kinship with Death and all his minions. I didn't feel abandoned anymore. I no longer felt like the failure I'd been portrayed as by my father. His jibes and insults still echoed around in my head, but that's all they were now - echoes. Lacking substance. The meat gnawed from the bones of his derision by the jaws of time. They say time is a great healer. I don't know about that, but Time, when feeling a bit peckish, can nosh away at something until there's only a rack of skeletal remains that not even CSI's Gruesome Grisolm can decipher. I found it comforting that the worms had feasted on my father faster than Time had upon his memory. At least the little wrigglers had got something out of him, even if it was mostly gristle and stringy fat. I doubted even in death he'd been particularly appetising.

So I didn't feel abandoned when I saw that I was standing alone in the nursery. That surprised me actually. I'd been clinging on to Joy, letting her lead me whichever way was loose, with barely a whisper or whimper. In that short time I'd seen a friend murdered, stolen a vehicle from someone I'd almost murdered myself, and teleported into the hands of the enemy.

The Enemy. Anyone would think this was a war.

Well, perhaps it was, although I still had no idea why there was a conflict of any kind. Connors couldn't know that I knew either of his treatment of me or his killing of Jeremy. Why was I being hunted? *Was* I being hunted, in fact? Perhaps the doctor was simply worried about me and wanted my safe return so he could continue my treatment. And perhaps he taught Sunday School and could ride a tightrope on a unicycle backwards whilst blindfolded. He knew about me. He knew what I was. Probably more so than I did, because I had no idea. But he'd tested me. He'd made me into his personal laboratory rat and had been teaching me to run through his maze, without using my feet. And I could only imagine he wanted that part of me for himself. Somehow.

It was a war. There had already been casualties - one seagull and one careless driver springing to mind. But how to end it? I couldn't see a treaty being signed or a surrender (unless it was my own). There'd be no amicable shaking of hands and downing of weapons. He was out to get - or be - me and I was out to... not let him. Wow I sounded so 'GRRRR' sometimes, like the Hulk bursting forth from his pants. I'd been basically imprisoned, experimented upon and stalked, and all I could come up with was that I wanted to not let him. It had to be more than that. Not let him? Was I going to just tell him?

"Don't do that anymore Dr. Connors. I don't like it."

"Oh, sorry about that. Don't worry, I'll leave you alone."

"Why, thank you Doc."

"No problem, but please don't call me Doc."

Hardly.

There was going to be pain. Possibly more death. I just had to make sure it wasn't my own. Easy, no?

No.

I had to stop him. Find out what and why, and bring him to a screeching halt faster than my old dog Lady when she ran to the back door and saw all this white, freezing cold, snowy stuff. She'd never experienced it before and stopped so quickly the message didn't get from her head to her back legs fast enough to prevent her backside carrying on over her head and into the snow beyond. Naturally she then ran back in, jumped on the sofa and shook herself dry. I hoped I'd have more success with Connors than I did with Lady. He probably wasn't that bothered by snow so it would take a little more to stop him.

But what more did I have? What could I do? One may think what couldn't I do. Here's a guy that can leap tall buildings in a single teleport. Who could push a bus through a post office storefront with less effort than it takes to sneeze. One would be correct. Apparently I could. And apparently I could control it. But I didn't know how. Apart from the occasional feeling of composure, it was an entity all of its own. I no more held it in check than I did set it free. The control was uncontrolled, and in fact controlled me. But maybe that was a good thing. I should set this beast within me free and let it wreak the havoc it wished until it was sated. And Connors would pay whatever price that involved. I was in the perfect place. The madhouse under the guise of the mendhouse. I didn't think

Bender Benny and Company would mind being released from their torment. I could wipe out the whole place in a heartbeat. Take Connors and his whole shitbang, including myself, on the very merry way into nothingness. Oblivion wasn't just a ride at Alton Towers, it was also a place where nobody knows your name - mainly because there was nobody and nothing there to know you.

I could do that. Except I couldn't, could I? I didn't know how. And besides that, whatever he'd done, I put myself under his 'care' to stop myself doing precisely that. I wasn't him, and I wasn't going to let myself become him. Well, if I could help it anyway. Best intentions were better than none at all, weren't they?

Joy? She'd already proven she could read my mind, so I didn't feel the need to shout out loud. Luckily. I'm sure I would have found that a good number of others had suddenly changed their names to Joy and I'd be surrounded by all manner of people who really didn't bear any resemblance to my sister. I called out mentally, hoping the sound would carry through the skull and veins and flesh to seek her out wherever she might be hiding. I listened to the sound of my voice as it echoed around in my head. I couldn't tell whether it was still rattling around the confines of my bonce or was out there running around free, playing hide and seek. I wished for the latter but expected the former. Nonetheless, I called out again.

I was greeted by silence. Ok, perhaps the feelings of abandonment hadn't completely left me. Perhaps they, along with Joy, were simply hiding in the shadows, peeking out when I wasn't looking, waiting to run up and whack me over the head.

I remember once my mum hit me on the back of my head with a roll of kitchen foil. I'd been messing about having a laugh - pretending to be a bee, I think, making silly buzzing noises around her. She hit me a touch too forcefully and apologised "I didn't mean to come so hard..." It took a good while for us to stop falling about laughing, and for me to stop feeling horrified that my own mother knew such a phrase. It was one of the few times when the sound of laughter echoed around the house. And afterwards it did seem to echo, fading into the emptiness that was the house's normal psyche.

That moment, that few seconds of hysteria (probably more profound because of its usual absence), was genuinely funny, even if it was in a you-had-to-be-there kind of way. This wasn't funny. Not even in a having-to-be-there kind of way. In fact this was a having-*not*-to-be-there moment! Well, maybe there was some dark humour to be scavenged from me finding myself lounging on the tongue of Pinocchio's whale, especially as I'd brought myself here. I didn't really see it though. I just needed to find the kindling to get it to spit me out.

Anyone got a match I could borrow?

Didn't think so.

Right. Sort this. That was the plan. Not the same kind of plan that the A-Team's Hannibal loved to come together, but perhaps one Howlin' Mad Murdoch would have been happy with. Joy or no joy, that was the question. Right now, the answer was no Joy, so no joy. I felt as if I'd become, in a very short time, reliant on my sister. Perhaps her sudden disappearance was a good thing. Perhaps this would be the making of me. As long as it didn't make me into either a mass murderer (ignoring my past) or a corpse, then I guess I could be happy. If I could figure out what happy was. No. Turn my frown upside down. At the least into a grimace, if nothing else.

I shouted out again in my head. Less a (mental) gob open yell than raising my voice and calling. She had buggered off. Whether she'd ran away or thought of something more pressing than her brother's impending death and destruction was up to her. I was on my own, and though I wasn't my first choice for company, I was all I had.

Go Team Me.

Give me an 'S!'

Give me an 'I!'

Give me an 'N!'

What have you got?

Good question. About time we found out.

Joy wasn't answering my calls. Maybe she was doing some supernatural version of call screening and hadn't bothered to turn on the answering machine. She'd said, about a million years ago, that a storm was coming. Up until moments ago I'd assumed she was going to be my umbrella. Well, hey-hey-hey, if I was going to get wet, or even swept away by the downpour, then so be it.

I looked up at the sky. The stars stared back down. I wondered if they could see me; if they were like the Norse gods; Zeus or Odin (mixing my deities) looking down, moving me like a chess piece. Sin to Queen's Bishop One. It sounded like a radio call to my backup team of Navy Seals. Well they were probably down the club having a party. They wouldn't be answering. And the stars may as well sit back and enjoy the show. I was going to figure out Checkmate in as few moves as possible even if it killed me.

Hmmm..... Anyone fancy a game of draughts or snakes and ladders? Kerplunk? Russian Roulette?

Star light, star bright, why does it have to be so shite?

Where to start? I didn't know whether to try and get out of the nursery and make my way back home - either by foot or attempted teleportation - or to go and find out what Dr. Connors was really up to. Gather my thoughts or plough in recklessly? I was never one for recklessness really, much preferring the more measured approach. I'd think before acting rather than wading in all guns a-blazing. I would have betted on being hit by any stray bullets in any shoot-out that may have resulted, and that was the case here. I knew something had to be done. But I also knew I might, or rather would, get hurt in the meantime.

It's strange how things can spiral out of control. A simple suicide attempt had morphed into murder and experimentation and fear. Yes I was afraid. Who wouldn't be? If you knew Jack the Ripper was hunting you down, you'd be clenching your buttocks quite a bit, reaching for the Kleenex. If Crippen was creeping around, you'd most likely want to take a shower rather than a bath, preferring Bates' knife to Crippen's acid. Not that I knew whether Connors was in the lofty leagues of such serious slaughterers, but I wouldn't be surprised if he aspired to be reworked in wax and displayed amongst the killers, politicians and other monsters that populated Tussauds' darker domains. Why couldn't I have a better hold on the situation though? If my suicide had worked, would Jeremy still be alive? Would it have stopped Connors in his tracks, Lady-esque? Would the world have kept on turning, oblivious to the sudden lack of me? Would Thor have thrown his hammer out of the pram for losing a pawn? Chaos had spun its spidery web around me and caught me in its trap. And now it was pulling off my legs one at a time and snacking on me. Finger licking good.

If only I could - if only I *dared* - toss a coin. Head you win, tails I lose. Flip and catch. Once upon a time that would have been so easy. Once upon a time the coin was leaving my hand and spinning through the air before I knew it had even left my pocket. Once upon a time little girls followed white rabbits down holes in the ground while witches hid out in gingerbread houses. Rats danced the conga behind pipers piping and wolves slept soundly in Grandma's bed. And, my, what big eyes they had. Oh, and ghosts haunted their lunatic brothers, and windows into the past existed amongst the hills.

Oh yeah, that wasn't once upon a time. That was once upon a yesterday.

It had been quite some time since I'd had any cash in my pockets, much like the Queen. But, unlike Her Majesty, I didn't actually have any pockets. Given my previous experiences with certain coinage, I wasn't too eager to have a pocket full of shrapnel - mainly because shrapnel of other kinds was usually involved. Even if I wanted to flippy-flop-catchy-monkey, I couldn't. For me, it wasn't a case of money burning a hole in my pocket; it was a case of money burning the whole of the world.

Should I stay or should I go now. If I went would I be followed? Either way there would be trouble. My secret hidey-hole that was my parent's house had been discovered so I assumed nowhere was safe. Had that information been siphoned out of me during one of my sessions with Connors? Who knew what else he might have drugged out of me. Well, the Doctor knew, of course. He probably even knew that I like my bacon crispy and my boxers fitted. Home was definitely out then. But if he knew things that I didn't even know I knew then how did I know what I knew myself?

Erm...

I'd begun to rant with myself. My mind was spinning out of control, trying to catch up with the situation itself. I didn't know which would win the race, but it was fast becoming obvious that I'd be the one who lost.

Right. Walk out of here and figure this out or stay and...

Voices.

Poo.

Chapter Eighteen

Typical, wasn't it. For six days out of seven, this building was deserted. Apart from the mist of a hundred water jets and the occasional buzz of an insect meandering amongst the plants, this was as quiet as a mausoleum. And I had to bring us - or rather, right now, myself - here right at the time that Glenn Rafferty, of Rafferty's Garden Services ("No tree too tall nor root too deep, your garden perfect we shall keep"), was being escorted in for his weekly spruce up. He knew his stuff, did Glenn, but then he had been in the business for so many years he may well have pruned the Eden's Tree of Life. The nursery wasn't a window box by any means and it would normally take a whole heap of tendering to keep it from wilting and dying. Glenn Rafferty literally did have green fingers, in the way a hundred a day smoker has fingers the colour of mustard dipped in pepper. He was so in tune with plants I wouldn't be surprised if he had conversations with them and understood when they spoke back. He probably even went down the pub on a Friday evening for a game of dominoes with the rhododendrons and a pint of bitter. I assumed rhododendrons drank pints, not halves - they were thirsty plants after all.

Glenn was an OK guy. He was nice in a wholesome, genial way. He'd had a lifetime of caring, and it reflected in his demeanour - a gentleness that could calm, perhaps, even an Audrey II.

But the patients of the institute scared the gladioli out of him. Pure and simple. In his bag, along with his gloves and secateurs, was most likely a roll of toilet paper in case a freako-psycho-sicko might jump out and eat his head. Or say "Hi," or something equally horrific. He'd fill his pants faster than my dad could down a shot of whiskey. His fears were entirely irrational. I could only think of one patient who had professed to be a cannibal, and he thought he was a dog, so he ate pooch rather than person. Any other patients were normally in such a state of doped-up dormancy that Glenn had more to fear from a Venus flytrap than Fido Freddy. Of course if said flytrap turned out to want to drink his blood and burst into song, thinking his name was Seymour, we all had a problem.

If Glenn Rafferty, of Rafferty's Garden Services (You grow it, we'll mow it - he had at least a dozen different business cards, each with their own little 'humorous' - or 'humerus' in his case - ditty) were to walk in and see me, he'd scream like a banshee and spray me with weed killer, before running for his life. It had happened. A patient, I forget who, had fallen asleep by the indoor (not that there was an outdoor here) rockery and water feature after a visit from the local mayor. A simple newspaper, care in the community, propaganda-fest. The most docile residents had been allowed to wander - almost freely - around the nursery, and the staff was informed to keep them gainfully occupied in play-gardening. No trowels or flora were to be hurt, or used, in the making of this nonsense. After the mayor, his entourage and the journalist-cum-photographer had left, Glenn was brought in to undo any damage that the show-patients had caused. It was, to be honest, minimal. A few shrubs and bulbs had been pulled out, and someone had urinated in the fountain - which was understandable as they'd seen the little boy stood in the middle doing exactly the same. If they'd defecated it would have been another matter, but at least the gardener would have been along with his toilet roll to sort it out. In this case, he'd walked in, escorted as ever by an orderly, the orderly had left him to it, he'd discovered the sleeping beauty in the rockery, and his scream could have shattered glass. Even an aged set of lungs can reach the dizzy decibels of a scream when pushed, and Glenn's could pop an eardrum at twenty paces.

Since that fateful day, he'd refused to enter unless the orderly went in first and looked around. Initially, this happened. The orderly, especially if it happened to be Jeremy... oh God, Jeremy... erm... yes... especially Jeremy, would go up and down the aisles, in and out the greenhouses. Thorough. Not because, except for Jezzer, they were conscientious, but more so that they didn't want to calm down a whole ward of agitated patients who had been scared half to death by the screech of a ghoulie kicked in the goolies. It was only to keep Glenn Rafferty's, of Rafferty's Backbone Recyclers, testicles from leaping into his gut so hard they could have played tennis with his tonsils. After a while, though, they made less and less effort until a cursory glance around was often too much.

It meant I knew that it wouldn't just be Gardener Glenn who'd be walking through those double doors, it would be Garry, with the tattooed arms that had so scared Edith, the grandmother of the baby they'd found left in the Tesco trolley, pushed back into the trolley station. She'd even reclaimed the pound. The dragon really wasn't going to eat her whole, maybe just piece by piece. Or it would be Ian, skinny little Ian with his lank hair and his sly smile that made him look like he'd just killed a cat or abducted a schoolchild. It could even be Connors himself, making sure that none of his residents were hiding away, ready to urinate up the side of his money tree. Either way, Glenn wouldn't be alone and I was buggered.

I'll say it again.

Poo.

I clicked my heels together three times. They didn't spark a little and nothing happened. Go figure. I closed my hands, clenched my fists tight and my teeth tighter, and wished for home, or Barbados, or the skip that was always parked at the end of Number 27's drive. Nothing.

Poo.

My choice, it seemed, was taken away from me. My mind was made up by Fate and all her minions. The Gods, sitting up there on their stars, had fancied a laugh. Or I'd been hit with the shitty end of the shit stick and was now in need of my own supply of tissue.

Glenn...?

I looked around frantically. A key was pushed into the lock and jiggled, an almost musical jingle that made my nerves dance. There was a greenhouse nearby, but I knew the doors were kept shut by padlock. The ever-fluid boy was to my left, but his effluent was too shallow to dive into, and I wasn't a fish anyway. The hangar, for that was what the nursery almost was - you could pretty much park your plane in it with room to spare - was a haphazard maze of tables and display areas. A fountain stood next to a pile of shrub covered rocks which neighboured a long table covered in soil filled trays with various wildly coloured flowers sprouting forth. It was, supposedly, purposeful chaos created thus to keep the minds of the patients occupied and prevent them from becoming bored. In truth, the asylum's inmates would have felt all their birthdays and Christmases had come together if they'd been able to use the nursery as it was designed. But no. The slapdash arrangement was deliberate in that its chaos was mirrored in the minds of the patients. Connors wanted them to shy away. He wanted them to have a headache at just the thought of walking into what should been a place of serenity. It worked. On the day the mayor paid his flying visit, it was double doses all round just to get them shambling around and amenable. There was no wonder one fell asleep. He would practically have been a walking coma anyway.

I heard an irritated mutter and the jangling of the keys. It had gone from a jingle to a jangle, from musical to menacing in a second. Wrong key, I assumed. A moment's reprieve. I ducked, right where I was, and ran towards the door that the gardener and the orderly were about to come through. What else could I do? I could have stayed where I was, been captured, and figured things out as I went. And as Connors was sticking the needle into my neck, as he did with Jeremy, I could realise that perhaps getting caught wasn't such a good idea. I could crouch in the shadows, holding my breath tighter than my dad would hold his giro, and hope that I wouldn't be seen. And after Glenn Rafferty screamed in a voice that only dogs could hear, I'd realise that, as the needle went in, I maybe should have not risked capture. I couldn't leave the way I arrived, that doorway seemed to be slammed shut and bolted tighter than a hangman's noose, so I could only hide by the side of the door and hope I could sneak out whilst they were looking into the room. Luckily it was still fairly dark, so night-time was my friend.

Oh.

Night.

Hmmm...

I needed to wake up. Not that I thought I was asleep, but I needed to get hold on the grip I was letting slip. It was still dark. The stars were kicking back, watching the show. The chances of fraidy-cat Rafferty coming in here after dark were smaller than the chance of Angelina Jolie calling me on a Friday evening and asking if I minded giving her a back massage because, you see, all that acting made her soooo stiff, and Brad just didn't have the touch. Besides, he was a gardener. He worked daylight, not night dark.

So it wasn't him. Who could it be? Connors? No, he wouldn't have had enough time to get here from the house, unless he could trip the light fantastic like me. And if he could, why would he want me in the first place?

I didn't have time to find out. I practically dived into the shadows in the corner by the door, just as the right key was found, inserted and turned. Clickety-click, I feel sick.

I held my breath. Again. It was getting to be a habit. I'd wish for gills, so I could breathe with my mouth and nose closed, silently, but I knew my own personal three wish genie was otherwise engaged in Disney cartoons. And he wasn't manically voiced by Robin Williams either. Not even Robbie. Kenneth maybe, all nasal and condescending. "You want me to what? Really, the people of today, think they can wish for anything!"

The door opened. The hinges squeaked quietly, as if they, too, were scared to make too much noise. The whole building, as quiet as it was, became even more hushed.

"Go on, it'll be fine," a voice hissed.

I knew the voice immediately. Jersey. I didn't think his name was actually Jersey, and he never wore anything other than t-shirts under his uniform, but I'd never heard him called anything else. Except perhaps Mr. Jersey by some of the patients, those that thought the orderlies were in charge and demanded respect rather than simply being fast food cast-offs. No, that was unkind. Dr. Connors didn't trawl very far up the (fast) food chain in his recruitment drives, but most of his employees weren't too bad. Jeremy was the only one I'd call decent, but others had varying degrees of apathy from not giving a flying fig to almost, if pushed, caring. Jersey was somewhere in between the two, depending on what he was after. He was so slimy I was often surprised he didn't leave a trail. Especially around Connors and the female or richer patients. He was the sort of person who'd make you want to wash your hands if he so much as walked past you, as if his aura was unclean. His voice, lowered, no doubt, because of the late hour, snaked over me, having the same effect. I felt like a bird on the beach after an oil spill.

I shuddered, not at the prospect of being caught, but at the feeling of my skin suddenly feeling slick and greasy.

"I don't..." A woman's voice. A stumble.

"Go on, I said. Quick!"

A pair of silhouettes entered the nursery, the first, small and obviously female, coming a little too fast, feet not keeping up with the rest of her. She fell forward, hand on mouth as knees met floor. She clearly knew to be quiet as barely a whimper, not much more than a gasp of air escaped her mouth as she landed. She was used to this. A veteran. The second was bigger, though not much more so. He was... spindly. I could already feel the oil making my feathers slick. I knew immediately who he was bringing to the nursery. He hung around her when he was on duty, treating her like his personal pet. She was quiet, unassuming, introverted. Caroline, that was her name. I knew nothing more about her, which was unusual. Normally everyone's conditions were the subject of much discussion. No one kept their particular version of insanity to themselves. Some like to brag about it, some even gloat that they were more tapped than the next person. Others told their tale as a sort of therapy.

A problem shared is a problem gossiped about, except no one really gossiped about anyone else. It was all just chit-chat. Non-judgemental, casual chat. You didn't go on holiday, you rarely saw your family, you, in some cases, didn't even know what day it was. Talking about each other's individual degree of dementia was often all you had. For me, my own personal problem was paranoia. It was the best I could come up with. I could have, I guessed, told it straight - that I could kill people with my thoughts even when I hadn't thought about it - but that was a step too far from mental to monumental. I wanted them to think I was unbalanced, not imbecilic. I wanted to be kept sequestered in my own little cell, with just enough chemical help to stop my demons becoming everyone else's. How this had progressed from that to this, from my voluntary, if not quite factual, incarceration to my being the fox with a thousand hounds sniffing out my tail, I couldn't guess. How Connors had discovered, unearthed or just beaten out of me my secrets was something I would have to ask him one of these days, maybe over tea and biscuits. I wonder if he liked chocolate hob-nobs.

Caroline was different. She spoke to people, had friends in here, but still, no one knew the real her. No one knew who she really was or why she was in the institute. She just turned up one day, sat quietly in a corner staring at the floor, and that's pretty much been it for her. She interacted with the others, including myself, wasn't nervous or jumpy, and had been known to have a sharp sense of humour, but if she was sitting in a room, even being the only one there, you could overlook her. Caroline blended in, like she was lost in the maze of Being and her inability to escape resulted in your eyes skimming over her, looking past her, forgetting there ever was a Caroline. It could easily be days between anyone saying more than three words to the girl, but she didn't seem to mind. She simply sat, in her chair, staring at the floor.

Jersey noticed her, but that was in the way a spider notices a fly. Once she was caught in his web, Jersey proceeded to pull her legs off one by one, slowly over the months, until she could barely walk without him. Figuratively speaking, of course. She didn't go from able-bodied to limbless, shuffling across the floor on her belly, she just lost whatever identity she arrived with. She was Jersey's when Jersey wanted her. *That* was noticed. *That* made her *be* noticed. But when Jersey wasn't there, in an abstract way, neither was Caroline. She faded into her seat as if she were part of its upholstery.

Now, Jersey was making her his own again. This time he was deflowering the wallflower.

It was like an episode of Lost or Coronation Street. Granted those two programmes were completely unrelated, but the appearance of polar bears in Jack Duckworth's bath tub or the Rover's Return being frequented by the survivors of an airplane crash or employees of the Dharma Initiative was not the issue. There hadn't been any opening credits and there wouldn't be closing ones either, but I could suddenly see how this was going to unfold. I realised who Jersey, the vile with the smile, reminded me of. More so than Connors, Jersey was Percy Wetmore, slimy prison guard who patrolled the Green Mile. A man you could despise simply by hearing his voice in another room. Yet, still he had his way. Still he, being an orderly and as such one of the Lords and Masters of the Institute, had the patients in his thrall. Still he could take Caroline from her bed where she'd be sleeping (for, if you weren't asleep after lights out, they had a pill that could help you with that) and bring her to the nursery. A nursery that should have been a place of caring for flora or children, not one of money making schemes and grand empty gestures. And not one of abuse and loathsome things that raped the smile from your face.

I saw it all, and not with a psychic sense of foreboding where I had a Final Destination style vision wash over me, more with a sick sense of inevitability. I was sure that the star players of this show would prefer to stay un-credited, though the cameras would still roll and nothing would be left on the cutting room floor to lower the certificate from 18 to U or even 13A.

The, gentle at first, urges and requests.

The softly spoken protests.

The gradual build up from friendliness to force.

The muted cries. The acquiescence. The tears and then the drugs that would wipe it away like a jay cloth on a spill on a kitchen worktop.

And the feeling of smug superiority that beat down the murmurings of guilt like Goliath turning to David and saying 'Is that all you've got?' before raising his mighty foot and stamping it down on his opponent's head.

I wanted Jersey then. Not in the disgusting way he wanted Caroline. I wanted him in the way David wanted Goliath. In the way I wanted the boy child-killing racer. I knew, in the way I know things, about all the Carolines that had gone before. And the Benny's too. And I knew, in the way I know things that I shouldn't and wish I couldn't, that Dr. Connors knew too.

I wanted Jersey.

I wanted Jersey dead.

I could stop him. I could step from the shadows and tap him on the shoulder.

"Put the girl down, Jersey. You don't want to do that, do you?"

"Sin! How you doing buddy? The girl? Sure, no problem. Sorry, got a bit carried away there. Won't happen again."

I could leap on him, pulling him back, forcing him to the ground as he would Caroline, smashing his face, breaking his neck the way Steven Seagal and countless other action heroes had taught me. Or I could sneak away, ignoring the drama playing out and

Caroline's plight. I could carry on with my planless plan and stop Connors, save myself and save the world.

Or 'D' - none of the above.

It was there before I knew it. The feeling. Creeping out of me like spiders from a dead man's mouth. And nothing like that. An EMP, an electro-magnetic pulse that would shut down all the circuits and generators that sparked and chugged in Jersey's dark heart and darker soul. And nothing like that. And nothing like a pocket nuclear explosion, small enough to just destroy the building and maybe the street but leave the nearby 24 hour supermarket untouched.

Well, you never knew when you might run out of milk.

The feeling, and I couldn't describe it as anything other than just that - a feeling - swept from me, finding cracks in whatever dam inside me held it at bay, making those cracks fissures, and the fissures holes. It had an insubstantial substance - there but not, real and utterly unreal. It roared but was voiceless as it hammered at Jersey. Then it was gone. My throat gagged, clenching so tightly I thought my tongue might snap, and the thunder faded.

Was the storm Joy had foretold actually in me? Thunder? It did seem as if a tempest raged in the pit of my stomach, but it could equally have been the gods having a bitch fight - pulling hair, slapping and clawing.

Either way, the sudden absence of force made me catch my breath and I gasped. Jersey turned and in the light from the gods' playground above I could see the shock in his eyes. And the blood. And from his nose. And his ears. Then his knees bent in different directions and he toppled backwards, his head making a dull thud as it connected with a gro-bag lying on the floor.

Dirt to dirt.

I looked from Jersey Dead to Caroline Alive and, in the same gods' glow, saw that she saw me, and that she smiled. Then her eyes closed and she, too, fell to the floor. There was no lifeless collapse, just a fainted fall.

I walked over to her and knelt. She'd made me smile too many times in the past, as quiet as she was, to realise, on waking, what could have transpired here. I searched through the jacket that Jersey always wore and the trousers that were almost undone until I found the syringe of forgetfulness he'd intended for his intended victim. In this I couldn't help, though it pained me, but agree with the corpse whose pockets I'd just pillaged.

I wiped the blood from Caroline's nose, there was just a little, took her arm and pushed up the sleeve. Then, as tenderly as I could with a needle, I administered the drug.

"Just a little prick," I whispered, "but he's gone now."

Now what? Should I leave the pair, dead and dazed, and run? Or hide? Or run and hide? Or hide them? Or risk moving them out of the nursery back into one of the many storerooms or vacant cells of the Institute? I certainly couldn't carry them both together. I wasn't a big, strapping bull of a man, I was just me. Strong enough but I'd never be a contender for World's Strongest Man, going up against Geoff Capes or Lars Van Danish or whoever was this year's champion. World's Strangest Man, maybe, but I didn't think there was a prize for that and I doubted they televised the championship anyway. Besides, Jersey would be a literal dead weight - not for any championship, just for moving him - and Caroline as good as. Eventually they'd be found and I'd be seen, and then the game was up before I'd had chance to roll the die.

I stood and looked around. Options, options, come to me, give me chances, one, two...

Over in the far corner was a wooden panelled box. Six feet square and five feet high with faded paintings of trees, hills and approximations of animals - a rabbit, a fox (that looked more like a map of Australia), what could have been a deer but what may have been a dog - adorning the sides. Flies buzzed energetically over its top, a simple handled cover, diving every so often to head butt the surface. The compost heap. Fermentation Central. On the odd times the patients had made it into this forbidden land, the box had become home to various items of clothing, including underwear, a wig, false teeth and even an equally false arm. The latter was the most curious as the only prosthetically challenged person in residence had a false leg, not arm. Barring that and those, though, Glenn used the compost heap religiously. Natural was best.

There was an extraction unit above the box that hummed and chittered and, for a moment, I was back on holiday in Luxor, Egypt. The scarabs were chattering to each other below my balcony as I looked over the Nile to the lit up mountains of the Valley of the Kings.. To the left, the south, the sun set, changing the sky to deep orange as, on the far bank, smoke rose from small fires. The feluccas drifted on the water, the occasional flash of a tourist's camera capturing the setting sun before the boats had to race back to be moored before darkness. It was a childhood dream come true and I'd gone with the woman of my dreams. Beautiful, sensual, funny and amazing in every way, Luxor and fiancée alike.

We hadn't fallen out, my fiancée and I. We couldn't fall out. But she did take the bus to work each day. The Number Five, usually.

A moan, a breath from Caroline snatched me back, thankfully, from the banks of the Nile to the banks of the compost heap. The extractor, I realised, sounded not so much like the casual banter of beetle buddies as it did like a frayed wire complaining that the electricity had to spark across the gaps and was tired of doing so, and warning that it might just fail if it didn't get fixed soon. Not wanting to argue with or risk the wrath of an irate fan, I made my choice.

I scooped up Jersey's body, then put him quickly back down as I realised I wouldn't be able to carry him all that way. I decided his mode of transport wasn't really going to bother him too much in his present deceased condition, so I grabbed his arms and pulled. His shoes squeaked too loudly along the floor so I had to stop to remove them, tying the laces to his refastened (by me) belt. Briefly, I wished I could teleport him as I could myself, but knew I couldn't control my own destination and didn't want him ending up in Jack Duckworth's bathtub - there wouldn't have been room, what with the polar bears. It felt like four days but was probably more like four minutes, with an indirect route thanks to the chaotic spread of tables and benches, before we, my passenger and I, reached the compost box. I was panting but didn't pause as I lifted the lid then dragged, pulled, swore and pushed Jersey's body inside.

I looked in before lowering the top. It was almost empty. I could hope that the gardener just threw rubbish in until it was full and didn't care to witness its decomposition. In that case, Jersey could be hiding in there for a good while before being discovered. I could hope, but I knew, with my luck, someone would walk in straight after I left with the sole intention of investigating the compost heap. The owner of the false arm, perhaps.

I hurried back to Caroline and was relieved to find her exactly as she'd been left. I'd half expected, or a little more than half, to find her gone. She'd be crawling along the corridor to collapse at the feet of a patrolling orderly or, even better, a returning Dr. Connors. She hadn't moved. She was even snoring softly.

Caroline I could carry, albeit not too gracefully.

Attempting the scooping again, this time with a much lighter and less deader person, I picked her up and threw her over my shoulder. No. That sounded like I manhandled her roughly. I didn't. She was delicate, in spirit as well as in body, and I couldn't bring myself to be harsh with her. She wasn't here by choice. I lowered her onto my shoulder, that was better, and I did my best, now that one was two, to slip out silently from the nursery. It was only then that I thought of CCTV cameras. I didn't know, had no idea, if any closed circuit sentries scanned the room with their beady black eyes. My long chats with Jeremy, from which I gleaned so much information I would never have discovered otherwise, being insane or dangerous or both, hadn't mentioned any such security.

Well, Dr. Connors was going to find out which was correct, insane or dangerous, and I looked forward to discovering that myself too.

As for the cameras, if they'd seen me it was tough and too late. If they hadn't, it was an unexpected bonus. One less thing on the catch me if you can list. One less way to grab Sin by the head and shake him until all his secrets fell out.

The corridor was in almost darkness. A high windowed hallway connected the nursery to the institute proper and, at this late hour, it was lit purely by starlight and the ambient almost-light of night time. That was fine with me as the fact that the whole corridor was, more or less, one long slice of gloom saved me the trouble of slipping from shadow to shadow. I reached the opposite end before I'd barely had chance to breathe then realised I'd been holding my breath. I let it out slowly through my nose and forced myself to breathe as normally as the weight on my shoulder would let me.

The double door at this end wasn't locked. It didn't have a lock. Each door had hinges, a hand plate to push either way and a kick board at the bottom for the times you had your hands full or you didn't get lucky with your wife the night before and didn't have a cat handy. I went to push it open but stopped. My fingers had made contact with the rectangle of metal worn smooth but dirtied by so many previous fingers.

This was it. Just as I could feel the thunder grumbling inside me, I sensed that somewhere there was a whirlwind on the other side of this door. Whether I was the dervish in question or whether it was Connors didn't matter. There would, most likely, be collateral damage. Casualties of a war I hadn't even known raged.

I could step through the door right into the face of the night watch, which was usually whichever orderly couldn't pay his rent that week and needed the extra cash. Or, in the case of Nathan, couldn't pay his dealer. Jeremy told me about him. Nathan's extensive crack habit was the only thing that stopped him being a patient himself. Once or twice a patient was allowed to do the rounds when there were no takers for the overtime or Connors wanted some free labour. Wayne Privet, who was so tired of jokes being made about his surname had tried to change it to his nickname 'Whippet' - he no longer wanted to be 'hedging his bets' - was an insomniac, and his perpetual lack of sleep made him jittery. A perfect candidate for the graveyard shift. The twilight tour. He wouldn't fall asleep on the job and his scream, if surprised, was loud enough to bring the whole house tumbling down. He suited his name, though - Whippet. He was lean and wiry. Less meat than a McDonalds. Wayne the Whippet wasn't the sort of person you could like, but you didn't dislike him either. His nervousness was infectious and just a few minutes in his manic company was enough to make your stomach churn and your skin sweat. He was still one of the gang however. A fully-fledged member of Us Not Them, so in that respect, he was okey-dokey, along with that pig in the pokey.

The Whippet, the Bender and the rest were, without even realising it, relying on me, The Reverend Sin. Perhaps my name suited me more than I'd known. Perhaps I was here to save them all.

Dr. Connors wasn't the clever, influential psychiatrist who took all in and ran a successful mental home. He was a monster. He was a killer. A puppeteer, with no strings to hold him down. He was who knew what else.

I paused, still, and took a deep breath. I held it. I had no choice but to hold it. I felt something change. Something in me. I looked up, out of the windows, up at the night sky, and I could have sworn, just for a second, all the stars had suddenly winked out as if the nine billion names of God had been found.

I don't have epiphanies on a daily basis. Not often at all. A sense of awakening to a knowledge that should have been there all along and that shocks you with its simple, but profound, enlightenment. When the stars came back on, if indeed they'd gone out in the first place, I knew.

From the beginning.

From the bus.

Chapter Nineteen

Barry Coombs. Loser extraordinaire. Lifelong welfare sponger, the type that had never had a job, or any intention of having one, but could still drive a car, smoke sixty cigarettes a day and drink a bottle of vodka a night. The type that was proud of it. I didn't know if buses had seat numbers, but if they had, Barry Coombs would have been sitting in, poetically almost, seat 13, top deck. He always sat on the top deck because, from being a surly schoolchild, he thought it was clever. Tough. Hard. He nearly always sat, anally almost, in the same seat. It was his place. His domain. He marked his territory by scrawling profanities on the back of the seat in front. He'd stub out his cigarette in the cushion next to him, but slowly so he could see the material burn. On that particular bus, because even though he always took the number five it wasn't always the same vehicle, he'd managed to almost finish burning the second 'R' of his name. On another he'd only completed the initial 'B'. On another bus still, Barry had written, in scorched circles, the full word and even managed to underline it in a line of cigarette burns that could have been the Morse Code for S.O.S.. The dots-and-joined-dots-to-make-dashes were deliberate. Barry was clever for knowing something like that, he thought. He was a brain. That was how he knew that today would be a good day. He was tired of not being able to feed his children properly on his fortnightly social payouts. He was tired of only being able to afford the cheap shop's own vodka and not the decent stuff. He wanted more than the crappy camel dropping fags he bought for £20 a sleeve from his mate at the house on the corner.

What could go wrong? Barry had a plan. Of course his plan had taken all of the time it took to eat a bowl of Frosties to work out. Barry didn't need to spend too much effort on his schemes. He was a brain. He actually called himself that but, if any of his ideas came to fruition, it was purely by chance. Barry was a brain. A legend. But only in his own head.

He knew how the Post Office worked, having cashed his giro cheque there for as long as he could remember. In fact, he was in there so often, over the years, he'd grown friendly with the staff. They must have liked him - they knew his name, the names of his children. Polite people don't do that. Friends do. So they naturally trusted him, he thought.

The gun wasn't his. Not exactly. He'd found it on the waste ground that had been allotments once upon a time. It was already loaded, but he'd never used it. The most he'd dared was to hold it in his hands, test the gun's weight and feel, ask if his reflection felt lucky, punk. Today, though, was a good day. A good day to fire a gun, or at least threaten to. A good day to earn a bit more dosh. A good day to become a man.

Barry had seen the drawers full of money. Too much money. There were ten counters, eleven if you counted the foreign exchange. He dismissed that. You couldn't buy fags or booze or be that man with funny money. Barry was a brain and, as such, wasn't greedy. One drawer full would do. Two at the most.

He didn't know that the woman, Maureen, behind the desk would sneeze in shock at the gun suddenly pointed at her, a sneeze that would make him jump and pull the trigger and empty the magazine before he'd had time to swallow that first spoonful cereal at breakfast. He didn't know that, even if he hadn't killed all those people, and shot his own foot, the cameras had seen it all and would grass him up to the police.

None of that mattered because I'd found a two pence coin and, after a simple flip and catch, the number five bus came to Barry instead of him going to the stop outside the newsagents and waiting until ten past the hour.

Each time there was something. Each time a wrong that needed righting or preventing. Even with the earthquake in Turkey. It wasn't just villages that had been buried under the trees and rocks and earth, or that had fallen into the crevices that opened and closed like a dragon's teeth. There had been a base. A storage site. A weapons cache. Not so much weapons of mass destruction, but still weapons of a huge amount of devastation. Much more than was originally thought and planned for. Much more than was caused when the Earth shrugged her shoulders and I tossed a coin.

The price of that something, that righted wrong, was enormous. Collateral damage was never acceptable, was it? Was it better for the family members of those who would have died at the hands of a terminal waster to mourn siblings or parents or children who had been murdered, or those who had died in an accident? Were the earthquake survivors better for receiving the world wide aid that came with a seemingly random natural disaster, or would they have preferred to be the nameless remnants of bomb and missile attacks from insurgents, possibly making one of the secondary headlines on the 24 hour news channels or page sixteen of a lesser read broadsheet? Did the needs of the many outweigh the needs of the multitude?

I couldn't answer. I couldn't do or say anything. I was frozen in the moment, rooted by the revelation. If the owner of the arm had come through the door right then, I was sure he would have taken me for a shop mannequin, one that he could move and dress and style, and all for only £99.99. I wasn't right, I wasn't wrong, I just was. Flip and catch went the toss of the coin. Heads or tails. Good or evil. Whichever I was, I couldn't help feel that a greater good was being served. Even down to the boy in the car in the trees.

I'd never had that before. The whole reason I had ventured into the grasp of Dr. Connors was because I felt I needed to stop myself somehow. I needed to numb the pain I felt when it happened, the pain of everything that had gone before revisiting me, saying 'Hi', taking my hand and ripping my heart out. Yes, I'd come to prevent it reoccurring but, being the honest man I tried to profess to be, I'd come here for more selfish reasons. I had admitted to myself into the insane asylum to keep myself sane. The jury, those good men and true of whom I've mentioned on occasion, were still debating on whether I'd succeeded.

It probably wasn't going to be a unanimous vote.

I wiped away the tears that drenched my face, not knowing where they'd come from. Had I cried? Was it Caroline? No, she was still unconscious. Anyway - in fact anywho-be-do - the moment had passed. Beautiful, to me, and profound, epiphany had returned to reality, passing the baton on so smoothly I barely noticed. I had changed. I *was* changed. Why then, why there? Why the moment had come at *that* moment I had no idea, but it had and I was no longer 'Sin-sin-sirree, there's no place for thee,' I was Sin. Not a superhero but... but good. Yes. I'd plead my case to that jury and I'd convince them. I wasn't a big bad wolf, ready to eat the little piggies.

But, Dr. Connors, I was going to blow your house down.

I pushed. The door opened smoothly and silently and I passed through the same way. I hoped that a plan might evolve, my mind making decisions whilst I was otherwise engaged, but it appeared that my mind was busy doing other things. Sudoku or something. I had no sense of what I might do next, but that was fine. I didn't have a bowl of Frosties to ponder over. I would take one step and follow it with another and see where they took me.

I couldn't take Caroline back to her room. I wanted to, to keep her out of harm's way, but it was too far. The risk of discovery grew with every second passed and with every step taken. I had to keep her with me. The injection had ensured that she was away making daisy chains with the fairies so I had no fears of her waking and causing a scene. He weight, though, seemed to be growing in direct proportion to the risk and I needed to get somewhere out of the way quickly.

For the first time in so long, if ever, I wished I had the coin with me. The two pence piece that had turned my life upside down, and me along with it, and which I'd tried so many times to rid myself of. I knew, now, that it wasn't the source of the things I could do, but I longed to feel its comforting footprint in my palm.

Oh well.

The corridor I was in now was dimly lit from bulbs hidden in the suspended ceiling. It cast my shadow in three directions at once and I was worried that, even if I wasn't seen, my grey-black partners would be. The corridor bent in either direction, curving away sharply. To the left were the rooms and padded cells that contained the patients - caged animals that were only allowed out at feeding or play times. The right curve led to the administration wing, a collection of storerooms, offices and treatment theatres. Right was right.

I might not have had a plan, but I did have a destination. The office of our illustrious leader. I wondered if there'd be an escape route from his office - a wardrobe with a secret passage at the back that led, if you stepped through, to the Seven Hills, our own version of Narnia. Chances were that it didn't. Joy had still not reappeared either, so she wasn't there to open a mystical portal for me to exit through. My own teleportation, on the other hand, didn't seem too far beyond my capabilities. Something *had* changed about me. The suspicion had begun with the bully in the street and his girlfriend. The rage built but I kept it on a leash, like a Rottweiler straining to attack a passing granny. In the nursery I had stopped Jersey from his desecration of Caroline and she had suffered, I hoped anyway, just a bloody nose in the back-draft. I didn't believe for one second I could control this, but I had an idea that it was no longer entirely uncontrolled.

I walked as quickly as I could, passing doors that I knew would be locked. Store Room 1. Store Room 2. Locker Room 1. Ladies Locker Room. Doors with similarly inventive names. I tested the locks on none of them. What would be the point? I only wanted one particular door and, before very long, that was the door I stood before.

Of course it was locked and, in lieu of a coin, I wished for a wand so I could cast a Potter-style spell. *Unlockiarmus!* I didn't have a wand, obviously, because magic didn't really exist, did it? I didn't even have a toothpick to wave about. A splinter wouldn't have been any good either. Magic was the fantasy of those who wished for more than that which they had. The desire for a greater power than that which turned on the TV magically at the press of a button on a remote control. Did I believe? I think I could be classed, based on my life story, as a convert. At the least an agnostic. Who was to say, in a world of teleportation, death by thought and infra red controllers, that you really couldn't wish upon a star?

The door was locked and I had no way to get inside. I swore at myself and Caroline. I ignored my self-deprecation and she didn't even hear it. Then I actually looked at the lock and had to stifle a laugh.

It was keypad entry. A combination lock with the numbers 0 to 9 and the letters A to D. A star, which was really an asterisk, and a hash were thrown in for good measure. It's strange how you can look at something once and see one thing, then look again and see something completely different. At first glance, with the weight of Caroline and the thrill of the chase rattling my heart in my head, this door was an impenetrable blockade, purely because of that locked lock. I hadn't thought about the code when I'd come this way with Joy, and I realised that it was nothing more than a temporary barrier - a brief respite and a chance to take a breath.

I'd been here so often with the doctor, for 'informal interviews and chats', that I'd seen him unlock his office many times. Tap-tap, tap-tap. A monotone beep accompanied each finger press to avoid recognition of the numbers selected, but a good few times I had been in a direct line of sight to the keypad itself. Dr. Connors was a brain. He actually was. Though Barry Coombs might ally himself with my tormentor, he was easily outclassed. Connors was, genuinely, a brain. Very intelligent and clearly cunning. But he was also as arrogant as Coombs. He thought he knew it all. He thought, especially in his line of work, he had people sussed. The populace would assume, Dr. Connors being so clever, that his entry code would be something equally clever. It wouldn't be his date of birth. His wouldn't be his credit card PIN number. It wouldn't be the number of times he'd been kissed, which wouldn't reach four figures anyway. No, it would be something that no one would think of. Something random and insightful. Which was why he chose none of those things.

I smiled, bizarrely under the circumstances, and pressed 1-2-3-4. There was a soft click and I let myself into the office.

Chapter Twenty

There were no lights on inside but, luckily, my friendly neighbourhood gods were still smiling down on me and, on this side of the building, Sister Moon, looking big and looking blue, had joined the audience. There was getting to be a bit of a group up there and some enterprising person could make quite a packet with a refreshments stand, or one of those boxes you put round your neck that had Cornettos and hot dogs piled high for equally piled high prices. Maybe a burger van would pull up selling tea, coffee and muddy liquid that passed as hot chocolate to wash down the pseudo-meat cheeseburgers. The light of so many spectators reflecting off the certificates adorning the walls allowed me to move towards the desk with ease. I hesitated, forever, at the chair that faced it. The chair Jeremy had been in as he faced his interrogator and his killer. Choice, as was usual, was not my friend and I had to put Caroline down somewhere. I wasn't going to just dump her on the floor, so the chair it was. As I stepped towards it, I thought I could still smell Jeremy, but it could quite easily have been death. Or Death. Maybe they all used the same deodorant or eau de lavatory. I wondered if, like the bodaches of Dean Koontz's Odd Thomas books, my friends were hovering in the shadows waiting for what was to come, drooling in anticipation. Fate, her fickle finger raised ready to pick the nose of my life and wipe it on her dress. Mr. Grimm, the Reaper, with his scythe rocking back and forth in his hand like a pendulum counting the seconds down to my doom. Or were the shadows clear and I was in this all on my own?

As gently as I could, I lowered Caroline down. The seat had groaned under Jeremy's weight, but she posed no threat to its stability. I hoped, by the end of all this, she didn't suffer the same fate as its previous resident.

First things always seemed to need to come first so, firstly, I needed to see. I had to take this chance to find out what Dr. Connors had done to me. And to see if I could use that to my advantage. As I sat at his desk I noticed something I hadn't seen before. Next to the perfectly ordered pencils was a new object. It was a clear cube of plastic or resin. Possibly even crystal. It was empty except for a single coin. A two pence piece. He'd turned it into a paperweight. I didn't know whether to laugh to be angry. It *was* laughable, but it also seemed a sacrilege. My coin was an object of such power. Not innately of course, as it could easily, I'm sure, have been a pound or a brick or a Big Mac. But it had woken me, the me inside that had been dormant for so long. The me that had so tempted and enticed Dr. Connors. To turn it into a desk ornament was... wrong.

I lifted it up and could practically feel the coin struggling to be free from its prison and return to my hands.

Sighing, I replaced the paperweight on the desk and moved my attention to the computer. I put my hand on the mouse and clicked. The monitor sprang into life, a taunting, teasing life. A 'you got this far, but you ain't getting no further' life. A rectangular dialog box. The username, Connors_H, already filled in and the cursor flashing beneath in the field that asked for Password.

This I hadn't seen before. This I had no idea of. I could try random words, his name again, the name of the dog he'd had as a boy (he'd called it Dog - it was less of a waste of thought apparently, even at ten years old) but I didn't know if it was three strikes and you're out. Three wrong turns and all the videos and documents would be lost to me forever. My hands hovered over the keyboard, wanting to press something - anything. I looked at the keys, hoping they'd leap out crying 'Press me! Press me!' I looked at the screen and the coin and even at Caroline for inspiration.

Caroline looked right back at me.

There was something odd about her face. Something unfocussed as if she were one of those 3D images, red and green pictures slightly offset that needed silly square glasses to fool the brain into seeing them jump from the page or screen. She was smiling at me, a blurred double smile that made her look like Batman's Joker, but a smile still. I wanted to rub my eyes. Perhaps tiredness or stress was affecting them. The trials and tribulations of sleeping in forests and killing in nurseries. I didn't though. My hands stayed where they were, hovering, waiting.

"Hey, Sin."

You'd think I'd be surprised. I, myself, would have thought I'd be surprised. I wasn't though. Not even slightly. I'd been immunised by a constant diet of big budget movies. And endless stream of Exorcist rip-offs or Grudge sequels. I didn't want to be showered in the projectile vomit of a demon possessed girl but, even with that, I wouldn't have been surprised. If it had just been me, my own talents, then yes, I'd be taken aback. Teleportation and a perverted sort of murder by decree were not normal, not by any means, but they were there. They were real. I couldn't deny the things I'd done even though they weren't rational, but they *were* real. Hollywood, in her many forms, had lured me from a young age, and she'd taken me in, and, in effect, numbed me to the magical. CGI could fold a world in on itself or turn a person blue. It could get you used to the idea of dead people talking through living. I wished Joy were here to explain this one. Not that she would.

"Hi, Jeremy," I replied.

"You're not surprised?" he asked.

I realised Caroline's mouth wasn't moving. Her eyes, on closer inspection, were still closed. She hadn't moved. If I'd laid her on the floor, Jeremy would still be sitting right where he was now. In the chair.

"No," I told him. "Not really."

"I am," he said. He didn't sound sad, in fact he seemed chirpy, his smile genuine. "I didn't expect to wake up dead. Saying that, being dead, I didn't expect to wake up at all!"

"You should meet my sister," I said. It felt odd. I was talking to the ghost of my dead friend, whom I'd witnessed being killed. I'd mourned him, however briefly, and part of my current course of action was the avenging of his death. I wasn't sad. Right then, I wasn't angry either. I was chatting to my friend, and I was smiling myself.

"I have," he replied. "She said to tell you 'hi'."

Way to wipe the smile off my face.

"You've met Joy? She said 'hi'?"

"Well, I've met her, but she didn't say 'hi'. She didn't say much of anything really. She just mentioned that you might need a hand."

I might need a hand? Was the afterlife some kind of Grand Central Station with everyone milling around waiting for their train into the Great Beyond? Was the Hereafter a pub where the souls of the dead met up for cocktails or the odd pint, the walls resplendent with random photos and those branded towels they laid out to soak up the spills, the bar complete with a bust of Queen Victoria? I could ask but I wouldn't be answered, so I didn't bother.

"Oh?"

"Yes. She said you might need my help, so here I am. Somehow. You're different to the rest, Sin. You were a friend."

I was pleased he thought of me the same way I did of him.

"I am dead, aren't I?"

The question shocked me. How could you not know? You wouldn't be going to work. Jeremy Kyle wouldn't be on daytime television, sorting the lives of the normal people; you and me and the queen makes three. Whether you sat around on clouds or walked along streets of gold, it still wouldn't be the same as life, would it? Surely you didn't just pass over into a complete replica of how it was before you died, including gone off milk in the fridge, car crash TV and bowel evacuations. Surely, please, you didn't need to keep stocked up on the Andrex, did you?

I could answer his question though. I wasn't one of the greater dead (was there a lesser dead?) so I wasn't held by the same rules, the same forced obtuseness. I could never do those cryptic crosswords in the papers anyway. My mind didn't work in the weird directions that were required to work out nine across, 'Man using mashie and spoon going round'. So I told him.

"Yes, my friend. You are dead. Connors did it."

"I thought so," he said. He still smiled, but the corners of his mouth, roughly overlapping Caroline's, dipped a little. "I thought I remembered being in here with him, but it's vague."

You should see your face, I thought.

"He was very interested in you, wasn't he? I read your file. Even tossed the coin. Was it all real? At one time I'd have said it was rubbish. The Institute was the right place for you. But you always seemed so... sane." He laughed. "It's hard to deny anything now, seeing as I'm sitting here talking to you!"

I could have told him no. I'm a patient in an insane asylum. I was rambling, of course. How could it be real?

"Yes," I said. "It was. It is."

"Well, Sin. You need to stop him. He's not a good man. Not at all."

So true.

"I will," I told him. "I just need to get on here. Connors used me, and I would guess he found out things about me. I need to find them out too."

"You need to find out about yourself?"

"I do, yes."

"Well you need the password then."

"I do," I said. "Yes..."

"I know it," Jeremy said, his smile back to full radiance. "I don't know really how, but I do know it. It's capital P, a, s, s..."

"... w, o, r, d?"

"That's it."

Typical. As obviously random as his office code number. The arrogance of genius. Tappity-tap-tap and Enter. The screen changed. I expected a bespoke window greeting me, one with multiple menus and commands that I'd have to navigate before I found what I was looking for. I was wrong. A simple, light blue background with standard icons along the left hand side and the word 'Start' at the bottom. Excellent. Windows, folders and files. Just how I liked it.

"Thanks, Jezzer. I appreciate that."

"I'd say anytime, Sin," he laughed. "But I don't think it's that simple."

I had no idea how simple it was. My sister had appeared, disappeared, reappeared and abandoned... I mean disappeared again.

That could have been choice, order or just 'cos. I didn't, and probably at no time would, know.

"Probably not, mate, but I appreciate it anyway."

"I know, Sin. I know. Anyway," he paused, his head cocked to the side, making him look like a wardrobe malfunction from the Hitchhikers' Guide to the Galaxy. They say two heads are better than one, but I doubted they meant when one was a ghost and the other asleep. "I think I have to go."

At least he could give me some warning that he was going. He didn't just vanish when my back was turned without waiting for it to turn.

"OK. It was good to see you. Thanks for the help." I took a breath. "I'm sorry about what happened."

"Me too, in a way. But, to be honest, in a way I'm fine with it. Being dead isn't too bad. It's hard to say, because it's not something you can actually experience. It's just something you are."

I could relate to that.

"Besides," he continued. "It can't be helped. It's done now. Just stop him Sin. I don't want, don't need payback, but just stop him, ok?"

I nodded. That was my intention.

"I promise I'll try."

"Good enough," he said. "Bye."

"Goodbye, Jeremy. Say hi to Joy."

Jeremy, or what was left of him as Caroline slowly became more solid, laughed.

"Don't need to."

Then he was gone.

Did they all go to the same school of awkward answers?

He'd gone. Caroline was once more in focus and I felt the loss of my friend all over again. The fact that it had happened here in this room, in that chair, didn't help matters. But no. This was the new me. The positive, good me. Jezzer was OK with his fate so I had to be too. Anyway, I had other things to deal with. Two fat ladies, clickety click. The computer screen was sparse. There were the usual icons for the Documents folder and Recycle Bin etc., but not much else. What there was, however, was sufficient.

A folder named 'Patients.' Let's try there shall we?

Simple structures were usually the best. Less chance for things to be lost or misplaced. In chaos lay frustration and aggravation. Luckily for me, Dr. Connors was a man of simplicity. He didn't subscribe to the idea that a tidy desk meant an untidy mind, or that a desk covered in files and paperwork and notes indicated a mind of regimented organisation. Calm and serenity in everything. Even murder. A double click on the icon revealed an alphabetised list of patients' names, surname first. Now I'd lost my second name a while back, maybe on a desk laden heavy with chaos, maybe in Tesco at midnight, amongst the shelf stackers and insomniacs, but I managed quite well with just my forename. Usually, when people heard that I was called 'Sin,' they were more engrossed in that than in than anything that might come after. That worked well enough, as Matthews linked me to my parents and that was something I didn't need to be reminded of. An abusive 'it was just a joke' father and a 'don't see, don't know, not bothered' mother where not things to be proud of. I knew I couldn't choose who sired me - you can choose your friends, they say, but not your family - but if I carried their name it was like I was wearing a sign around my neck, celebrating my deranged lineage.

Thanks, but no thanks.

In this instance, it would serve me, if only for the first time in my life.

I scanned down the list looking for 'M.' There were names I recognised and others I didn't. Once you came to the home, you usually stayed, the revolving door at the entrance providing you with a one-way ticket into drug induced emptiness. Twice, in my stay, new wings had to be built to house new patients, the intake was that regular. There were names, though, that I didn't know. Benjamin James. Collins Sarah. Why did that sound familiar...? Doherty David. Johnson Bernadette. These were strangers to me. The institute had been around for a good few years before I graced its doorstep so perhaps they and the other unknowns were Connors' success stories. Perhaps he had managed to actually cure or rehabilitate someone. I was genuinely surprised at the concept, having had the impression that the only person Dr. Connors helped was himself. I could only assume that there was method in his methods. They had to be useful to him in the outside world. He helped rid them of their demons and they helped him create a whole new set, complete with matching jackets and forked tails.

I was a cynic, I knew that, but my opinion of the doctor being the answer to my prayers had severely changed. I know knew him for what he was. A beast. A demon himself, in a non-supernatural but equally horrific way. So maybe he had helped them and David, Bernadette and James were all living out their naturals, eternally grateful to Dr. Connors for his aid. Grunt, grunt, flap, flap. Pigs may well soar through the clouds above. They may, but they don't. The price of bacon has most definitely not gone up.

I reached the 'M's' and looked for my name. There was a folder for a Mandy, first name Andy. Where his parents related, even tenuously, to my own? He was another stranger, but I knew the next name. Maxwell Peter. Peter had been beaten as a child. His mother had started the abuse, apparently after the six-year-old boy had knocked over his glass of blackcurrant juice just as the lottery numbers, a double rollover, were being announced. The glass was on the hearth of the fire and smashed as it fell. The lottery ticket was on the coffee table, completely remote from the fruit juice, but the distraction meant that his mother missed the bonus ball being called out. The ticket wasn't a winner anyway, with only one number - a fourteen - being circled, so it wouldn't matter what ball had popped up in the machine. But Peter's mother still blamed him for her losing. The glass wasn't the only thing smashed against the hearth that evening. Peter was clumsy as a child. His mother wasn't a tolerant woman. The lottery incident flipped a switch in her that made her think it was acceptable to punish her son by hitting him, or pushing him. A broken arm or rib, you see, would heal, so it was OK. The young boy's father didn't agree, not at first, but after not long enough thought 'in for a penny, in for a punch.'

It affected Peter as time went on. It might have been from that first night when his head met the fireplace much too hard, or it could have been one of the many times thereafter. He didn't learn too well. His speech slurred more and more. He became afraid of everyone. He thought every person he met was going to strike out. He was admitted to the institute to help him. It was for his own safety. He was brought here because he couldn't function as a normal person - whatever one of those was. But he played a mean game of backgammon and would give you his entire lunch if you were still hungry even if you'd already had three yourself.

Montgomery Paula was next. Matthews Sin was missing. Well, I wasn't missing, was I? I was sitting at the computer. I knew exactly where I was, but my name wasn't where it should have been. I suddenly doubted my knowledge of the alphabet and looked back then further on. Then I saw it. I wasn't under Matthews Sin. I was in a folder simply called 'Sin,' in capital letters, no less. Did Connors know of my abhorrence for my family name and respect my wishes for it to be forgotten? Grunt. Flap. Whatever the reason, I double-clicked on me. It was still night, but night had a habit of slipping unannounced into day so I had to keep moving.

In my folder were hundreds of files. There was one document - the letter I'd written when I escaped, scanned onto the computer with a brief addendum from Connors himself. It said how he thought it was all rubbish and I was, in his so-called professional opinion, insane. Well, thanks for that, mister. Thanks a lot. I didn't dwell on his lies. He obviously knew I wasn't insane, or even if I was, I was still telling the truth. It didn't matter now anyway. I'd written that letter as a suicide note. It was meant to absolve me and appease my conscience but did neither. It did, at least, convince Jeremy, so that was something. It prompted his death too, I guessed, but it also prompted his willingness to help.

Every other file, four hundred and twenty seven of them, were videos. I couldn't believe it. I could remember only a slack handful of times I'd been in his presence. Over four hundred was as crazy as I was supposed to be! Well, we were in the right place for crazy. Whether there were two thousand video files or just two was neither here nor there. They just needed to tell me something. They just needed to help me.

The files all had names rather than just sequential numbers so I clicked on one called 'Induction.' The media player started up and the video began. It was my first day here and my initial interview with the doctor. He'd been very genial, seemingly kind and gentle. He fooled me good 'n' proper and lured me into his web. I, for my part in the charade, lied completely and told a story of abject paranoia that, in return, seemed to fool him. He welcomed me into his care. I closed that file and looked further. I seemed so much younger then, felt a hundred years older now. There were a large number that were just called Treatment Room followed by a date. In some cases they were suffixed by an A, B or C to show I'd been 'treated' numerous times on the same day. To my knowledge days or weeks had gone by between visits to the treatment rooms or this, Connors inner sanctum. I opened a second file, picking one at random from around the middle, assuming my secrets had been discovered and the real fun had begun. There was no way I'd be able to watch every single one before sunrise or the return of Connors, whichever came first, so a planned attack seemed fruitless.

The chair. The table. The bolts fixing them to the floor. The slightly fishbowled view.

Chapter Twenty One

I was sitting in the chair, back to camera, my head slumped forward. One hand was on my lap, the other hanging loosely by my side. I wasn't chained, but from the look of me, shackles would have been redundant. Connors leant against the wall. His suit jacket was folded neatly on the table but otherwise he looked his usual pristine self. Even his dress sense was precise, sharp like it could cut you. In his arms he was stroking a cat. I wasn't aware of any feline friendliness (or any other kind) in the man, but the cat's purring could just be heard. He was looking at me, Connors, not the cat, in a kind of casual staring into space and barely seeing me way, as if he knew I was there, and I had been the subject of his attention, but his mind had wondered off to sunnier climes and was sitting by the pool, sipping a cocktail and reading the latest Clancy thriller.

"Sin," he said softly. He sounded warm, like a night time malted drink, perfect for soothing the worries and wearies of the day and sending you cosily off to sleep. I could feel its effects over the computer's speakers. No doubt, considering the volume of files, it had been used on me on many occasions and I was attuned to its soporific effects. I blinked and shook my head.

Not this time, Doctor.

On the screen I lifted my head slowly, drunkenly. It fell backwards until I was staring at the ceiling and I hardly recognised myself. My eyes were bloodshot, my face pale and drawn. Clearly Dr. Connors methods of care were working.

"Look at me, Sin." As gently spoken as it was, there was no mistaking the underlying authority in his tone. He was asking me nicely but he was ordering me just the same.

I complied, although it wasn't entirely effortless. I had to force my head upright and seemed to struggle to stop myself from lolling forward again. My head gave a little eight pint, three vodka and an Aftershock wobble and then managed to steady itself. I watched myself looking at the doctor on the screen. It was an alien, a pod person that just looked like me. But it wasn't me. I had no recollection. It was, though. It was me.

"Good boy, Sin. That's a good boy. How are we today?"

I, the 'I' on the computer screen sitting in a chair bolted to the floor, mumbled something I couldn't hear. I could have been telling Connors all was good, fine and dandy, everything in the garden rosy red as blood and coming up daisies, even though I preferred lilies. Alternatively I could have been telling him my cell was too cold and the mashed potatoes were lumpy. Oh and was there any chance of a new pillow? The one I had was doing no good for my back. I could, of course, have been telling him that life in the institute was a bag of spanners - it was heavy, would hurt if it whacked you over the head and it had all these odd sticky out bits. Oh, and he could shove it up his backside. Judging from Connors' expression, I guessed it was the former.

"Excellent, Sin. That's wonderful."

He pushed himself away from the wall and put the cat down on the table next to his folded jacket. He continued to stroke its back and scratch it behind its neck. It yawned and stretched and purred and then curled up to enjoy the ministrations.

"You see this cat, Sin?"

I stayed silent. Either I didn't see it or I didn't hear. Or I was too drugged up to respond.

"Sin, come on. Play the game. Do you see this cat?" A sliver of ice crept into his voice, chilling me and making the digital me sit up a touch straighter.

"Yes, doctor." I could hear that more clearly, the other me realising that he should take notice.

"Good boy," Connors said. He smiled but it had all the warmth of a scorpion. Never having held a scorpion, I didn't know if they were hotter than toast or colder than a bag of peas, but one would certainly get a frosty reception if it decided to come and sit on my tuffet. "Do you like the cat, Sin? Do you see how cute it is?"

Some words just didn't suit some people. If Sylvester Stallone ever uttered the words 'How sweet,' you'd probably ask him to repeat it, sure that you'd misheard. The same went for Connors. He and 'cute' just didn't go together. Other me didn't seem to see this and nodded languidly.

"It is, isn't it? Cute. Cuddly even. But would you believe, my friend, that this cat is evil? Would you believe that, Sin?"

Mumble.

"Sorry, Sin? I didn't get that."

I was beginning to wish he would stop using my name so much. I was the only other person in the room with him, so I'd hardly think he was talking to anyone else, but he employed the same techniques just before he killed Jeremy. Unfortunately, Other Me was doped and duped and hadn't witnessed his friends murder as I had. So...

Mumble louder.

"You wouldn't? I'm not surprised, really Sin. Not at all. Some things really are not what they appeared to be."

I understood that he was referring to me and the talents he was trying to exploit, but indirectly he must have also been talking about the treatment itself and he himself.

"It is, though," he continued, his voice almost a lullaby. "Evil as evil can be." Well, he would know evil - it looked at him in the mirror each morning. "This cat, this cute bundle of fur, Sin, hurt someone. Did you know that?"

I squirmed in my seat a little and shook my head.

"Well, you wouldn't know that, would you? But you believe me, don't you? You trust me?"

A pause, then a nod.

"Good. Very good." Connors smiled an icicle smile and leaned closer to me, leaving the cat alone. It was obviously content after the attention it had received so didn't move. Other me, however, flinched back slightly.

The doctor didn't notice or didn't care.

"It was a little girl's pet," he said. "A little girl who'd always wanted her own cat. She'd had it from a kitten and loved that little pussycat. She loved it, Sin. But then, one day..." He leaned right in to say the next two words, pausing for effect, close enough that I must have been able to feel his breath on my cheek.

"It changed."

Where was Bela Lugosi when you needed decent organ music?

He began to walk around the chair, circling me just as he had my dear departed,, but so recently... 'reparted'... friend. The serpent ready to strike. The scorpion ready to sting.

"One day," he told us, me and Other Me, "it was happy playing with its catnipped toys and balls of wool. The next it was, and there's no other word I can use, evil."

Round and round.

"It attacked her, Sin. It attacked that little girl. For no reason other than it felt like it, this here cat attacked her. It clawed her face, shredded it, scratched her eyes, bit her nose. That girl, that little girl, Sin, was attacked."

Round and round, dipping in and out occasionally to speak close to my ear. I was becoming agitated, shuffling in my chair, rocking, my hand no longer hanging down but joined with the other, rubbing and wringing.

"It clawed her eyes, Sin. Clawed them until she could no longer see. Clawed them until they were useless and blind. It scratched her cheeks until no flesh remained and it bit her nose until there was nothing left but bone and gristle. That's what this sweet, little cat did to that poor girl."

He stopped his circling and became the panther, ready to pounce. In the chair on the screen I stopped moving too. I thought that Dr. Connors, me and Other Me held our breath at exactly the same moment. Then he asked:

"What should we do about that, Sin? What should be done with a viscous animal capable of maiming a defenceless child?"

I, either of the me's, didn't move. Connors waited for an answer. It seemed he believed no more prompting was required. It seemed he was well versed in this.

"Kill it."

That wasn't me. It was, but it wasn't. My voice said the words but I couldn't believe they'd come from my mouth. I wouldn't, outright like that, callously, say to kill anything. Even if what Connors had said about the girl was true, and if it was then I was sorry for her, I couldn't just think that. Even with all I now knew and had seen of the eminent and psychotic doctor, I hadn't come here to kill him. Stop him. Kill him? Yes, I wanted him. I wanted him dead. It had even run through my head about the wheres and hows, but I couldn't kill him myself.

All the others had been accidents. Or if not accidents, they'd been unintentional. To me, anyway. I hadn't set out with the intention of anyone dying, not even Jersey. I only wanted to live my life, not pass judgement on the toss of a coin.

"What did you say?"

"Kill it."

Round and round again.

"Well, my friend, I can see your reasoning. Who's to say it won't happen again? Who's to say the taste of blood hasn't turned this cat for good? But how? How would we do that? I couldn't. I couldn't kill a soul. I've dedicated my life to others. To those poor unfortunates who find themselves under my care, for whatever reasons. People like yourself, Sin, who need my help."

In the chair I was silent, but I could see, from the incline of my head, I was staring at the cat.

"Perhaps you could help, Sin, as I try to help you. Do you think you could?"

A nod. Definitive.

"Thank you. I knew I could rely on you. I really did. But how? How would you stop this evil?"

How indeed.

Other me looked at his, my, hand, then back at the cat.

"Of course. Why didn't that occur to me?" He was standing next to me. his hand on my shoulder. "You have your special way, don't you my friend. Go on then. Give that little girl her retribution."

Other me, whom I had to believe didn't know what he was doing, had to because I couldn't remember it so it didn't happen and I was drugged and Connors was... Connors, sat upright, leaned forward and stretched out his hand, fingers splayed, towards the sleeping cat.

I, the real I, waited. I could see Connors waiting too. The cat slept. I expected it to explode or suddenly screech as its eyes started oozing blood. But nothing happened.

"Come on, Sin. Come on son. You can do it. You know how." The doctor was bent close to his ear. I could no longer think of him as me. A whisper that was almost not picked up: "Do it."

Sin leaned forward, both hands out now. His head went down in concentration. He was trying. He was attempting to force it out. It wasn't coming. The beast within wasn't leaving his cage, even with the door wide open.

"Come on," Connors insisted. His teeth were clenched, his voice tight. "You know how. Don't try. Don't think. Just feel it. Just do it. Just let it go, then, when you're done, just stop it. You know, Sin. It's like breathing."

Sin took a breath then. He lowered his hands and let the breath out.

I wasn't fast enough to click the 'X' to close the video. I sat, cold, afraid. What else had Connors made me do? Had it been confined to pets or other animals? Or had James Benjamin or David Docherty suddenly had no further need for the doctor's care. I closed my eyes and forgot to control my own breath, short and ragged.

Then...... You know when you look at something and see one thing, then look again and see the same thing, then *don't* look and see something completely different?

I clicked up a folder level, back to the list of patients' names. Scrolling back up the list I looked at each one in turn, just to be sure I wasn't mistaken. Then I stopped. I wasn't mistaken, no matter how much I wanted to be. Managing to find my way to this office, with Caroline over my shoulder, without being caught. Having seen, previously, the code to gain entry so I wasn't left standing in the corridor twiddling my thumbs, waiting for Christmas. Jeremy, the last person I expected to see, not least because he was dead, providing me with the password I needed to gain entry to the video file cache. And then, out of hundreds, finding possibly the one file that told me what I needed to know about myself. There could, quite easily, have been many like that, where Connors had to prompt Other me - I couldn't deny that it *was* me in the video, though it was a past incarnation after which I was mistakenly brought back as myself rather than a butterfly or a dolphin into performing like the circus act he'd made me.

It seemed Fortune had joined my gang, cosying up with Fate and Mr. Grim to watch over, support and laugh as I fell flat on my face. She'd thrown her magic fairy dust to help me on my way, but now, as she liked to do, had turned her other cheek and slipped a whoopee cushion under my arse.

Johnson Bernadette was the name at the top of the screen but that wasn't of even the slightest interest to me, whether I knew her or not. My eyes were fixed on one particular name. Below Bernadette's. After Johnson in the alphabet. Like mine, a single capitalised word.

JOY.

Can your blood run cold? Is there an internal thermostat that drops your body's temperature down a few degrees, from 39°C to scared to hell? If there was then someone had just grabbed my dial, given it a twist and kicked me all the way to -273° Terrified.

Joy.

I moved the cursor over my sister's name. I had to look. She couldn't have been here. I'd have known, somehow. If she hadn't told me, Connors would have, or I would have heard her name mentioned at least once. There had been nothing. I went to click the mouse button.

"Hello Sin."

Chapter Twenty Two

I should have been surprised, again. I was intent on the computer screen, drawn in like Carry-Ann in Poltergeist, sucked into the hellish world that Connors and I were creating on the monitor. I should have fair leapt from my skin, skeleton and flesh departing company like a banana peeled. My heart should have stopped beating in my chest, becoming a rock faster than Medusa could blink. But I wasn't and they didn't. Instead of being shocked, I was expectant.

"Hey doc."

"How are we today?"

I looked up, not wanting to take my eyes away from my sister's name on the screen but not having a choice. She couldn't be on there. It was a mistake. A coincidence, but I wasn't going to allow Connors to see my confusion or fear. I was going to look him in the eye. Steady, sharp and, mostly, ready. As I felt none of those things, if he saw through my feint I was probably done for. If I wasn't already anyway. My mind had still not come forth with a plan, so I was playing it by ear, not that my ears were particularly musical or that good with plans. Our eyes met across a room crowded with tension and apprehension that bordered on anticipation. He was smiling, of course. He had his prey in his grasp. He could reach out and snatch me from my seat and, with a little medicinal help, I'd be his once more.

Or so he thought. I was sure that, given an injection, I would be amenable to his wishes - his own little lap dog, sitting up and begging for him to pet me or have me do tricks for him. Things had changed, however. I was no longer under any illusions about him. I no longer felt he was the nice, genial, dedicated man that had welcomed me into his fold. He could drug me, confine me, strap me up and tie me down, but sooner or later (and I could wait), I would have a chance. Just a single second would be all it took. At some point his guard would fall, the drugs would wear off, the straps wouldn't be as tight as they should. Then it would be his nose that bled. His ears and his eyes.

He might decide to kill me now. Catch me unawares and slip me a needle like he did Jeremy. I doubted that though. He hadn't finished with me yet. I, however, had finished with him. I didn't have to go find him because he'd come to me. This was his office, his lair, but it was on my terms. His smile told me he didn't realise that. His smile said that he believed he had the upper hand, ready to slap me down, to swat me like the fly he thought I was. It said 'Look at me, trust me, like me'. Another day, another me, I would have. I, along with many others, would have fallen for his smarm. Not this day. This day, as Barry Coombs had once thought before his fate was decided on the turn of the screw and the flip of the coin, was a good day. Whether I lived to see the sunrise as dawn broke out in her morning chorus or whether I finished this night having a take out with Mr. Grim didn't matter. Connors would not be smiling. Somehow I would ensure that the take out would be for three and if I was dining with the Reaper, then he would be joining us.

I leaned back in the chair, trying to be casual. I wanted to not care, or make it not appear that I did. I wanted to be fine and dandy and chilled. Crack open a beer and snack on some tortillas whilst flicking through the latest edition of Stuff magazine. I didn't want to feel threatened, or to make it appear that I did. Admittedly, I felt anxious to a certain extent - here I was face to face with a man who was my own internal demon externalised. A man who killed because he wanted to. A man who experimented on people under his care and let those people be debased and humiliated by those in his employ. A man whose smile and manner and lies allowed him free rein on his desires.

"Good, thanks," I said. I wanted his smile to falter, to grab a hammer and smash his confidence. It didn't. Obviously the confidence was arrogance shrouded thinly in surety. I'd have to see what I could do to change that.

"Excellent," he said. He spoke as a snake would to the charmer for which it had become tired of dancing. Not that Connors had been the dancer. No he'd been the maestro and I had been his performing monkey, cap in hand collecting coins and lives. He was sly and stalking. He should have spoken with a lisp to complete the illusion.

He was just inside the door, a door I didn't hear open or close. Dressed immaculately, he was an imposing figure, with his cloak of superiority wrapped tightly around him. It wasn't his height nor his pushed out chest, but his manner. He demanded respect just because. He took a step forward. Any other time I would have flinched, but not this time. I felt like He Man against Skeletor. I had the Power. The video I had just watched told me what I needed to do, or how to do it anyway. All of them must have been like that - Connors forcing me and goading me into demonstrating what I could do. Training me, knowing the drugs would make me forget until he needed me to remember. When I first came here, I wanted their help to forget too, so I supposed he was doing, in a way, exactly what I wanted him to do. I hadn't signed up for the extra curricula activities like Maths Club or table tennis or slaughter, thank you very much. I was fine with a simple drug and detain, and when that wasn't working, an escape and (self) execution. He was the doctor, the brain, the puppeteer and the perfect gentleman and, whether or not he was a baker or a candlestick maker, he was a butcher to boot. Even here, in his office when the game was up, the cards were on the table and we were the jokers in the pack, he couldn't drop the facade. The game wasn't up, not really, and our cards were still held closely to our chests. He didn't know what I planned. He couldn't, seeing as I still didn't know myself. He didn't know that I'd witnessed the death of Jeremy. I didn't know if he had a syringe full of death juice. He didn't know which video I'd seen. Neither of us knew what the other was thinking, but I DID know that he still thought I was his little plaything, I'd just come off the tracks for a moment and he was going to put me back in place and let me chug along on my way, with his feeding the fire and tooting my whistle. I don't wanna play no more.

"You caused me a little bit of stress, you know."

Shame. Pity it was only a little.

"I knew you'd come back, though. This is your home, Sin. We're your family. Where else would you go?"

Anywhere else sounded good to me. A furnace, Outer Mongolia, Scunthorpe even. I would even chance Meadowhall on Christmas Eve.

"I'm sorry I'm so predictable, Doc." I could have been respectful, sounded fearful to fool him into thinking I still belonged to him, but I really couldn't be bothered. The fear was gone. It wasn't replaced by hatred or anger, it was just a void of feeling. An empty space waiting for an in-rush of emotion but not even experiencing an in-trickle.

"Come, now, Sin. That's not you. Cocky and arrogant? It's unseemly."

He was right, cocky and arrogant wasn't me, but perhaps cooky and confident was. And I didn't care if I was unseemly or not. Let me be. Let me be a tosser, foul mouthed and farting, fagging the day away. Who was he to even pretend he knew me. The me he knew was a drugged up sideshow freak that he had created. If he didn't like the un-drugged 'normal' me, then that was up to him.

"Like I said, Doc, sorry."

Connors paused and looked at me for a long moment. He was slowly walking forward, advancing. I felt myself waiting, almost straining forward to pounce on the pouncer. I wanted him in my own grasp. I wanted to shake him and make him see what he'd done. But he wouldn't. He wouldn't see or understand that what he was doing was wrong. As far as he was concerned, I guessed, his egocentricity raised him above the paltry moralities of me, you and the postman. The kind of people who might step on an ant, but would feel guilty about it. The kind that might wish for someone to be dead, but would balk at the thought of sticking in the syringe or stabbing the knife. He stopped by the chair, his hand leaning on the back next to Caroline's head. I stared at it, thinking, if it touched even a single hair on her head, I'd happily break those fingers, snap the hand off at the wrist.

"That's fine, Sin. We'll let it go. You've been through a lot, running away like that, but now you're home so it's all fine."

My eyes, his hand.

"Thanks Doc. I appreciate that. That's the kind of man you are, eh?"

"Well, I try to..." The corners of his mouth were turned up but his brow was furrowed down. "Ah. You were being facetious. Seriously now. It honestly doesn't become you."

Death didn't become me either. As much as I could do things that were extra ordinary, I didn't see myself as extraordinary, so Goldie Hawn and Meryl Streep might be able to fight Death, but it would be a battled I'd lose if he tapped me on the shoulder and beckoned his bony hand.

"I apologise," I said, sitting up straight. I knew I wasn't imposing to someone like him, but I could at least put on a good show.

"Accepted. So, my boy, did you enjoy your little adventure?"

Adventure? Was that what it was? I try to kill myself, end up killing others, meet my dead sister and see the man before me murder my friend. Very adventurous. Enjoy? Hardly.

"It was ok," I said with a shrug. "I would have preferred a beer and a movie."

"I'm sure you would. Wouldn't we all." I doubted he would even look a pint of lager in the eye. He would be wine all the way to the gutter. "But what now, Sin? What are we going to do now? Are you going to let me help you? Can I help you? Or are you going to run off again? If you do, you know I won't be chasing after you again. I did it this time because I was worried about you and wanted to make sure you were safe. You'll be on your own."

On my own. What a horrific thought. Me, with no one there to hold my hand, to keep me company, to... oh, hold on, I'd spent my life on my own. I was used to it. And the thought that he might bugger off and leave me alone? Gave me warm tingles. Clearly, he was talking out of his bottom. He was excreting verbosity, that was for sure. If I did "run off again," he'd be chasing my tail like the hounds after the fox, sniffing me out so he could have me for lunch. I didn't have any intention of running anywhere, not anymore. This was the final chapter, the end game. Whether it be checkmate, house or the dawn of the apocalypse I didn't know and didn't care. This office may as well have been an arena, a screaming, bloodthirsty hoard spectating, panting for blood, a king holding his hand out, thumb extended to decide the fate of the combatants in the center. Well I wasn't Maximus Glutious Wotsicus and I didn't have the legs for a toga. And, I was done being on display, an exhibit in a cage so Connors could poke a stick at me to get me to perform.

How to answer. Tell him where to shove his help? Make him angry and take my chance to... do whatever? Follow his lead, accept his help, then take my chance to... do whatever? Or just not answer and... well... do whatever? I told him the truth.

"I'm not going to run, Dr." I looked him in the eyes. They sparkled, the flame of a gunpowder trail Guy Fawkes would have be proud of lighting them up. Big badda boom. I wanted to see tiredness in them. I wanted to see him weary. It might have slowed him down, muddied his thoughts. Given me the chance to do my thing. If this was a Hollywood blockbuster and if I was Will Smith or Brad Pitt, I'd probably have been doing my thang right then, rather than just my thing, spinning out one-liners like a spider on its web. But it wasn't. And I wasn't. I also didn't think I was as sharp as the doctor. I was me and he was he. I had to wait and see who would be the one to be cut first. And there's me out of plasters.

"That's good, Sin. I'm pleased to hear that. But what about my offer of help?"

I was tiring quickly of this play, but I hadn't pulled an ace to help me win the hand. All I had was those jokers, and they weren't the rib-tickling kind. In a second your mind can change its... erm... mind, flipping from one decision to an opposing one before you can blink, with little more impetus than a whisper of breeze. My mind wasn't flipping but I caught a choice in the palm of my hand.

I leaned back. "Thanks, doc, but I'm good. I appreciate the offer but I feel I must decline."

My mother always told me manners cost nothing. She told me that with every clip around the ear and slap on the back of my head.

Connors didn't say anything. I tried to read his expression, but his face was a picture of calm. A felucca floating stationary on the waters of the Nile. A reaction would have been nice. It would have been polite to show fear, concern, perhaps a touch of anger. There was nothing. The hint of a smile was all.

"That's fine. Really. If you don't want my help, that's up to you. You do realise, don't you, that I can't let you leave? You're a danger."

I was a danger, I knew that very well. People had died, innocent and guilty alike. That was the whole point of me coming here, and trying to kill myself. The person whom I was most a danger to, however, was the good doctor himself. I didn't think he was aware of that. I tried to appear calm myself, to mirror the impassive mask on his face. Inside my insides were roly-polying and handy-standying like a child at his first junior gym class. I could almost feel the bubbles fizzing in my belly popping out on my face to show just how un-calm I really was. I had to stay my hand from touching my cheek.

"Well, we can maybe talk about that," I said. Of course we could. Over a Starbucks. In the park.

"Maybe." He obviously didn't agree. Oh well. He wouldn't be offering to pay for the coffee then.

He looked down at the chair he was standing next to, as if seeing it for the first time.

"What do we have here?" he asked. "A little late night fun? Does Sinny have a girlfriend?"

Sinny? Had he really just called me that? I think my grandmother had called me Sinny once upon a long time ago, but no one else had ever thought to sweeten my name quite like that. My teeth were ready to rot at the amount of sugar he'd ladled on. And no...

"Sin does not have a girlfriend," I answered. "She was going to be a little late night fun for one of your employees, and I felt I should intervene."

"That Jersey," he laughed, hollowly. "Ever the joker."

He knew. I thought so.

"Yes," I said. "Hilarious."

"So, what does she know? Has she seen you? Has she seen what you can do?" He licked his lips then, a flick side to side. His eyes widened and the placid exterior became a touch wilder.

What I can do? He was admitting he knew?

"What I can do?" Play dumb, for now. Change the subject from the sleeping Caroline.

"Come now, my boy. I think the time for reticence is long past, don't you?"

Oh yes. Long gone. Hundreds of videos past.

"So you know." Softly, softly, catchy monkey. Or spider. Or snake.

"I assume," he said, lifting his hand from the chair to smooth down a strand of hair that was sticking up, "that you know I know. The fact that you are sitting in that seat and have just been watching one of our therapy sessions sort of indicates that."

Well, yes. I guessed it would. I probably wouldn't have been playing Freecell. I nodded. I planned (hey, me with a plan - who'd have thought it) to say as little as possible and let him say as much as possible.

"That's better. There's no point in hiding things is there?"

None at all. But did he just know I knew, or was he aware that I *knew*. I had seen him instruct me in the noble art of murdering a moggy. Whether I could put that instruction into practice remained to be seen, but I could bet we both had a few little secrets tucked away. Well, mine were few and little, he still had one the size of his ego, and it was represented by that one word on the screen. Not my name, but my sister's.

JOY

I shook my head in agreement. There was no point in hiding anything, but we both still would. Dishing all the dirt would only serve to lay any advantage I had slap bang in the hands of mine enemy. It wasn't definite that I even had an advantage, but I certainly wasn't going to give it up if one such existed.

Connors sighed and looked to the floor. "I believe I may owe you an apology."

That surprised me. An apology from him? Connors the Mighty? Did he even know what the word signified? He could quite easily have believed he was offering me a wedgie or dinner at the Savoy. Well, maybe not the latter - he'd know what that was. He'd be well in with the Family of Funny Handshakes and Rolled Up Trouser Legs. He'd know what fine wine, fine food and fine women were, whatever the cost. And a wedgie implied a sense of fun that was sadly not just lacking but faily non-existent. Wow. He must actually know what 'sorry' meant! We live and learn. Whether he was serious about it was still in doubt, and I wasn't naive enough to give the benefit.

"Oh?" I prompted.

He looked back at me, then down at the still sleeping Caroline. His hand was still next to her head, and he lifted it to move some stray hair from her eyes. My hands clenched tightly, as if I could punch him from where I sat. He looked at me and the smile returned.

"You sure you don't like her in that way?"

"No, doctor. I don't. I just don't want you to hurt her."

He laughed out loud, his head back and his perfect teeth on display. What was so funny?

"Hurt her? My dear Sin, how could I hurt anyone? I only want to help people!"

The way he 'helped' Jeremy. The way he was 'helping' me. He left his hand on her head, stroking her hair the way he had the cat in the video.

"Sin," he continued, "I don't know where you get this idea that I'm a bad man! I'm not evil. I'm just here to help, that's all."

Of course. How could I doubt him.

"The way you helped me?" I half wanted to stay quiet and try to lead his conversation into the realm of treatments and intentions and sisters, and half wanted to yell and scream and tell him I wasn't his pet monkey, I wasn't his lab rat, I wasn't his personal injection of Death. I walked the fine line between, arms held out to balance me as I teetered and tottered to and fro.

"Help you? Of course I helped you! Sin, you have no idea. What have you seem, hmmm? What have you watched on there. Surely you must know that I was trying to guide you."

What I'd seen wasn't so much guidance as taking me, blindfolded, by the hand and pushing me over a cliff, watching me fall. Should I tell him? Admit I understood how to use what I could do - even though I hadn't quite figured out just how to apply that knowledge? Or not say a word. I hadn't seen anything, Officer. It was like that when I arrived. The bloody knife in my hand? It's a plant, and not the flowering type - more the de-flowering. I would have liked to have been better at making up my mind. Why couldn't it be like making a bed? Tidy the duvet, fluff up the pillows, then slide in all cosy. My mind felt like a bunch of children had used it as a trampoline.

Take a breath, make a choice. Flip and catch.

"I saw," I said quietly staring at his stroking hand, "you make me kill a cat."

He was about to say something but my bluntness gave him pause. There was no point in hiding anything, but he still expected it as part of the cat and mouse merry-go-round. Well, stop the world, I wanted to get off.

"Yes," he admitted slowly. "I did do that, didn't I?" He licked his lips, as if in preparation for the coming meal. "What was the story I gave you? I can't remember. There were so many I had to make up to get you do just get into the spirit of the game. It really did grow tiresome, you know."

Made up? Game? Rein it in... Rein it in...

"It attacked a little girl. That's what you told me. It'd tasted blood and wanted more."

"Oh, I know that feeling very well, Sin. I can see the lure of vampirism, in fact. Power and lust all on a sip of blood. It's addictive, even if only metaphorically. Do you remember any of it?"

I shook my head.

"Nothing at all?"

Another shake.

"I'm impressed. My little cocktail worked better than I expected. I thought it would mask your memories to a certain extent, but I couldn't have hoped for a full blanket. Granted," he said, softly as if talking to himself, "your own mind would have helped with that, if the things I had you do were that bad..." He paused and his eyes went wide, manic, windows into his dark soul. "But you certainly seemed to enjoy it at the time!"

Enjoy it? Yes indeed. A party and a half of full dairy blood. From the video I'd seen, I'd been badgered and goaded until I snapped. If that was enjoyment, make mine a double. I didn't respond. How would you counter that? Whilst watching myself on the screen, I could at least see why I gave in. I could understand how his provocations had pushed me into killing the cat and probably a great deal more. He'd lied, pure and simple. Fabricated a story to get me to follow his bidding. From the sounds of it, each of those video files told a similar tale, and it was like a warped version of Jackanory. Instead of a well known face telling a story, making up the voices for the characters, Connors was inventing fairytales where I was the Big Bad Wolf and his victims were the little piggies, wrapped in scarlet blankets made from the cloak of Little Red Riding Hood. His victims, not mine.

I stayed silent. I wasn't going to rise to whatever he might tell me. I knew the situation. I'd checked myself in to a hotel Hitchcock would have been proud of, and the resident psycho in charge had discovered my little fibs regarding my reasons for being there. He'd used that knowledge to his advantage - and I still wasn't sure what advantage that was - and people (and animals) had died. And he'd killed too. At least mine wasn't in cold blood. Mine was just... there. I'd escaped, and he'd come after me, not wanting to let his pet off the leash. I knew, just as well as he. So I didn't say anything.

Dr. Connors watched me. I think he tried to pretend he wasn't doing so - he was simply looking, but I could feel him watching me. His eyes weren't just resting on my face like tired feet would sit casually on a foot stool, they were crawling over my features, trying to detect any fear or intention, like ants over a donut, ready to rip it apart so they could take the little pieces home to dine on. In another life or reality he could have been my saviour. A parallel universe might exist where the mighty psychiatrist was a paragon of perfection, the shining example of his trade where he reached out to the crazies and with one touch, healed their woes. On the other banana, he might be a bastard in every dimension he deemed worthy of his presence.

"You're not going to come quietly, are you Sin?"

So there we had it. A threat thinly veiled as a threat. The leopard hadn't changed his spots, he'd just cast off his fluffy woollen coat. Softly, softly, eaty monkey. I tensed, expecting an attack of some sort. My spidey-sense was asleep or non-existent, I wasn't sure which, so I had to keep my guard up against low flying hypodermics.

Again, I kept my silence. Let him think what he wanted. He was right, I wasn't going to go quietly. I was going to take him with me and I assumed one of us might possibly have been screaming.

He laughed. He seemed to be enjoying this himself but I supposed he would be. He had me back. He had me in his den and had nothing to worry about. So what if I'd seen what he'd done. So what if I'd learned how to control the devil inside. Did it matter that I could wipe him out without moving or saying a word? Not to him. He was in control purely because he was always in control. That was what and who he was. He spoke and others listened. He walked and others followed. He said and others did. His was the will and the way and he left everyone else to be the straw and the hay, chopped down shoots worthy of nothing more than being food, bedding and toilet facilities for horses. He expected to play our little game and then lead me gently by the throat back to my cell, with a shot or two of Risperdal and coke to tease me into pacification. He was going to be surprised.

"Come now, boy. We've been friends for so long, gone through so much, and you can't even engage in a simple slice of adult dialog? That's a little rude, don't you think?"

"I'm not in a particularly talkative mood, to be honest," I told him with a shrug.

"I can understand that. You'll be tired. Why don't you go an have a lie down? Rest a bit and we can chat more tomorrow?"

"I'd rather not," I said. "I don't mean to offend you, but I'm not entirely sure you'd let me wake up again."

Not a laugh, but at least a smile. "Don't be silly, Sin. Of course I'd let you wake! You're far too precious to me to harm you in any way."

I won't harm a hair on your chinny-chin-chin, said the Big Bad Wolf.

"Precious?"

"Of course! Don't you know how special you are? Haven't you seen what I've helped you to do? OK, so I had to tell a few white lies to push you in the right direction, but we... you... have achieved so much!"

"All you've had me do is kill people." I'd seen one video, true, and it was a cat not a person, but I couldn't believe it was an isolated incident nor that it was restricted to the feline persuasion. He'd murdered my friend. He knew about Jersey's late night habit

He shook his head emphatically. "You're so wrong, Sin. So wrong."

He was so sure of this, I almost didn't believe what I'd seen, and what I felt I knew. But then he continued.

"That's not *all* I've had you do! Not by a long way."

My stomach lurched upwards and I had to fight the urge to throw up. I felt like I had just been about to step off a cliff and had been yanked back, although, in effect, I'd been pulled off the cliff into the abyss below. For a second I had almost believed him, fell for his winning smile and subtle tones. Then he'd put the boot in with a big fist.

He must have seen my reaction, thought he had me completely, as his eyes fill with a sparkle I'd not seen before. I was the spider he was pulling the legs off.

"Come on, boy. You must remember something. All the fun we've had! If it wasn't for you, this hospital would have closed long ago and I'd most likely have been struck off. Thanks to all your wonderful help, we've a roaring trade in Lunacy, and I'm one of the most celebrated in my field! You should be proud of yourself!"

My anger, and the beast that shadowed it, circled about just beneath the surface of my control. How dare he make me responsible for whatever macabre games he'd played. I'd been his unwilling and unknowing minion, forced to do whatever he wanted me to. I had nothing to be proud of. I hated myself for what he'd made me do. Fortunately, I hated him more.

"I have nothing to be proud of."

Connors moved forward to sit on the arm of the chair he was leaning against. He didn't even look at Caroline, but he reached down to pat her hand. It looked absent-minded, an automatic, caring thing to do. I was sure that wasn't the case. Nothing he did was automatic or absent-minded.

"Again, Sin, you're wrong. You don't know what you've done, so how can you know it's something to be ashamed of? You may well have healed a hundred sick or saved a thousand. Don't put yourself down so much."

"Have I, then? Have I saved anyone?"

"Well, you saved me."

Wow. Whoopee. Whoop-de-doop. Go me. I could have punched him. Or worse. Or better, depending on your point of view.

"You don't seem pleased." No, really? "Well, I suppose that's to be expected. It'll be a surprise for you, no doubt."

He was doing his speaking-to-you-but-actually-to-himself thing again. Looking at me but not seeing me. Talking through his thought processes as if having a conversation with himself was preferable than one with me. Which it probably was. When I talked to myself, answering those voices in my head (the ones we all have, not the crazy ones - I ignored them... mostly), I tended to waffle, my thoughts meandering along like a stream of consciousness until they opened up into a sea of contemplation where I'd either walk on water or drown, down amongst the seaweed and the shipwrecks of my past ideas. Maybe Connors' little chat with himself would follow a similar course and he'd open up to me, telling me what the flip was really going on.

In films, the bad guys (that's him, not me, remember?) almost always told their victims the plan. Just before the poor wretch (that's me, not him) was shot, pushed off the roof or wrestled the knife out of the Big Bad Wolf's hand and plunged it into his heart, all would be revealed. In reality, I really didn't know if that kind of thing happened. I wouldn't, myself, give the game away just in case that knife did get pulled from my hand and thrust into me, only with my dying, gurgling breath to see my cunning plan unravel. I, though, wasn't a megalomaniac, or I didn't think I was. Thus, I didn't want to take over the world and it was only by accident and incident that I seemed to want to destroy it.

"To think," he continued, seemingly oblivious, now, to my presence, "We almost had it all, and then you had to go and spoil it. Things were going so well and you had to run away like a frightened little boy."

The look he gave me was like daggers slicked with snake venom, dipped in fire. He knew exactly where I was and was talking directly to me. I needed to remember who faced me. He wasn't me, nor was he anyone else. He didn't do oblivious.

I pushed myself up straighter. I'd slouched down, trying to appear indifferent, but I needed, whether it was a good idea or not, to face him off. Not in the Travolta/Cage way as I didn't want him peeling my face off - I liked it just how it was (well, perhaps with a little more hair, but that's it), but I had to show some backbone before he ripped it out, skull-spine-'n'-all, like the predator he was.

"I didn't run away," I said, my voice calm and level, at least in my head. "I left. And *we* didn't have it all, you did. You just used me to get what you wanted, whatever that was."

Connors face cracked in a smile the Joker would have been proud of and I, like the Batman, wanted to wipe it clean off.

"Oh, Sin! My boy! You really have no idea, do you? You're sitting there, in *my* chair, no less, and you just don't know. You've been through my files - private, I might add, but I'll let that go. Didn't the computer tell you anything?"

I shook my head. Let him think I didn't know what was going on, which I didn't. Don't let him know what I did find out, not until it was too late.

He laughed. I was glad he was enjoying this. It was a real gigglefest. He shifted his position on the arm of the chair, his hand leaving Caroline's. I kept my stare on him, not giving away the fact that I was very aware of how vulnerable my friend was next to him.

"Well, should I let you in on the secret? Or should I keep it to myself and just take you back to your cell, give you a few drugs and carry on regardless?"

I'd like to see him try that one. But he was a man of many means, and I was sure he'd not be sitting there without any way to follow through with his threats.

"That's up to you, doctor. If you want to tell me, you will, if you don't, then you won't. I'm sure you already know which is which anyway."

"I didn't realise you were so perceptive, my boy. Well, you're right. I do know, and I'm going to give you a treat. I'll tell you."

I was shocked. He didn't have a gun on me, nor a knife. I wasn't in chains with a laser slowly burning a line up between my legs and nor was I submerged in a tank with sharks circling ever closer. So this really did happen in reality. Who'd have thought it. Not I, yer 'onour.

"Don't be surprised. I've told you before. Granted then you were under my drug induced spell, but I did spill those beans all over you. Why not? You weren't going anywhere, and you still aren't. You're mine, Sin. From the moment you walked in here with that half-arsed story of paranoia, you were mine."

He stood and started to pace in front of the desk, his back to the chair Caroline was in. What was it about people and pacing? Were you trying to catch up with your thoughts? Chasing them in an endless circle until you finally had them back in the grasp of your mind? He wasn't looking at me, or at least his eyes went from me to the floor to the room about us, and if I'd had a weapon I could fairly easily have used it. But I didn't. Not a real one. Not one I could have taken in my hands and smashed the back of his skull in with, accompanied by a satisfying crunch. That sounded bloodthirsty, I know, but this man, even though I didn't know the details, had to be stopped. is it bad to kill a killer? What about those police marksmen who take one shot to explode the back of the head of the man who's killed a school full of pupils and holed himself up with the staff, murdering one an hour until they're all gone and he blows his brains all over the coffee maker and box of Fox's crinkle creams. Are they bad men? Are they evil? Or are they heroes. Not that I counted myself a hero. Not heroic. Vindicated, maybe.

One hand was in his pocket, the other gestured as he spoke.

"I knew, you see," he said as he walked. "You weren't paranoid. You didn't have the right level of desperation to begin with. You were drawn, and you were tired, but you weren't in despair. Apart from that, though, I knew who you were. Your legend precedes you, as it were."

He saw the look in my eyes. he knew me? But I was nobody. A nameless, faceless nonentity who just happened to be able to do some not very nice things.

"Yes, Sin. I knew who you were. I could have danced when you came into my office and asked for my help. And the fun I had with you. Who knew one man could offer so much?"

I went to speak, to ask how he could possibly know me before we even met, but he raised a hand and I automatically obeyed the signal. He still commanded that much from me in that he was above me and I was to fawn at his feet. Or at least that was the initial reaction, before I gave myself a mental slap in the face for behaving in such a way. My pause was long enough for him to continue, so I let him. I'd have to make sure I had my chance to ask my own questions.

"It took time, you know. We didn't get it figured out straight away. And there were a few mistakes, especially when we moved to people. So much more complicated."

He saw my frown and leant forward on the desk, facing me directly.

"Don't worry," he said. "We were careful. I pay certain members of my staff very well, and choose them carefully for the way I can use them and for what I can use against them." He pushed himself away and resumed his pacing. It was almost hypnotic, back and forth in front of the desk. I was becoming entranced, concentrating on his words. "You were my prize. For all my years of hard work, battling with those who didn't understand my techniques or agree with my views. I knew, one day, I'd be able to prove them wrong. Of course," he said with a wink that made me want to poke his open eye out, "they didn't know about our little arrangement."

He began tapping the side of his head as he walked, as if he were Morse coding the thoughts into his head, or his finger was a woodpecker drilling down to all the gooey stuff inside.

"Once you came to me, whether by fate, coincidence or your sister..."

"My sister!?" I couldn't help the exclamation. How did he know Joy? Why was her name on his computer? Did he know where she was now?

He waved his hand to shush me. "Yes, yes. Your sister. Don't get too excited. I don't think she really brought you here. It was probably a coincidence, or some form of divine intervention in repayment for my years of dedication. God knows I deserve it. Either way, once I had you here, you helped me with a few experiments to find out what we could do with you, and then we were away! It was so simple in the end. And apart from the two who discovered what we were doing, and the one who was just because I felt like it, there were very few deaths. Good job, really," he laughed. "It was getting hard to find stray cats."

So. There had been more cats that I'd killed for him. And people too, it seemed. Should I have felt nauseous? Should I have wanted to vomit? Cry out? Perhaps. But I didn't. I felt nothing but hate. My sense of shock and outrage was fading rapidly. I was only angry now. I was only waiting. The pouncee was becoming the pouncer. The kickee, the kicker.

He ranted on. He must have been enjoying the sound of his own voice, a sound that was starting to grate on me like fingernails on a blackboard or a knife across a ceramic plate.

"It didn't take long for me to figure out the right buttons to push to point you in the right direction. You're a fast learner, boy. I don't know why you couldn't work it out for yourself, but no matter. We did it together, which was nice. A true bonding experience, don't you think?"

No.

He stopped again and looked at me, an eyebrow raised. "I suppose I'll have to spell it out for you. You've done this so often, with such... finesse... I can't believe you don't remember a thing. I ought to go into business with my cocktail. I could imagine a big market out there for a drug that left you suggestible but unaware."

Again, the pacing and the head tapping.

"It started off, you know, with a few patients who came in with fairly minor, treatable illnesses. Some depression, a little paranoia - the real kind not your phony version. If you messed up and they started bleeding from their nose or dribbling out of their ears whilst staring at their groin, so what? Obviously they were worse than they thought. If you cured them, you could then *make* them dribble from their nose or bleed from their ears, and we'd keep them here, with the money rolling in, until they either died or were no longer needed. And, as you no doubt *do* remember, Sin, not many leave."

He stopped his tapping and both hands went into his pockets.

"Unfortunately, the intake was too low. Not enough crazies in the world to keep us going. I wanted to expand. I wanted to become a haven for those whom the world called Lunatic. And if there were no lunatics, then I'd just make them. Or rather, we would. You and me, Sin. What a team. We've extended the Institute three times just since you've been here, you know that? Three times. And the funding and sponsorship has gone through the roof. Do you realise, I have so much money, I don't know what to do with it? Do you realise, I'm practically a celebrity? Even the Prime Minister has called me for advice. Me! And it's all thanks to you. I actually thought that, if I were to meet him, I could make him a patient too. Then we would be firmly on the map. Forget the Priory and all those other clinics for the fashionably addicted. We would be the place to be, and I would be known all over the world." He pointed at me. "And you, my dear boy, would be standing right behind me, unseen of course, helping make it all happen."

His face was alight with excitement and the thrill of what he was telling me. I shouldn't have been surprised that a lunatic was in charge of the asylum, but I had to admit I was. This was all about fame and money. His grand scheme, his murders and manipulations were all down to celebrity. How sad. How... anticlimactic.

"Money?" I asked. "This was down to money?"

"Sin," he said with what sounded like a cackle. If he'd have been green he would have been the evil brother of the Wicked Witch of the East. "How can you make this so simplistic? How can you make it sound so inane? Money? Is that what you think?" I nodded. I didn't think it was that at all. It was greed, but not just financial. "Well," he continued, "perhaps at first. And reputation. I was getting nowhere. My dream of being renowned was simply that, a dream. I wanted more. I wanted prominence. Notoriety even. But then you came along. Your sister helped. She made people like me, listen to me, but it wasn't enough. You took it further. Made it possible. It's all thanks to you."

My sister again. He was throwing her into his discourse as if she were a piece of flotsam to be tossed overboard, ignorant of how this would, and did, make me feel. I didn't even know Joy played any part in this, and now I was discovering she had taken my place before I knew such a place existed. He wasn't slowing enough for me to ask, and besides, he was in mid flow. As much as I needed to know my sister's involvement, I still needed him to carry on. Which he did.

"You, my boy, made people *need* me. When people didn't come to me, I went out to find them. I'd never been in a public house in my life, but needs must, and the clientele was perfect. The right mix of the desperate and the despised. The supermarket. The back streets of Riby Square, where the prostitutes would try to force themselves on me night after night. Oh, Sin. The things I had to endure! I still feel unclean. A needle in the neck, or a drug in the drink, and then you would do what you did so well. And there'd be one more patient to tend to. We're on the verge of being the biggest mental home in the country. If we keep this up, it will be the world. Eventually, Sin, with your help, it literally will be the world! I've only used you on a maximum of five people at a time. More would be too noticable. But who knows what you can do? Who knows the real extent of your power? The right push from me, and you could even turn the whole planet into one big asylum! Think of it, Sin. Think of it. The whole world one big slobbering mess, with only me to help them all. Well, apart, I suppose, from a select few. I'd need some support from staff, I suppose. But you'd keep them in line for me, of course. But best to stay small for now. Build things up slowly, eh? There's plenty of time for the rest."

Stunned. How else can I describe how I felt? He wanted to make everyone in the world mad. He wanted to be psychiatrist to billions. I didn't know what to say. All of the despots in all of the Bond films paled into insignificance next to Dr. Connors. His was a vision of gargantuan proportions. The thing was, I didn't know what I could do. What if he was right? What if I could cause everyone on Earth to suddenly become a variation of my friend Bender Benny? It sounded preposterous, but so did teleportation and causing a bus to drive into a post office.

I just didn't know.

But what about Joy?

"What about Joy?" I had to ask. I had to know. "What did you do to her?"

"I didn't, Sin." He wasn't laughing. He wasn't smiling. He was no longer pacing or tapping. He was standing, facing me. "You did."

"Me?" I was hoarse. My throat probably constricted, my eyes probably wide, I didn't know. I wasn't me anymore. I felt apart from myself, as if I couldn't bear to be a part of what he was going to tell me.

"Yes, Sin. Don't you remember? I can't have two of you here. That's far too dangerous, even for me. You were more use than she. Your sister had served her purpose."

"So you killed her?"

He smiled then. "No, Sin. You did."

I jumped up from my seat, pushing it backwards against the wall, moving to climb over the desk to grab him, but he was faster. His hand was on Caroline's throat, a syringe in his other, needle to her neck.

"I wouldn't."

I stopped. My heart was beating in my head. I could hear it in my ears.

He was looking at me, a Cheshire cat smile.

"Saying that," he said, and his thumb moved to push the plunger in.

My hand went up, my mouth uttering... something. Caroline was no longer sprawled in the chair asleep. She was gone. The syringe fell to the seat and rolled onto the floor. Connors gasped, then smiled again. He stood up.

"Where is she?"

I shook my head. I couldn't speak. I knew, but I wasn't going to tell him, and I didn't trust myself as to what I might say. Caroline was fine. She was miles away, in bed. My bed at my parents house. She was safe. She'd wake up in the morning and remember none of what had happened. Jersey, Connors, the institute would be a half remembered nightmare. The fact that she didn't know who's house she was in, nor how she had got there, nor the past few months of her life wouldn't matter. Her eyes would open and she would just be.

Connors bent and picked up the syringe off the floor. It was still full. He looked at me and shook his own head.

"Oh, Sin," he said sadly. "We could do so much."

He was faster than me, I knew. I'd seen. But as he leapt for the table at me, my eyes flicked to the paperweight. It was empty. In my clenched fist, I felt something familiar. Something comfortable. Round. Metal. Warm. His eyes followed mine and widened as he saw the same vacant space in the crystal cube. When he looked back at me the two pence coin was already curving through the air. I caught it in the same instant his hand grabbed my throat and his needle touched my neck.

Re-using a hypodermic. Didn't he know the risks?

"I wouldn't," he whispered.

But it was already too late.

Because I had.

Because I could.

Thanks to him.

Epilogue

"I didn't want to be picking up the pieces, Sin. I wanted to make sure there were no pieces to pick up."

She stood in Dr. Connors' office in front of his computer. She stared at it for a long moment. Her name, in capitals was still on the screen.

JOY.

She clicked off the monitor and walked around the desk, although she could quite easily have walked through it. She liked to at least pretend to be normal.

She looked down at the floor, then bent down to where the two pence coin had rolled and come to rest.

Sin's sister straightened and held out her hand. A tear fell as her thumb slid under the coin and flicked.

Flip.

And...

Catch.

###

About the Author

A writer of many prize winning short stories and poems, Shaun Allan has written for more years than he would perhaps care to remember. Having once run an online poetry and prose magazine, he has appeared on Sky television to debate, against a major literary agent, the pros and cons of internet publishing as opposed to the more traditional method. Many of his personal experiences and memories are woven into Sin's point of view and sense of humour although he can't, at this point, teleport.

Shaun lives with his one partner, two daughters, three cats and four fish!

Shaun can be found on the internet at http://www.shaunallan.co.uk, followed on Twitter at @singularityspnt and can be found on Facebook at http://tinyurl.com/shaunallan

Mortal Sin – Sin Book Two

Coming Soon

Chapter One

A foetus, at approximately 18 weeks old, can begin to hear sounds from outside the womb. Bones are in place, not just in the inner ear. Fingernails emerge to protect the fingertips and hair sprouts forth - eyelashes and mopatop alike rather than just the soft down that keeps the skin safe from being immersed in amniotic fluid for three quarters of a year. Eyelids are still fused shut, but, before too long, the unborn child can tell the difference between light and dark, shadow and sun. Soon thereafter fingerprints form, identifying the baby more uniquely than any Max, Isobella or Princess Tinkerbell label slapped on by the parents, sticky side down, could ever do. At what point, though, does the foetus become self-aware? How many weeks is it, from the moment the sperm wheedles its wriggly way into the heart of the egg until baby bump sits up - or swims up - and thinks, therefore is?

Or is it simply the fact that neurons are firing, like midnight on New Year's Eve, that gives a person mind, body and spirit? Even though thoughts stumble unbidden through the still forming brain, senseless voices in a chaotic void, does thought itself, recognisable or not, give Being?

Is the mind an entity in itself, trapped in the confines of the body? Or are those neurons actually an electrical cage, with the soul, whatever form it might take, crying out at the bars?

From conception to death, is the body a prison from which the spirit strains to be released? And if that is the case, birth isn't necessarily the beginning, and death is certainly not the end. Maybe

Life is purely a sentence, incarceration for crimes unknown. A judge and jury sit sequestered, passing judgement and Life means just that. You've committed a crime so despicable that the ultimate punishment is to walk the Earth trapped in a shell of flesh, bone and blood. And when the bone breaks, down will come body, spirit and all.

Centenarians. They must be the ones who were the real nasty pieces of work. They are the ones given the longest sentences, forced to stay in this world for a seemingly unending amount of time, until their bodies no longer work without help and their bowels work with absolutely no help whatsoever.

Does that make suiciders the escapees?

Or are we simply batteries for the machines, with our world a video-on-demand stream of virtual unreality? There are no babies. There is no consciousness. And life after death is just another re-run, just like the omnibus edition of Coronation Street on a Sunday afternoon.

Would that mean killing your own mother wasn't Matricide but was actually Matrixcide?

We could be, of course, infinitesimal dots standing on slightly less infinitesimal spots circling each other in a ball around a cat's neck.

I don't know. Of course I don't. I doubt anyone does, or has ever. The whole how-why-what-and-who-be-do has been debated on the world stage, in pubs and at the footy match - to no avail. The battles that have decimated millions in the name of whichever god the warring parties held in reverence have never faced the question of what if...?

What if there is only one, and the Kurgen told the Highlander the truth? What if they're all sitting up there, playing chess, knocking down the odd pawn, whilst drinking tea and nattering about last night's Formula 1?

Do we ever find out? When we finally exit this reality, coffin lowered into the ground, set alight or body eaten by rats, do we discover that the answer isn't 42? Or even that it is?

Douglas Adams could be the only person to have ever been graced with the ultimate answer to the ultimate question. Well, one of them, anyway. Along with why are we here, what comes next, what came before and what's for dessert.

I'll take the Key Lime Pie, please. With cream. The squirty kind.

Chapter Two

I remember floating.

Chapter Three

And burning.

Chapter Four

And, somehow... I remember nothing.

I wouldn't have thought you'd be able to remember nothing. It's like, what lays beyond the edge of the Universe? How can there be an complete absence of something? An exit of existence? It can't be comprehended, but when you think of it, you can sense the edge of the idea. You *can* almost comprehend it. It's just outside your grasp, and you can reach and you can grab but you can't quite take hold.

But I remember it.

After the fire there was... nothing. I want to explain it. I want to express it, but I can't. How do you describe a feeling? It's like a game of Taboo, where you have to help your partner guess a word without using the 5 main descriptors. How do you tell someone what *hot* feels like without using words like 'heat'? And if there *are* no words?

Nothing was like... nothing. No taste or feeling or sound or any semblance of light. Not floating but not standing. Not spinning right around like a record, baby.

Nothing was like a whole load of *not*.

And after the Nothing came... not nothing. It seeped in slowly. I'm not sure which came first the chicken or the light. There wasn't a great booming voice demanding "LET THERE BE SOMETHING!" It just came. Like opening your eyes after a good night's sleep, blearily welcoming the sun but not really realising it's there standing right in front of you, slapping your face trying to wake you up.

For a long time, although with no reference or feeling of Time's passing it could have been a heartbeat - if my heart were still beating, that was all there was. Dawn had cracked, as she is prone to do, in silence and was oozing in like smoke under the door of a burning building. I couldn't see as I wasn't even sure if I had eyes. I don't think I was actually aware that I *was*. I was a foetus, embryonic in knowledge and sense.

Still in silence, a growing feeling of me washed over, a breakwater of sensation on a morning's tide. It's spray was refreshing although I had yet to know that I had a body or a mind... or what refreshing could mean. I think I welcomed it. I'm sure I didn't shy away.

At least I don't think I did.

After the floating, after the burning and the nothing... I became.

Became what? Just became. I wasn't then I was. I didn't then I did. I wasn't asleep, but I did wake up.

You know the deal. Except, no. You probably don't. No-one will. Unless you've died and been brought back. Resurrected. Crossed the Styx and Paypalled the Ferryman. How could you? Did some really see tunnels leading to a great white light? Did your belated family or friends stand on the precipice of Life and Afterlife and tell you that it's not your time yet so skedaddle back into your body and don't be so eager?

Or was it simply darkness? An absence of everything? Nothing? You are, then you're not then, lo and behold, you are again. A yo-yo of You. A bounce of Being. A loop of Life.

Maybe, like with the Gods looking down, playing chess, poker and asking if they want sugar in their tea and one chocolate hob-nob or two, there was a party going on and we were all invited. Dress smart but formal, no trainers.

I don't know. And I don't know why I'm even contemplating it. Do I think I died? I'm not sure. I don't remember being, I just - sort of - remember *not* being.

But that's all. That's all I do remember.

Or did.

Who I was, not just in name but in essence, where I was from - they were gone. Not even a grey area that clouded my knowledge like a dirty window. Gone completely. No hint or whisper or vague shadow. Just... well... nothing.

Nothing and I were becoming friends. Not quite beer, pizza and movie buddies, but at least more than nodding acquaintances. If we met on the street we'd stop and chat about last night's TV, that morning's Jeremy Kyle, the price of fuel. We'd say sure, pop round for a coffee. Drop me a text or an email. Facebook me. And neither would, but that'd be ok. It'd be understood - unspoken but realised.

Chapter Five

I found myself - literally - sitting on a beach.

People do that, don't they? Not necessarily on a beach, the tide slowly inching forwards to soak you where you sat - doing it in little increments so you didn't notice. But otherwise, people go away to 'find themselves'. They've lost their way in life so they, often mid mid-life crisis, feel the need to rediscover their path.

I always thought it was a pretentious excuse to whinge. Find yourself? Lost your way? Get a grip and live in the real world. Normal people don't have the luxury of noticing if they're lost or not. Life and all her furry friends gets slap bang right in the way and creates a total eclipse of the heartache. Muddle on and grow a pair.

Then I lost myself. Then I was reduced to a husk - a shell on a beach, one that no self-respecting hermit crab would look twice at. A slum on the shoreline of the crustacean.

But, rather than the self-reproaching misery of the standard self-loser - much of which is probably rooted in Munchhausen's attention seeking syndrome - I had actually been removed. My 'me' had been separated from my 'I' and both had lost track of my Self.

I could only assume this, though. I could only guess that there had been something before the now. We don't just pop into existence, do we? Spontaneously appearing on the Number 5 bus on the way into town to visit the Post Office or buy some cookies? No. We have to go through the foetal development first, growing fingernails and hair, drinking amniotic fluid like it's a mojito. Then we have to be squeezed through what amounts to a toilet roll tube to be ejected screaming into the big wide scary world.

Thus, I couldn't have merely materialised, fully grown and dressed, cross legged on the sand.

Perhaps I was a John Doe. Along with losing myself I'd lost my memory. Just because I couldn't remember didn't mean the memories weren't there. They could be hiding, waiting for my back to be turned so they could leap out and go 'BOO!' And we'd laugh and frolic and tumble about like we were eight year old siblings at the park on a summer's day. But that wasn't the case. I could remember, even though the memories were more feelings than solid thoughts in my head. The floating, the fire, the awakening. I knew I had been something or someone before, but I didn't know who or what. But I did know I hadn't simply forgotten. It hadn't been a bash on the head or some other trauma.

I had been *not*.

I had been.... erased.

And now one of the gods had paused in their game and put down their drink, picked up a pencil and scribbled me back. And that's how I felt. Scribbled. A three year old had been trying to draw a mister that wasn't just a stick man, and had then coloured it in, not being neat enough to stay within the lines.

So I went from *NOT* to... *AM*? *IS*? Or even, am or is. No capitals. No Great Exclamation! No "Sin is IN the building!!" Simply not there to there. No to yes. There, wherever 'there' might be, to here.

Wherever 'here' was.

I felt fuzzy. Like I said - scribbled. I wasn't yet awake, though my eyes and ears and head were open. I was in a fog. In fact, I was the fog. Although that would be great for getting past locked doors, tendrils of my smokey self sneaking underneath, it wasn't doing me much good staring at the sea with sand creeping into all my nooks and crannies. I felt like the ocean breeze could lift me from my sandy seat and carry me away. And I didn't care if it did.

I felt apart from myself, like I was a stranger I'd just met in the street. Nod a 'hi' and walk on by.

Sin's Blog

Samples from the Diary of a Madman

Slush, Grit and Gristle

Slush, grit and gristle. That's how she always referred to it. She often had a way with words that reduced everything to its base contents. And slush, grit and gristle was pretty much what the meals they fed us consisted of. All wrapped up in a uniform grey colour that really appealed to the appetite. Granted normally there wasn't much gristle in there to keep you going - that smacked too much of being a substantial meal, and we couldn't have that now, could we? Then we'd all end up with bursts of energy and you might actually have to look after us.

Can't have that. Lethargy was too strenuous for some of us residents. The Institute had a policy of calm and that calm was instilled by regular doses of irregular drugs and meals that looked - and usually tasted - like they'd already been scoffed, digested and excreted. Yummy, scrummy in my emaciated tummy.

She didn't complain though. Not about pretty much anything, and, being pretty, she would have had a certain amount to complain about. Especially with Jersey being her orderly of choice - his choice not hers. Slimier than a snail on speed with a much harder shell. You felt like a gull caught in an oil spill if you so much as heard his voice. He liked her. Too much. But she didn't complain. The bruises faded before they were replaced with new ones and abortion? What abortion?

I didn't find out what she was here for until after she'd gone. She never said and, if you didn't say you weren't asked. Mostly, patients here liked to talk about their illnesses and woes. It was a form of therapy that far surpasses the 'care' that Connors and his lackeys provided. A problem shared is a problem halved, so they say. Not so in this place. In some cases, a problem shared is a problem taken on as your own and escalated to whole new levels of insanity. But still we talked. Still we shared. What else could we do?

But not her. Quiet. Almost camouflaged by her stillness and reticence. Barely moving so much so that your eyes missed her as you looked around the room. She blended in. She was magnolia in a room of scarlets and oranges and puces. Whatever colour *puce* is. Sounds like someone just vomited. But when she was gone, we noticed it. When she was gone, the lack of her tranquillity - that you really didn't notice while it was there - was palpable. She was the eye of the storm. An island of serenity that drew others to it like Lost's.

It's not always the fathers. It's not always the uncles. Sometimes it's the brothers or the sons or the dad's drinking buddies. In her case it was the mother. Does violence beget violence like Adam and Eve begat Cain, Abel and Seth? I would guess her mother was violated as a child, or perhaps as an adult, and abusing her daughter was her escape - her vent. But one push, one slap, one intimate intrusion too far and the camel's back shattered into a thousand pieces. And she ended up here. For possibly the first time in her life she didn't have to huddle in the corner or fear both falling asleep and waking up. She didn't need to be afraid. Not even of Jersey. Jersey was scum, but he greased his way in, not drove through like a truck.

We don't know how she did it. We don't know why, really. Though I suppose we do. But they carried her body through the recreation room like a trophy... or a warning.

R.I.P. Caroline.

Slush, grit and gristle. She always called it that. Not sure she was just talking about the food.

* * * *

Luscious Lily

With the help of some purple paint and three imaginary friends, Luscious Lily tried to change the world.

Lily, of the Luscious kind, was probably one of the more outgoing patients I've met. Well, less probably, more certainly. She was never backward in coming forward, said what she thought and danced almost all the time. Even on the days when MTV wasn't on the TV, and after Tuesdays had died their dismal death, Lily de Lush seemed to have a song constantly in her head. Her feet were never still, her hands waved as if she was part Mexican and her body swayed to a beat no-one could hear but her.

And she was away with the fairies.

The phrase could have been coined - two pence or otherwise - especially for her. Lily's entry into this non-exclusive club was her genuine belief that, when dusk fell and all was quiet, a secret doorway opened in her room and the elves and pixies came to take her to play. Whether that room was at her home or in the asylum, the door would appear and playtime would begin. She would, apparently, spend her time in this other land, snorting fairy dust and dancing.

How she managed to get her hands on the purple paint, I have no idea. To my knowledge, you could get any shade in the institute as long as it was white. The only place that had anything other than blinding was the nursery, but that oasis of greenery was off limits to all except when visiting dignitaries or big money spenders were around and it had to look like is was being used for the patient's therapy. Which it wasn't. I can't imagine - and I can imagine most things - that there had been an odd tin of Precocious Purple, vinyl silk, lying around in the corridor. She managed to get her hands on one though. Somehow.

Maybe it came through the secret magic door with her...

Anywho, once Jeremy (luckily it was him and not one of his illustrious colleagues) went to collect her the next morning, she was bathed in paint and her room covered in hand daubed musical notes. Lily was no longer Luscious, she was lavender. The paint dripped and smeared together to hide much of the stanzas, but it appeared that she had composed a concerto of some sort. No-one tried to piece it all together to find out if the opus was awful or genius. It, and she, were hosed down and scrubbed until spotless once more. When asked where she had found the means to make the mess, she insisted her friends, of which there were three, had given it to her, and that they had said she should write down the song in her head. She was bringing music to the masses, a song to the silent and colour to the crazy. Even though she spent a long stretch in Room 101, she was unrepentant. But then, her special doorway opened anywhere.

Strange. Weird. Bizarre. Pick your adjective. You couldn't help, though, but be infected with the drum of Lily's feet and you could almost be sure you heard the music in her head. It was a little like the overflow of noise from someone listening to music on the bus. You can just hear the beat and a touch of chorus. With Lily, if you were close enough, you could sometimes swear you heard it too.

And rumour, along with its brother-in-arms gossip, reported that she had once woken with grass on her feet. Seemingly from whatever field or meadow was on the other side of the door.

But that, dear fellow lunatics, was impossible. Much like causing a bus to smash through the window of a post office with the toss of a coin and the bite of a Big Mac. It doesn't happen. Except it does. At least the bus side of things does. Hence my appearance within these hallowed walls. Who am I, considering the things I know and can do, to say that Lily, Luscious as she is, is nuttier than a bar of Snickers, all wrapped up in chewy caramel? Who am I, in fact, to say that any of the surrealities that exist in the minds of my friends are not actually real?

For all I know, when all is quiet and darkness falls, a crack of light starts in the wall. It opens wide and Lily's gone to dance and play in the garden beyond.

But I doubt it. Probably, Lily, who is quite easily the most attractive patient in here, hence her Luscious pseudonym - red hair and green eyes that sparkle in even the brightest light - is a chicken short of a kebab and lives in a world all of her own invention.

To be honest, though, I don't blame her.

To be honest... I wouldn't mind visiting occasionally.

* * * *

The Light in the Attic

The light in the attic was noticeably different - it had a strange pink hue.

I remember it even now. It glowed with a faint pulse and there was a low hum that accompanied the glimmering.

I think I was around 8 years old at the time. I was the worn-down brunt of my father's jokes. The steady stream of strangers that came and went through the back door were often entertained by his playful banter at my expense and his rough'n'ready prodding. They never saw the bruises from the prodding - verbal or physical. They just laughed as they ruffled my hair. I tried to ignore it all, just as I tried to ignore the pricking at the corners of my eyes.

I'd never let my father see me cry. Only Joy, my sister, ever saw that. And she understood. She had it too, in her own way.

I was never allowed in the attic, though I never actually wanted to go up there. It was dark. It was dusty. Dad told me that monsters slept in the shadows and, if you put a step wrong, your foot would go through the ceiling and you'd be trapped. Then the monsters could feed on you as they wished. They'd chew on your fat and gnaw on your bones until all that remained was your eyes - they left them until last so you could watch them eat you.

I stayed away.

The odd creaks and muffled voiced that I heard from up there only served to confirm what Dad said.

At night I would listen to the sounds. I'd imagine the monsters staring at me from hidden holes, shuffling around with their stomachs growling, desperate to dine on 8 year old boy.

Then the light up there changed. It had always been yellowy-orange. Whenever Dad went into the attic with a bag of clothes or old toys - moaning that they should be taken to the tip rather than be shoved up there where they'll be forgotten about until the next owners moved in - he'd pull the cord for the light. It would be 'light' coloured. The same way my bedside lamp was. The same way the bulb in the living room was.

But then it changed. It became pinkish. And the hum started. And the strangers visited.

On the day of my ninth birthday, Dad wasn't there. Mum told us, my sister and I, that he'd been eaten by the monsters that hid in the shadows, and that we should listen to what Dad had said - NEVER go up there. Not that we would.

Dad wasn't there for a long time. I cried, then. He always treated me like he hated me. He always acted as if I embarrassed him. But he was always, still, my dad. Then he came back.

He hadn't been eaten by the monsters. That was just a joke my mother had said. He'd been staying in a hotel that was so safe they put bars on the windows.

The pink glow had gone. So had the monsters, Dad said. But we should still never go up in the attic.

Just in case they ever came back...

Find more great books from Fantasy Island Book Publishing
at http://www.fantasyislandbookpublishing.com

Lightning Source UK Ltd.
Milton Keynes UK
UKOW041555221012

200989UK00001B/37/P